Pucky, Prince of Bacon

ALSO BY GEORGIA DUNN

Breaking Cat News
Lupin Leaps In
Take It Away, Tommy!
Elvis Puffs Out
Behind the Scenes with Burt

Pucky, Prince of Bacon

GEORGIA DUNN

 A **BREAKING CAT NEWS** ADVENTURE

Andrews McMeel
PUBLISHING®

FOR MY DAUGHTER,
GUINEVERE FAILLACE.

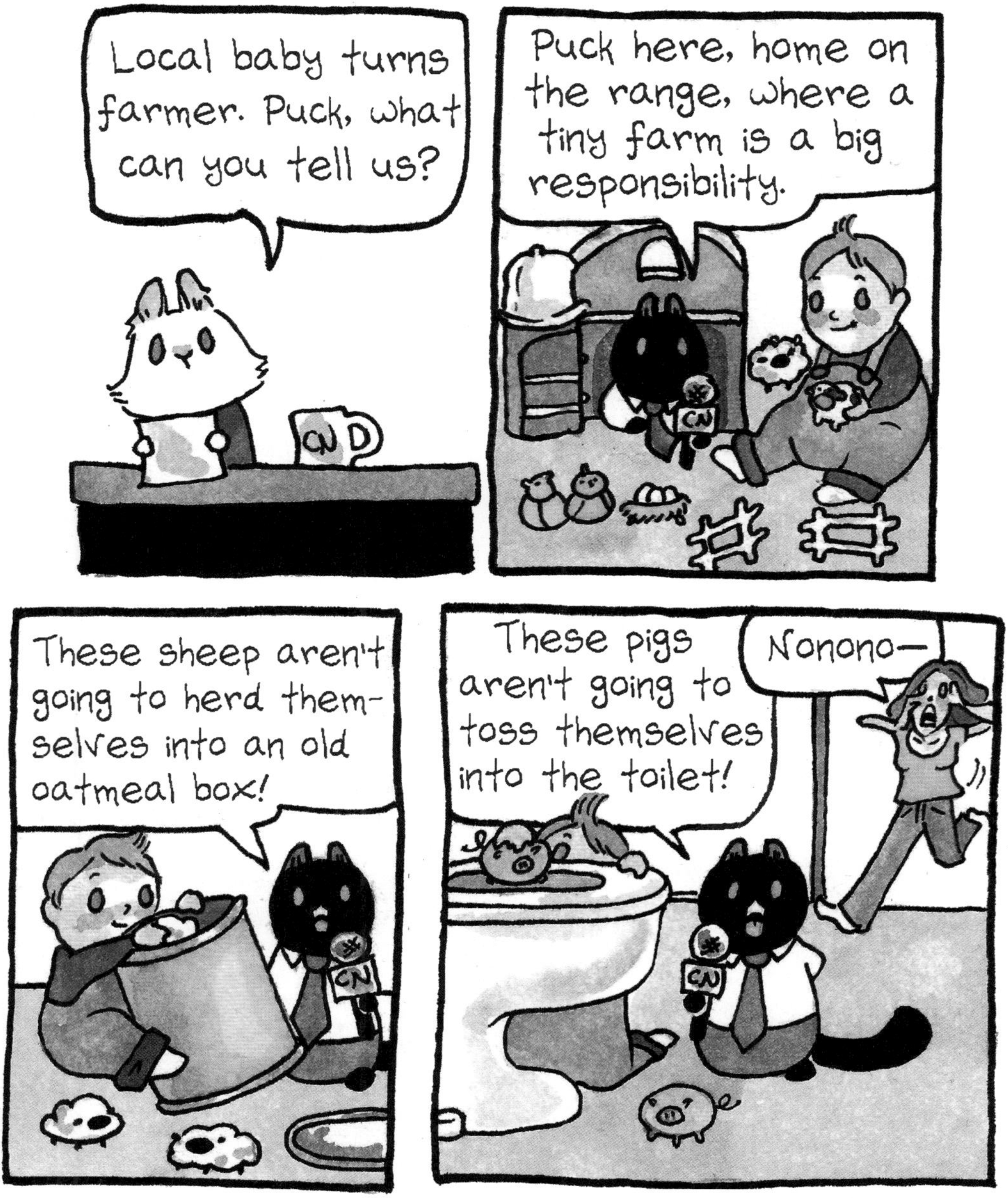
Local baby turns farmer. Puck, what can you tell us?
Puck here, home on the range, where a tiny farm is a big responsibility.
These sheep aren't going to herd themselves into an old oatmeal box!
These pigs aren't going to toss themselves into the toilet!
Nonono—

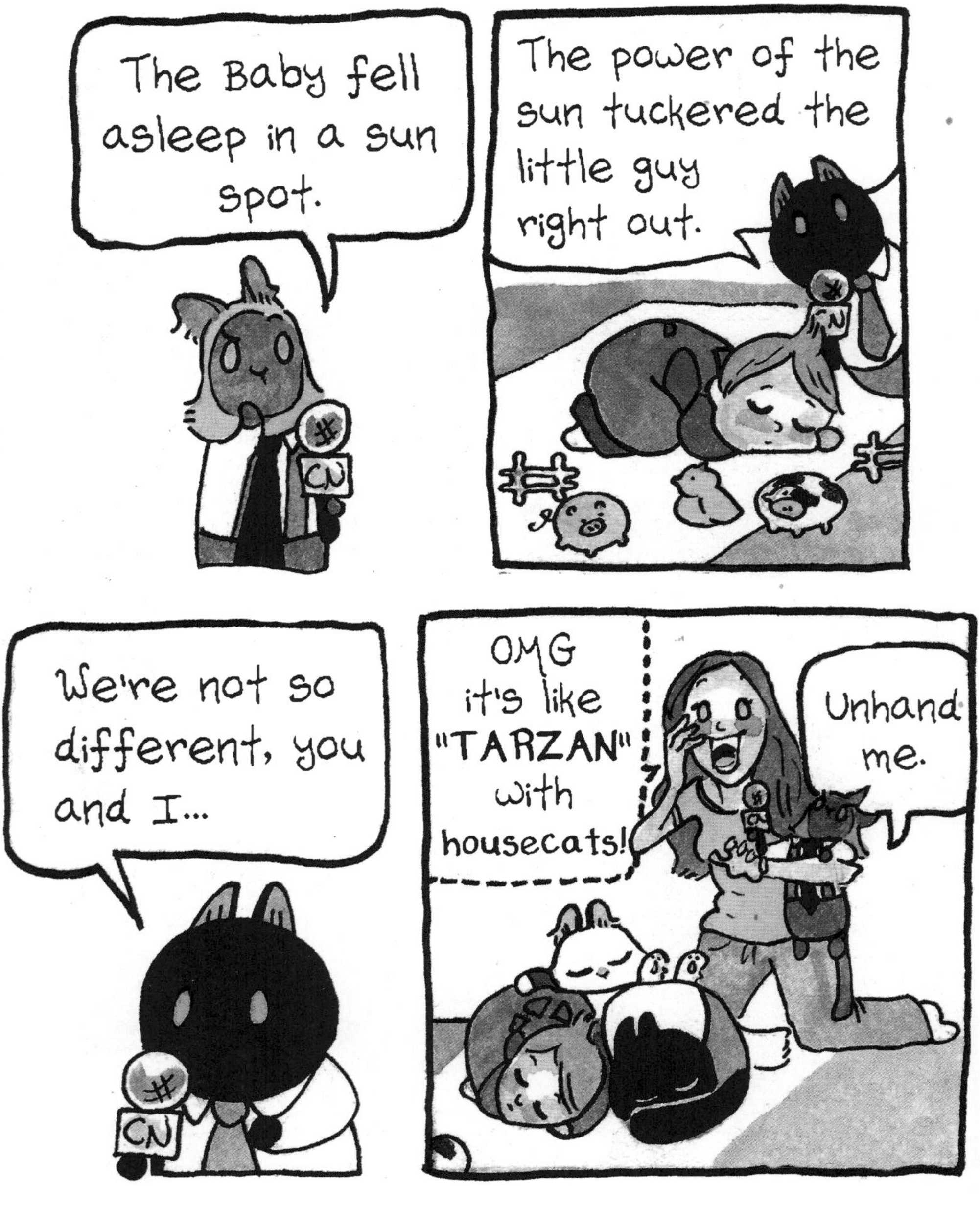
The Baby fell asleep in a sun spot.
The power of the sun tuckered the little guy right out.
We're not so different, you and I...
OMG it's like "TARZAN" with housecats!
Unhand me.

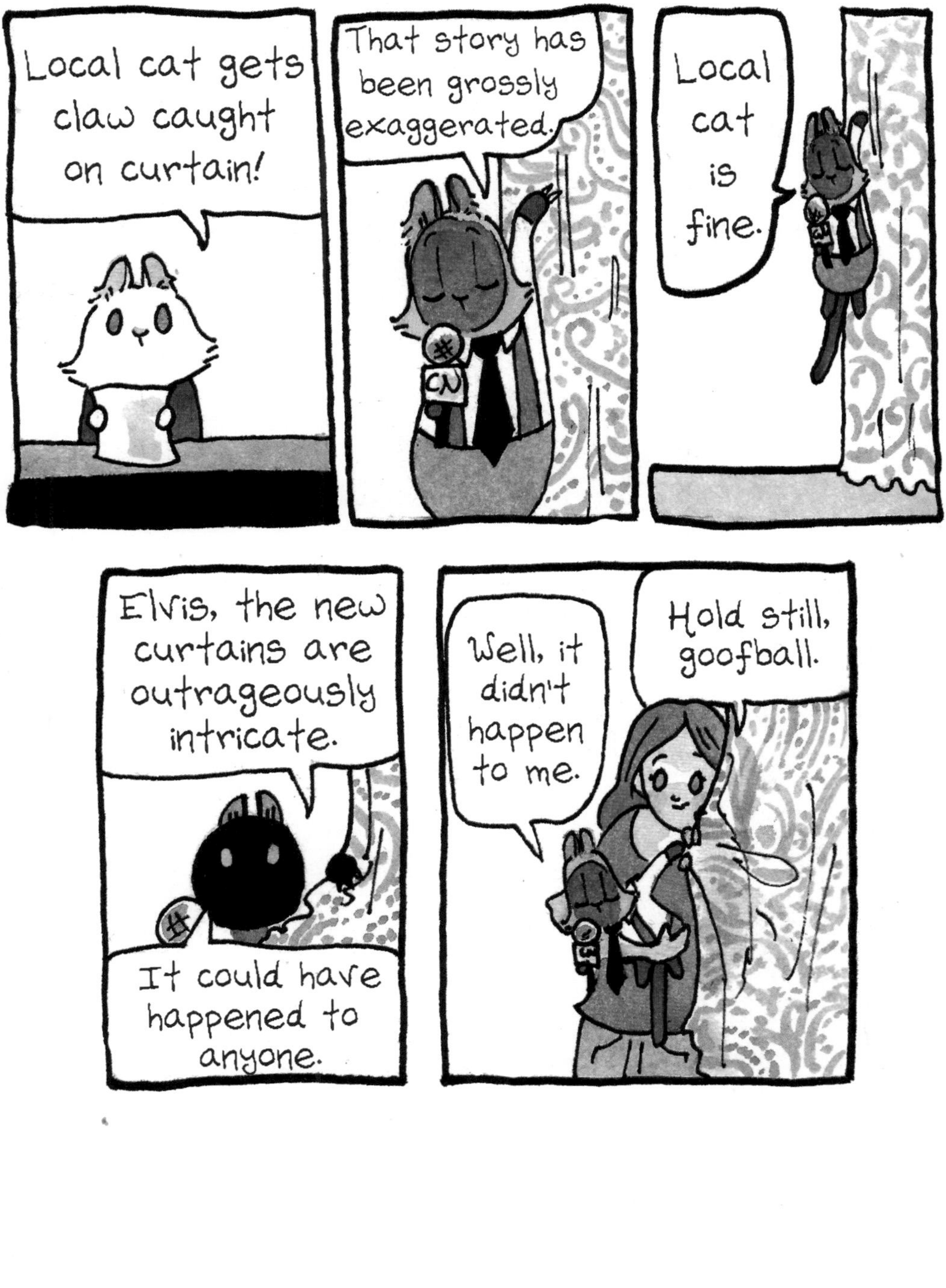
Local cat gets claw caught on curtain!
That story has been grossly exaggerated.
CN
Local cat is fine.
Elvis, the new curtains are outrageously intricate.
It could have happened to anyone.
Well, it didn't happen to me.
Hold still, goofball.

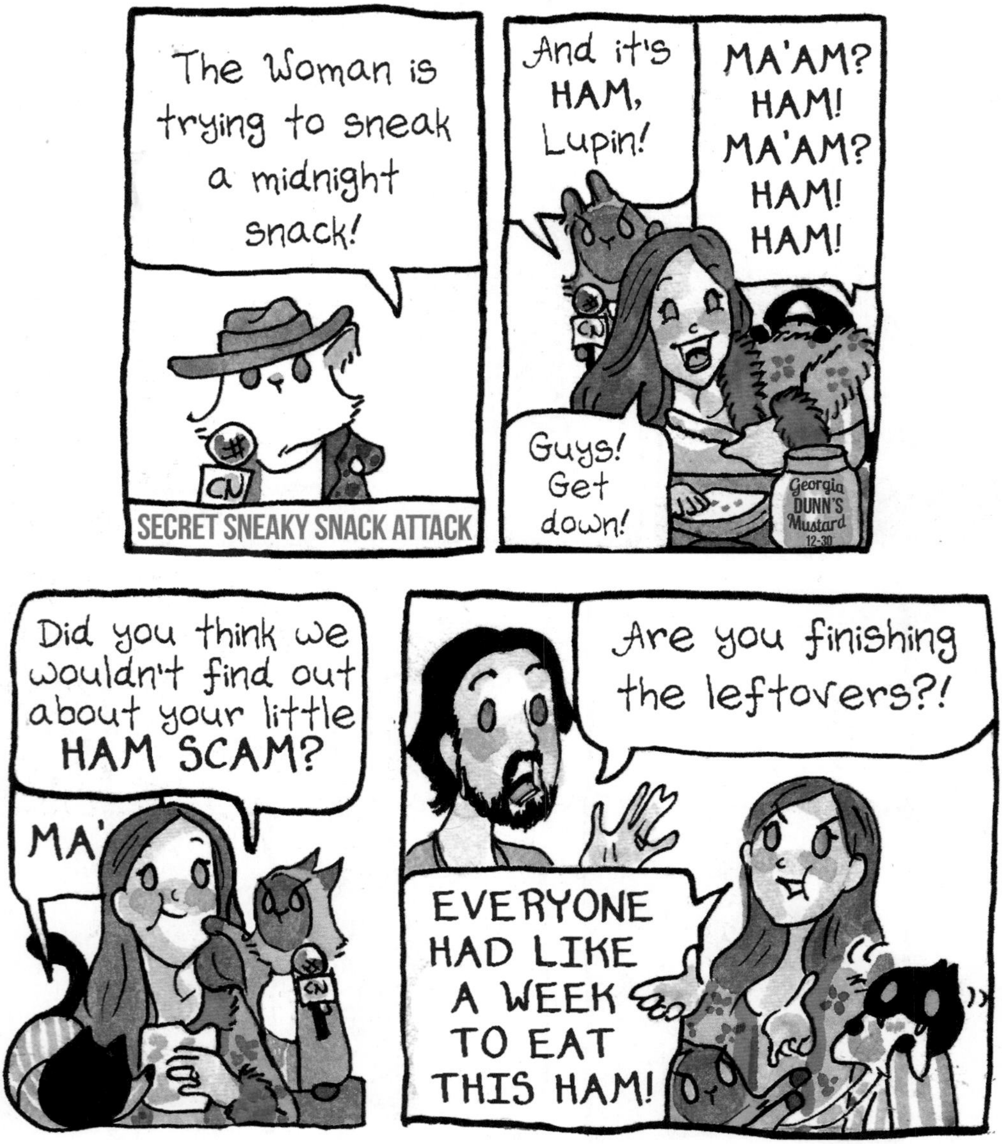
The Woman is trying to sneak a midnight snack!
SECRET SNEAKY SNACK ATTACK
And it's HAM, Lupin!
MA'AM? HAM! MA'AM? HAM! HAM!
Guys! Get down!
Georgia DUNN'S Mustard 12-30
Did you think we wouldn't find out about your little HAM SCAM?
MA'
Are you finishing the leftovers?!
EVERYONE HAD LIKE A WEEK TO EAT THIS HAM!

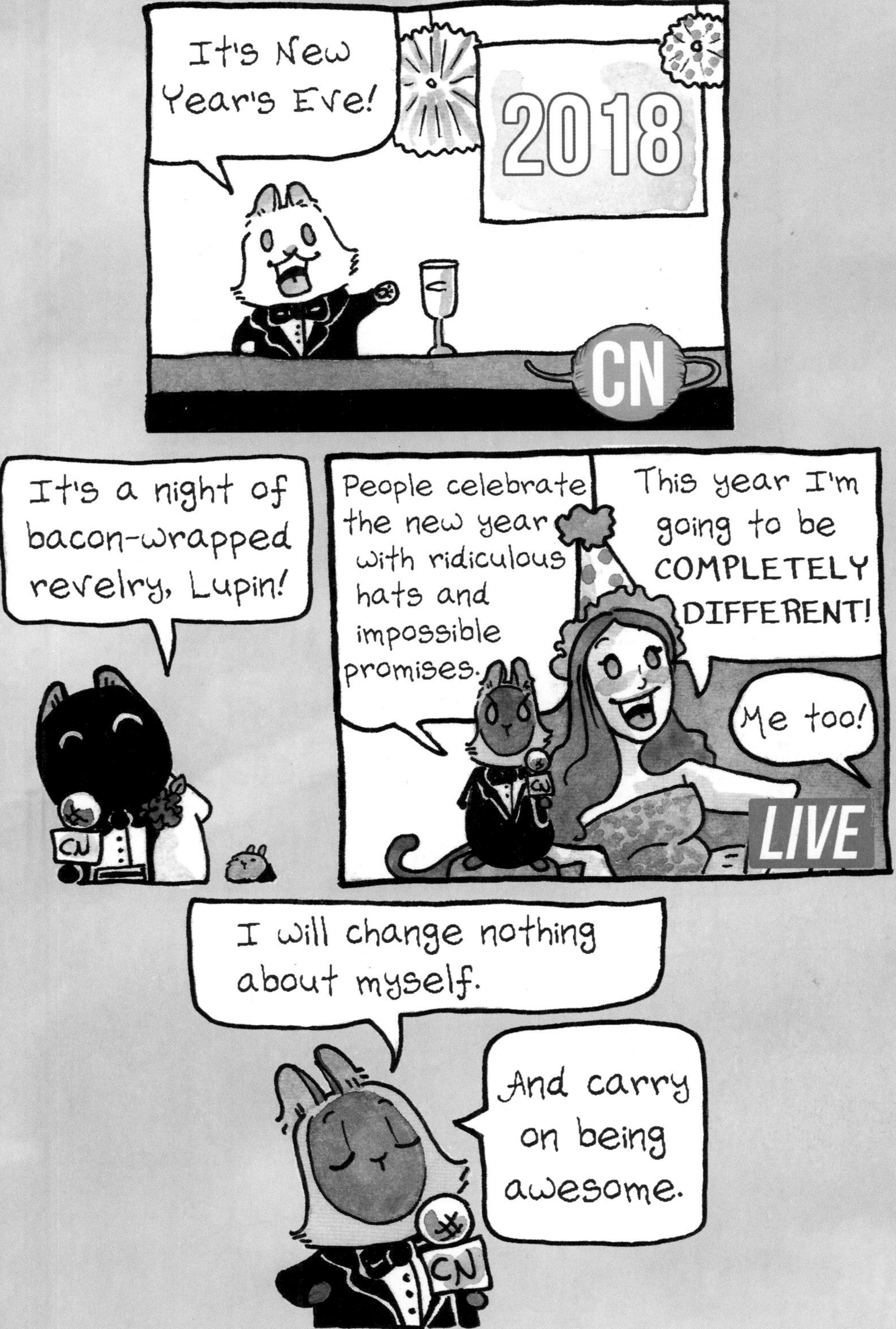
It's New Year's Eve!
2018
CN
It's a night of bacon-wrapped revelry, Lupin!
CN
People celebrate the new year with ridiculous hats and impossible promises.
This year I'm going to be COMPLETELY DIFFERENT!
Me too!
LIVE
I will change nothing about myself.
And carry on being awesome.
CN

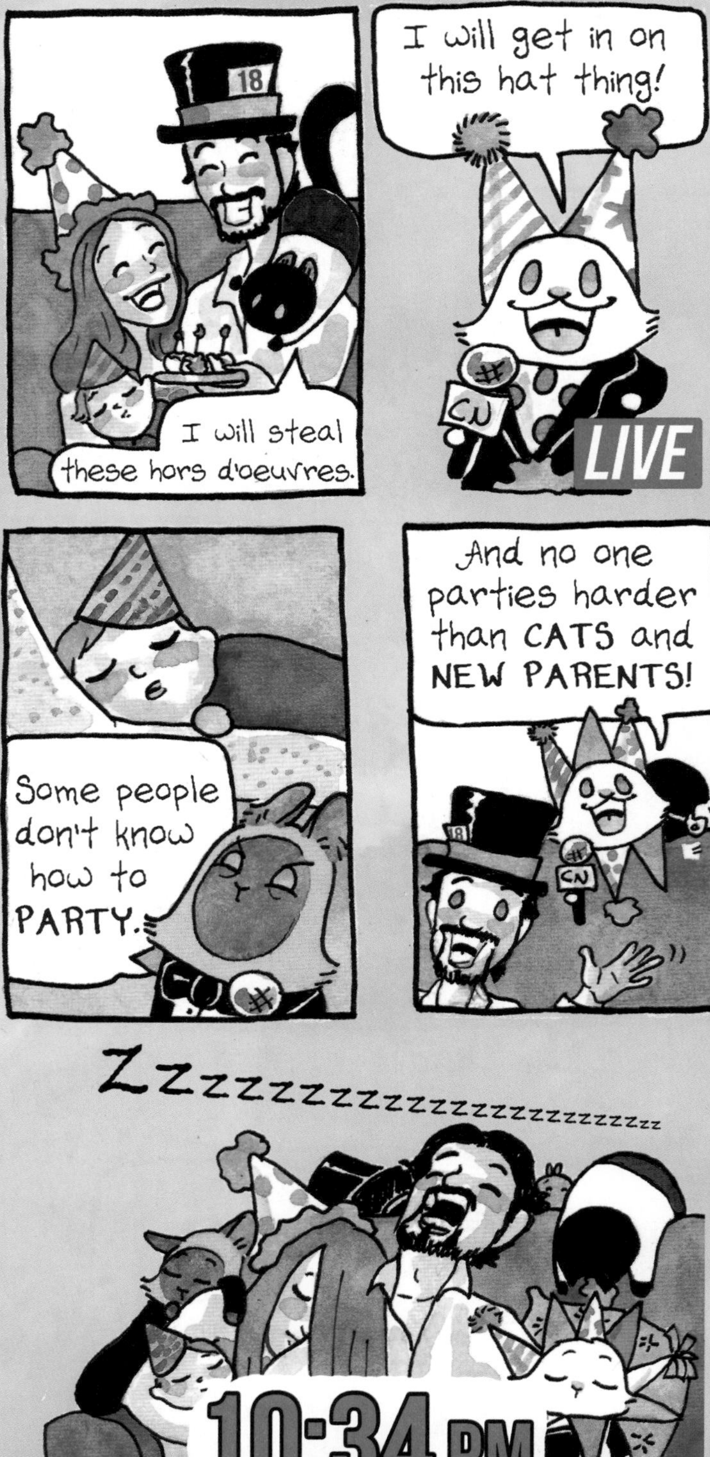
I will steal these hors d'oeuvres.
18
I will get in on this hat thing!
CN
LIVE
Some people don't know how to PARTY.
And no one parties harder than CATS and NEW PARENTS!
18
CN
Zzzzzzzzzzzzzzzzzzzzzzzzzzz
10:34 PM
Happy New Year!

The Woman made a resolution to spend more time on her yoga mat this year!
CN
Good
We are here to help...
20 minutes of staring at the ceiling on a yoga mat...
Is still 20 minutes on a yoga mat.
I'm very good at this!
CN
Good Boy
CN
CN
Georgia Dunn 1-2
RESTING MOM POSE • LET THE MIND GO BLANK • HOW LONG HAS THAT STICKER BEEN UP THERE?

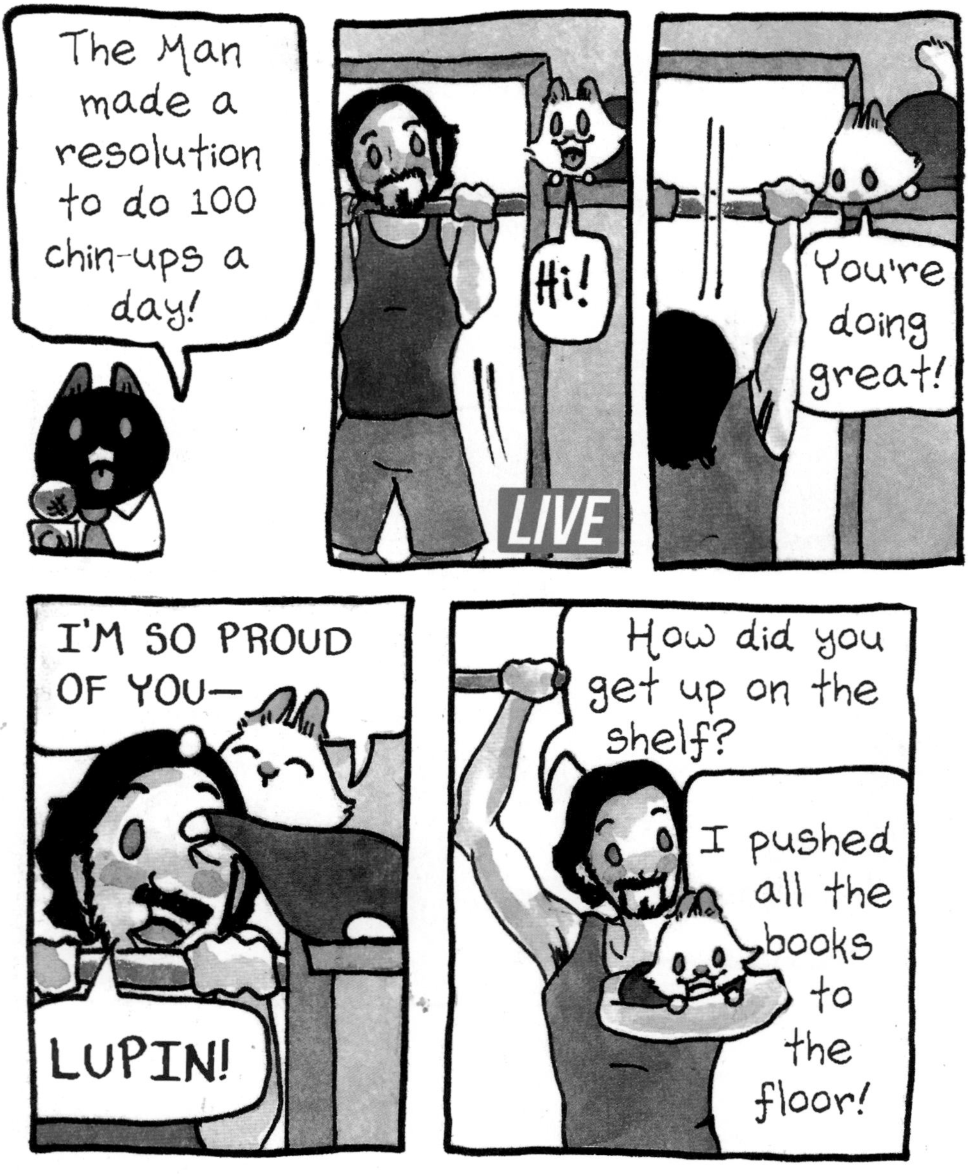
The Man made a resolution to do 100 chin-ups a day!
Hi!
LIVE
You're doing great!
I'M SO PROUD OF YOU—
LUPIN!
How did you get up on the shelf?
I pushed all the books to the floor!

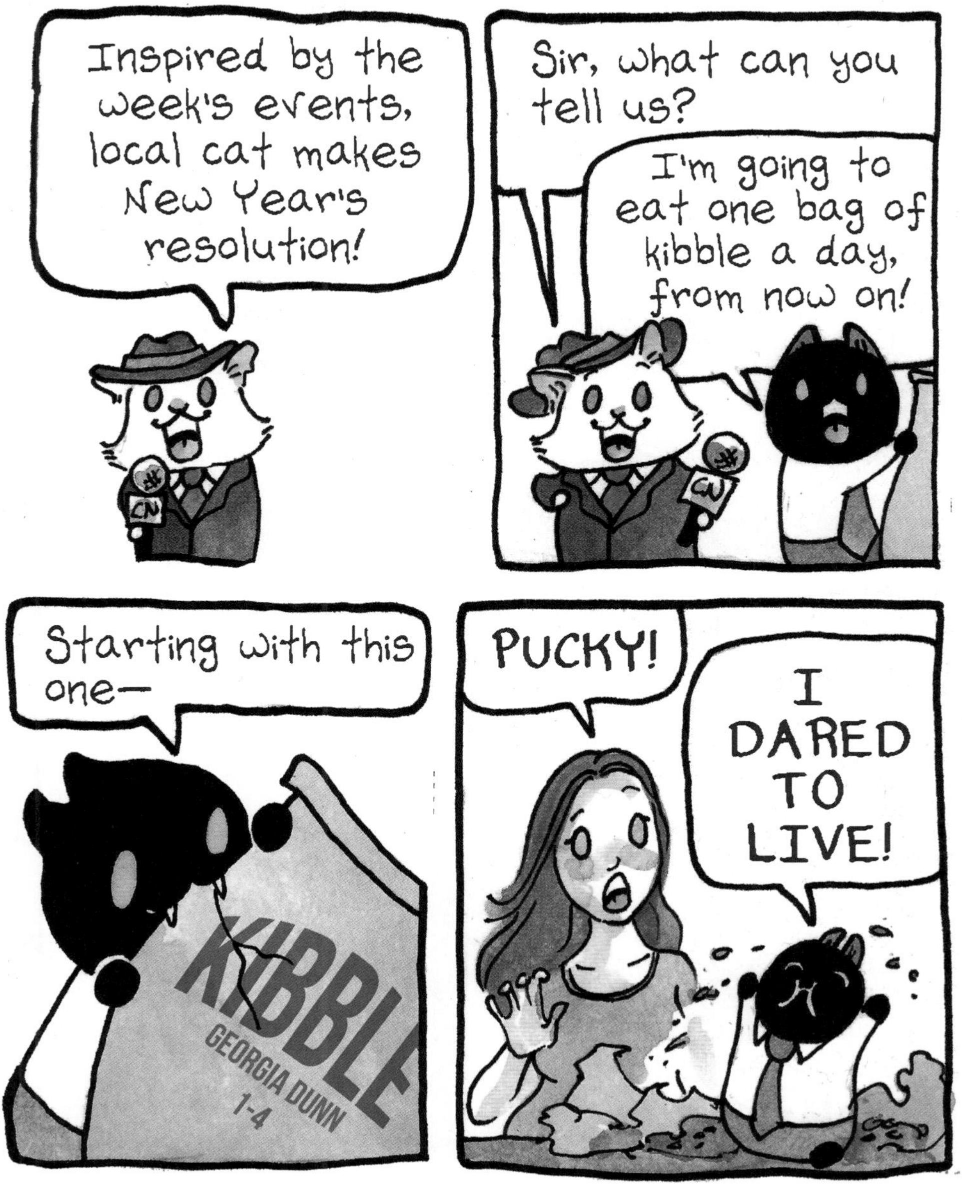
Inspired by the week's events, local cat makes New Year's resolution!
CN
Sir, what can you tell us?
I'm going to eat one bag of kibble a day, from now on!
CN
Starting with this one—
KIBBLE
GEORGIA DUNN
1-4
PUCKY!
I DARED TO LIVE!

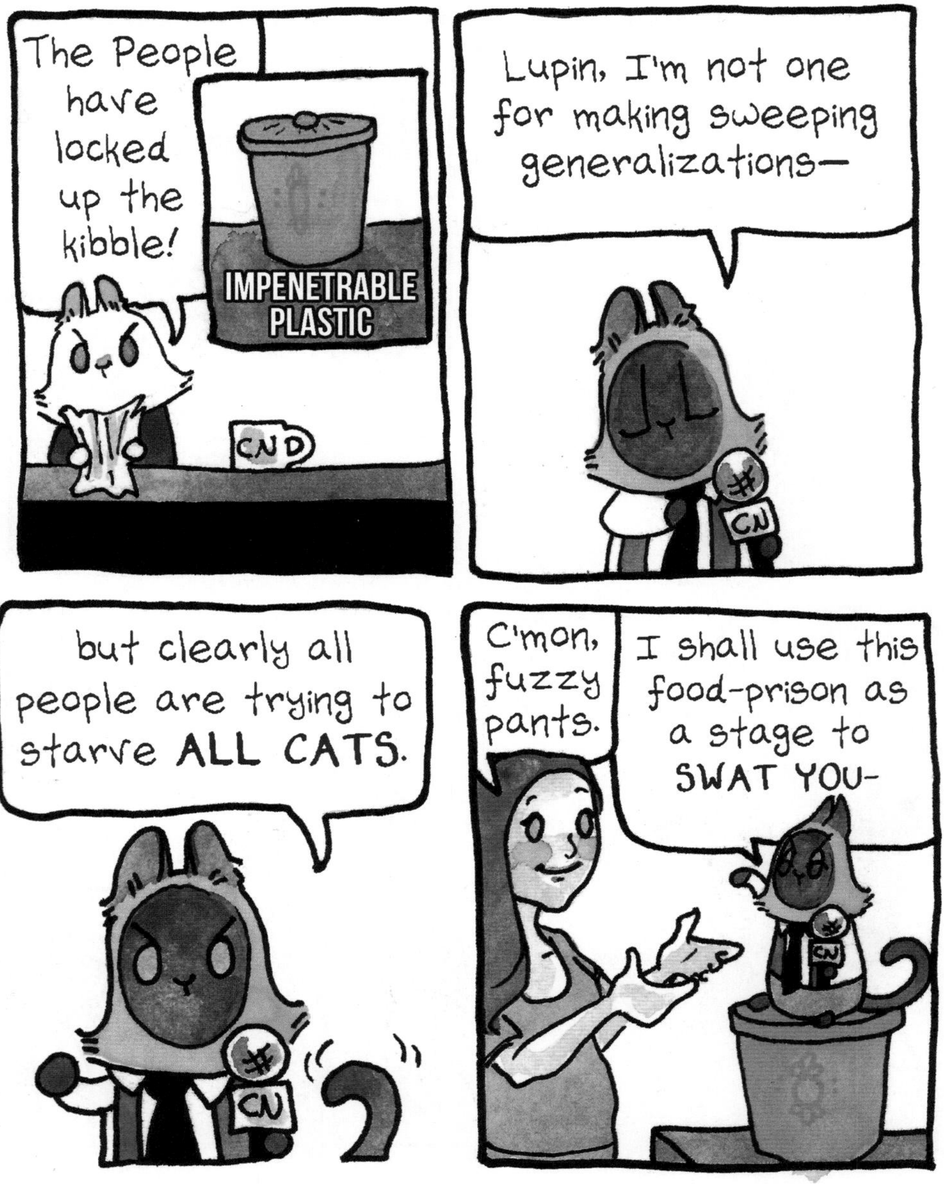
The People have locked up the kibble!
IMPENETRABLE PLASTIC
CND
Lupin, I'm not one for making sweeping generalizations—
CN
but clearly all people are trying to starve **ALL CATS**.
CN
C'mon, fuzzy pants.
I shall use this food-prison as a stage to SWAT YOU-
CN

It appears to be a model from the late '70s.
Seals in fresh-ness, seals out break-ins.
Can it be defeated?
Not anytime soon. It will take careful planning. And thumbs.

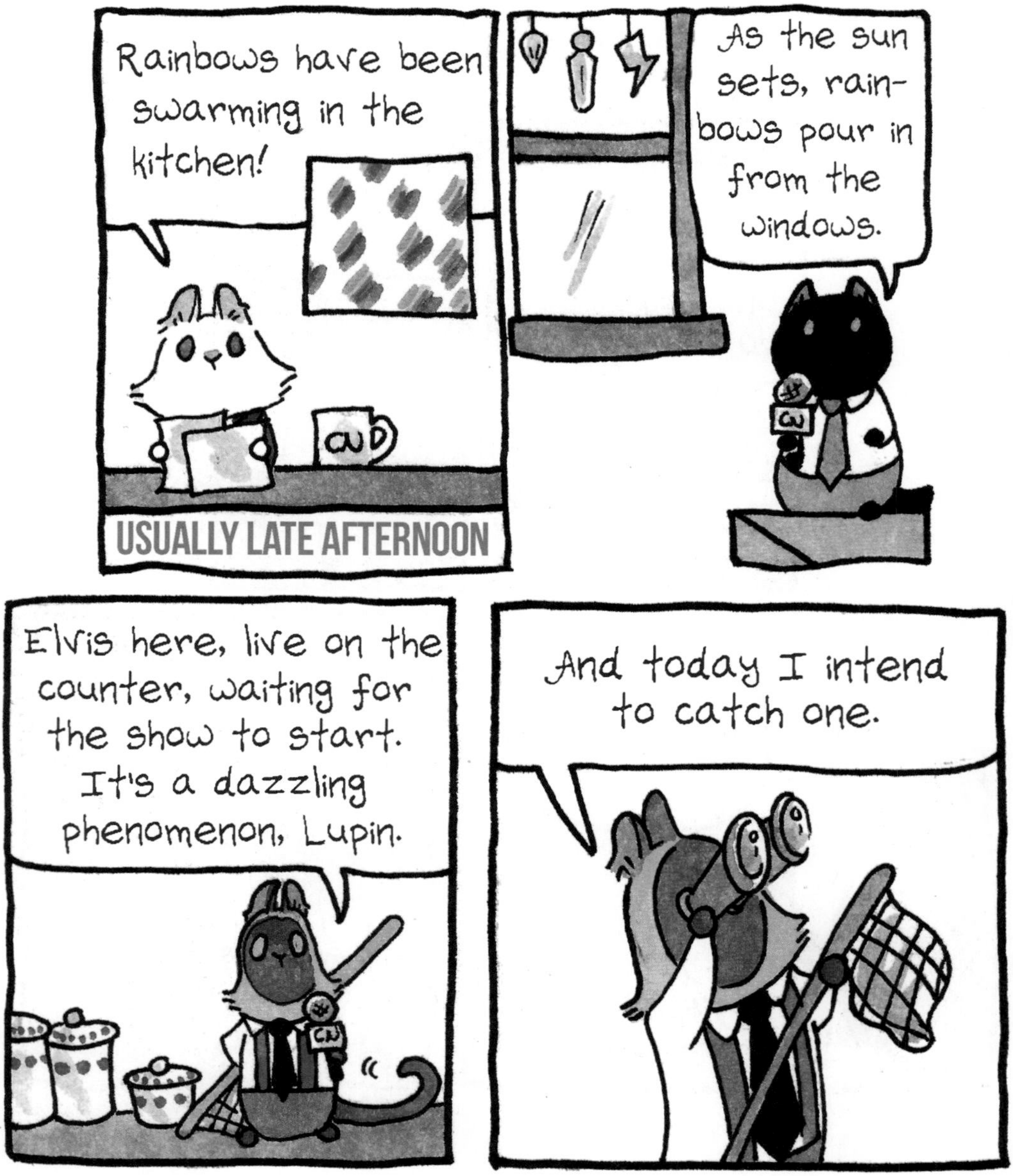
Rainbows have been swarming in the kitchen!
USUALLY LATE AFTERNOON
As the sun sets, rainbows pour in from the windows.
Elvis here, live on the counter, waiting for the show to start. It's a dazzling phenomenon, Lupin.
And today I intend to catch one.

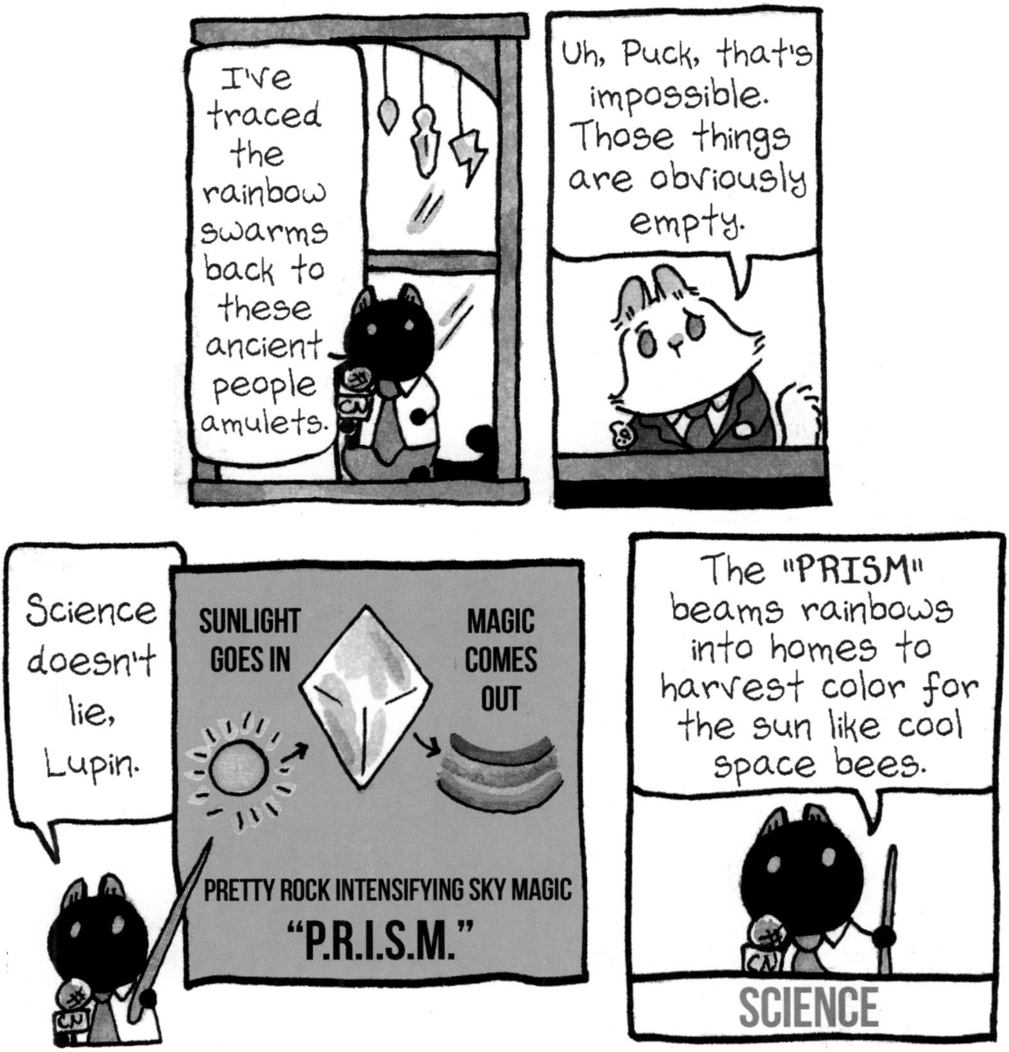
I've traced the rainbow swarms back to these ancient people amulets.
Uh, Puck, that's impossible. Those things are obviously empty.
Science doesn't lie, Lupin.
SUNLIGHT GOES IN
MAGIC COMES OUT
PRETTY ROCK INTENSIFYING SKY MAGIC
"P.R.I.S.M."
The "PRISM" beams rainbows into homes to harvest color for the sun like cool space bees.
SCIENCE

...IT BEGINS.

I'm going to see about this FOR MYSELF...

BITE BITE BITE

Lupin?

BITE BITE BITE

I CAN SEE EVERY COLOR.

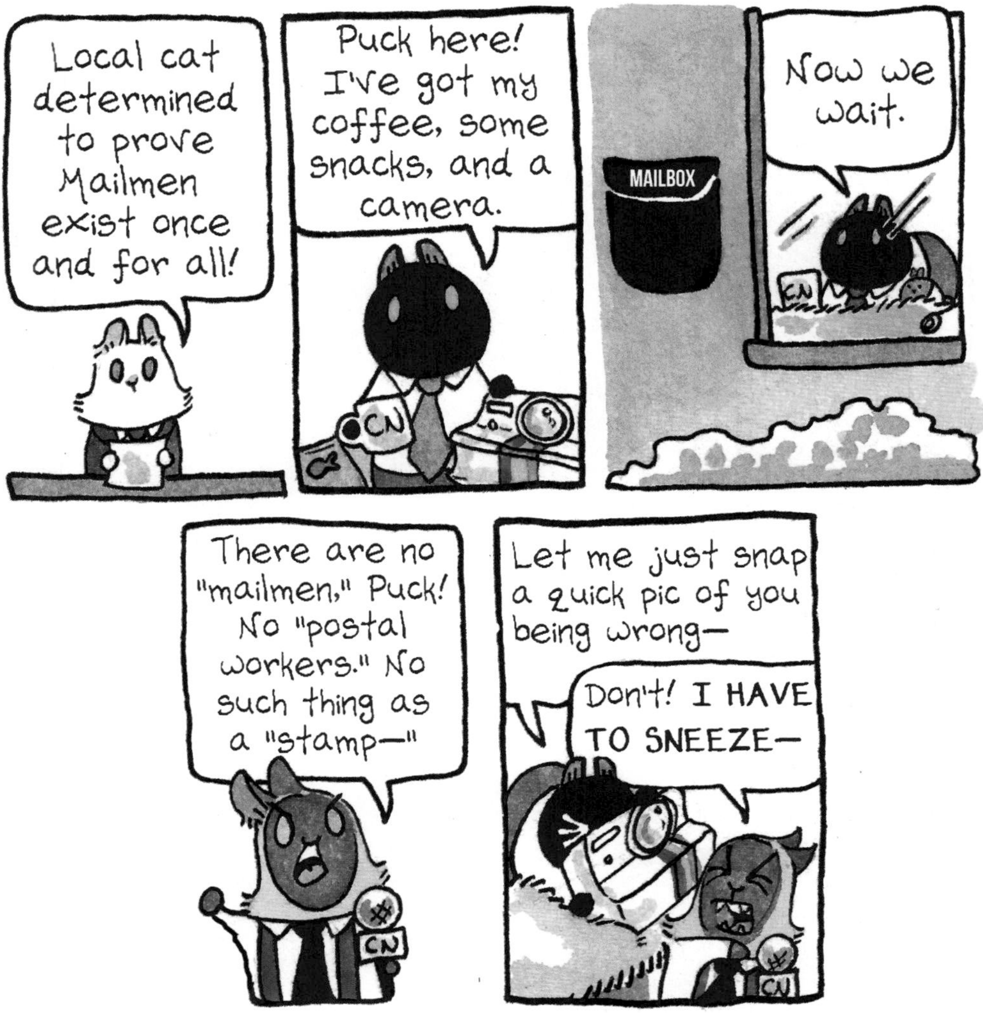
Local cat determined to prove Mailmen exist once and for all!
Puck here! I've got my coffee, some snacks, and a camera.
MAILBOX
Now we wait.
CN
There are no "mailmen," Puck! No "postal workers." No such thing as a "stamp—"
CN
Let me just snap a quick pic of you being wrong—
Don't! I HAVE TO SNEEZE—
CN

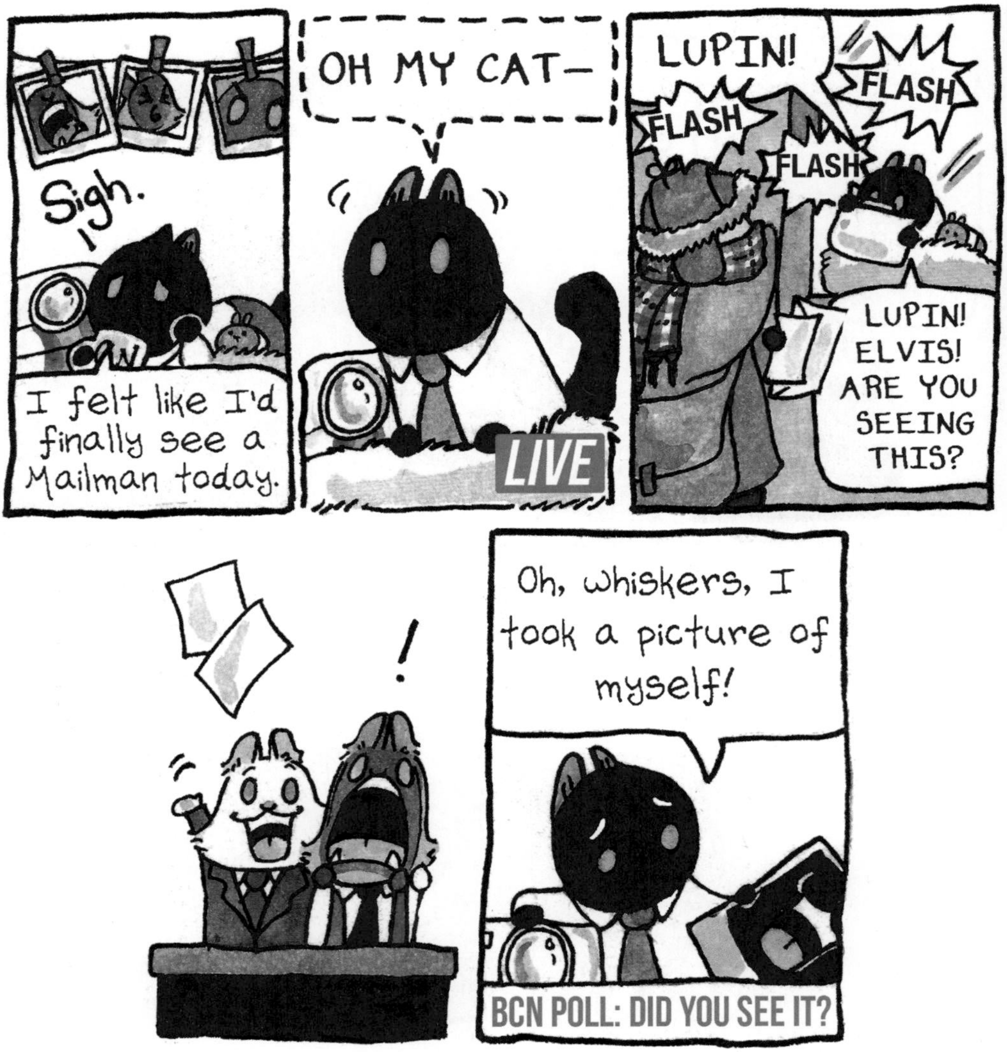

Sigh.
I felt like I'd finally see a Mailman today.
OH MY CAT—
LIVE
LUPIN!
FLASH
FLASH
FLASH
LUPIN! ELVIS! ARE YOU SEEING THIS?
!
Oh, whiskers, I took a picture of myself!
BCN POLL: DID YOU SEE IT?

The litter box is being changed.

Here's Puck on the scene.

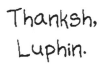

Thanksh, Luphin.

I'm live where crews-sh are hard at work cleaning the litter box-sh.

Crews could stand to give a little more NOTICE.

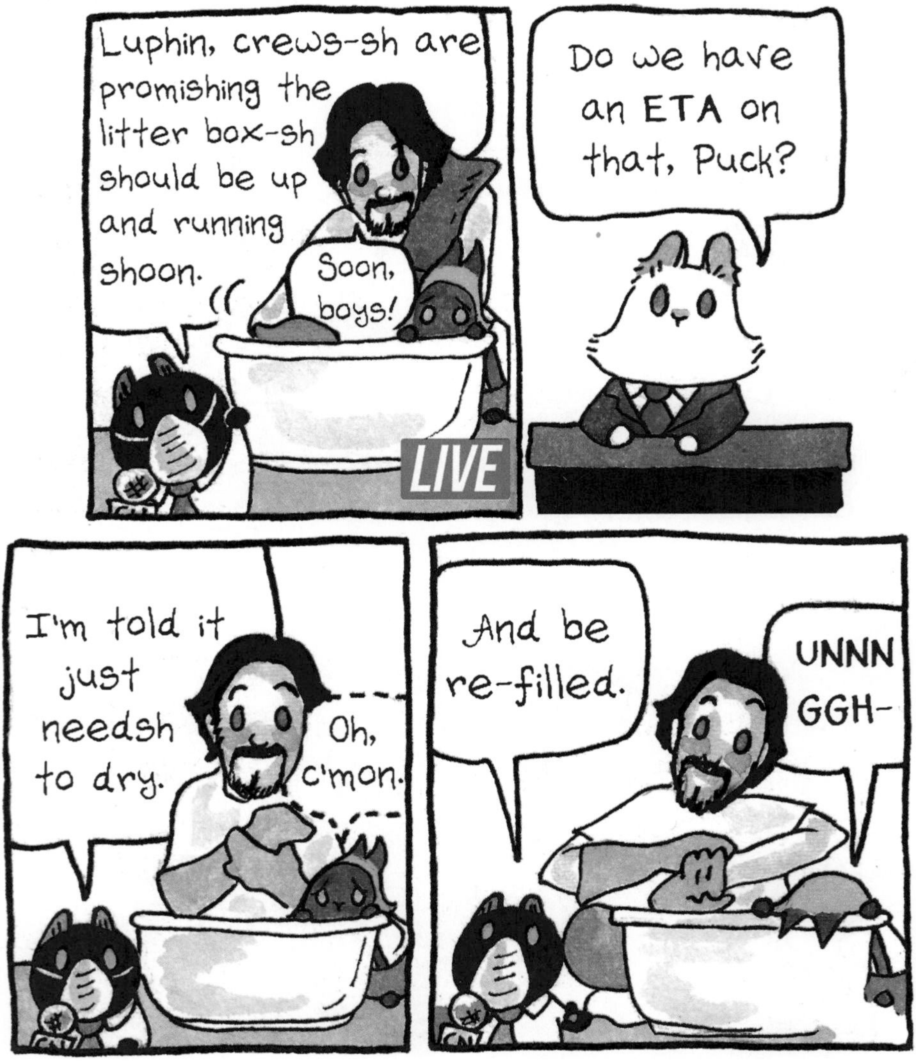
Luphin, crews-sh are promishing the litter box-sh should be up and running shoon.
Soon, boys!
LIVE
Do we have an ETA on that, Puck?
I'm told it just needsh to dry.
Oh, c'mon.
And be re-filled.
UNNN GGH-

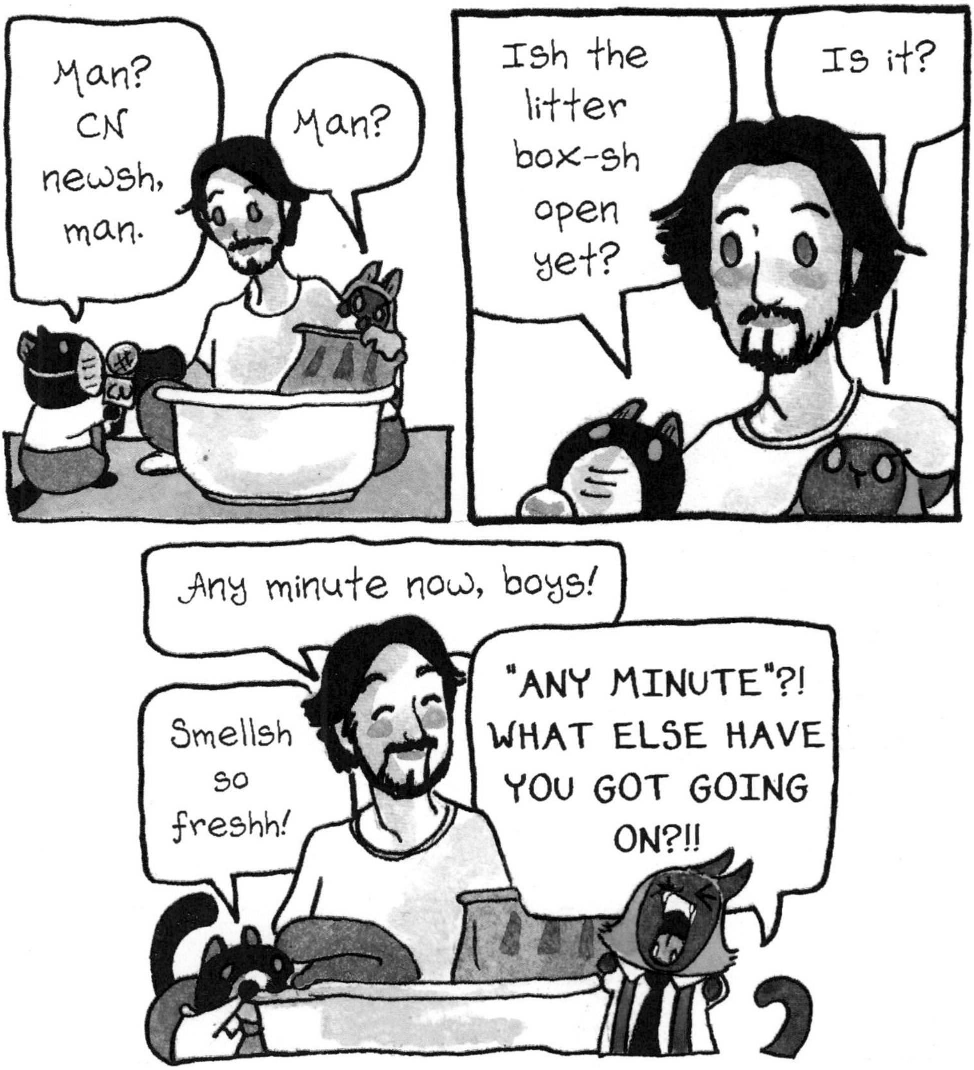

Man? CN newsh, man.
Man?
Ish the litter box-sh open yet?
Is it?
Any minute now, boys!
Smellsh so freshh!
"ANY MINUTE"?! WHAT ELSE HAVE YOU GOT GOING ON?!!

Reportsh are coming in that the litter box-sh ish back online!
CN
It'sh a glorioush day!
What's the pass-word?!
"MURDER."
CRUNCH
Relax! It's not what you think!
I'm just here to kick out litter!

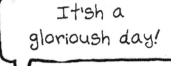

This is a CN news emergency broadcast: Two vacuums are out at the same time!

• VIEWERS URGED TO REMAIN UNDER BUREAU •

RRRRRRRRRRRRRRR

Lupin, in an unpredictable nightmare scenario, the people upstairs and our people are vacuuming at the same time.

RRRRRRRRR

SHELTER IN PLACE • DO NOT ATTEMPT TO RABBIT KICK VACU

RRRRRRRRRRRR?

It's like some kind of mating call.

RRR! RRRRRR?

It's exactly like that, Elvis.

21

Note how the throat bag inflates to display its bright colors.
MATING RITUALS
DANCES IN A ZIG-ZAG PATTERN
SHINES BRIGHT, ALERT EYE
PUFFS THROAT BAG
OF THE COMMON VACUUM CLEANER
RRRRRRRRR
Its mighty roar seems to say, "Mmm. You sound interesting. Tell me more!"
CLEAN HERE OFTEN?
RRRRRRRRRR
It's like being the third wheel on the world's loudest date.
RRRRRRRRRR

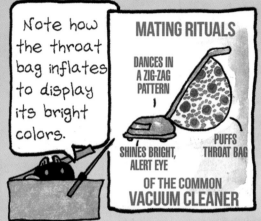

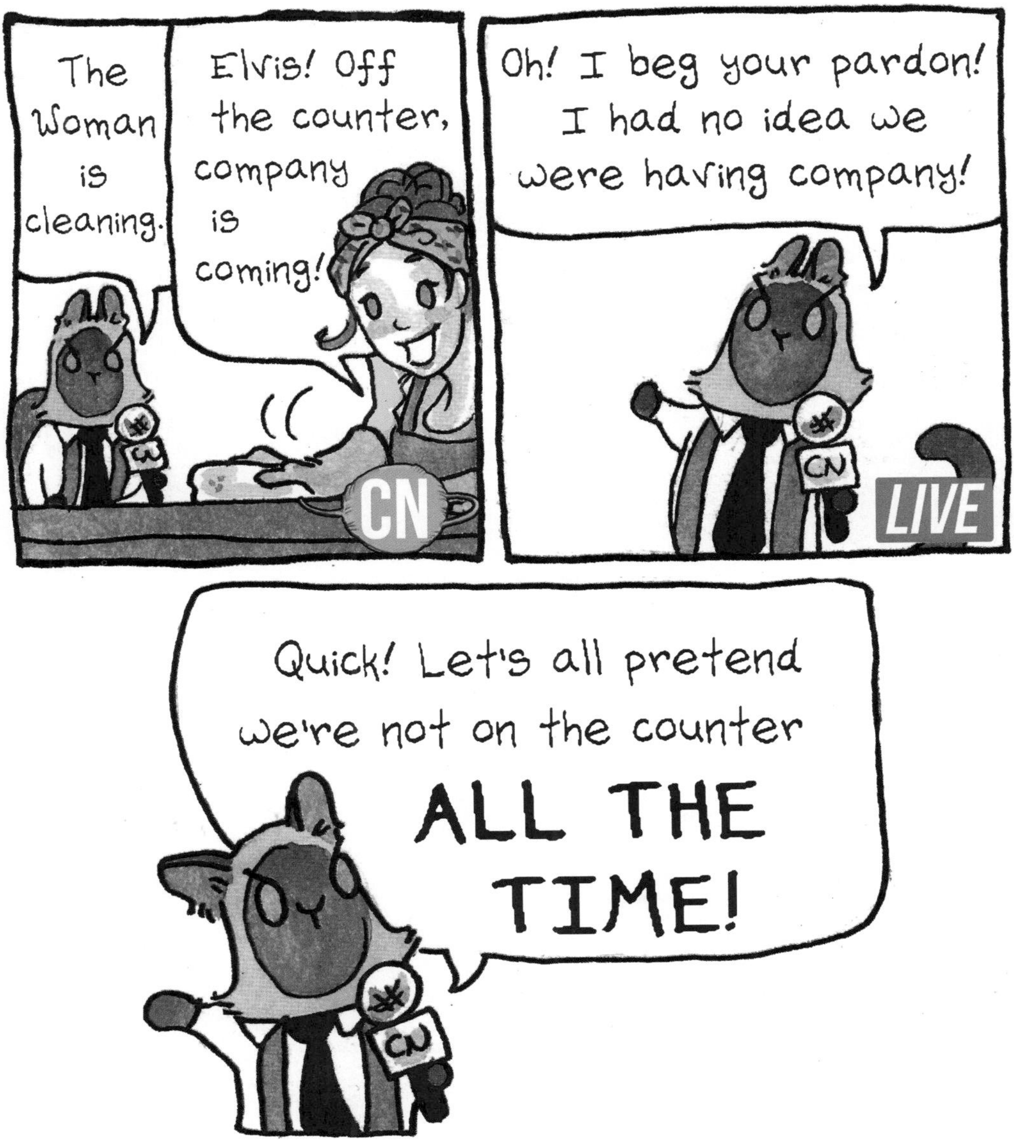
The Woman is cleaning.
Elvis! Off the counter, company is coming!
CN
Oh! I beg your pardon! I had no idea we were having company!
CN
LIVE
Quick! Let's all pretend we're not on the counter ALL THE TIME!
CN

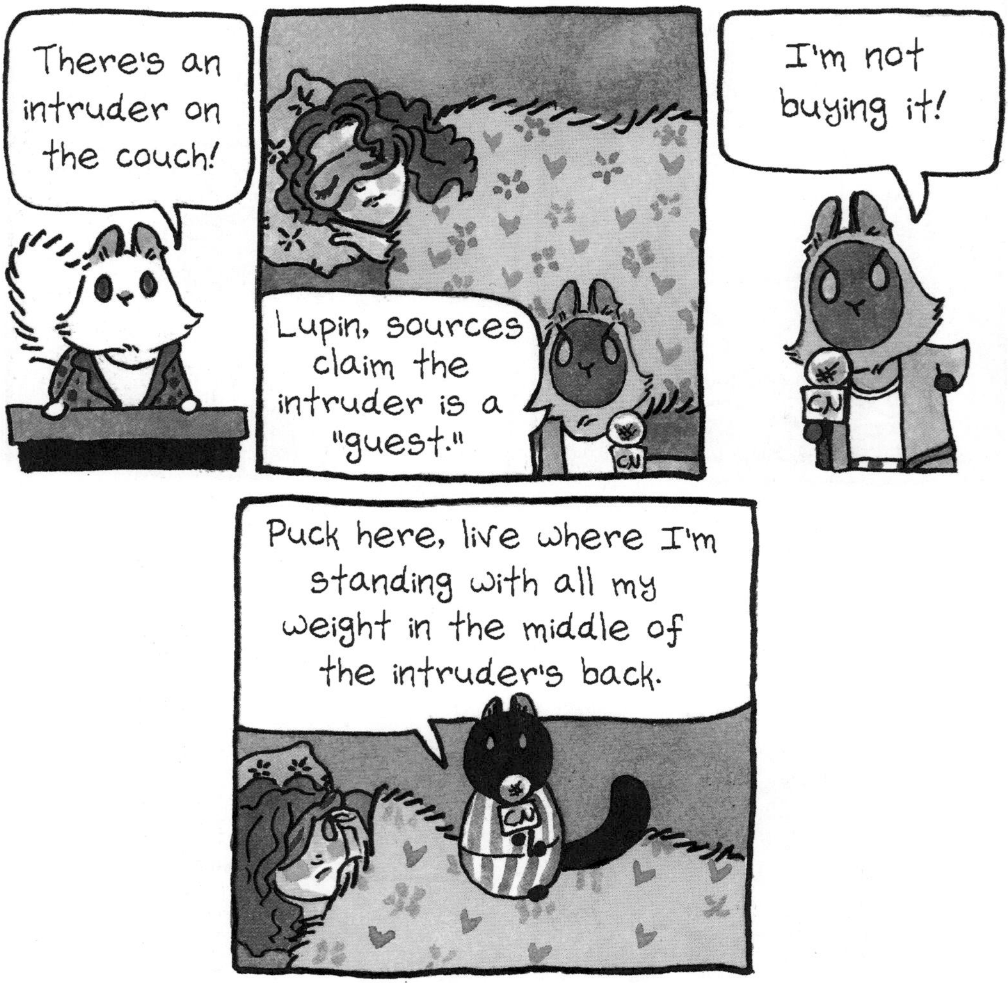
There's an intruder on the couch!
Lupin, sources claim the intruder is a "guest."
I'm not buying it!
Puck here, live where I'm standing with all my weight in the middle of the intruder's back.

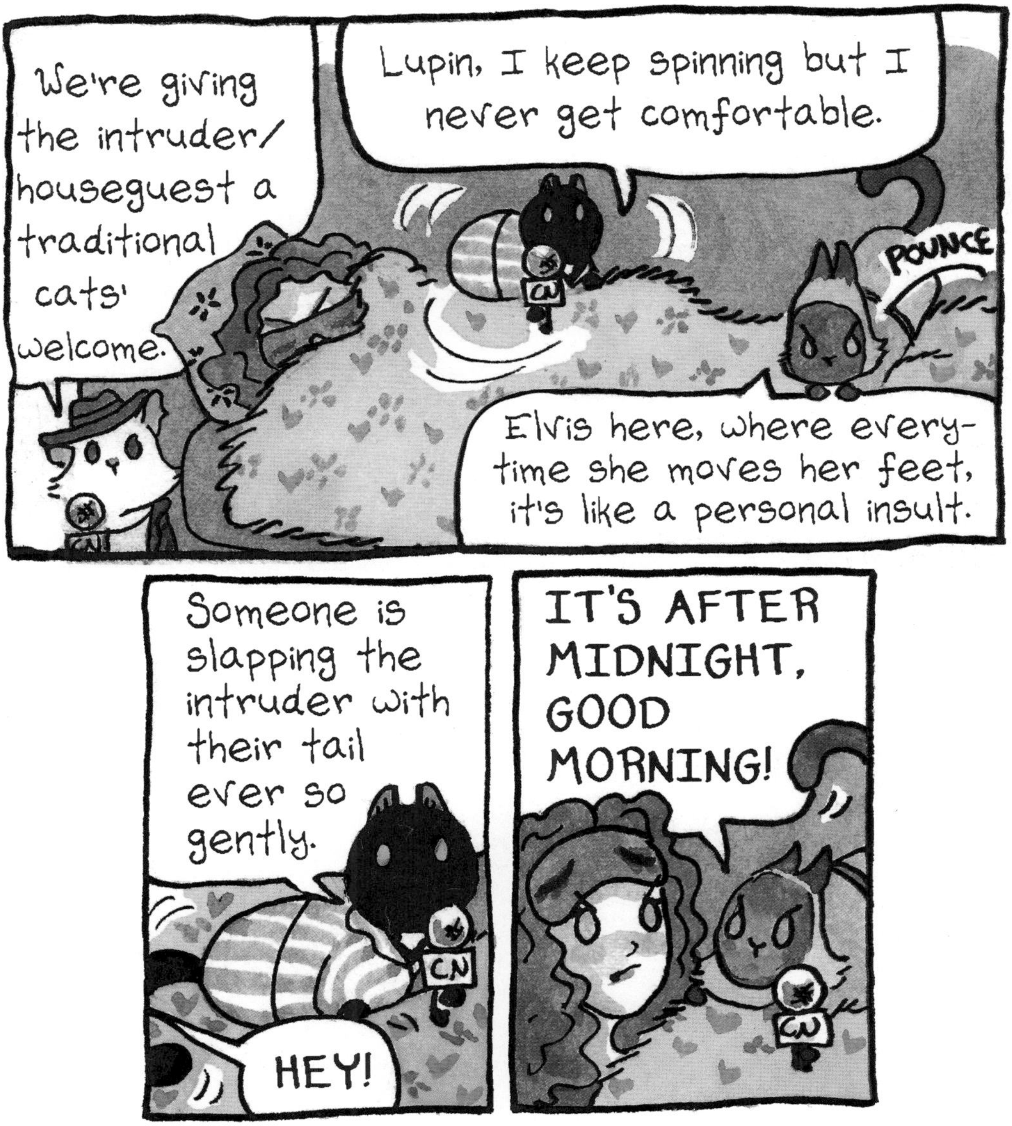
We're giving the intruder/ houseguest a traditional cats' welcome.
Lupin, I keep spinning but I never get comfortable.
POUNCE
Elvis here, where every-time she moves her feet, it's like a personal insult.
Someone is slapping the intruder with their tail ever so gently.
HEY!
IT'S AFTER MIDNIGHT, GOOD MORNING!

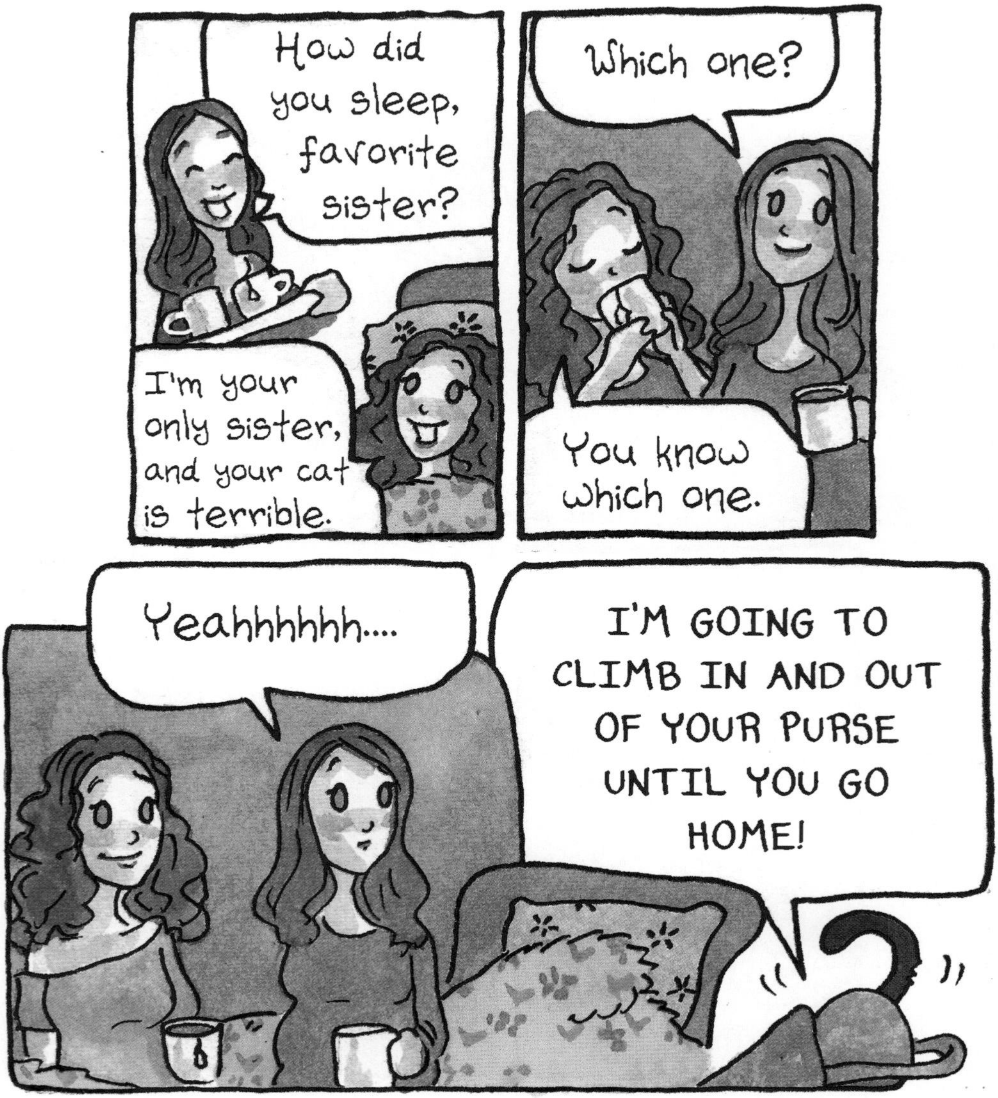
How did you sleep, favorite sister?
I'm your only sister, and your cat is terrible.
Which one?
You know which one.
Yeahhhhhh....
I'M GOING TO CLIMB IN AND OUT OF YOUR PURSE UNTIL YOU GO HOME!

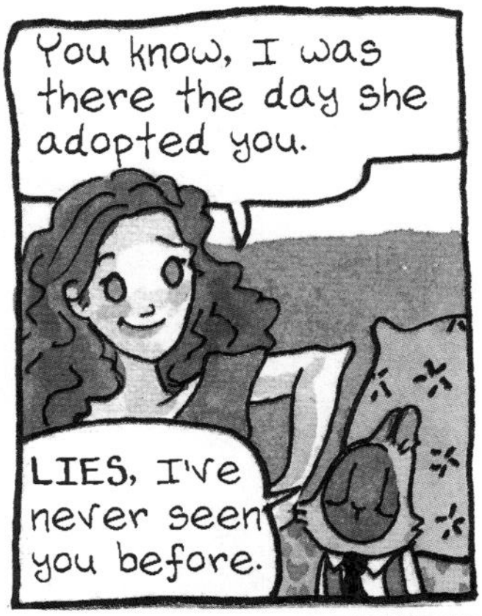
You know, I was there the day she adopted you.
LIES, I've never seen you before.

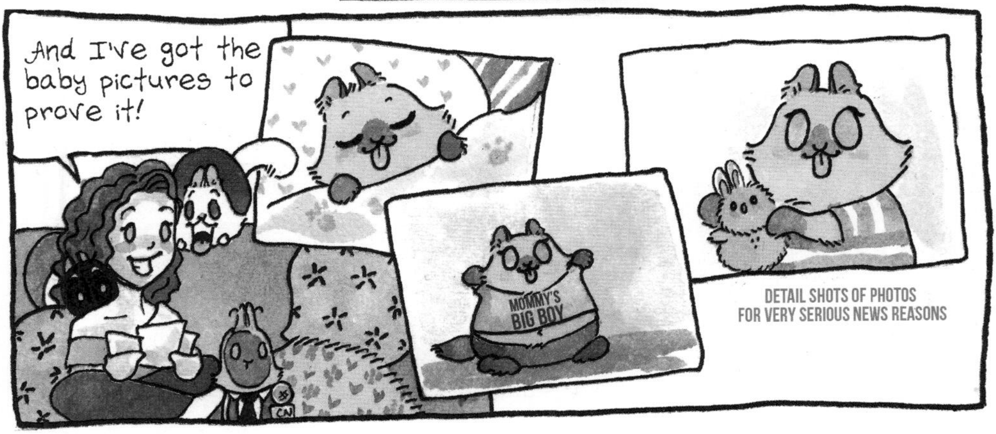
And I've got the baby pictures to prove it!
MOMMY'S BIG BOY
DETAIL SHOTS OF PHOTOS FOR VERY SERIOUS NEWS REASONS

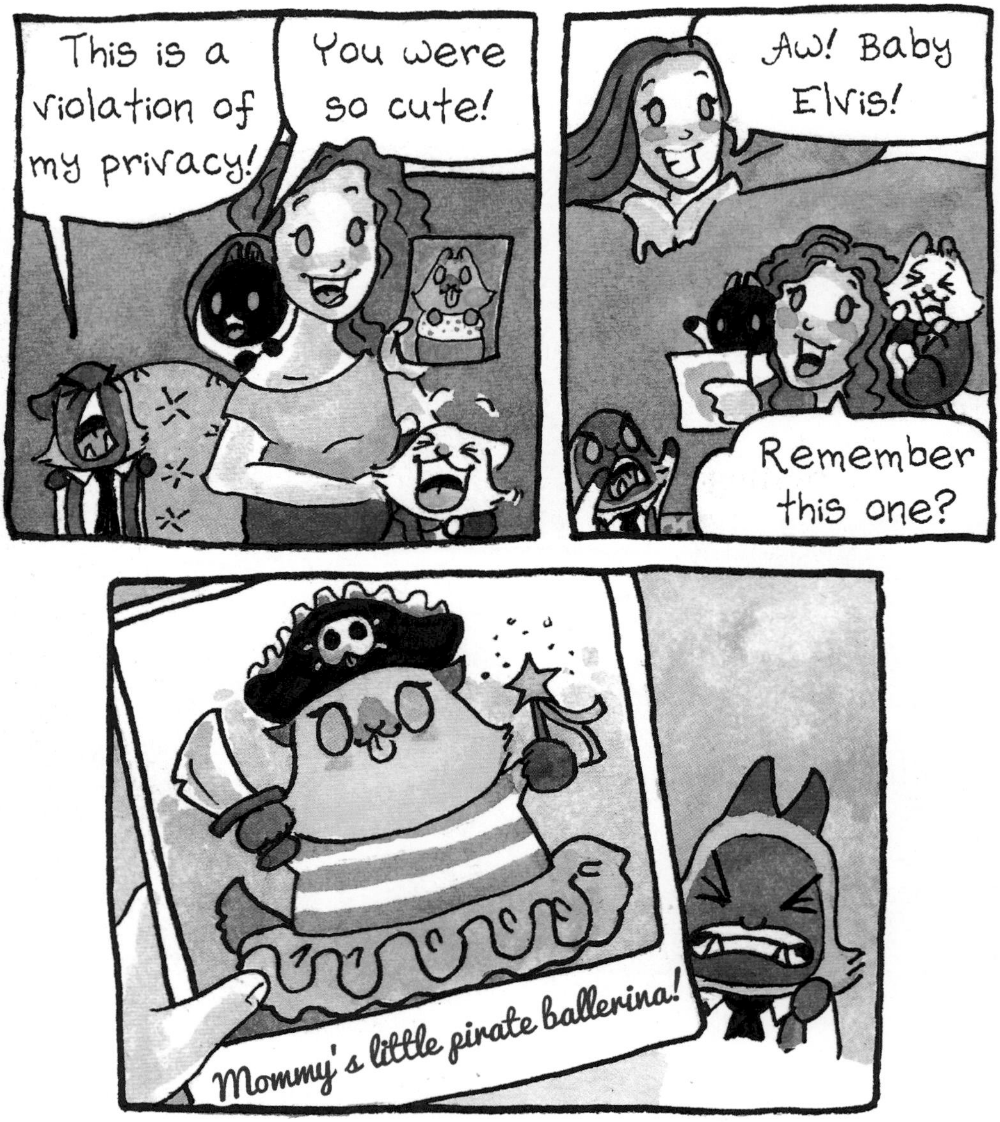
This is a violation of my privacy!
You were so cute!
Aw! Baby Elvis!
Remember this one?
Mommy's little pirate ballerina!

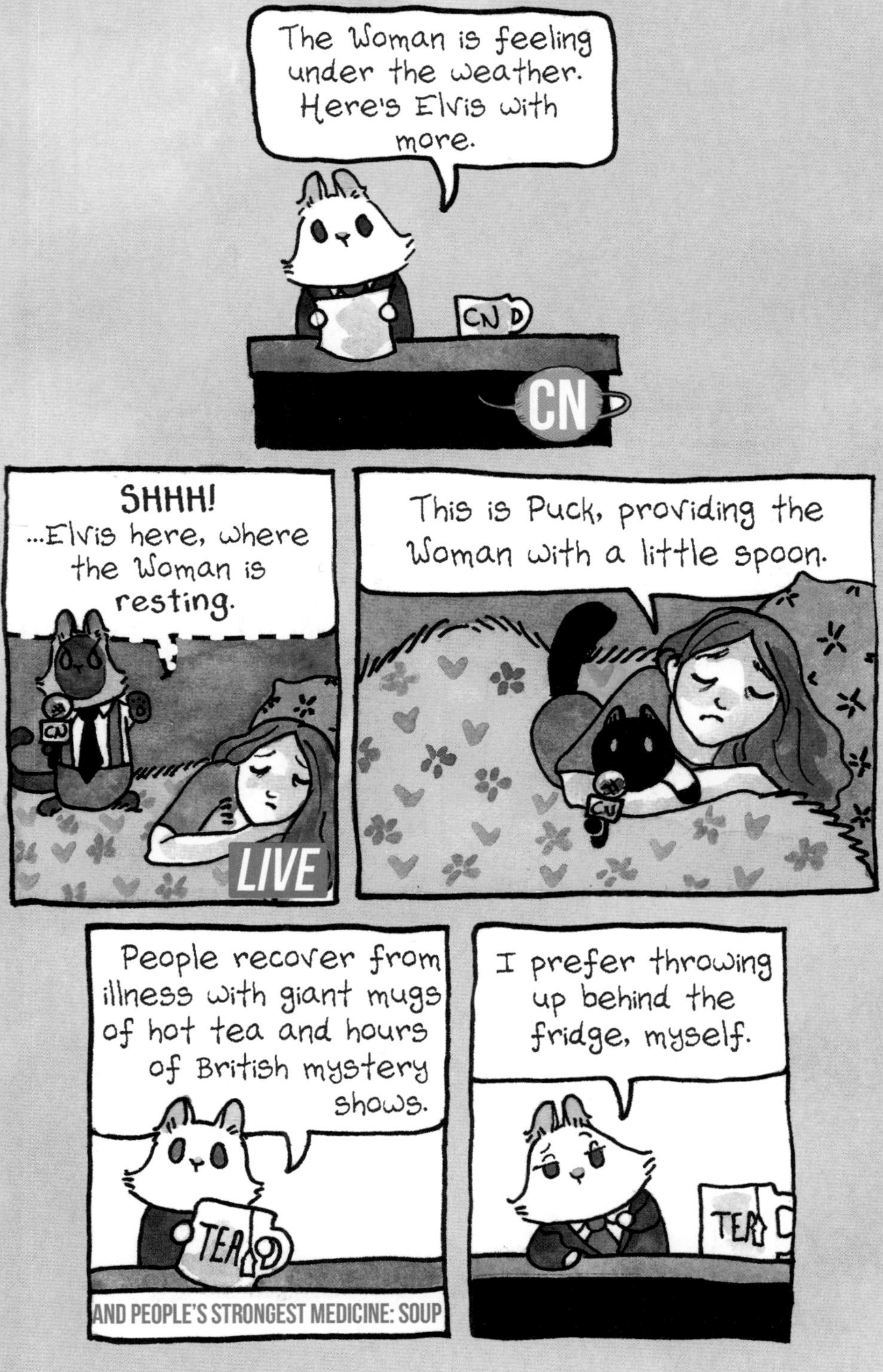
The Woman is feeling under the weather. Here's Elvis with more.
CN
CN
SHHH! ...Elvis here, where the Woman is resting.
CN
LIVE
This is Puck, providing the Woman with a little spoon.
People recover from illness with giant mugs of hot tea and hours of British mystery shows.
TEA
AND PEOPLE'S STRONGEST MEDICINE: SOUP
I prefer throwing up behind the fridge, myself.
TEA

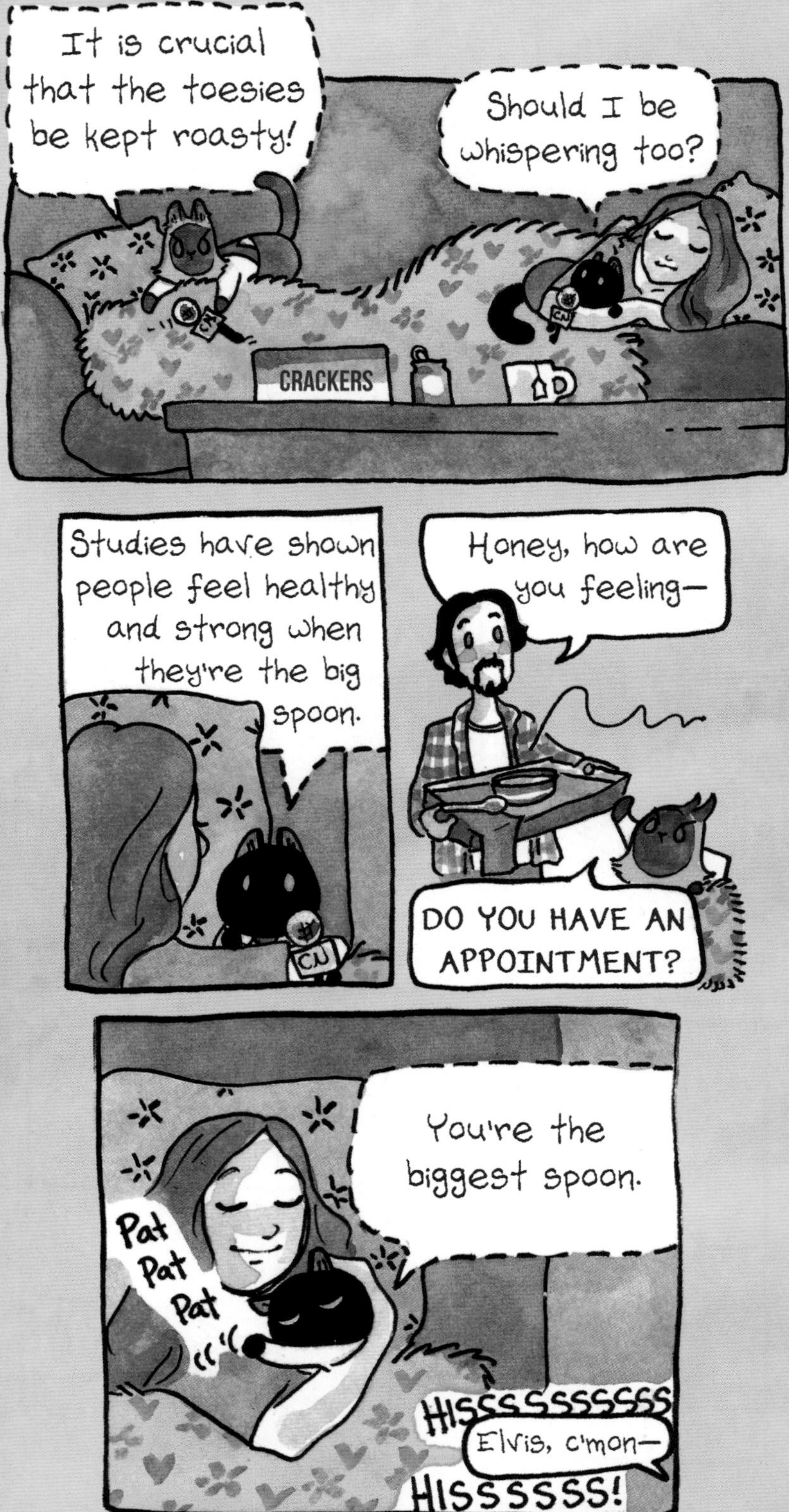
It is crucial that the toesies be kept roasty!
Should I be whispering too?
CRACKERS
CNJ
CNJ
Studies have shown people feel healthy and strong when they're the big spoon.
CNJ
Honey, how are you feeling—
DO YOU HAVE AN APPOINTMENT?
You're the biggest spoon.
Pat Pat Pat
HISSSSSSSSSS
Elvis, c'mon—
HISSSSSS!

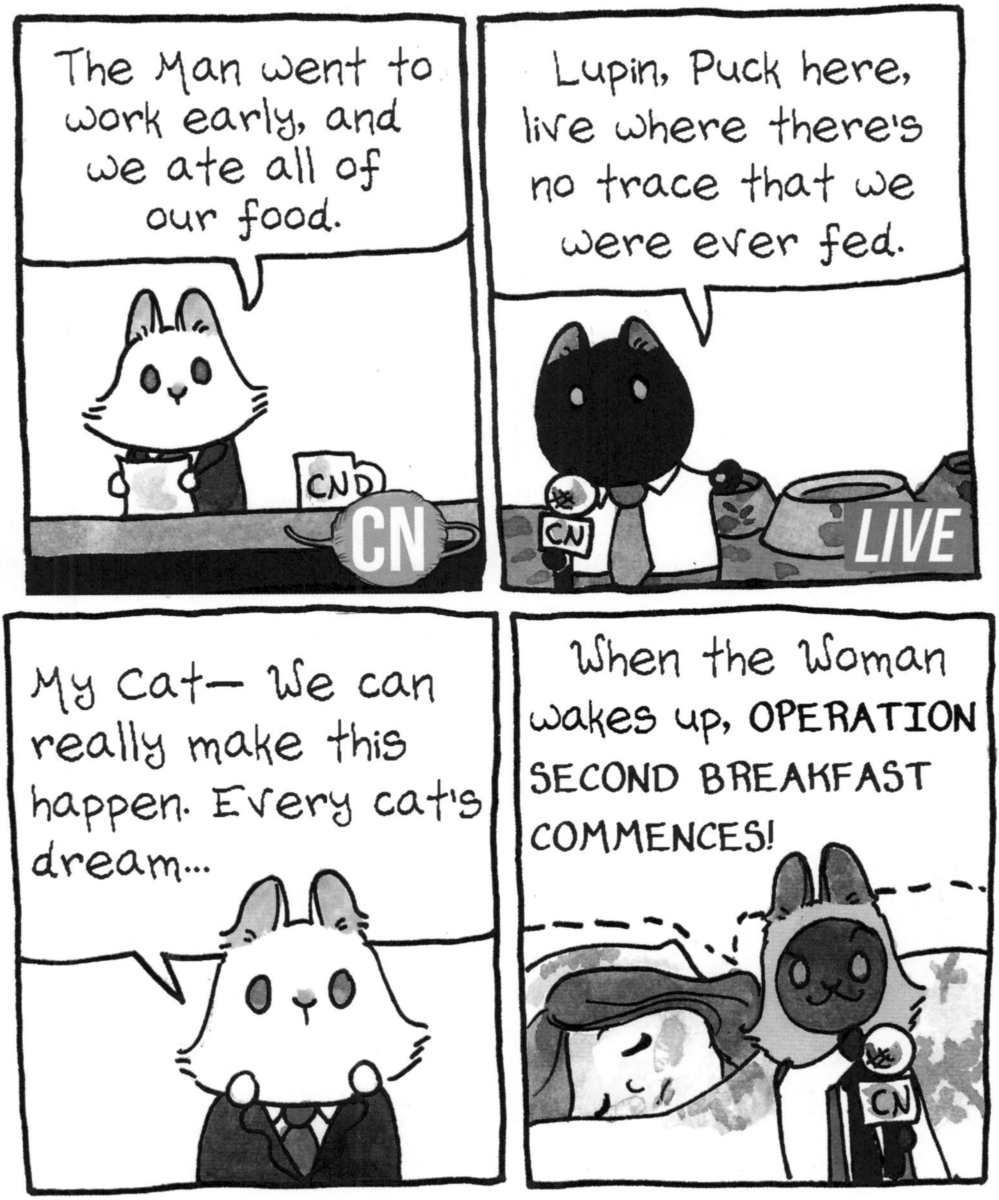
The Man went to work early, and we ate all of our food.
CND
CN
Lupin, Puck here, live where there's no trace that we were ever fed.
CN
LIVE
My Cat— We can really make this happen. Every cat's dream...
When the Woman wakes up, OPERATION SECOND BREAKFAST COMMENCES!
CN

Ma'am? CN news, Ma'am.
MA'AM?
Elvis? What time is it?
HALF PAST BREAKFAST O'CLOCK.
Haven't you been fed?
I have to be honest: No.
I HAVEN'T BEEN FED IN YEARS.

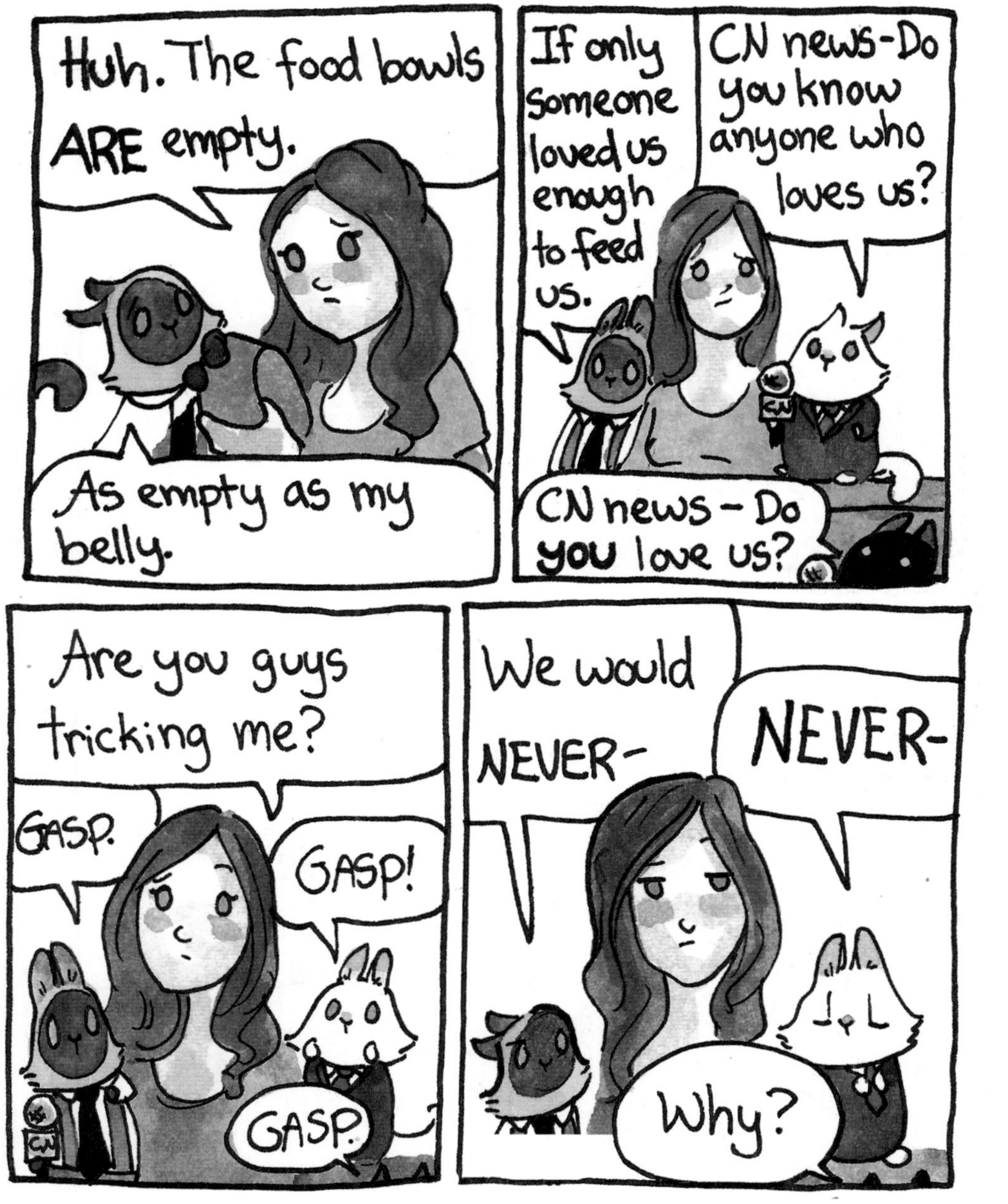
Huh. The food bowls ARE empty.
As empty as my belly.
If only someone loved us enough to feed us.
CN news-Do you know anyone who loves us?
CN news - Do you love us?
Are you guys tricking me?
GASP.
GASP!
GASP.
We would NEVER-
NEVER-
Why?

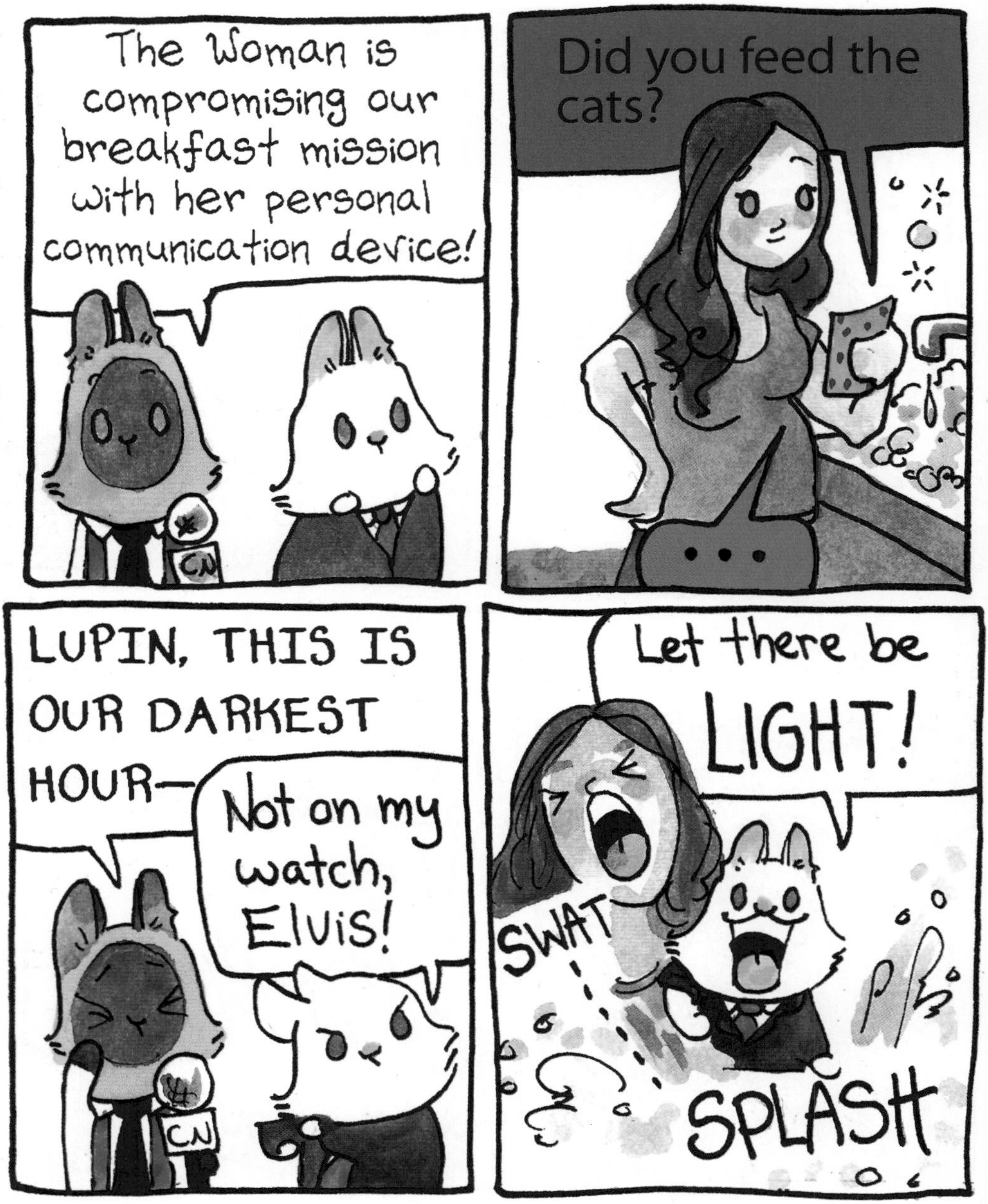
The Woman is compromising our breakfast mission with her personal communication device!
CN
Did you feed the cats?
...
LUPIN, THIS IS OUR DARKEST HOUR—
Not on my watch, Elvis!
CN
Let there be LIGHT!
SWAT
SPLASH

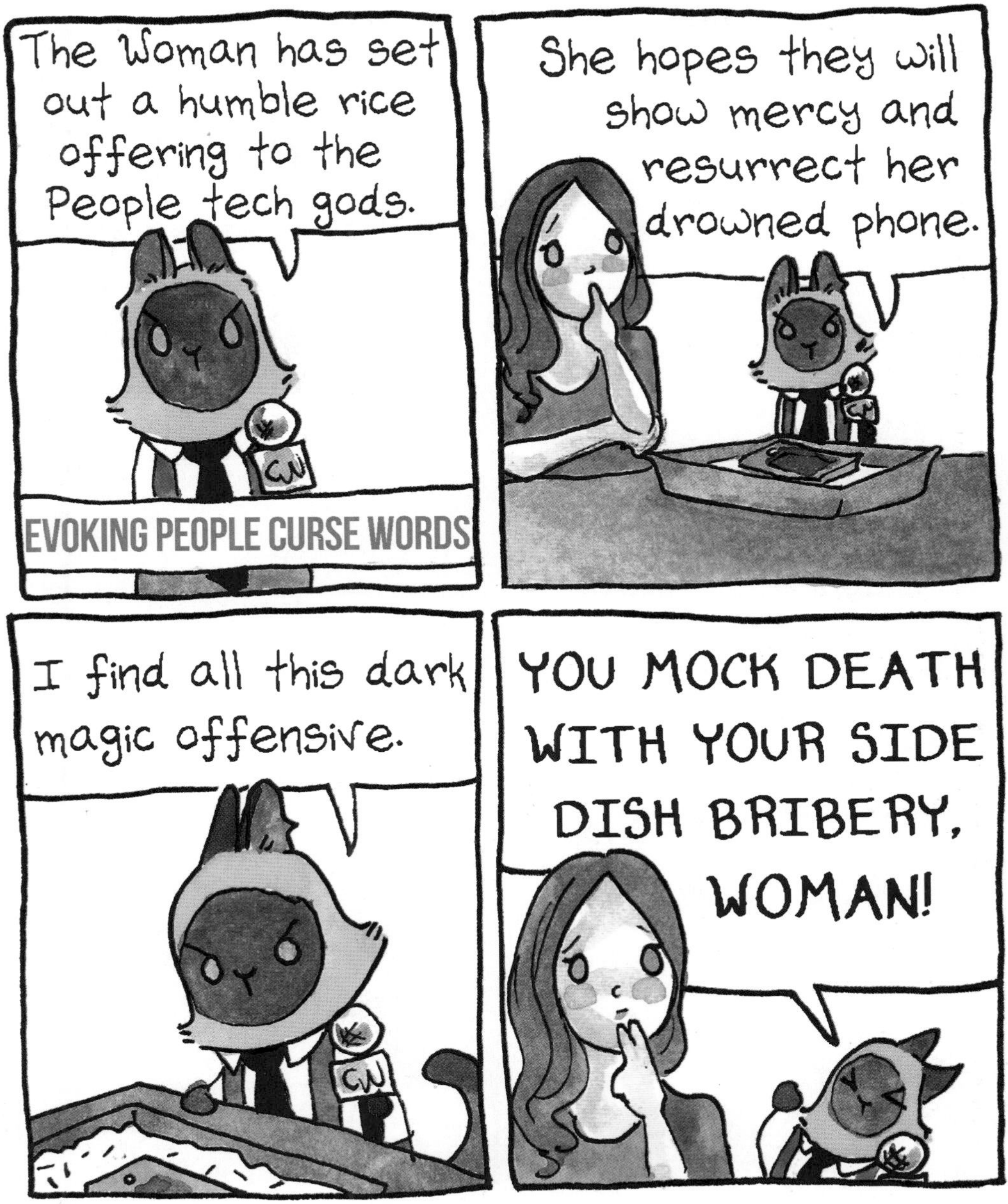
The Woman has set out a humble rice offering to the People tech gods.
EVOKING PEOPLE CURSE WORDS
She hopes they will show mercy and resurrect her drowned phone.
I find all this dark magic offensive.
YOU MOCK DEATH WITH YOUR SIDE DISH BRIBERY, WOMAN!

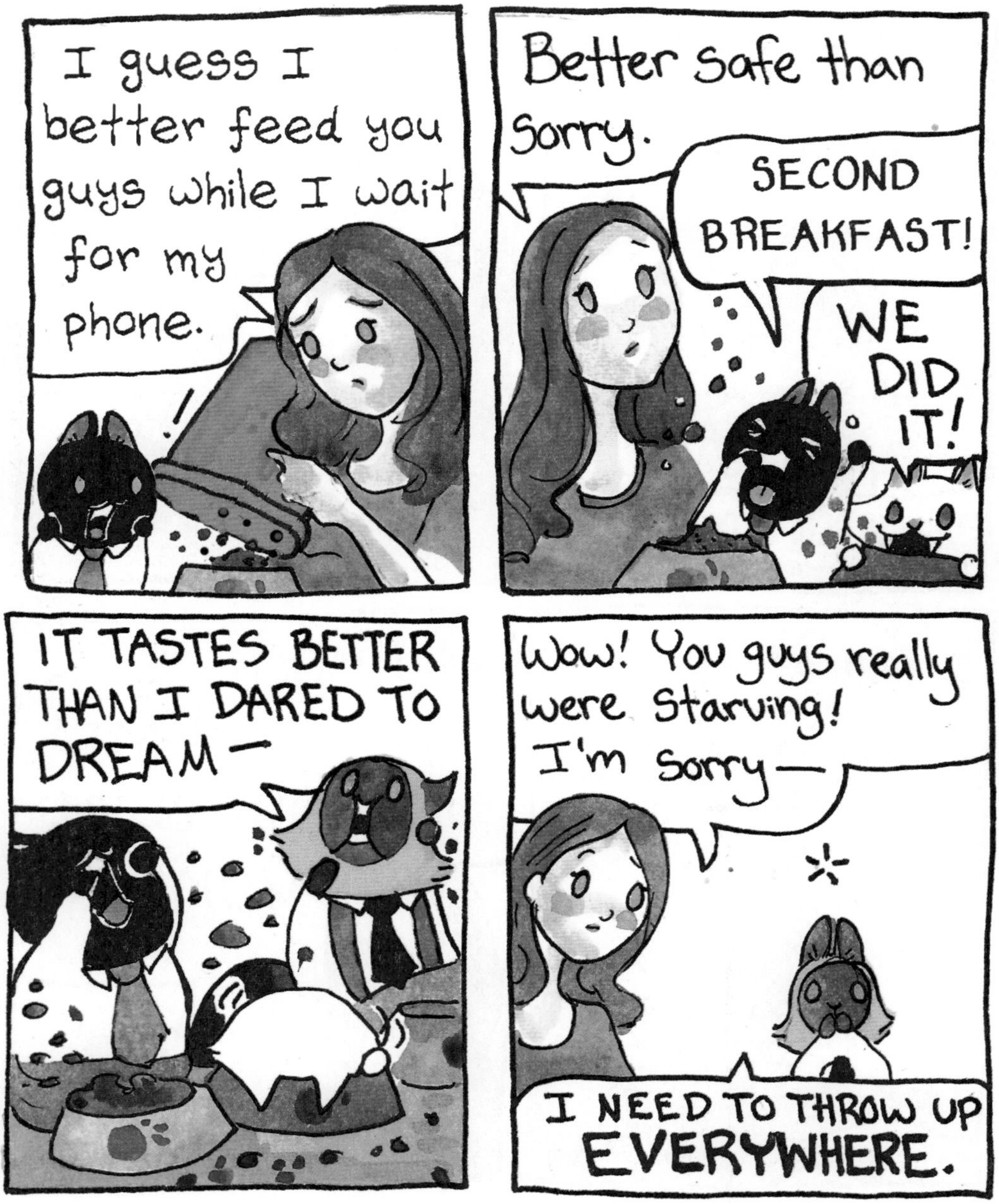
I guess I better feed you guys while I wait for my phone.
Better safe than sorry.
SECOND BREAKFAST!
WE DID IT!
IT TASTES BETTER THAN I DARED TO DREAM—
Wow! You guys really were starving! I'm sorry—
I NEED TO THROW UP EVERYWHERE.

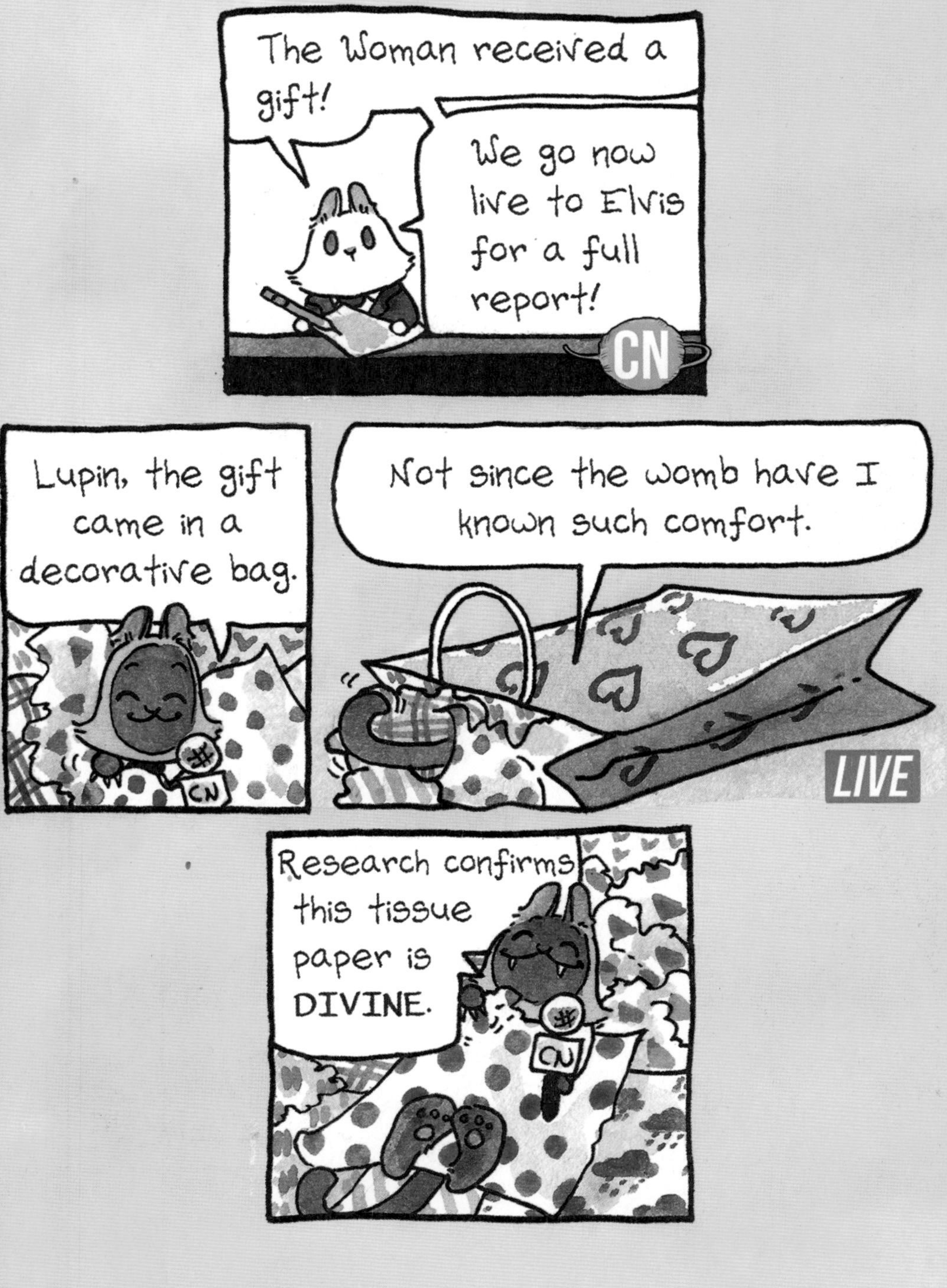
The Woman received a gift!
We go now live to Elvis for a full report!
CN
Lupin, the gift came in a decorative bag.
CN
Not since the womb have I known such comfort.
LIVE
Research confirms this tissue paper is DIVINE.
CN

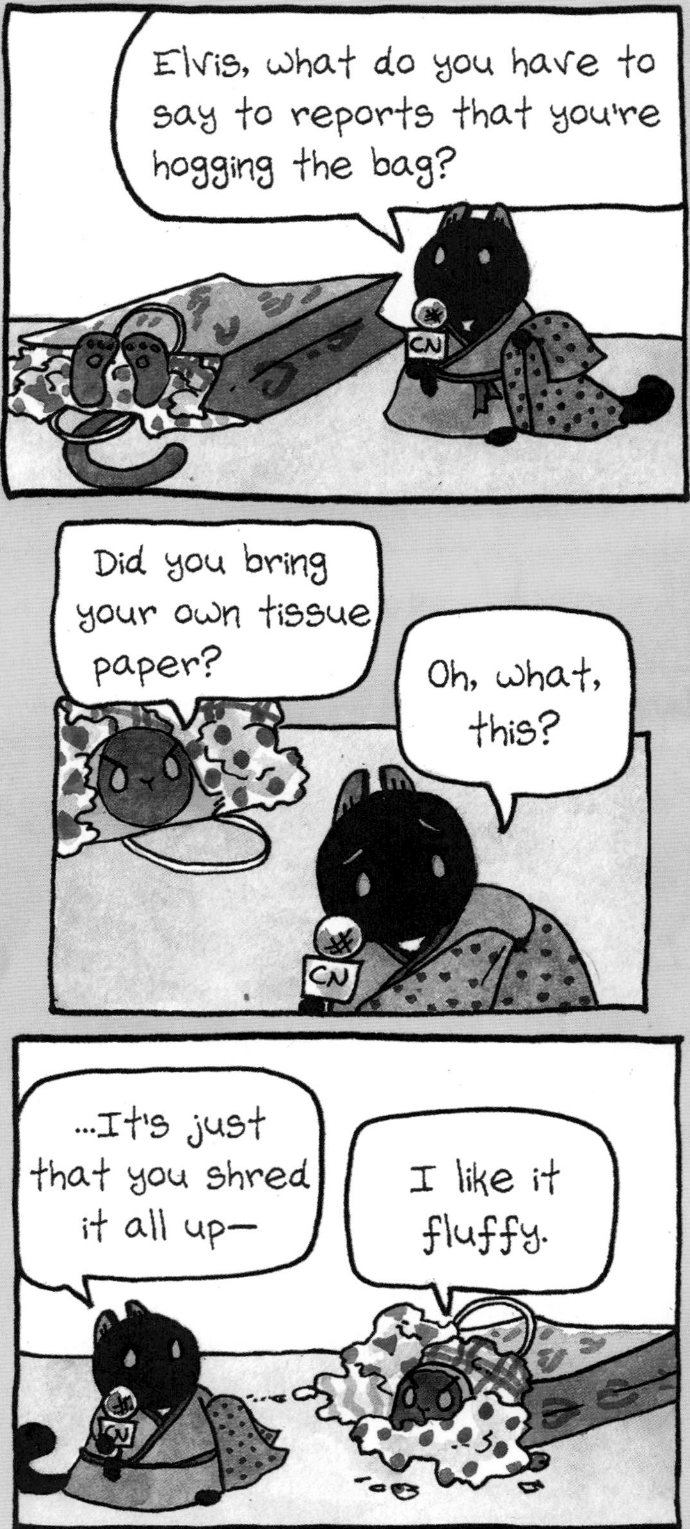
Elvis, what do you have to say to reports that you're hogging the bag?
Did you bring your own tissue paper?
Oh, what, this?
...It's just that you shred it all up—
I like it fluffy.

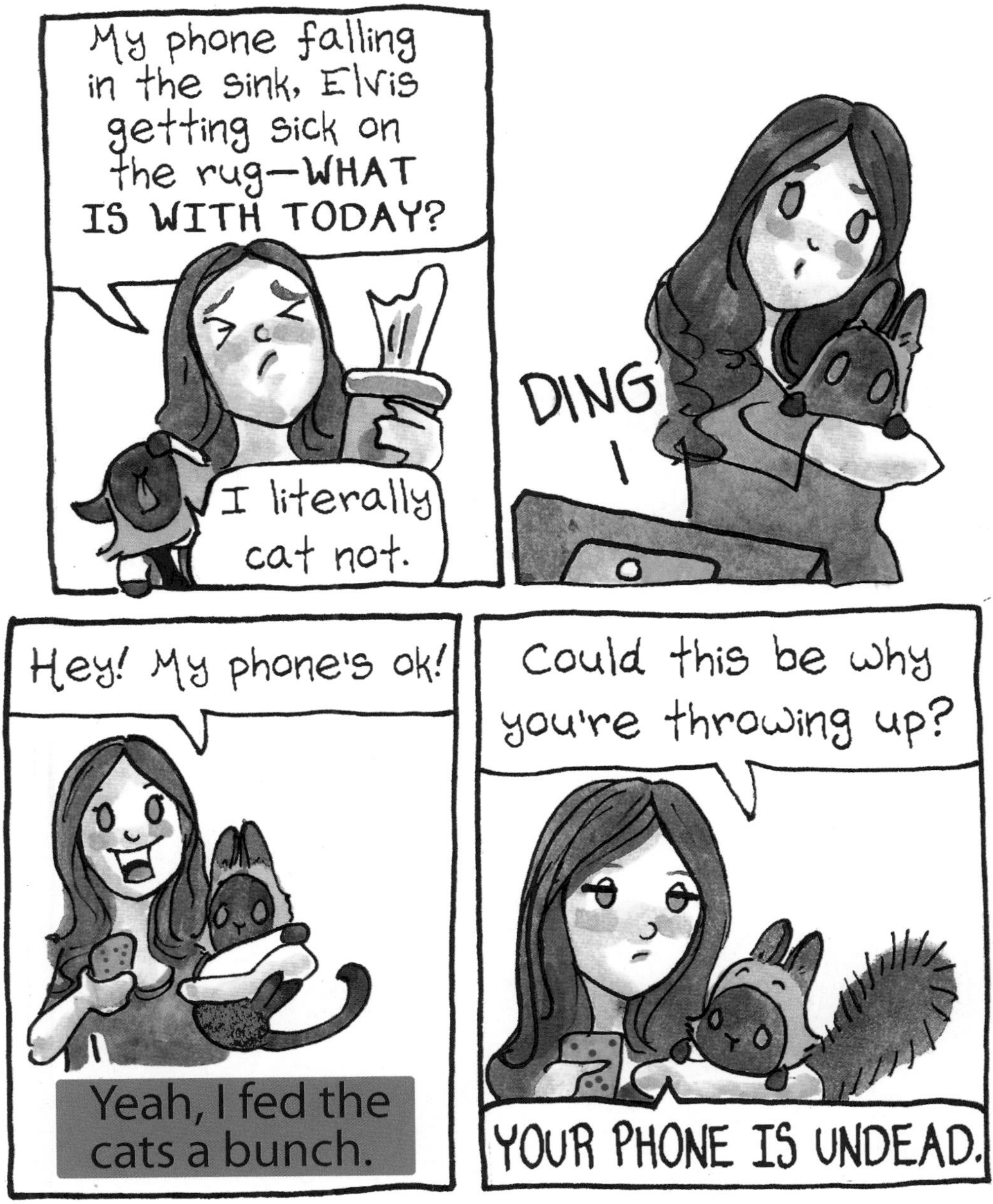
My phone falling in the sink, Elvis getting sick on the rug—WHAT IS WITH TODAY?
I literally cat not.
DING
Hey! My phone's ok!
Yeah, I fed the cats a bunch.
Could this be why you're throwing up?
YOUR PHONE IS UNDEAD.

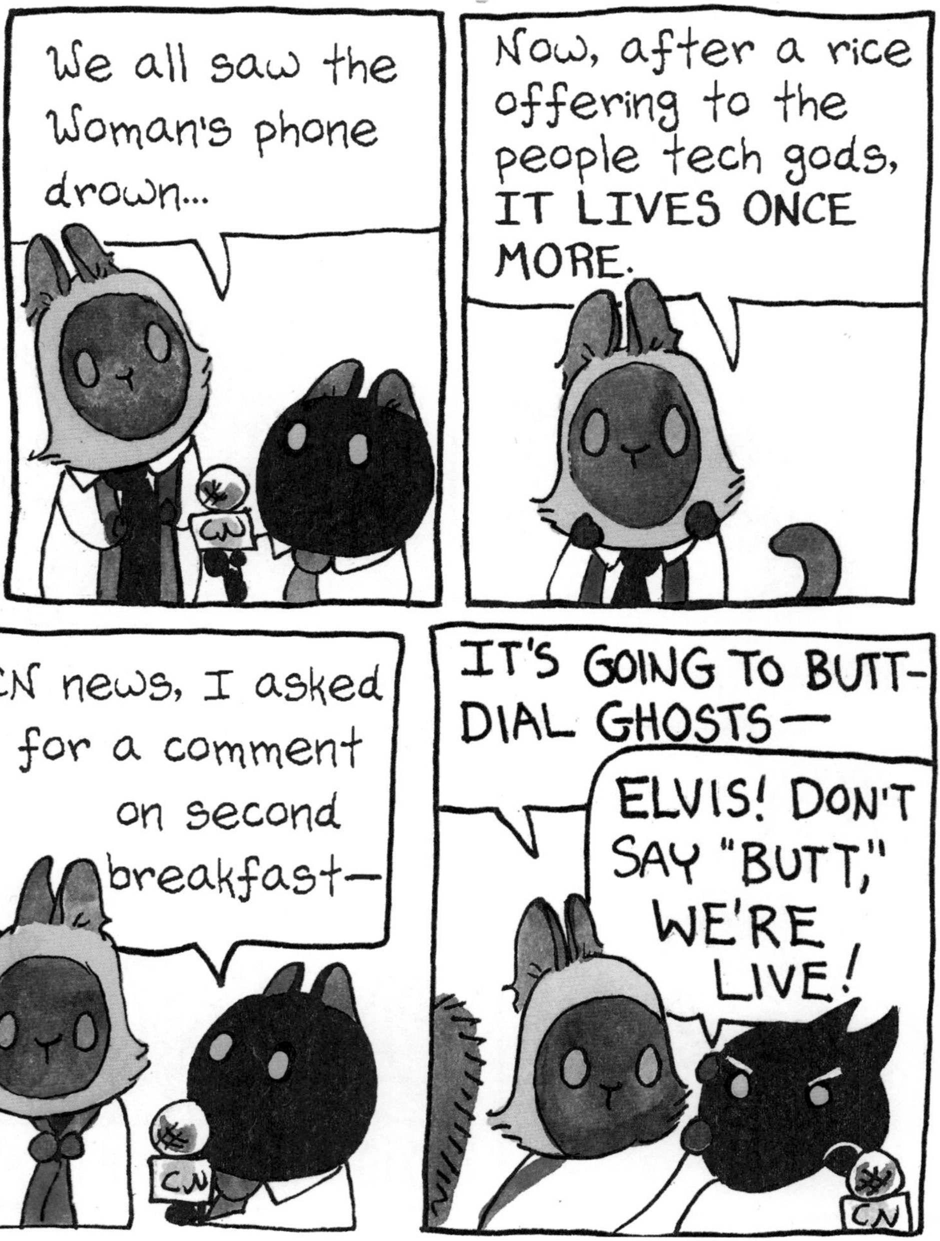
We all saw the Woman's phone drown...
Now, after a rice offering to the people tech gods, IT LIVES ONCE MORE.
CN news, I asked for a comment on second breakfast—
IT'S GOING TO BUTT-DIAL GHOSTS—
ELVIS! DON'T SAY "BUTT," WE'RE LIVE!

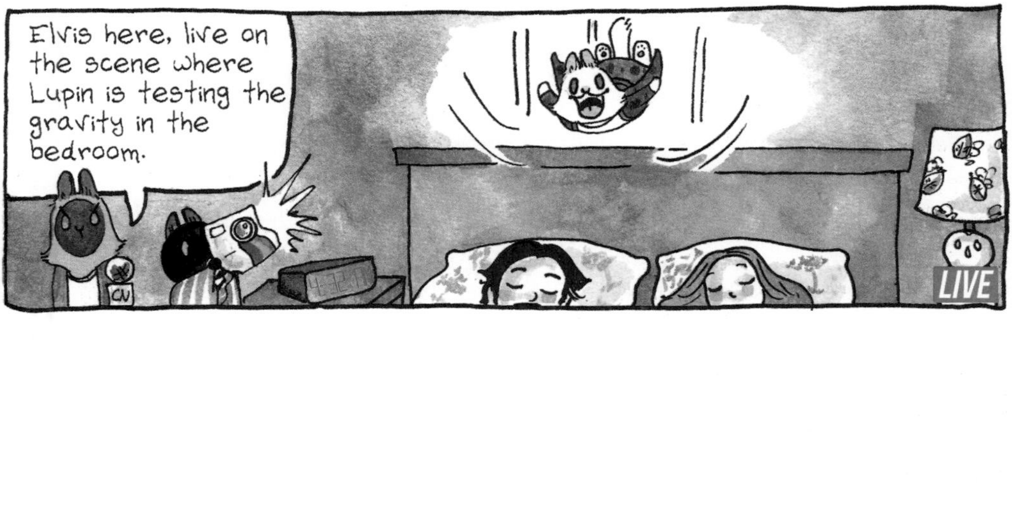
Elvis here, live on the scene where Lupin is testing the gravity in the bedroom.
CN
LIVE

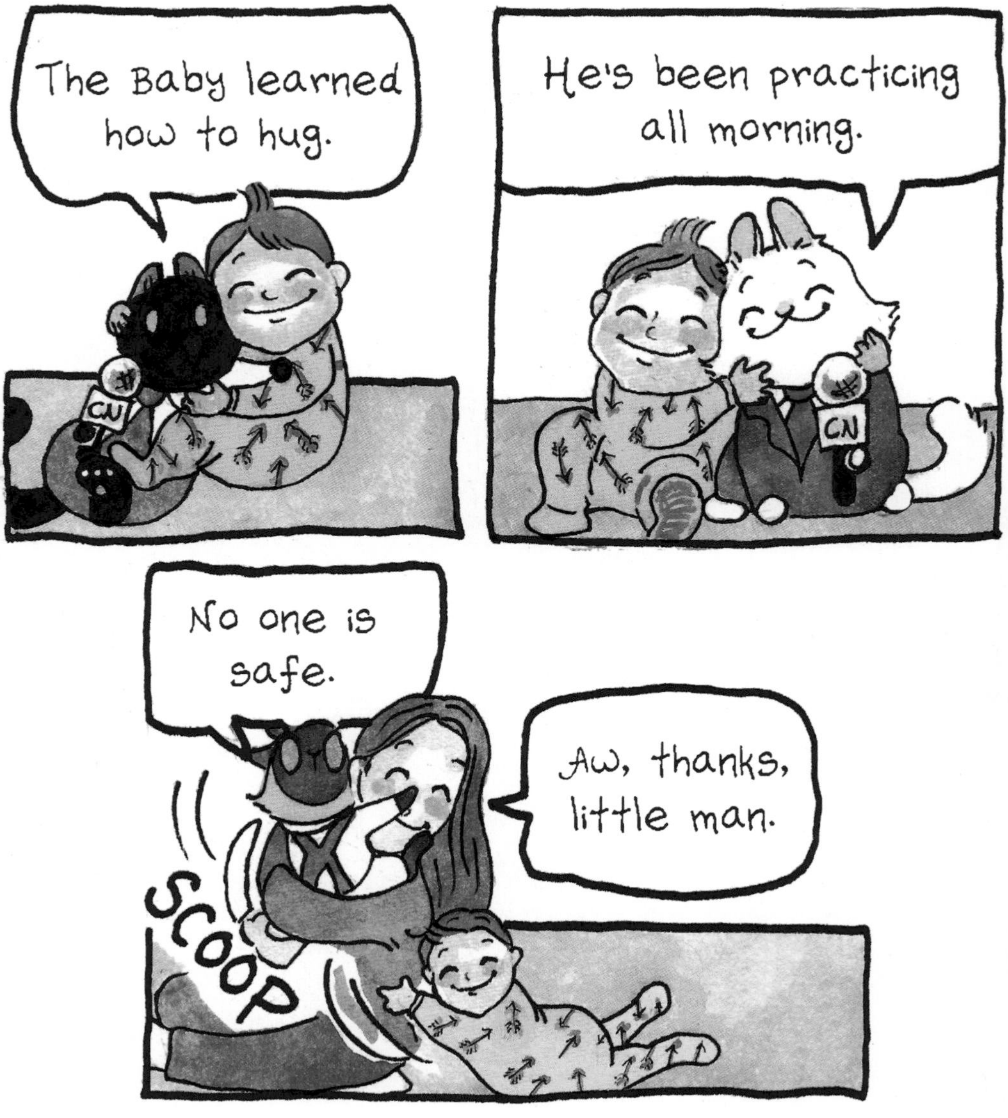
The Baby learned how to hug.
CN
He's been practicing all morning.
CN
No one is safe.
Aw, thanks, little man.
SCOOP

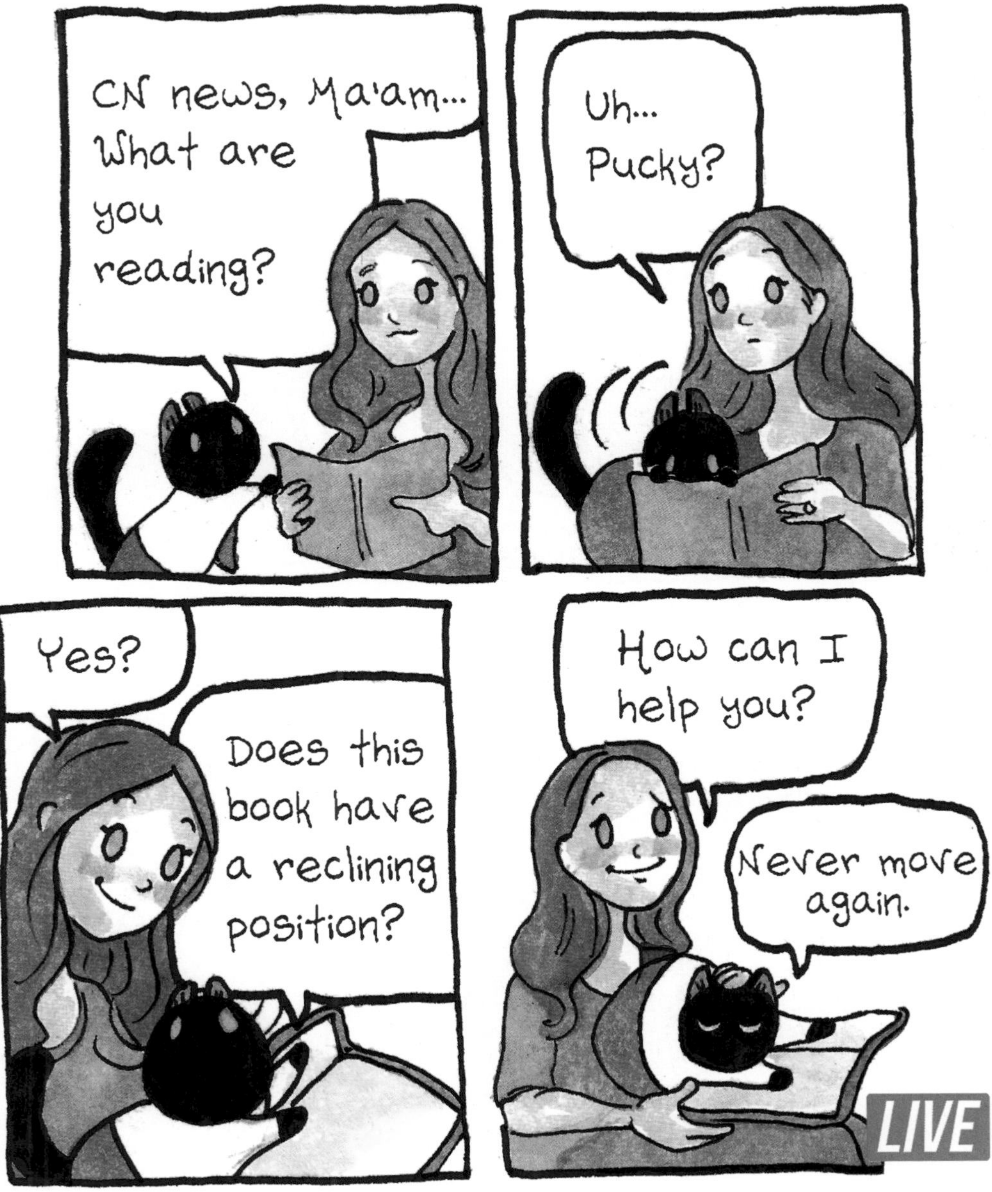
CN news, Ma'am... What are you reading?
Uh... Pucky?
Yes?
Does this book have a reclining position?
How can I help you?
Never move again.
LIVE

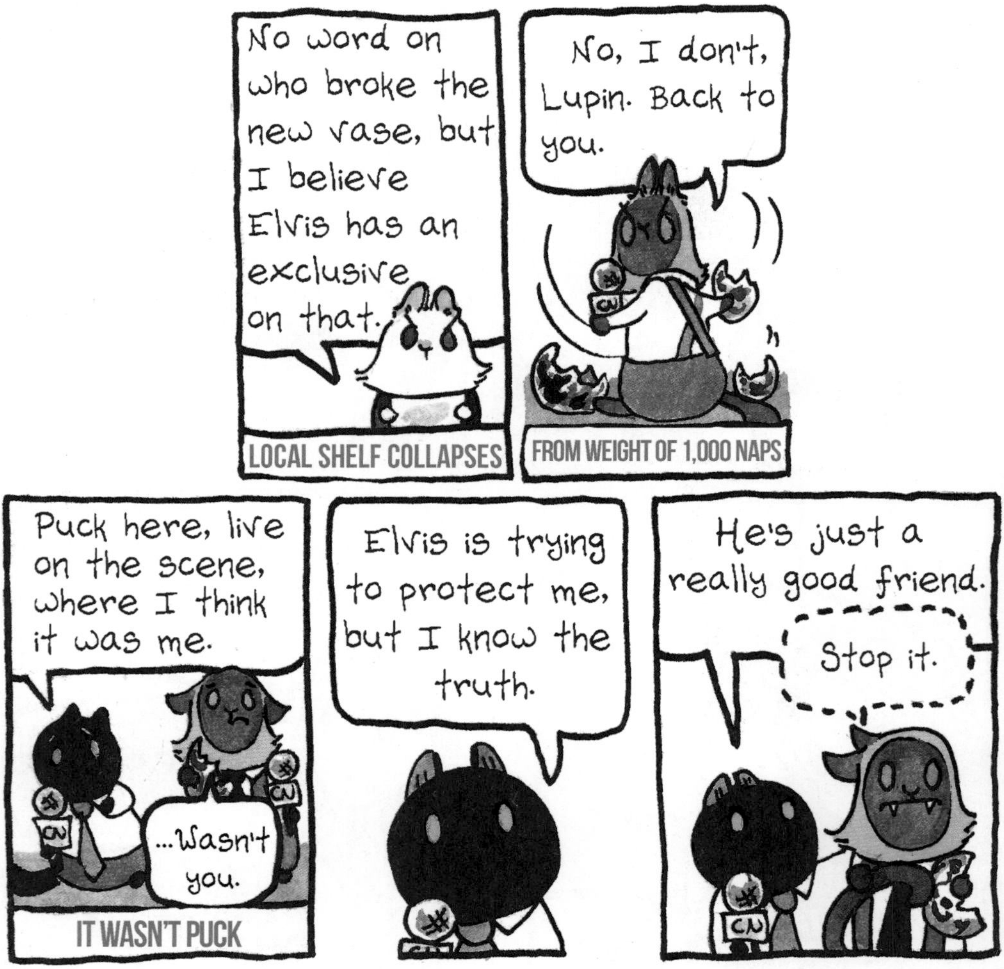
No word on who broke the new vase, but I believe Elvis has an exclusive on that.
LOCAL SHELF COLLAPSES
No, I don't, Lupin. Back to you.
FROM WEIGHT OF 1,000 NAPS
Puck here, live on the scene, where I think it was me.
...Wasn't you.
IT WASN'T PUCK
Elvis is trying to protect me, but I know the truth.
He's just a really good friend.
Stop it.

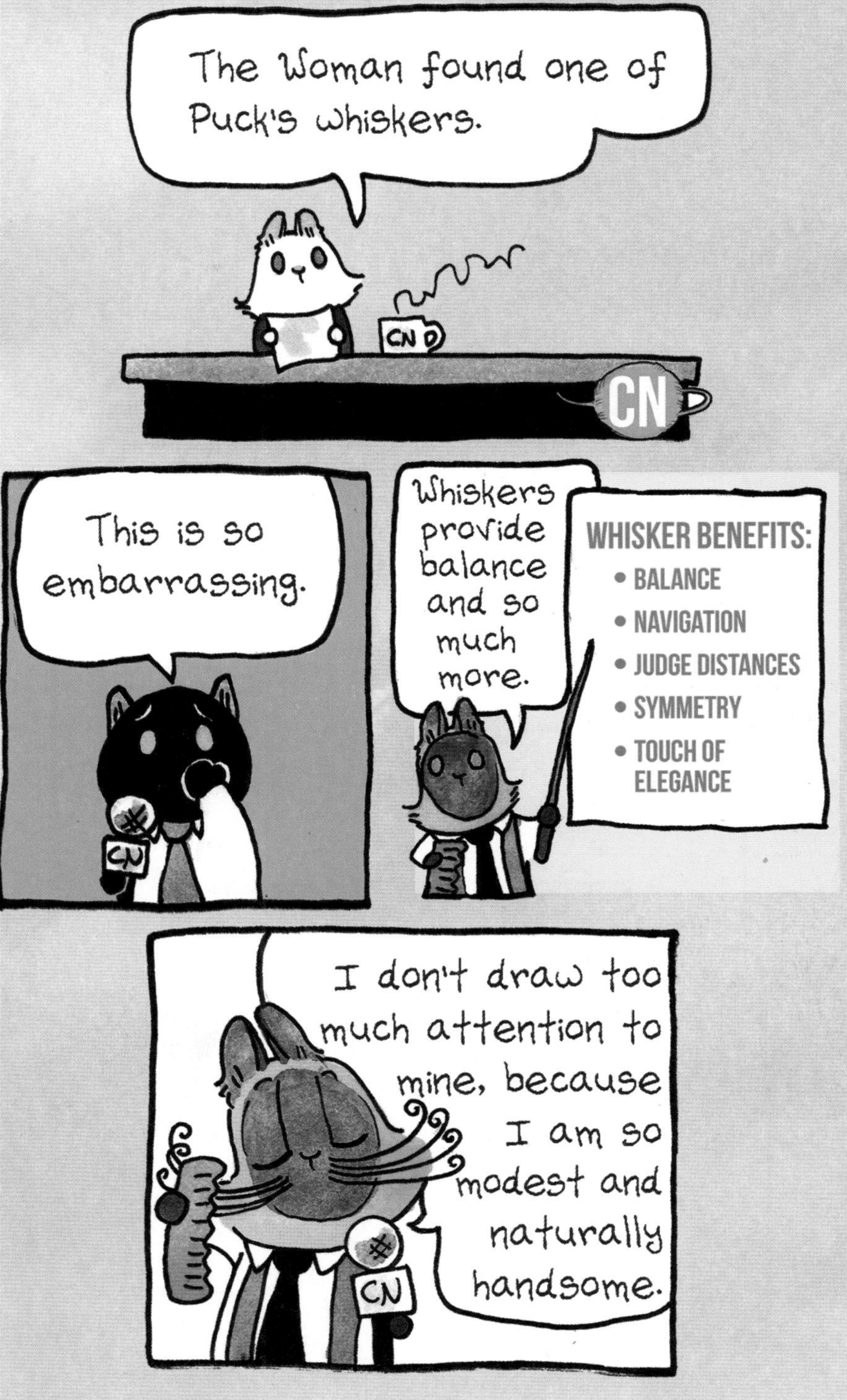
The Woman found one of Puck's whiskers.
CN
CN
This is so embarrassing.
CN
Whiskers provide balance and so much more.
WHISKER BENEFITS:
• BALANCE
• NAVIGATION
• JUDGE DISTANCES
• SYMMETRY
• TOUCH OF ELEGANCE
I don't draw too much attention to mine, because I am so modest and naturally handsome.
CN

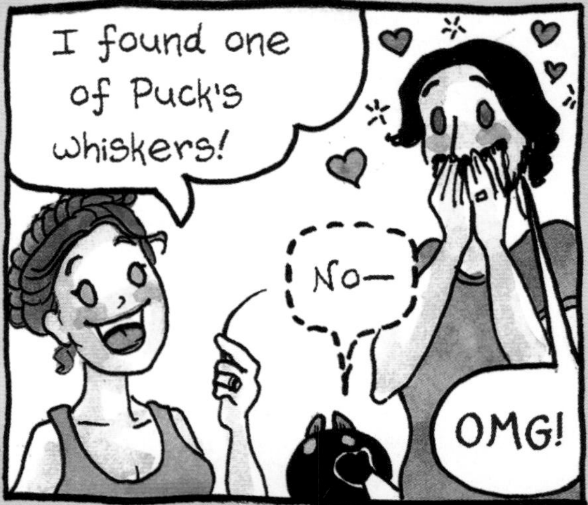
I found one of Puck's whiskers!
No—
OMG!

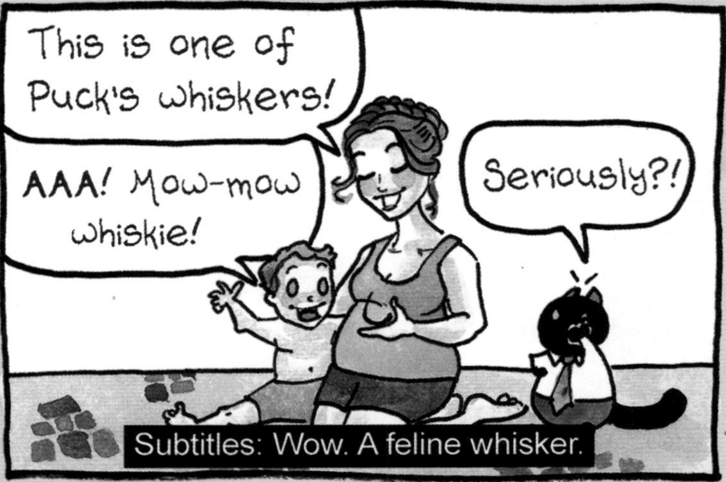
This is one of Puck's whiskers!
AAA! Mow-mow whiskie!
Seriously?!
Subtitles: Wow. A feline whisker.

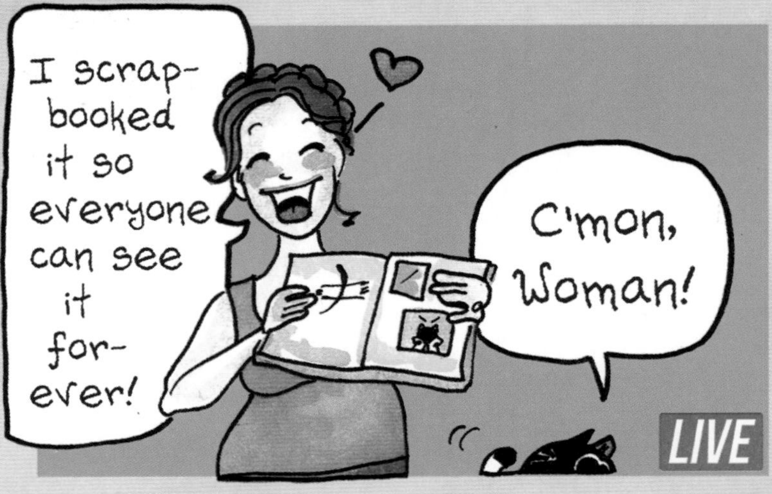
I scrap-booked it so everyone can see it for-ever!
C'mon, Woman!
LIVE

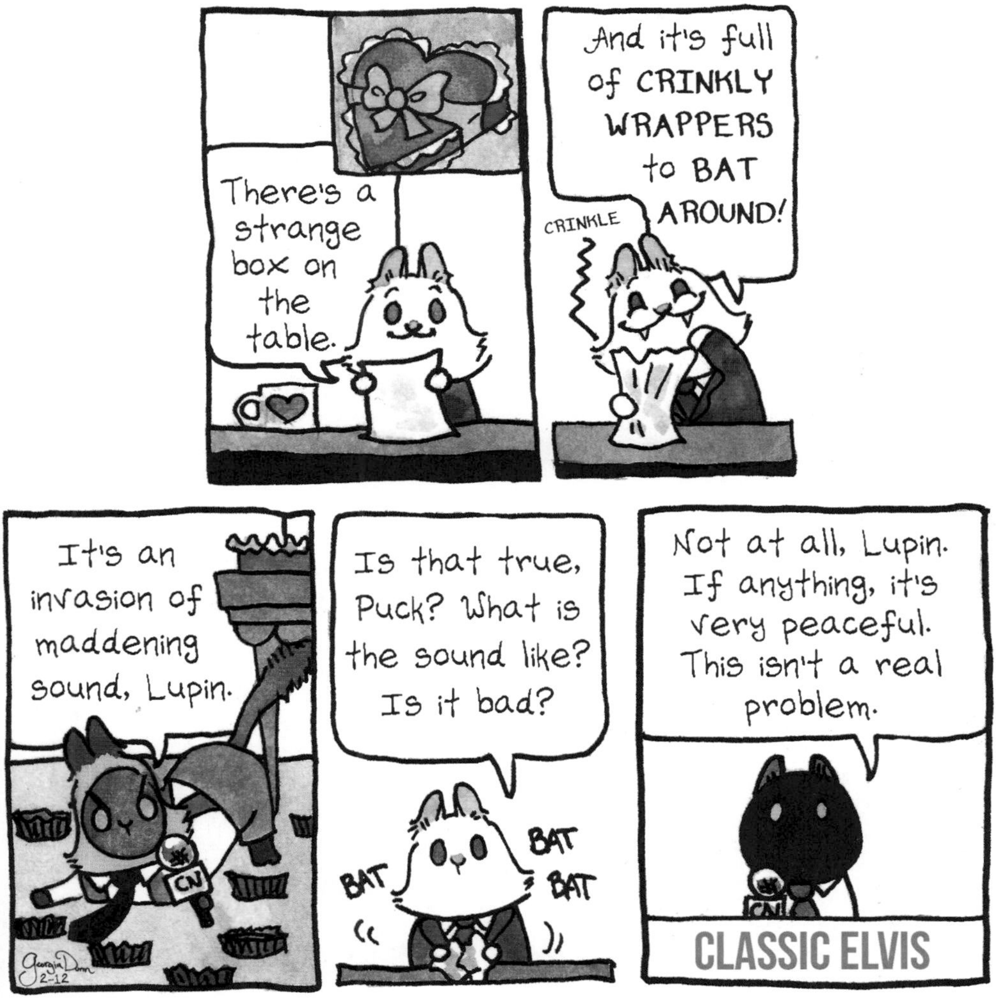
There's a strange box on the table.
And it's full of CRINKLY WRAPPERS to BAT AROUND!
CRINKLE
It's an invasion of maddening sound, Lupin.
CN
Is that true, Puck? What is the sound like? Is it bad?
BAT
BAT
BAT
Not at all, Lupin. If anything, it's very peaceful. This isn't a real problem.
CN
CLASSIC ELVIS
Georgia Dunn 2-12

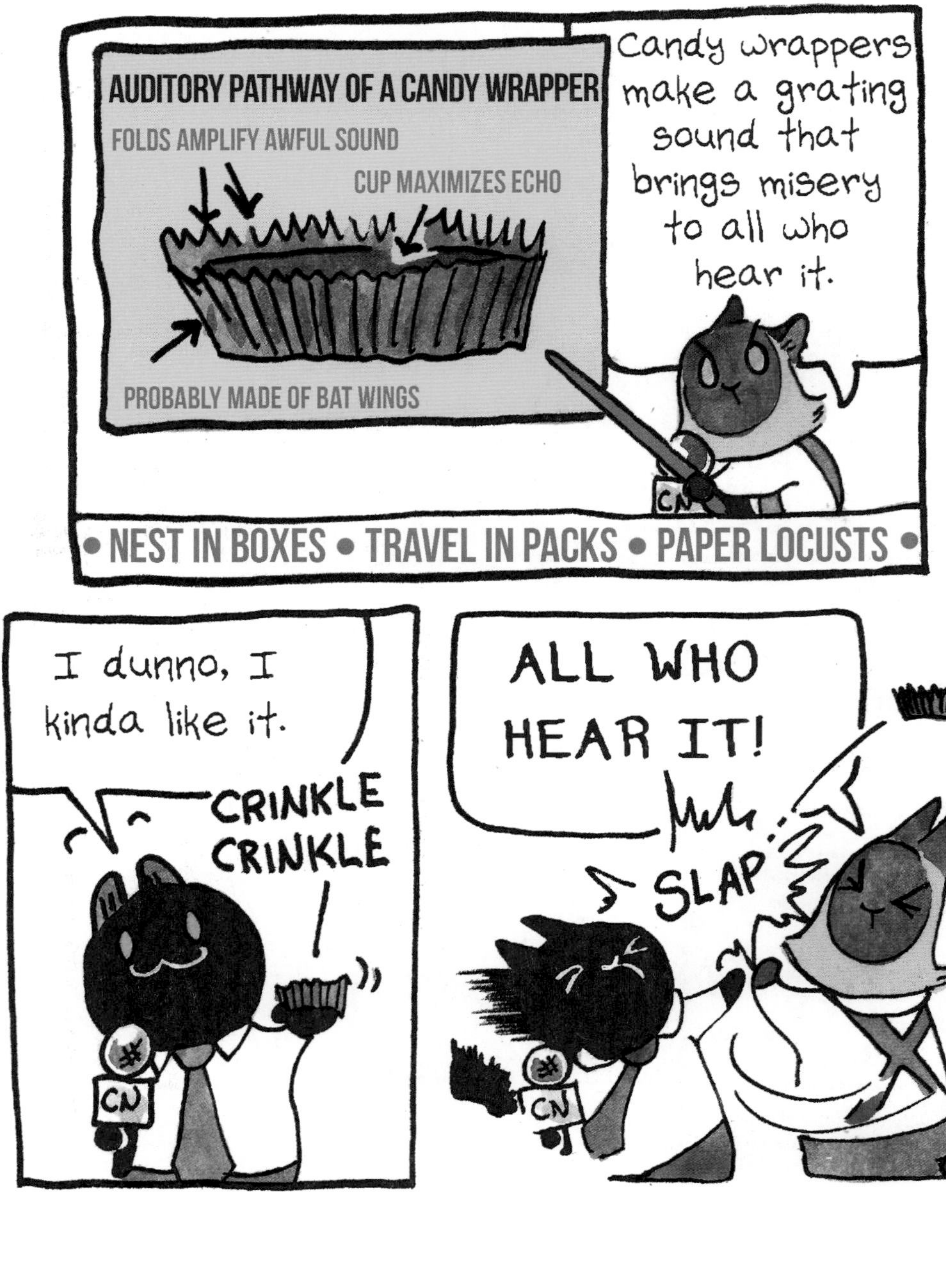
AUDITORY PATHWAY OF A CANDY WRAPPER
FOLDS AMPLIFY AWFUL SOUND
CUP MAXIMIZES ECHO
PROBABLY MADE OF BAT WINGS
Candy wrappers make a grating sound that brings misery to all who hear it.
CN
• NEST IN BOXES • TRAVEL IN PACKS • PAPER LOCUSTS •
I dunno, I kinda like it.
CRINKLE CRINKLE
CN
ALL WHO HEAR IT!
SLAP
CN

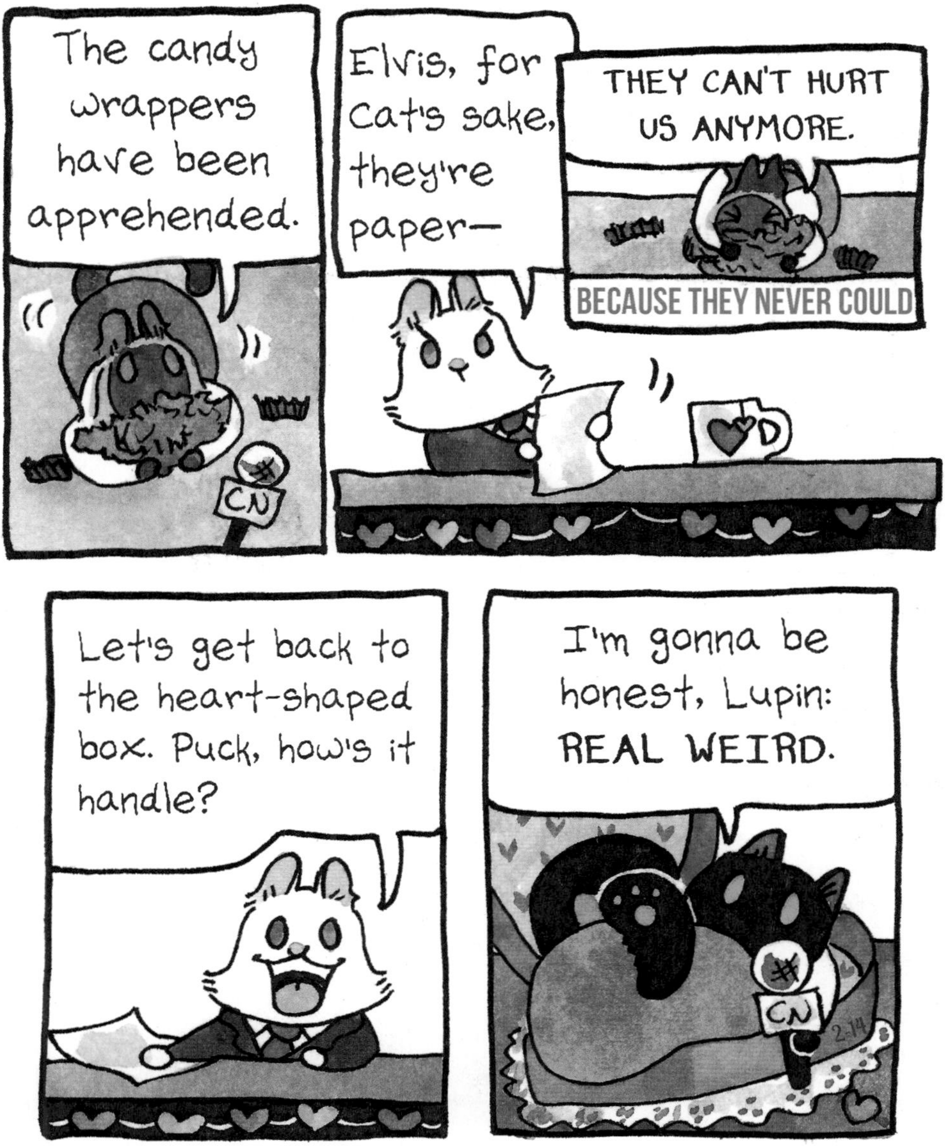
The candy wrappers have been apprehended.
CN
Elvis, for cat's sake, they're paper—
THEY CAN'T HURT US ANYMORE.
BECAUSE THEY NEVER COULD
Let's get back to the heart-shaped box. Puck, how's it handle?
I'm gonna be honest, Lupin: REAL WEIRD.
CN

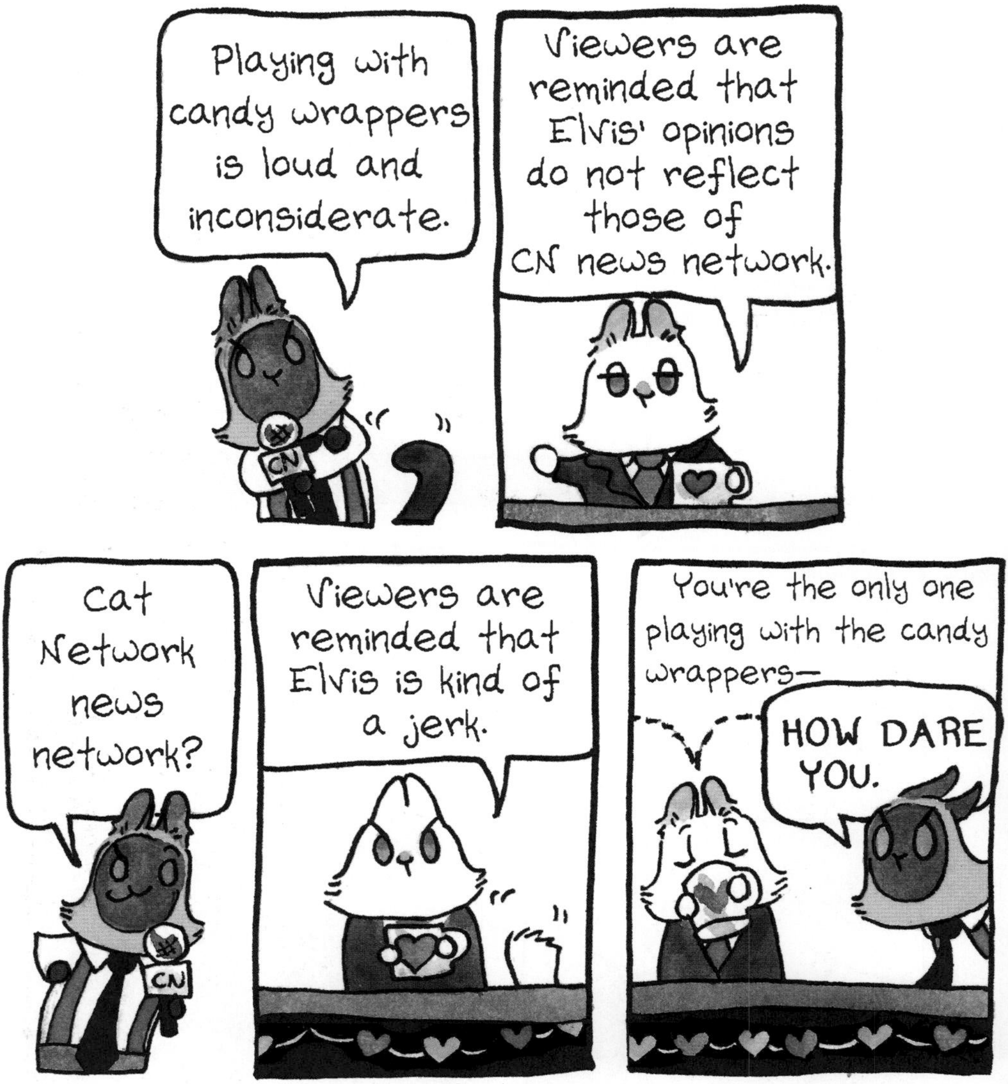
Playing with candy wrappers is loud and inconsiderate.
Viewers are reminded that Elvis' opinions do not reflect those of CN news network.
CN
Cat Network news network?
CN
Viewers are reminded that Elvis is kind of a jerk.
You're the only one playing with the candy wrappers—
HOW DARE YOU.

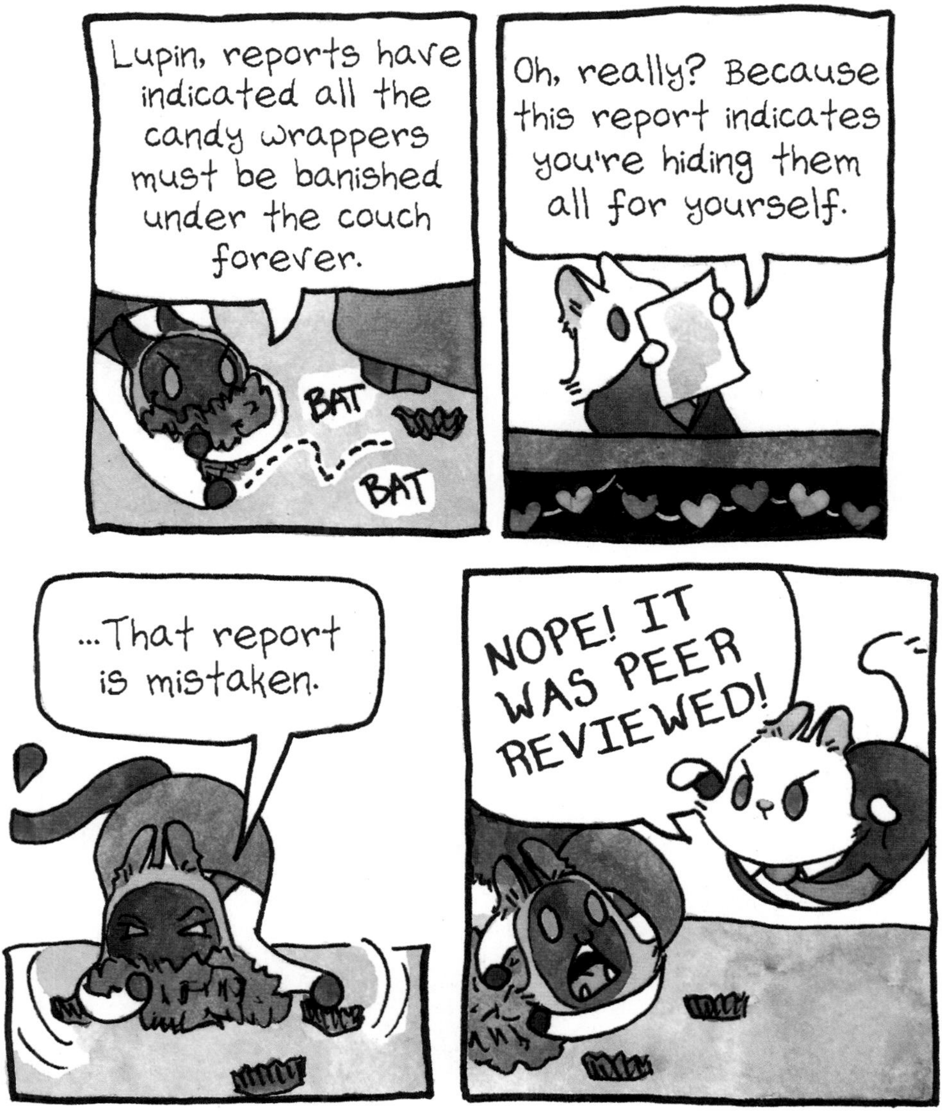
Lupin, reports have indicated all the candy wrappers must be banished under the couch forever.
BAT
BAT
Oh, really? Because this report indicates you're hiding them all for yourself.
...That report is mistaken.
NOPE! IT WAS PEER REVIEWED!

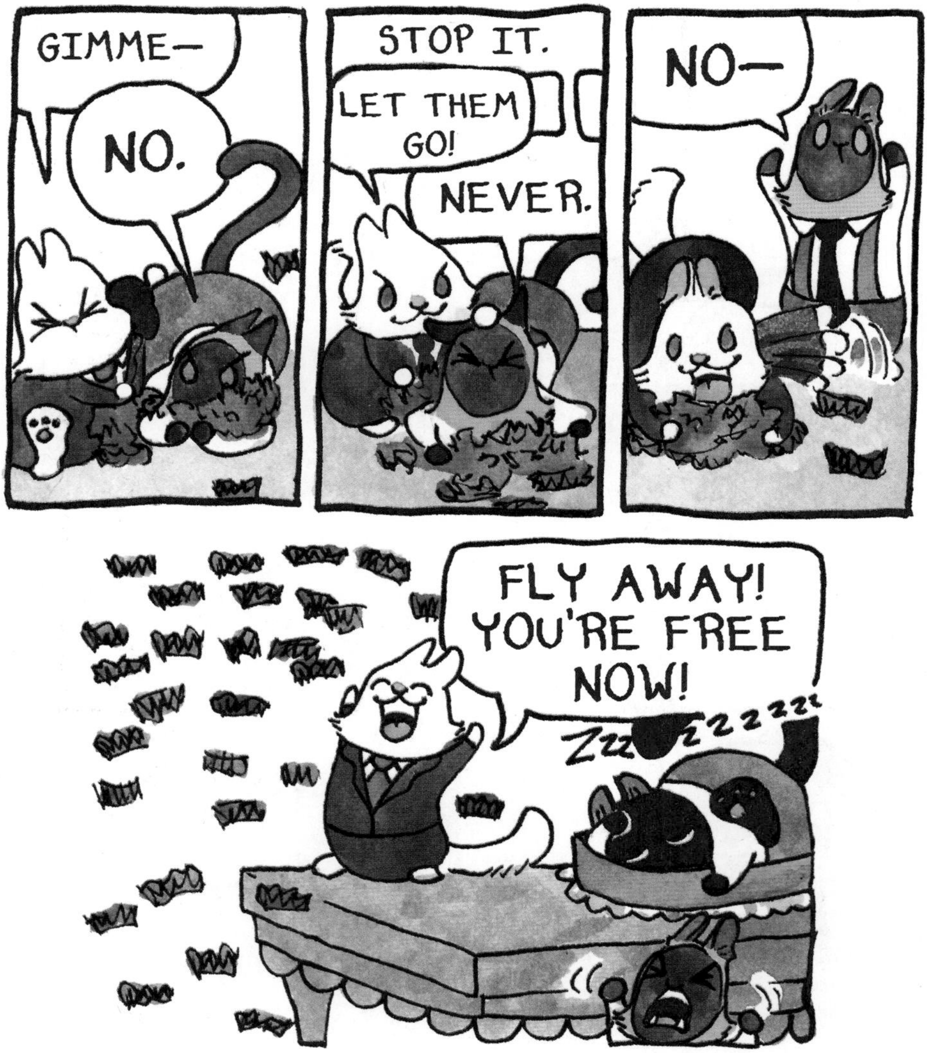
GIMME—
NO.
STOP IT.
LET THEM GO!
NEVER.
NO—
FLY AWAY! YOU'RE FREE NOW!
Zzz
zzzzz

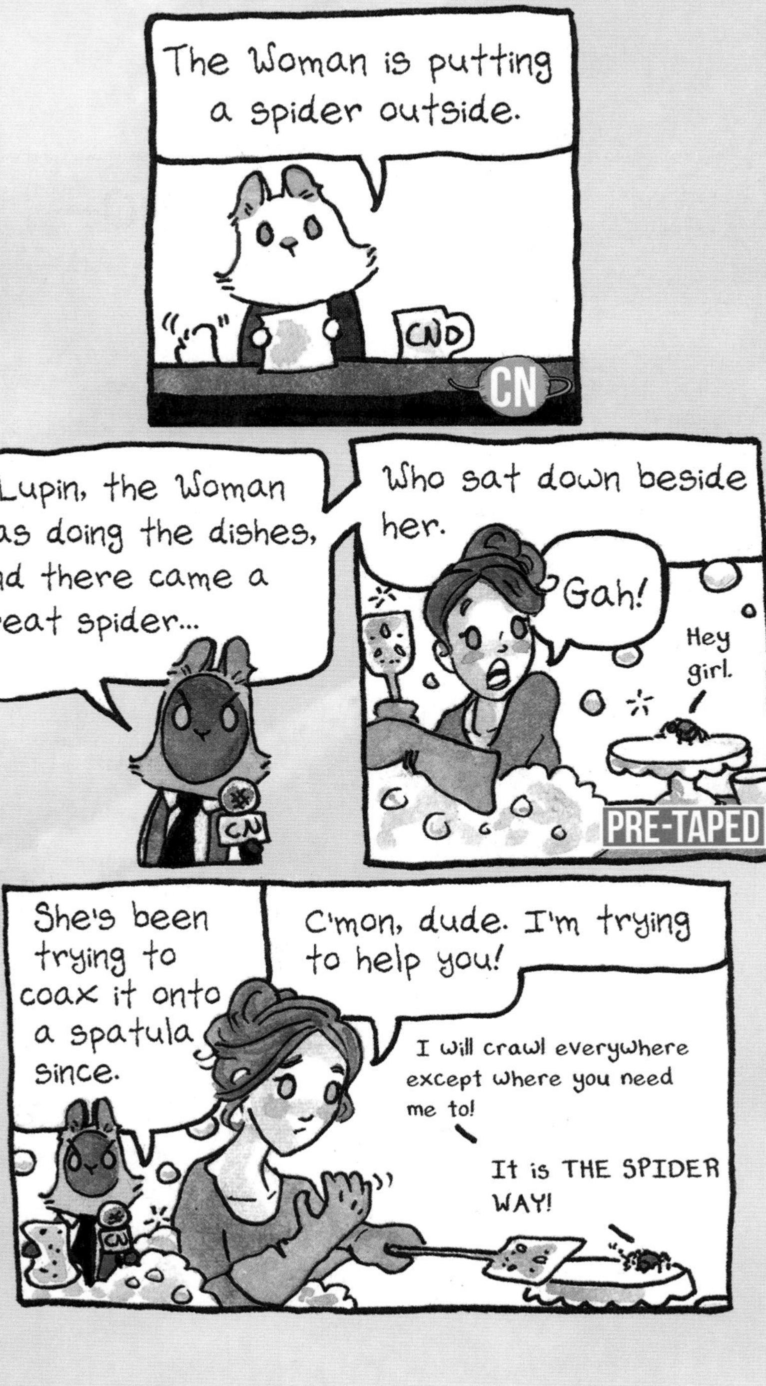
The Woman is putting a spider outside.
CN
CN
Lupin, the Woman was doing the dishes, and there came a great spider...
CN
Who sat down beside her.
Gah!
Hey girl.
PRE-TAPED
She's been trying to coax it onto a spatula since.
C'mon, dude. I'm trying to help you!
I will crawl everywhere except where you need me to!
It is THE SPIDER WAY!
CN

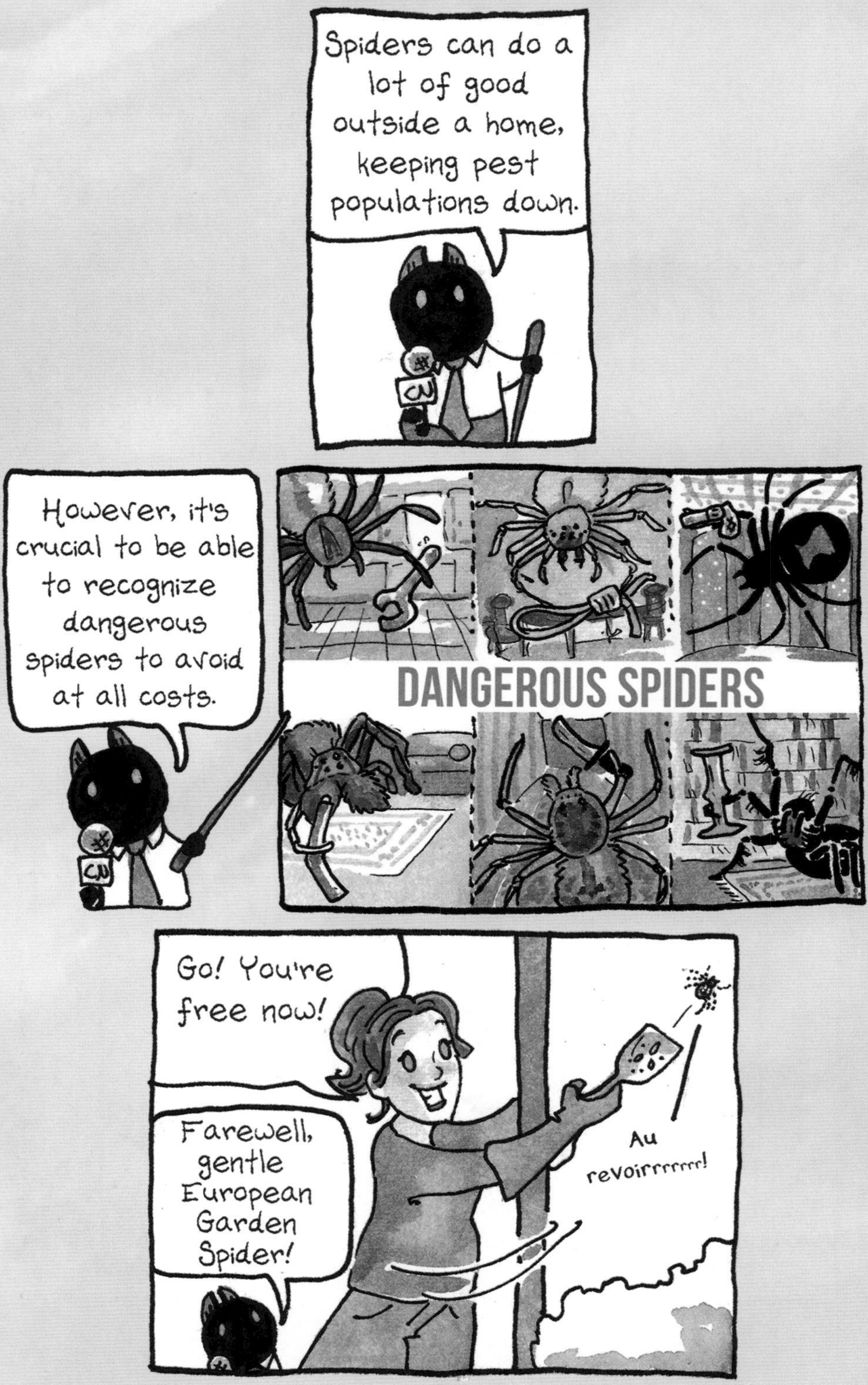
Spiders can do a lot of good outside a home, keeping pest populations down.
However, it's crucial to be able to recognize dangerous spiders to avoid at all costs.
DANGEROUS SPIDERS
Go! You're free now!
Farewell, gentle European Garden Spider!
Au revoirrrrrrr!

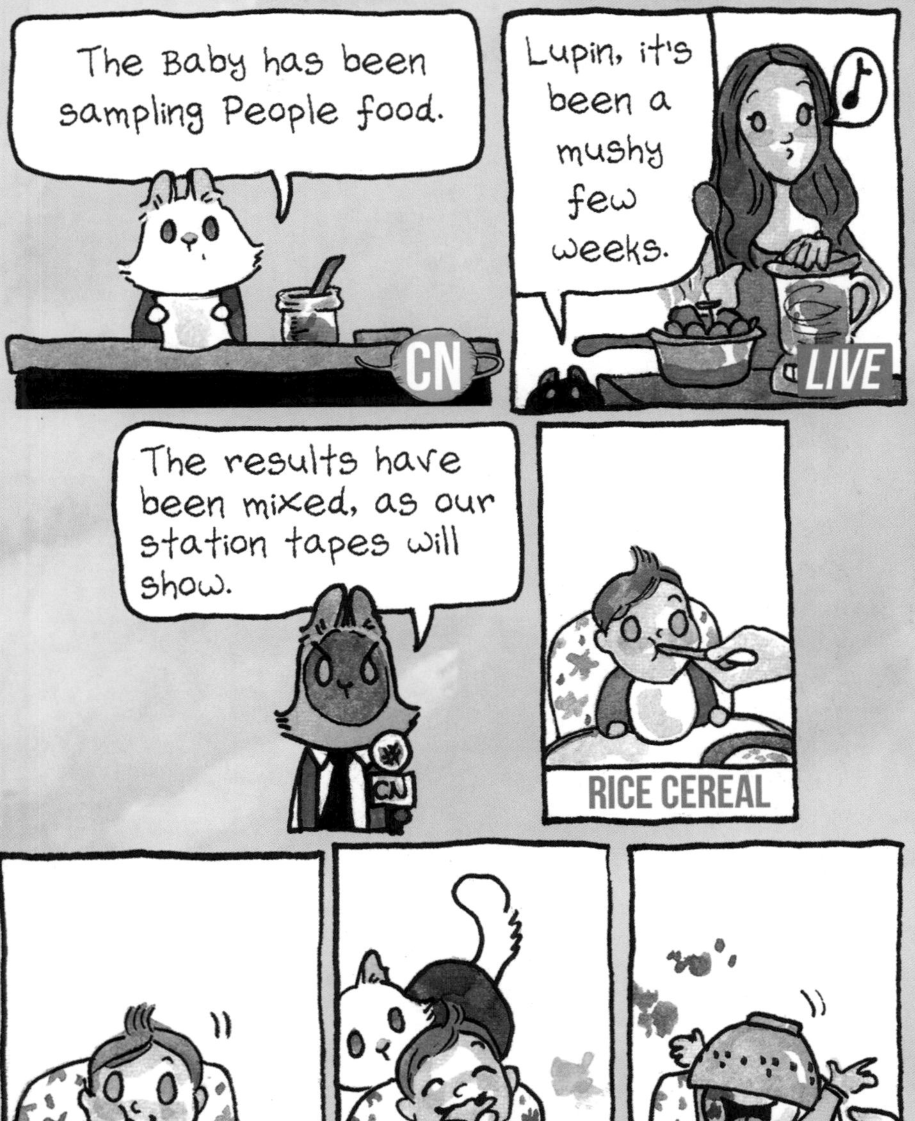
The Baby has been sampling People food.
CN
Lupin, it's been a mushy few weeks.
LIVE
The results have been mixed, as our station tapes will show.
CN
RICE CEREAL
BANANAS
APPLESAUCE
AVOCADO

CARROTS
BEETS
CHICKEN
Aw, who's Mommy's good little boy?
Lupin, it's me.
CN
UP NEXT: SWEET POTATOES

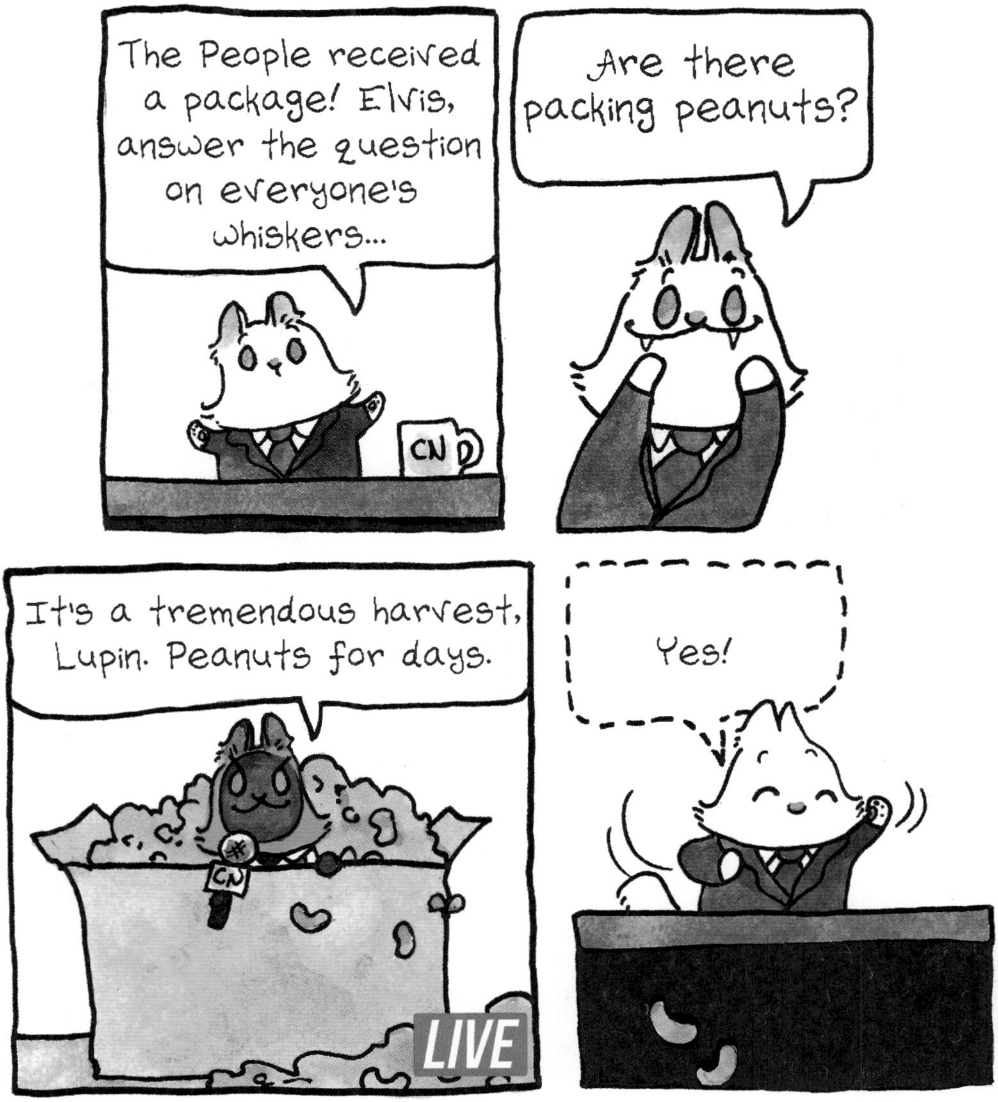
The People received a package! Elvis, answer the question on everyone's whiskers...
CN
Are there packing peanuts?
It's a tremendous harvest, Lupin. Peanuts for days.
CN
LIVE
Yes!

Here's Puck with more on packing peanuts.

Packing peanuts are infinite and multiply when you look at them.

People hate packing peanuts, yet mail each other boxfuls all the time.

Back to you, Lupin.

LIVE

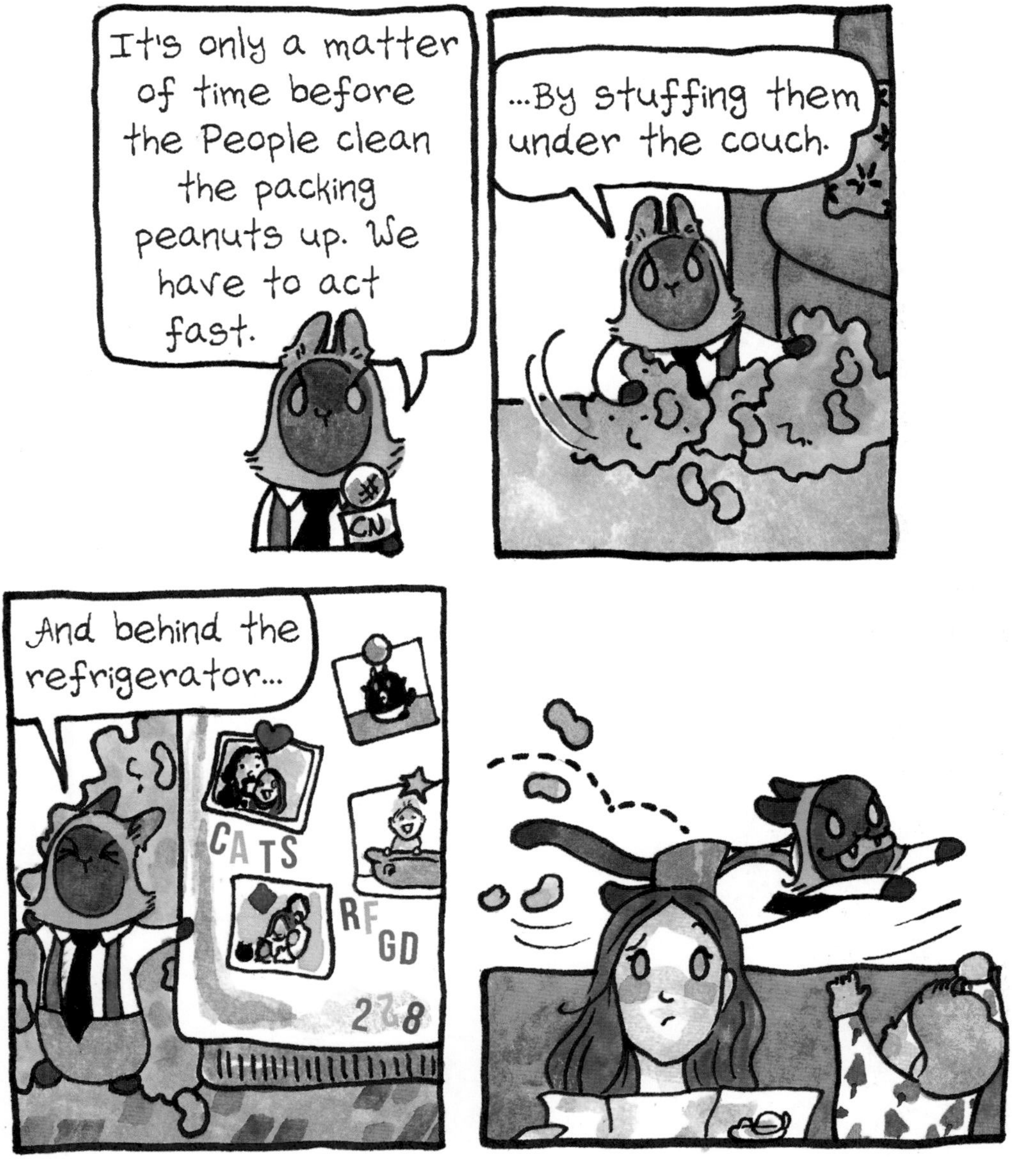
It's only a matter of time before the People clean the packing peanuts up. We have to act fast.
CN
...By stuffing them under the couch.
And behind the refrigerator...
CATS
RFGD

Packing peanuts increase their volume to fill whatever space they occupy.

It closed just fine a minute ago!

Honey! The cats got into those styro-foam thingies! Can you get me the broom?

I am part of the infinite...

LIVE

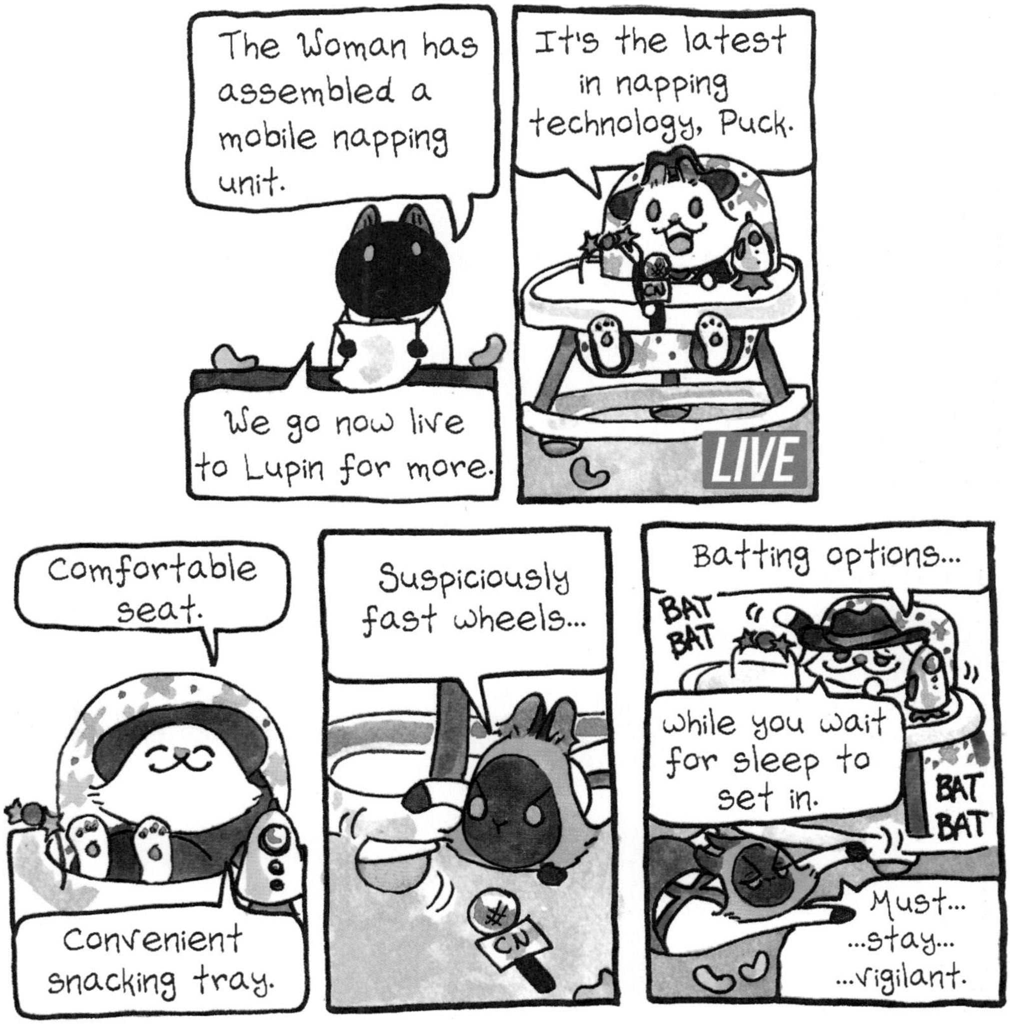
The Woman has assembled a mobile napping unit.
We go now live to Lupin for more.
It's the latest in napping technology, Puck.
CN
LIVE
Comfortable seat.
Convenient snacking tray.
Suspiciously fast wheels...
CN
Batting options...
BAT BAT
while you wait for sleep to set in.
BAT BAT
Must... ...stay... ...vigilant.

The Man has to sweep.

It's a dire situation, Puck.

CN PACKING PEANUTS KEEP APPEARING

The Baby and Lupin fell asleep at the same time...

creating a rare opportunity to sweep without anyone chasing the broom.

SQUEEEAK

CRINGE

CAN THEY DO IT?

SUCCESS! THEY'VE PULLED IT OFF, PUCK!

AIR HIGH FIVE

CN GETTING HANG OF THIS PARENTING THING

The Woman is trying to take pictures of us.

No word on why a grown woman would try to photograph cats, Lupin.

...But there was much mention of "cheese."

Since ancient times, people have created images of their cats.

The madness continues to this day. No one knows why.

♥ 312 🐾 327

Mommy's happy boy, snoozing in the laundry!

Oh, c'mon.

Elvis, everyone knows the Egyptian cat gods demand frequent images of cats to grow and maintain their power.

IT'S WHY THEY CREATED THE INTERNET

That... Yeah, wow, that sounds about right.

YUP.

Skinny elbow!

The Man does not like salmon.

But he does like the Woman.

Honey! This salmon's terrific!

Really?

I couldn't keep it on the plate!

CHARLATAN! What else have you lied about? IS THAT EVEN HER BABY?!

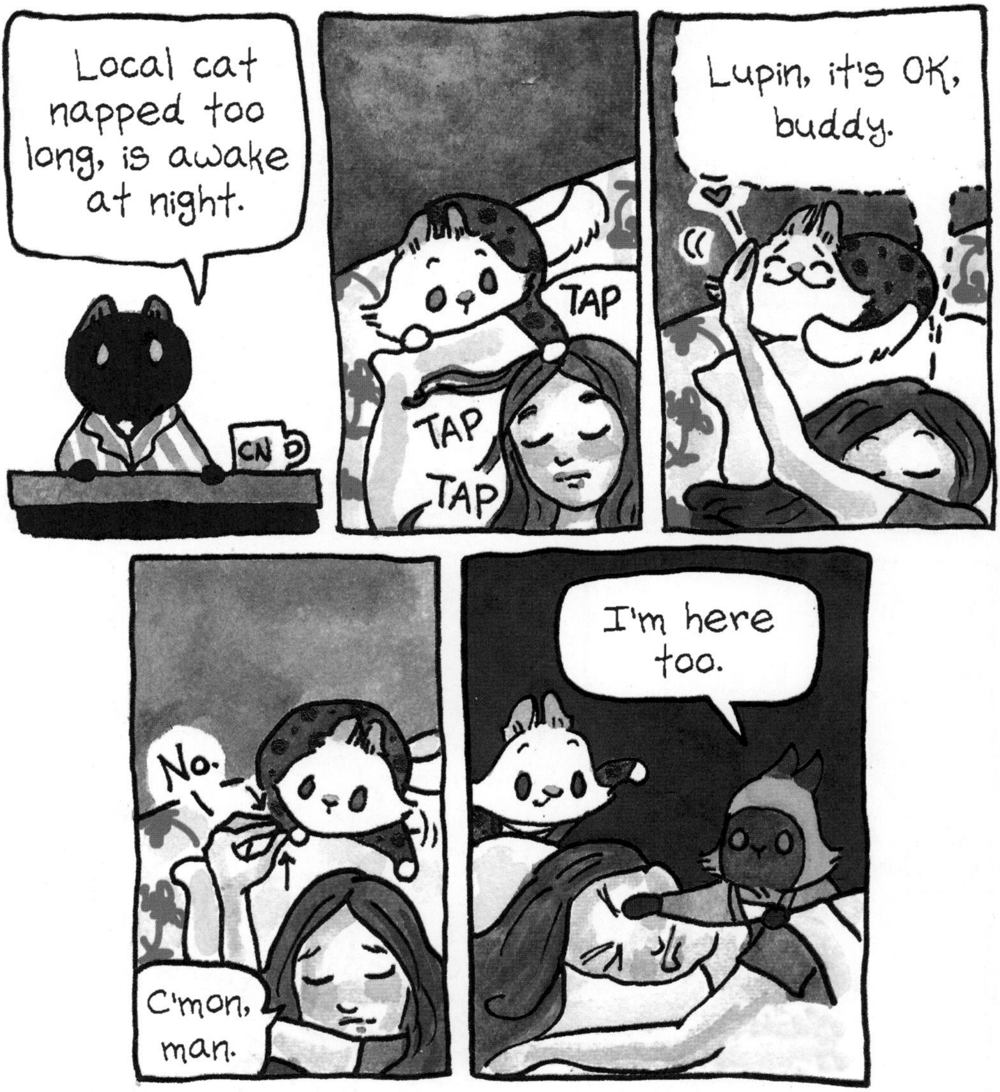
Local cat napped too long, is awake at night.
CN
TAP
TAP
TAP
Lupin, it's OK, buddy.
No.
C'mon, man.
I'm here too.

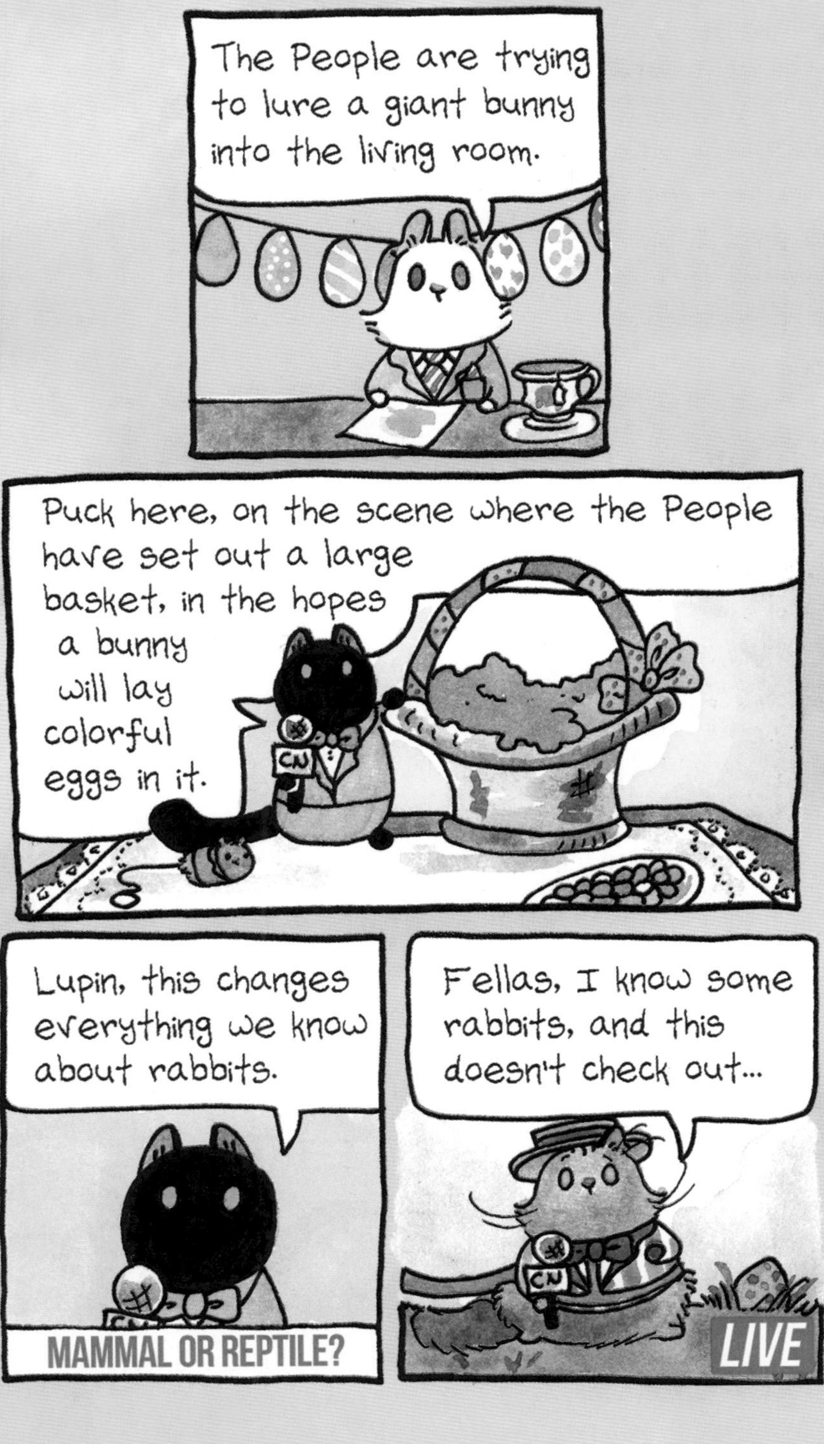
The People are trying to lure a giant bunny into the living room.
Puck here, on the scene where the People have set out a large basket, in the hopes a bunny will lay colorful eggs in it.
CN
Lupin, this changes everything we know about rabbits.
MAMMAL OR REPTILE?
Fellas, I know some rabbits, and this doesn't check out...
CN
LIVE

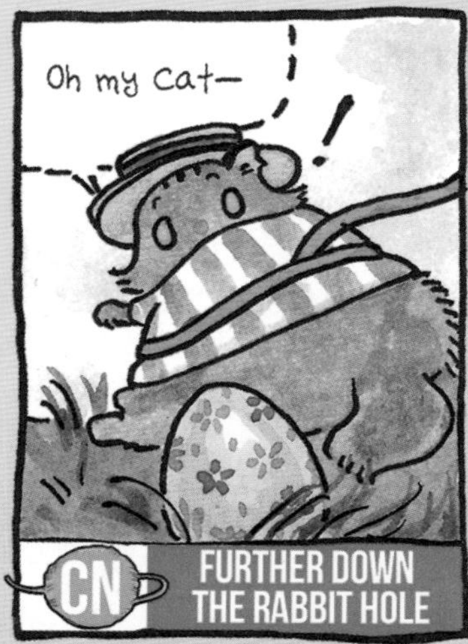
Oh my Cat—
!
CN
FURTHER DOWN THE RABBIT HOLE

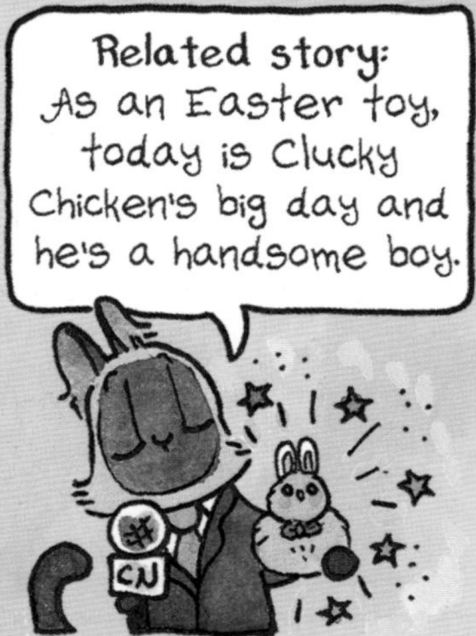
Related story:
As an Easter toy, today is Clucky Chicken's big day and he's a handsome boy.
CN

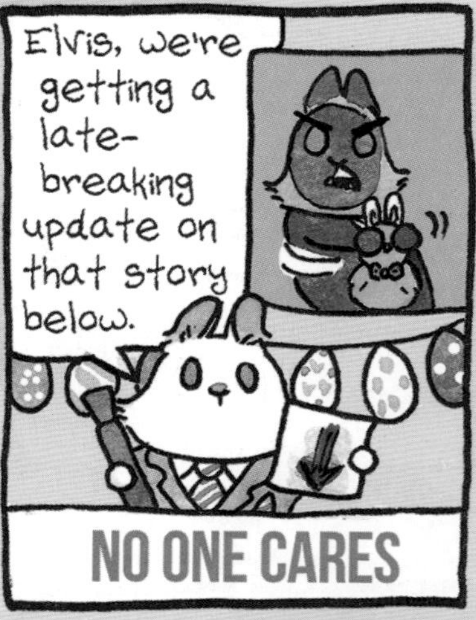
Elvis, we're getting a late-breaking update on that story below.
NO ONE CARES

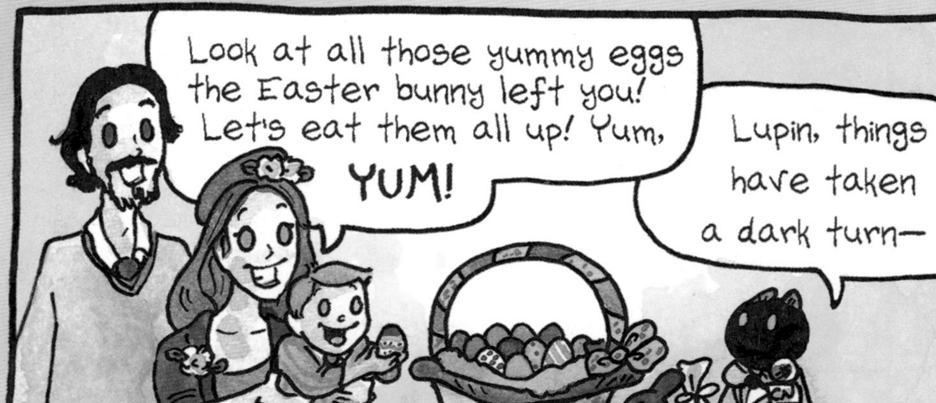
Look at all those yummy eggs the Easter bunny left you! Let's eat them all up! Yum, YUM!
Lupin, things have taken a dark turn—
CN

The Woman finally has a quiet moment to herself.

Ahh hhh.

Which means it's time for **BCW!!!**

"BEST CAT WRESTLING"

LUPIN!!

THWUMP!

BCW
BEST CAT WRESTLING

WHAT

Someone cue my entrance music!

MY CAT! IT'S BIG FLUFFY TOMMY BEE!

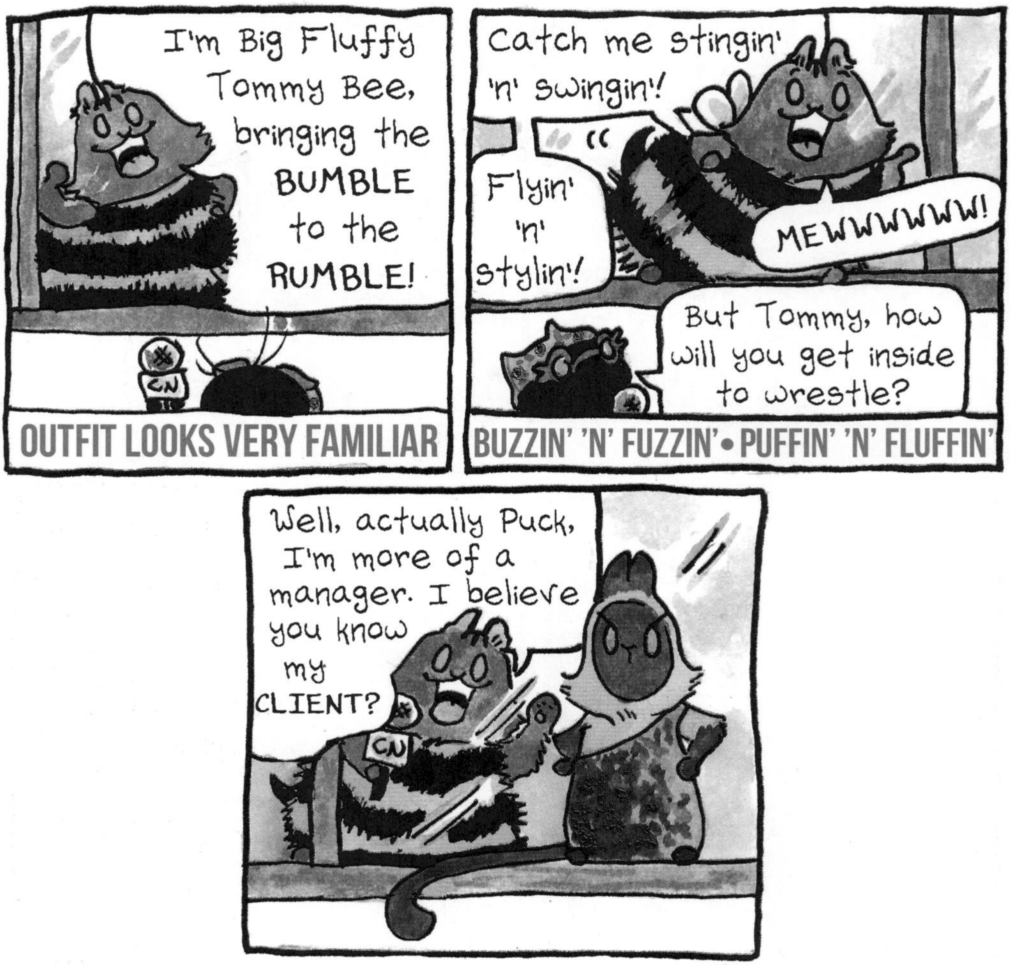
I'm Big Fluffy Tommy Bee, bringing the BUMBLE to the RUMBLE!
CN
OUTFIT LOOKS VERY FAMILIAR
Catch me stingin' 'n' swingin'!
Flyin' 'n' stylin'!
MEWWWWWW!
But Tommy, how will you get inside to wrestle?
BUZZIN' 'N' FUZZIN' • PUFFIN' 'N' FLUFFIN'
Well, actually Puck, I'm more of a manager. I believe you know my CLIENT?
CN

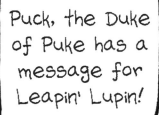

Puck, the Duke of Puke has a message for Leapin' Lupin!

Lupin, I'm sick of you spilling the Woman's tea and knocking over plants!

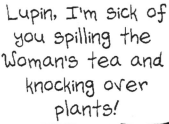

Shredding up curtains, batting car keys under the bed, eating books, licking that spot on the floor in the kitchen DAY and NIGHT—

Lupin, what do you have to say?

Tea gets spilled all the time.

That's the world we live in.

BCW
BEST CAT WRESTLING

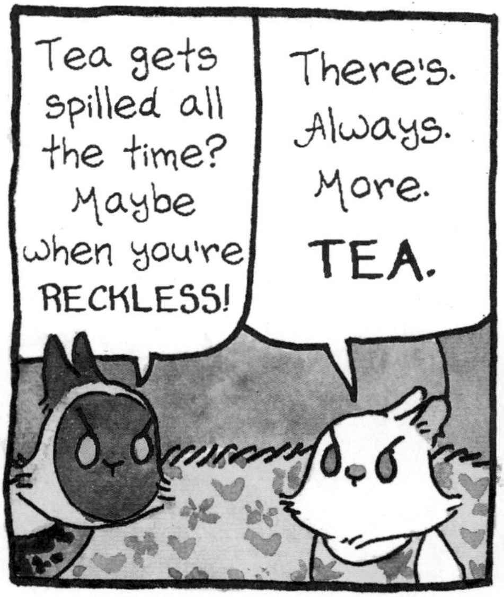
Tea gets spilled all the time? Maybe when you're RECKLESS!
There's. Always. More. TEA.

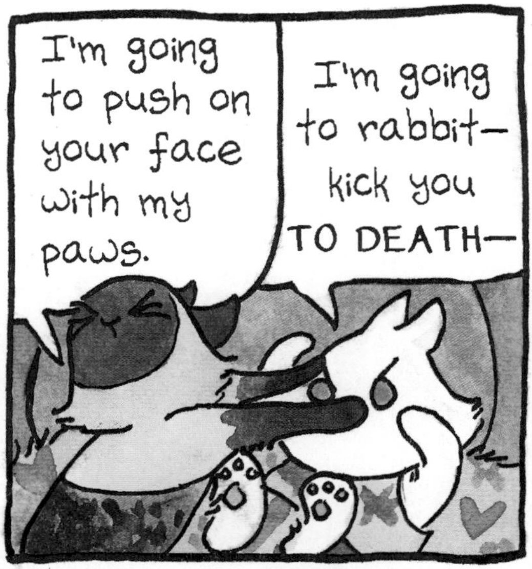
I'm going to push on your face with my paws.
I'm going to rabbit-kick you TO DEATH—

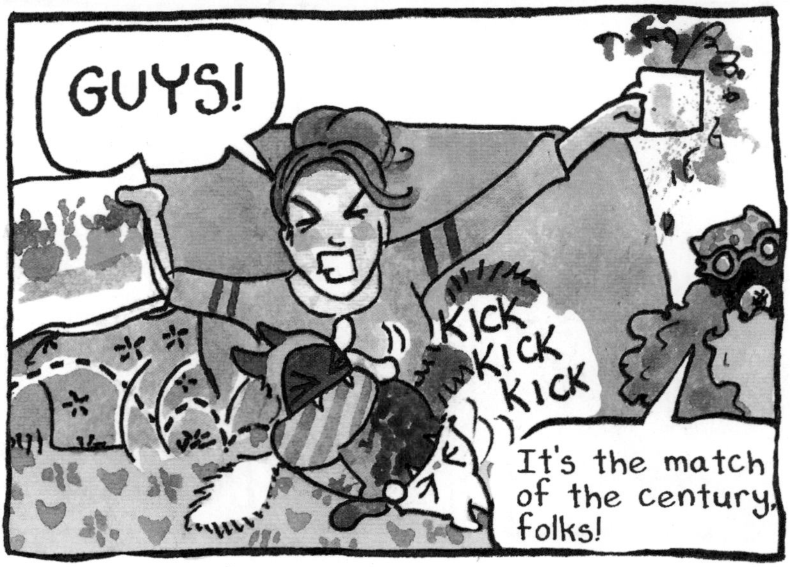
GUYS!
KICK
KICK
KICK
It's the match of the century, folks!

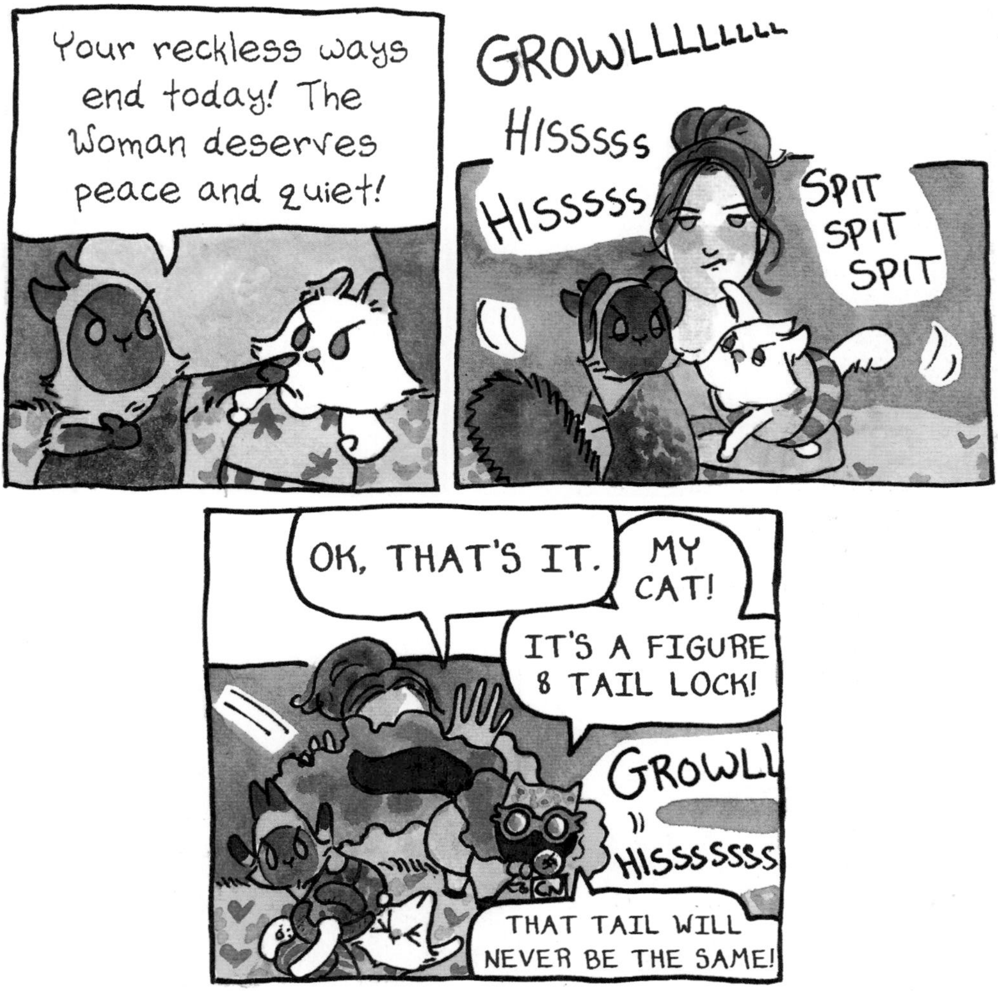
Your reckless ways end today! The Woman deserves peace and quiet!
GROWLLLLLLLL
HISSSSS
HISSSSS
SPIT SPIT SPIT
OK, THAT'S IT.
MY CAT!
IT'S A FIGURE 8 TAIL LOCK!
GROWLL
HISSSSSSS
THAT TAIL WILL NEVER BE THE SAME!

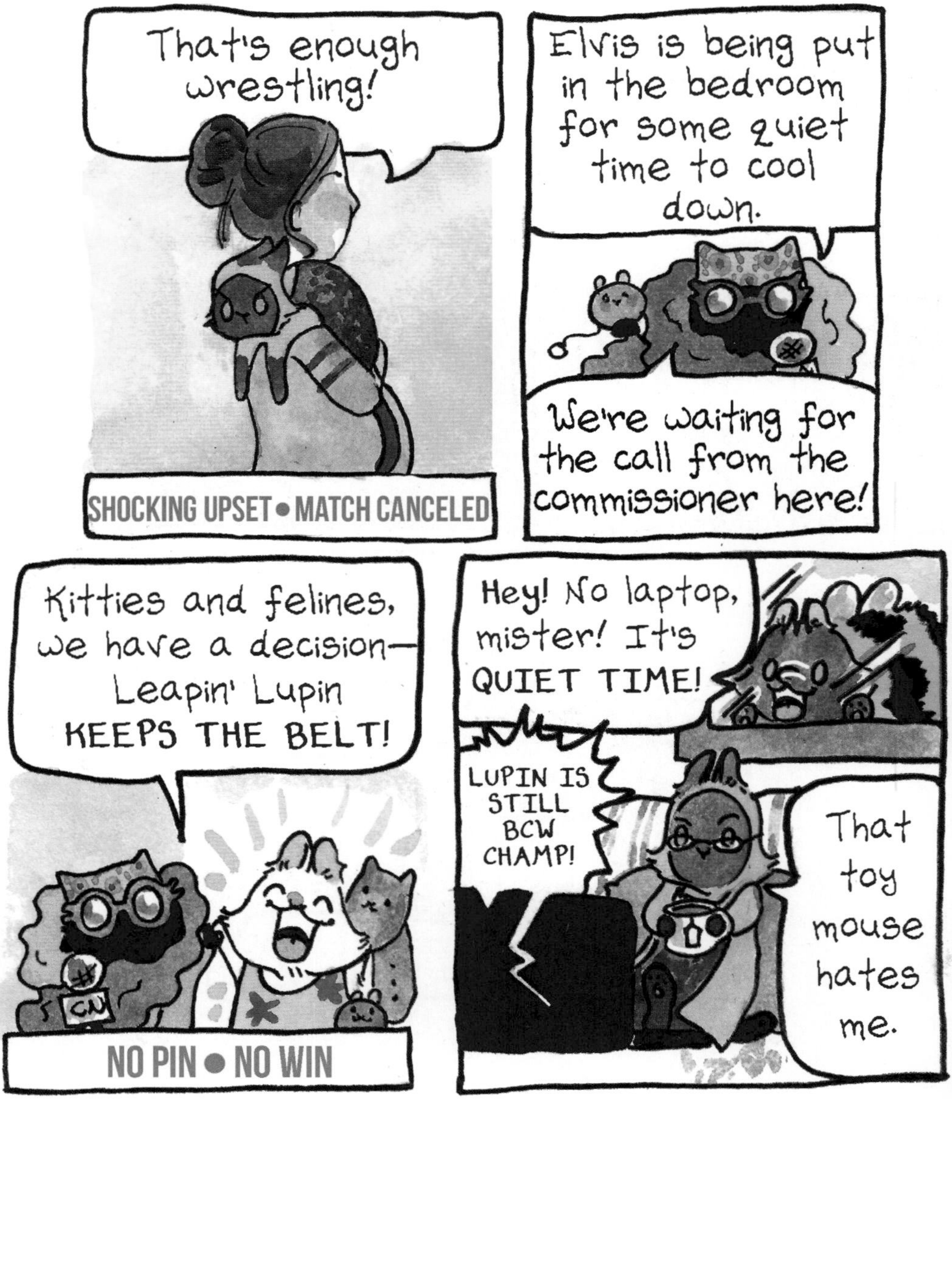
That's enough wrestling!
SHOCKING UPSET • MATCH CANCELED
Elvis is being put in the bedroom for some quiet time to cool down.
We're waiting for the call from the commissioner here!
Kitties and felines, we have a decision—Leapin' Lupin KEEPS THE BELT!
NO PIN • NO WIN
Hey! No laptop, mister! It's QUIET TIME!
LUPIN IS STILL BCW CHAMP!
That toy mouse hates me.

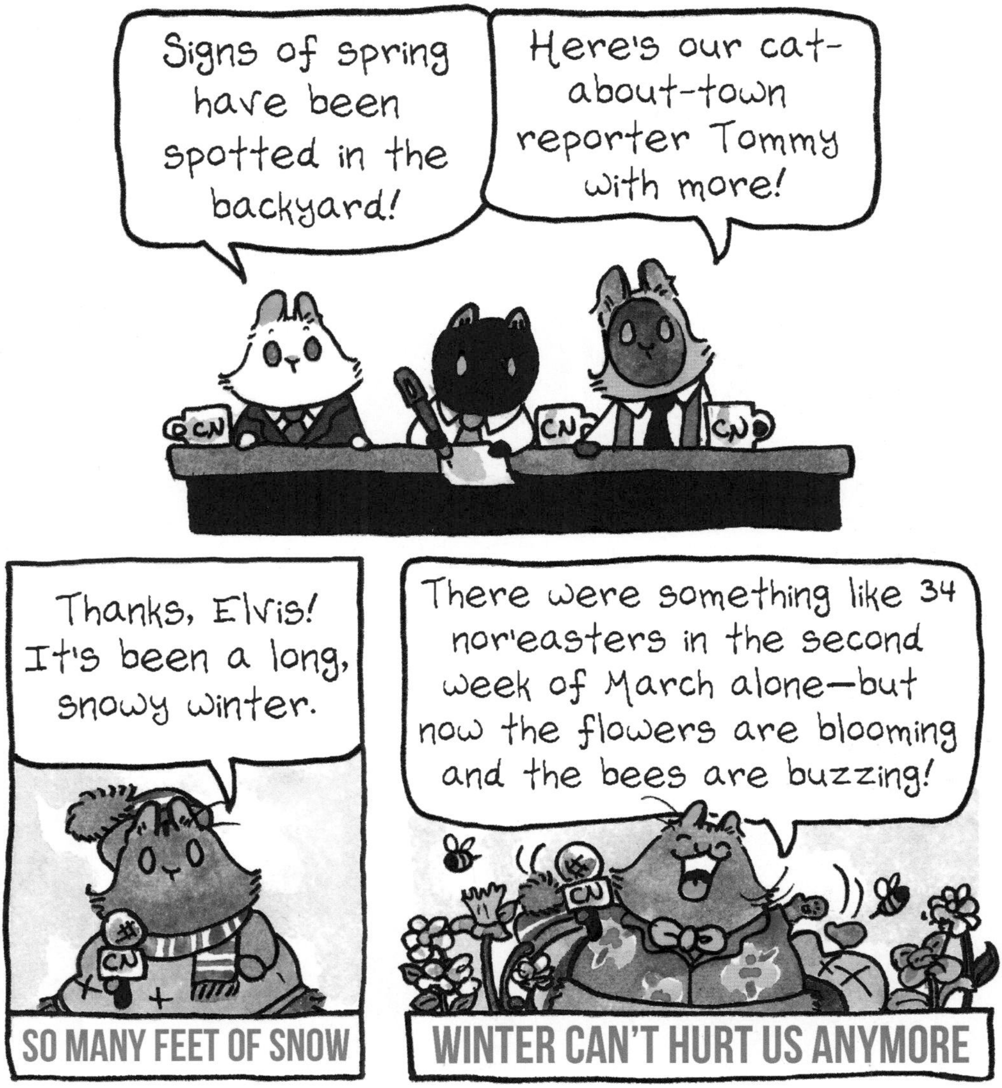
Signs of spring have been spotted in the backyard!
Here's our cat-about-town reporter Tommy with more!
CN
CN
CN
Thanks, Elvis! It's been a long, snowy winter.
CN
SO MANY FEET OF SNOW
There were something like 34 nor'easters in the second week of March alone—but now the flowers are blooming and the bees are buzzing!
CN
WINTER CAN'T HURT US ANYMORE

Signs of spring are all around us!

The sun is shining.

The wormies are squirmy.

The snow is making its slow, graceful transformation into mud and debris.

SPARE CHANGE & LOST CAR KEYS SOON TO EMERGE

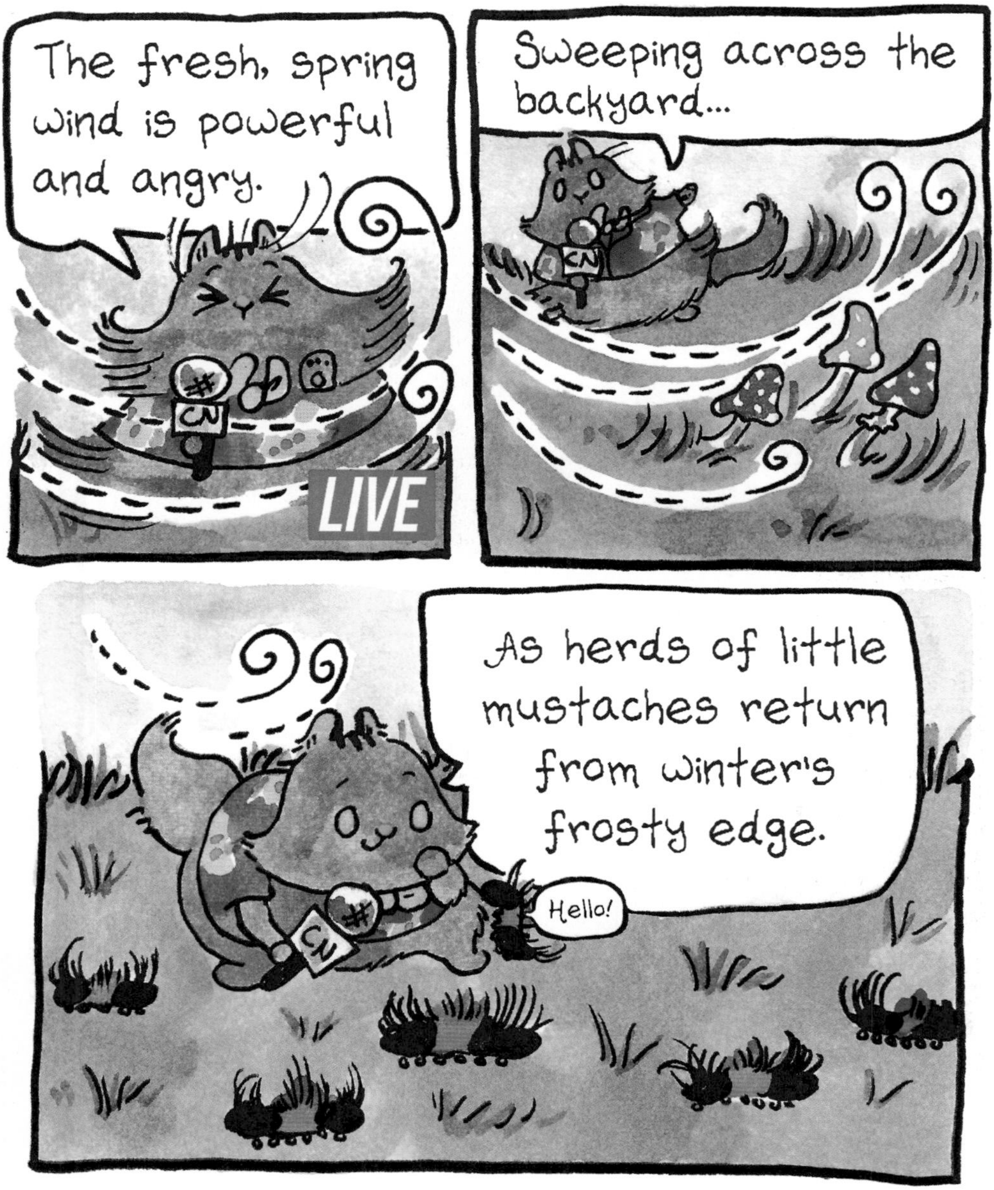
The fresh, spring wind is powerful and angry.
#
CN
LIVE
Sweeping across the backyard...
CN
As herds of little mustaches return from winter's frosty edge.
Hello!
#
CN

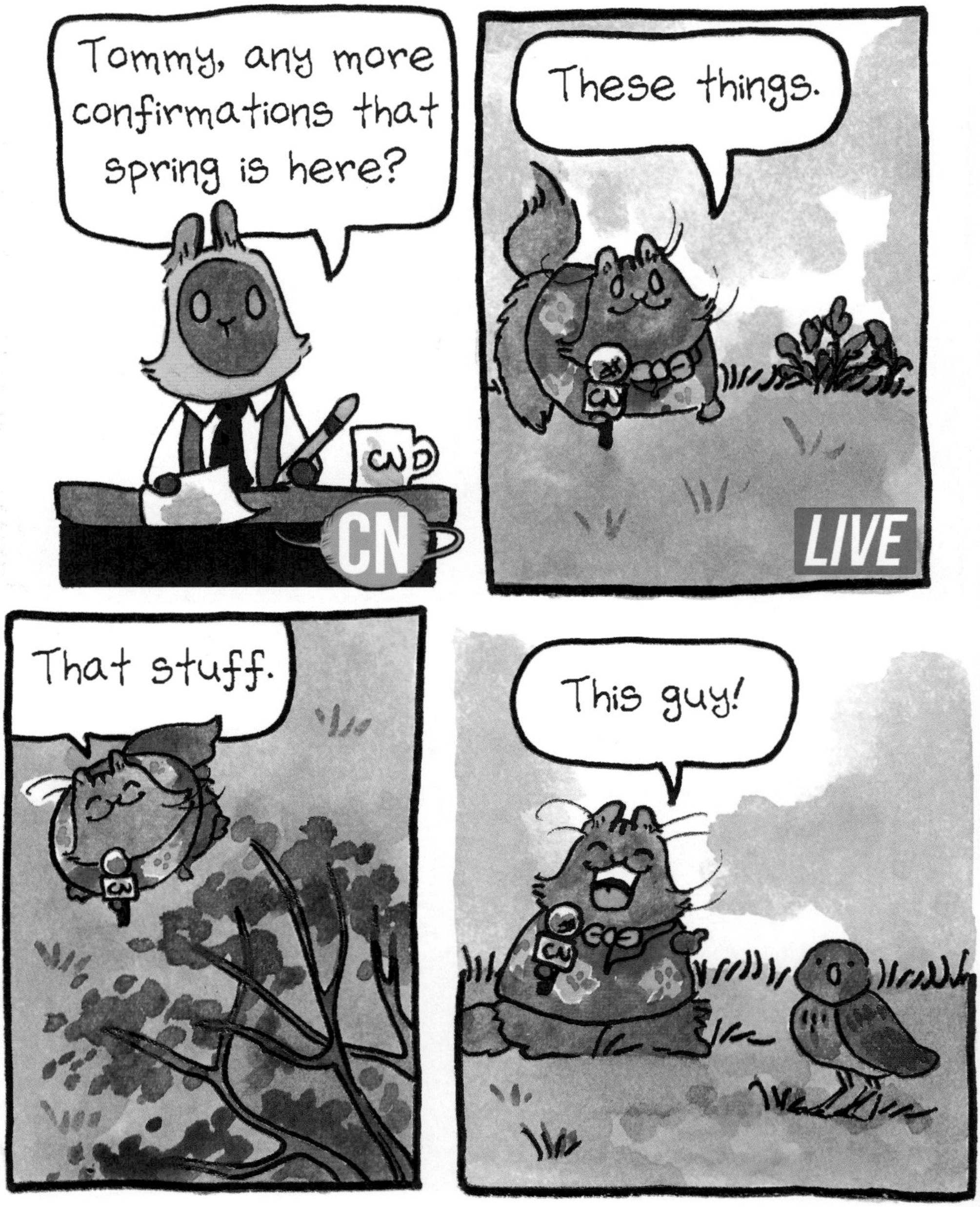
Tommy, any more confirmations that spring is here?
CN
These things.
LIVE
That stuff.
This guy!

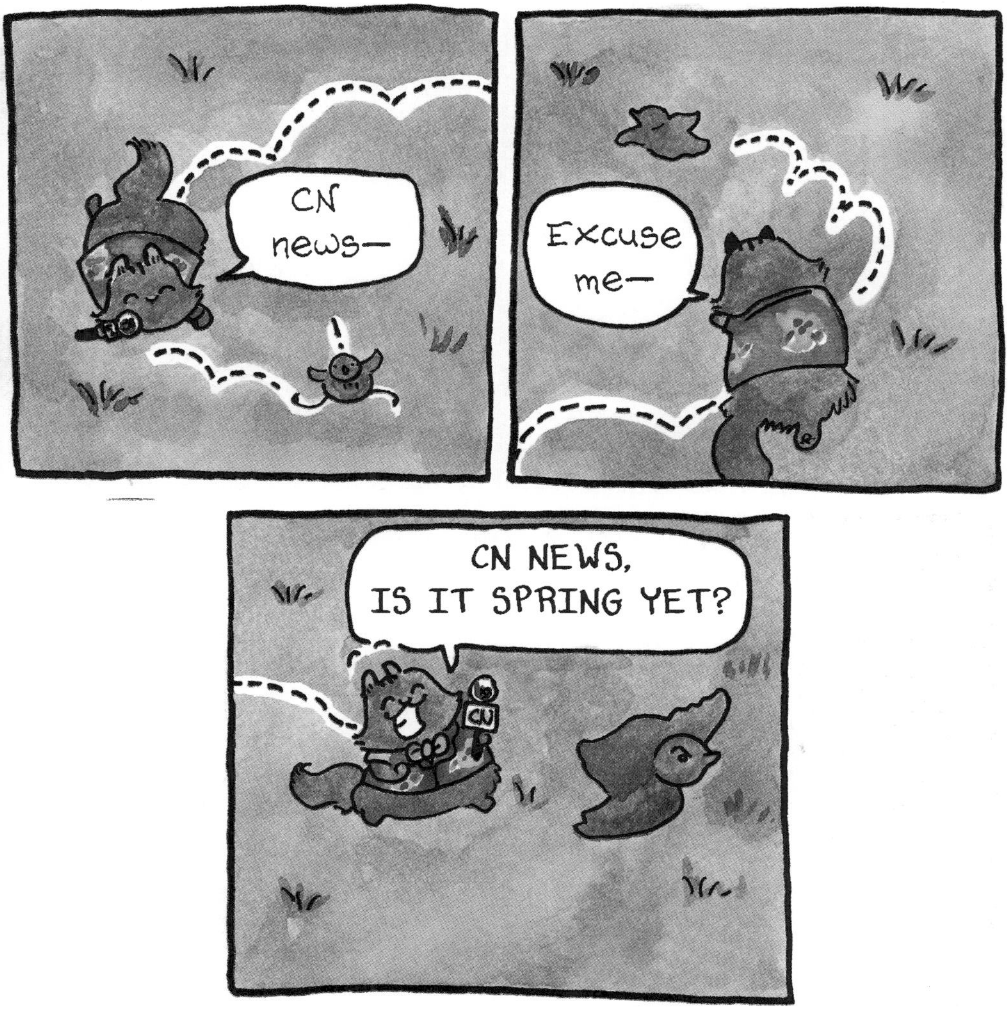
CN news—
Excuse me—
CN NEWS, IS IT SPRING YET?

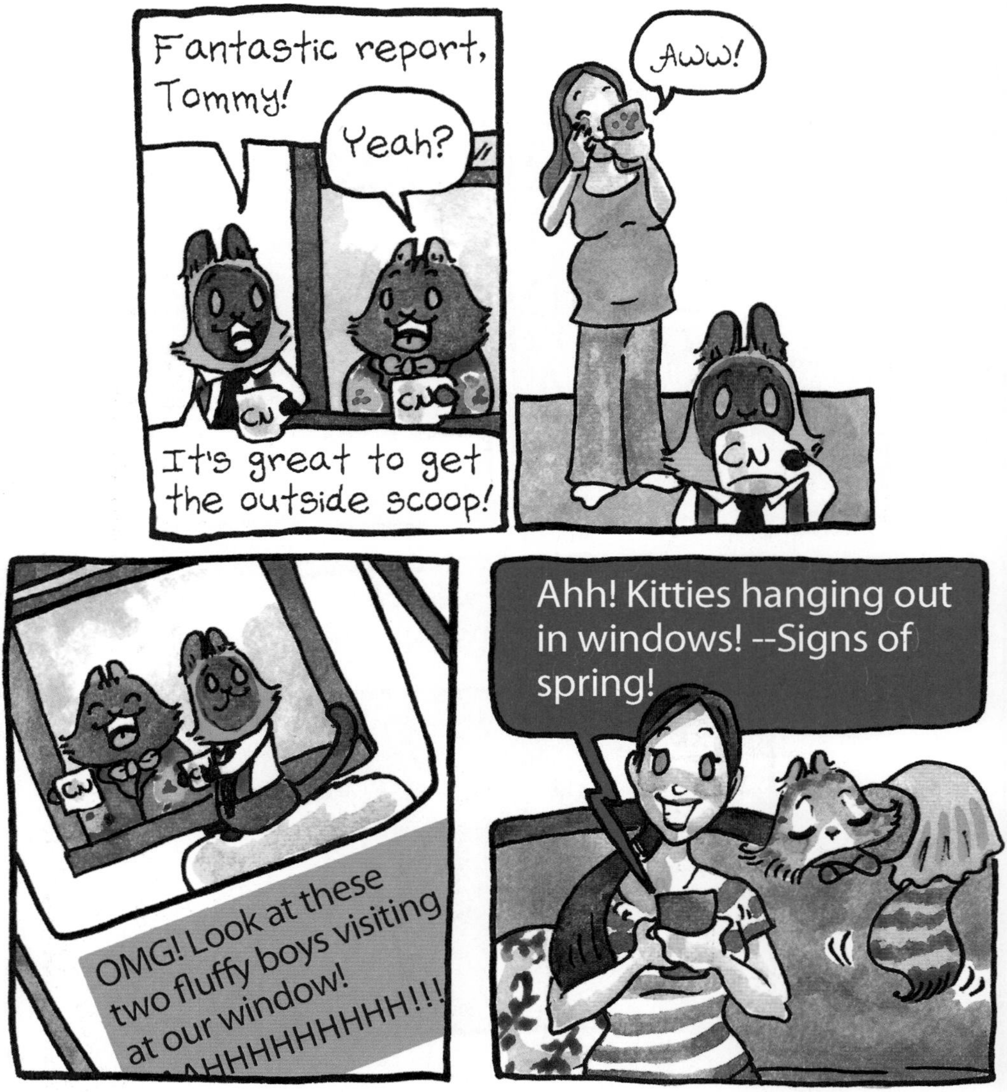
Fantastic report, Tommy!
Yeah?
CN
CN
It's great to get the outside scoop!
Aww!
CN
CN
CN
OMG! Look at these two fluffy boys visiting at our window!
AHHHHHHHHHH!!!
Ahh! Kitties hanging out in windows! --Signs of spring!

It's cookie season! ...Elvis?

CHANCE OF OATMEAL RAISIN

Lupin, they say you can't buy happiness.

Well then, what's in all these boxes?

COOKIES
COOKIES
COOKIES
COOKIES
COOKIES
COOKIES
COOKIES
COOKIES

The "Future Lady Cubs of America" is an organization of creative, thoughtful People-kittens.

And they are terrific little business-women.

I like to freeze the lemon-mints!

They're great in the summer!

With a glass of lemonade!

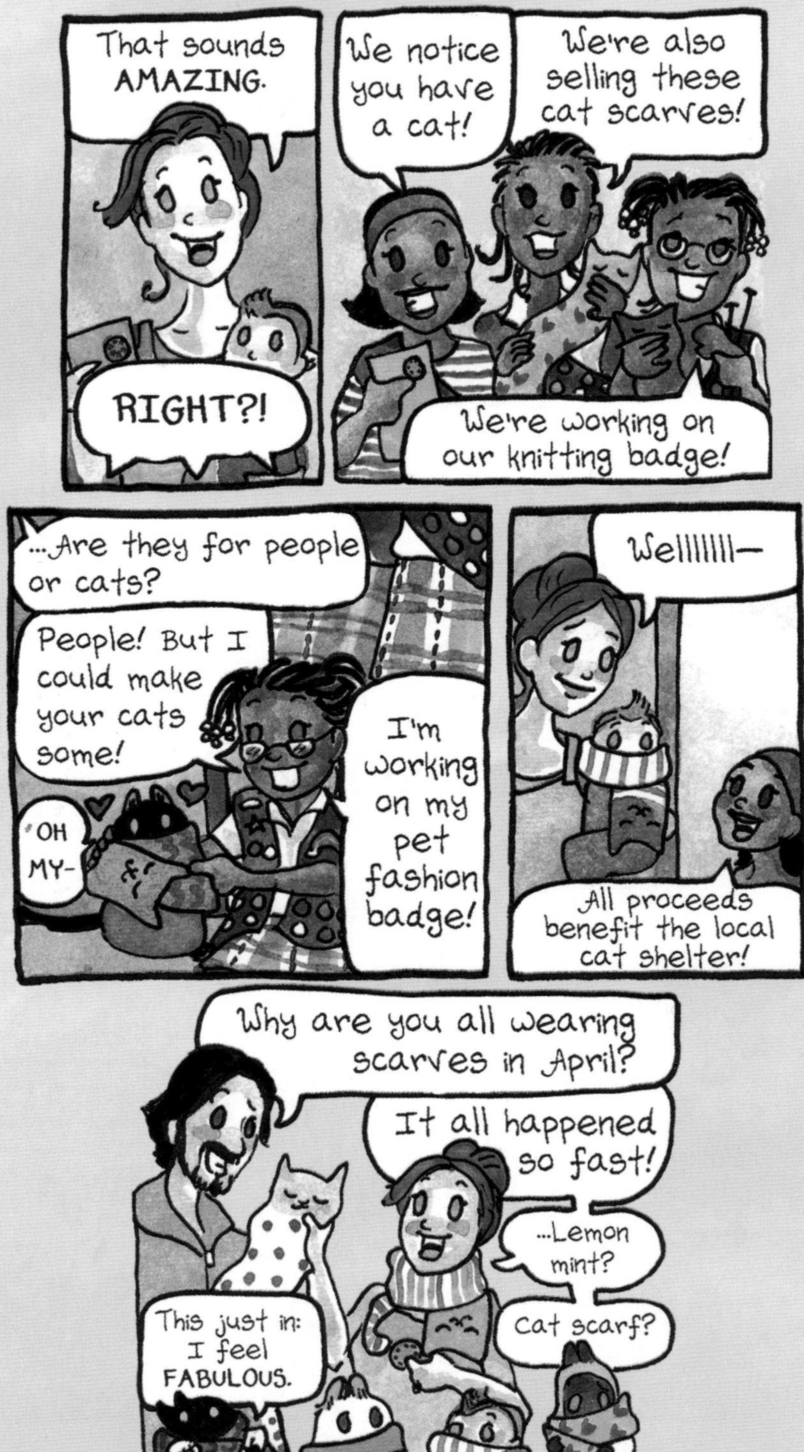
That sounds AMAZING.
RIGHT?!
We notice you have a cat!
We're also selling these cat scarves!
We're working on our knitting badge!
...Are they for people or cats?
People! But I could make your cats some!
OH MY-
I'm working on my pet fashion badge!
Wellllllll—
All proceeds benefit the local cat shelter!
Why are you all wearing scarves in April?
It all happened so fast!
...Lemon mint?
Cat scarf?
This just in: I feel FABULOUS.

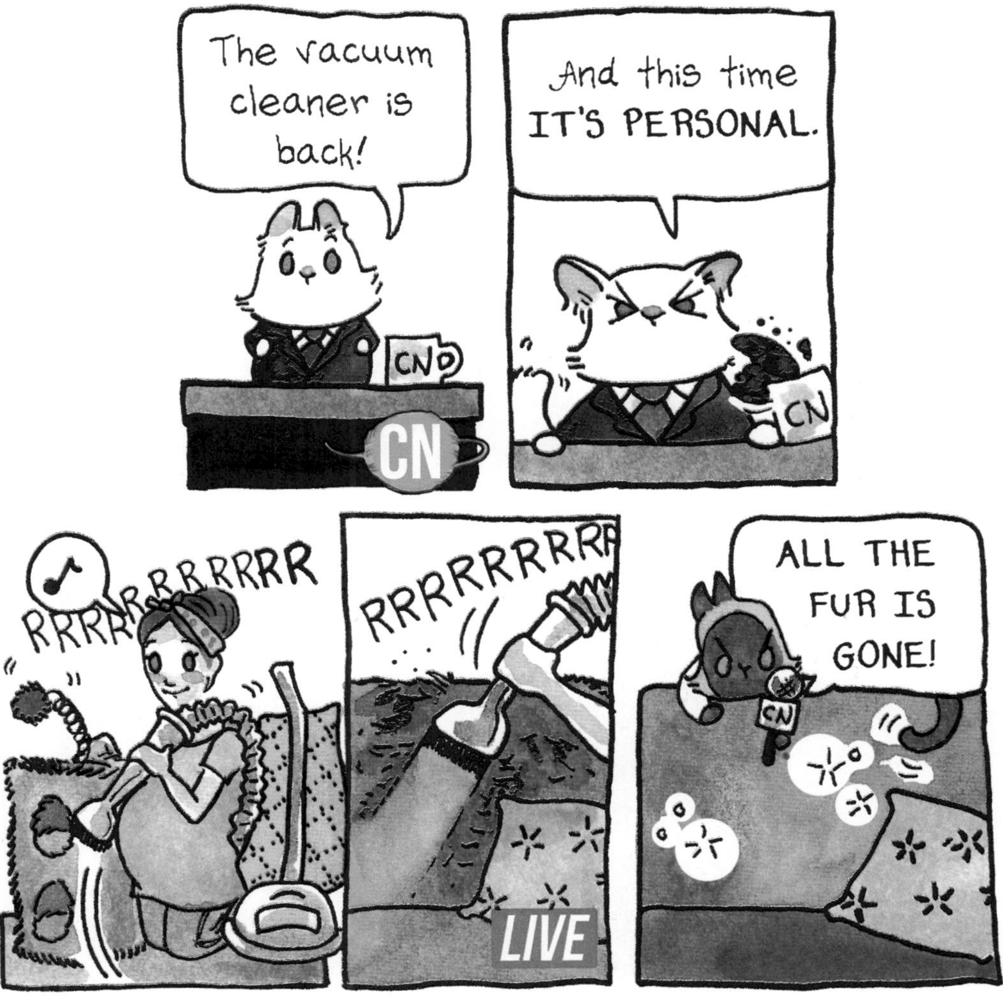
The vacuum cleaner is back!
CN
CN
And this time IT'S PERSONAL.
CN
RRRRRRRRRRRR
RRRRRRRRRR
LIVE
ALL THE FUR IS GONE!
CN

Lupin, **hours of** covering the couch with **fur** have been ERASED.

I can only shed so much.

Good luck when company sees an unmarked couch and assumes it's theirs!

How much fur do you think I have?

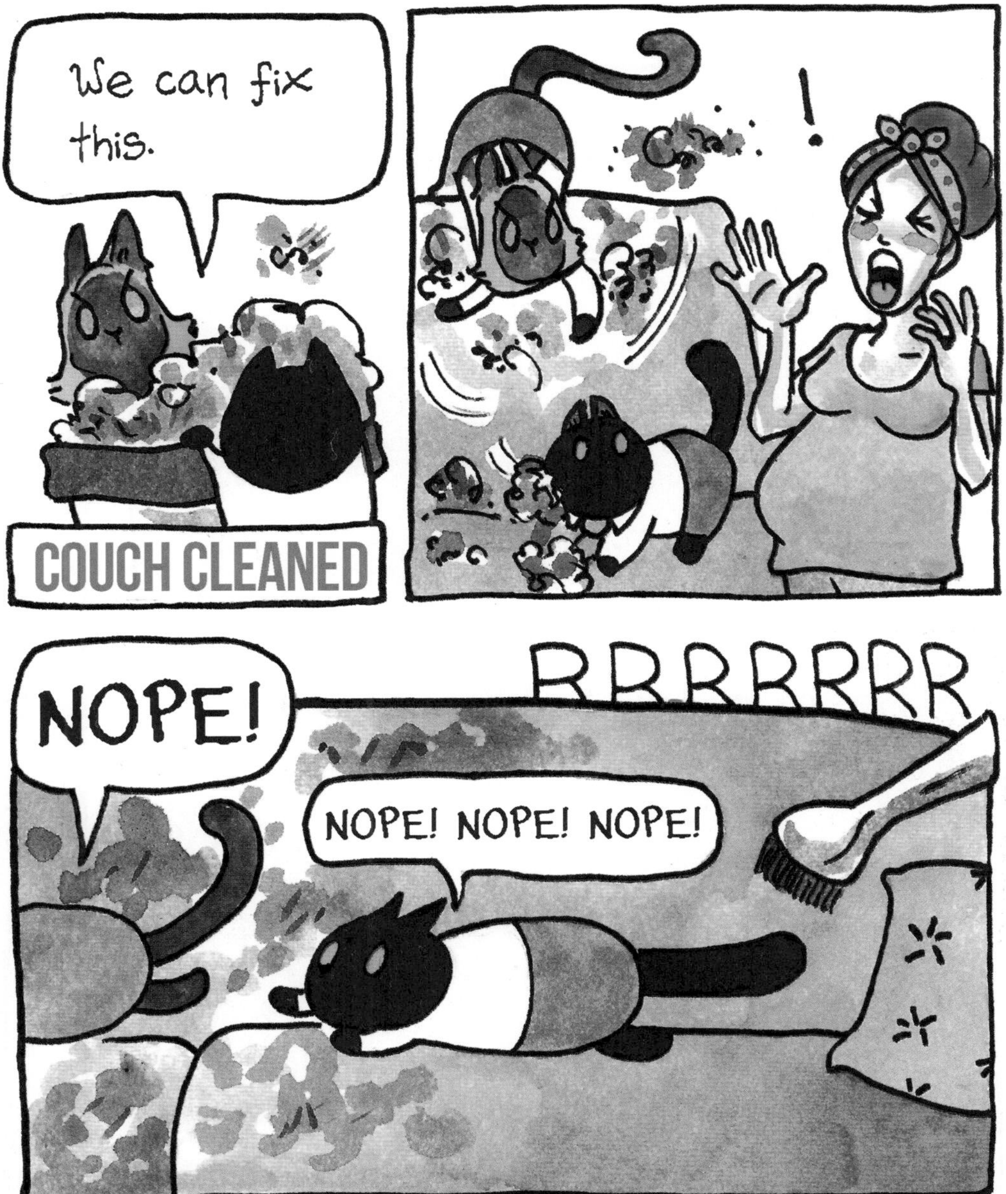
We can fix this.
COUCH CLEANED
!
NOPE!
RRRRRRR
NOPE! NOPE! NOPE!

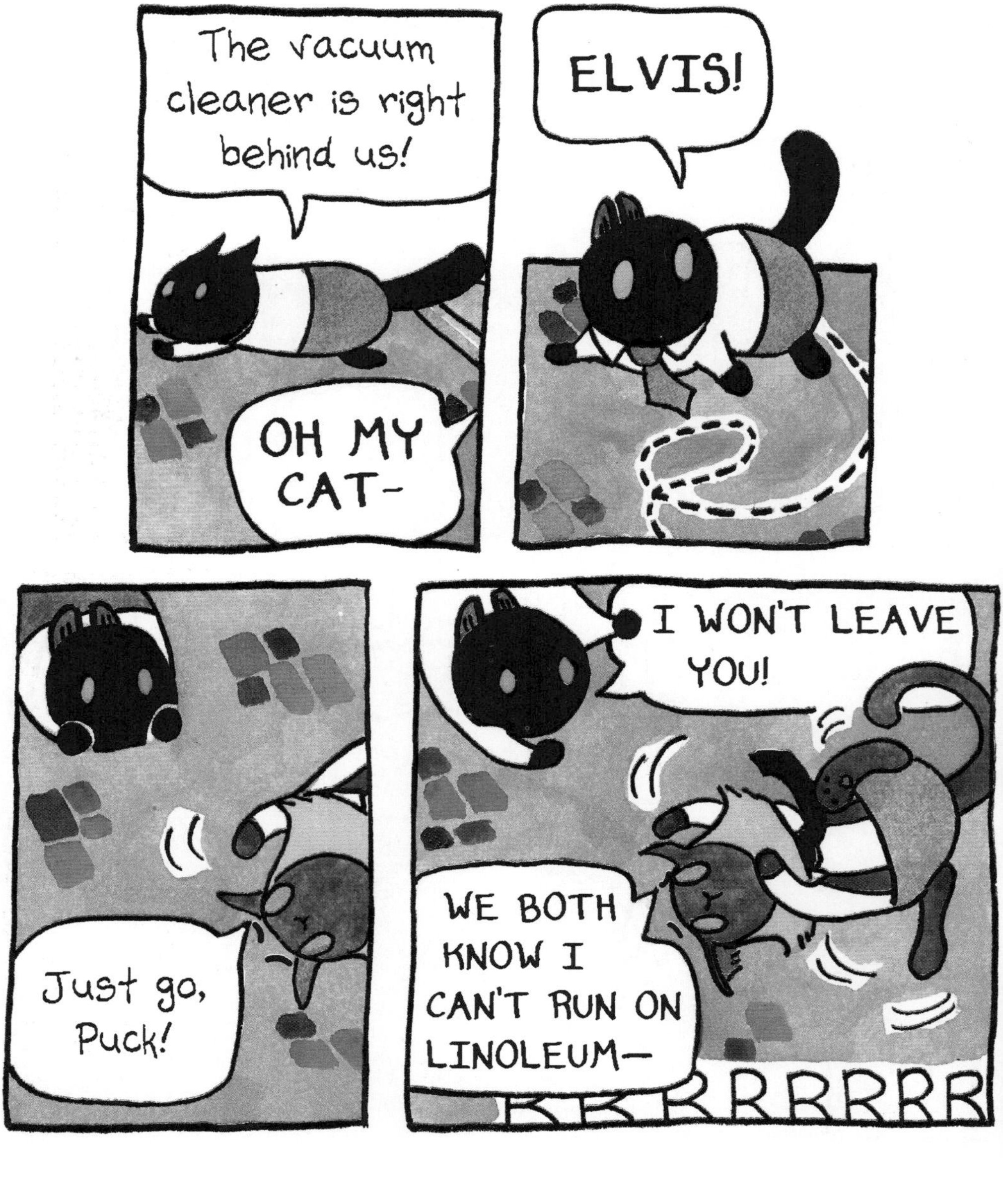
The vacuum cleaner is right behind us!
OH MY CAT-
ELVIS!
Just go, Puck!
I WON'T LEAVE YOU!
WE BOTH KNOW I CAN'T RUN ON LINOLEUM—
RRRRRRRR

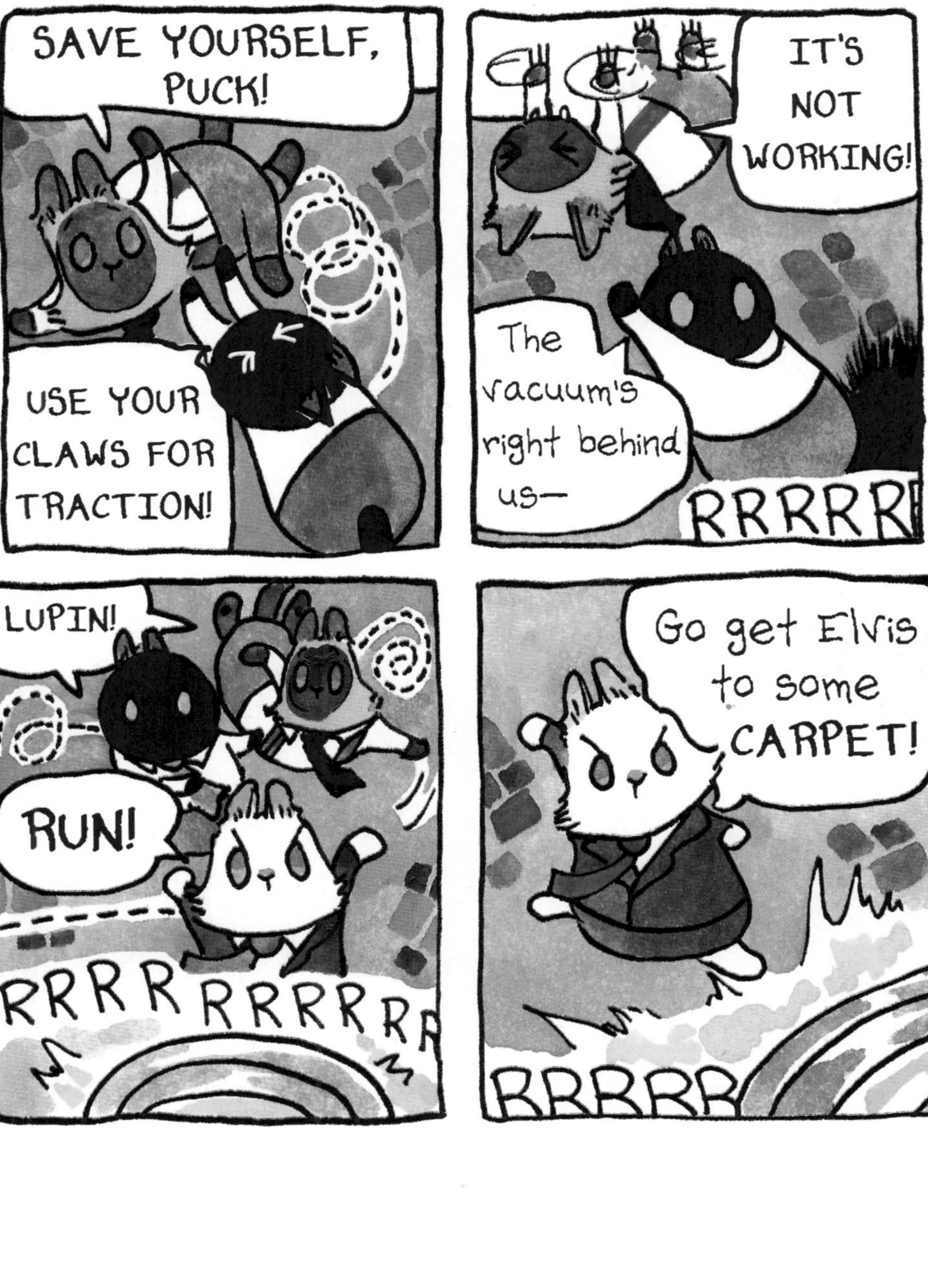
SAVE YOURSELF, PUCK!
USE YOUR CLAWS FOR TRACTION!
IT'S NOT WORKING!
The vacuum's right behind us—
RRRRRR
LUPIN!
RUN!
RRRR RRRRRRR
Go get Elvis to some CARPET!
RRRRRR

I lost the vacuum! We're safe... for now.

But for how long? Aren't you tired of running?

Of hiding?

What do you mean, Lupin?

I mean I've HAD IT.

We're putting an end to the vacuum cleaner, ONCE AND FOR ALL!

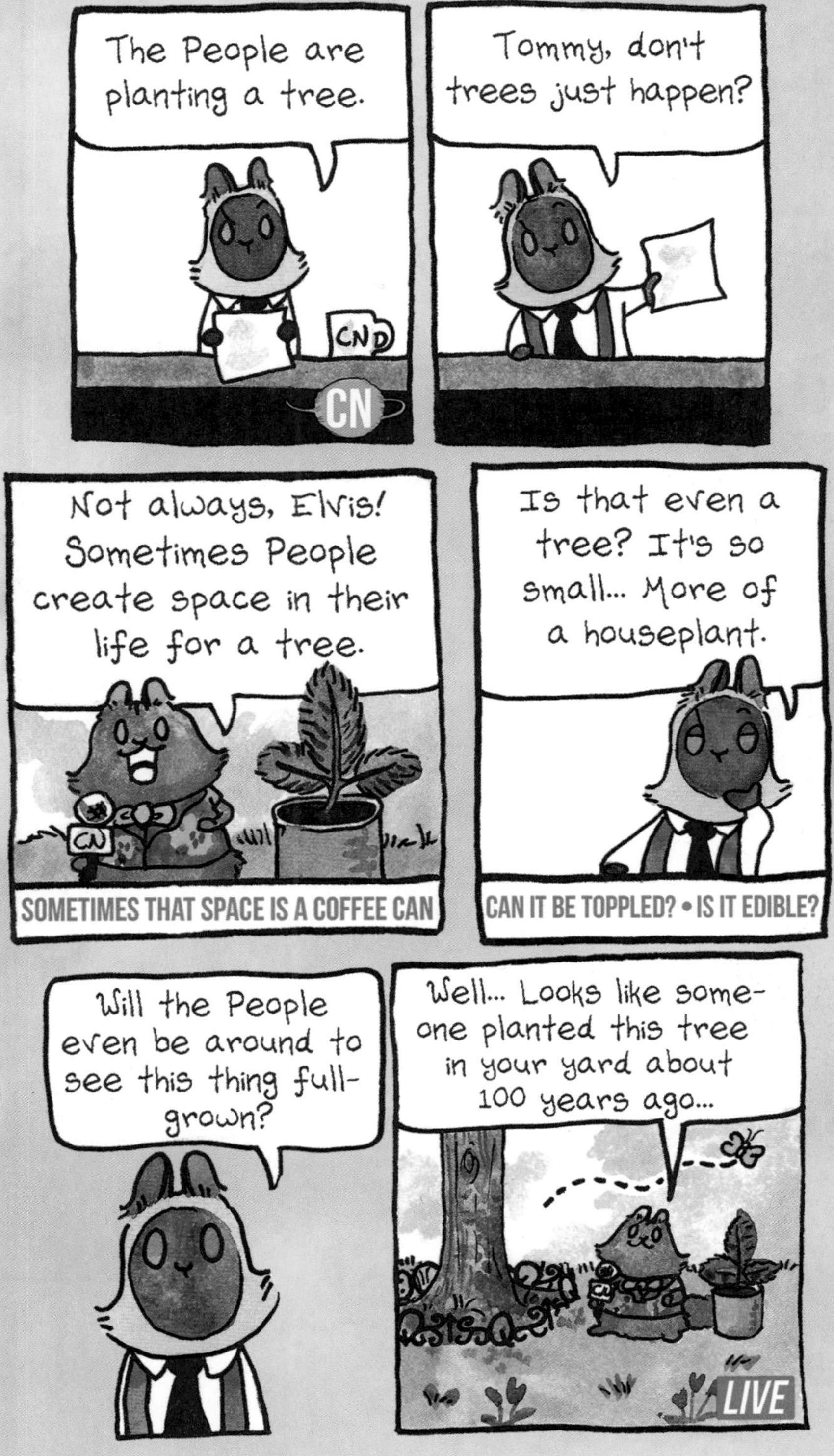
The People are planting a tree.
CND
CN
Tommy, don't trees just happen?
Not always, Elvis! Sometimes People create space in their life for a tree.
CN
SOMETIMES THAT SPACE IS A COFFEE CAN
Is that even a tree? It's so small... More of a houseplant.
CAN IT BE TOPPLED? • IS IT EDIBLE?
Will the People even be around to see this thing full-grown?
Well... Looks like some-one planted this tree in your yard about 100 years ago...
LIVE

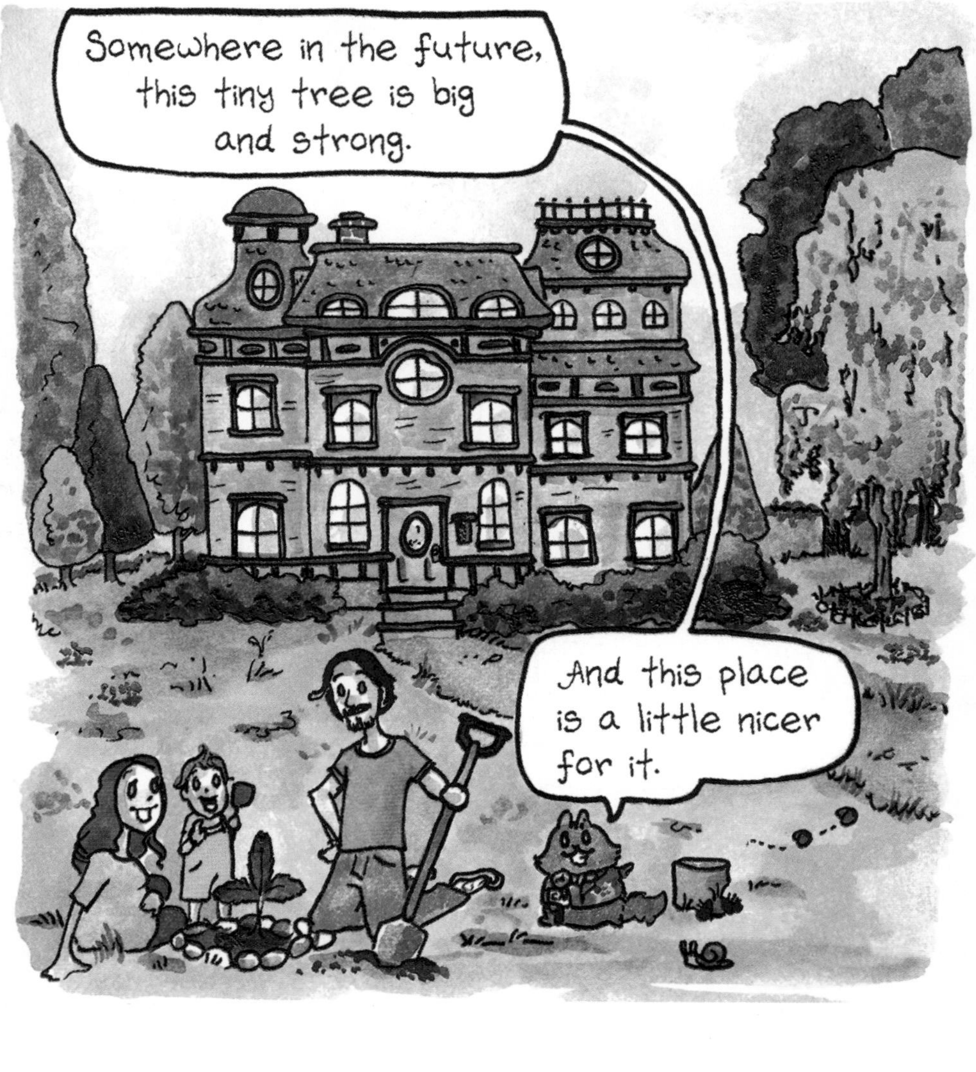
Somewhere in the future, this tiny tree is big and strong.
And this place is a little nicer for it.

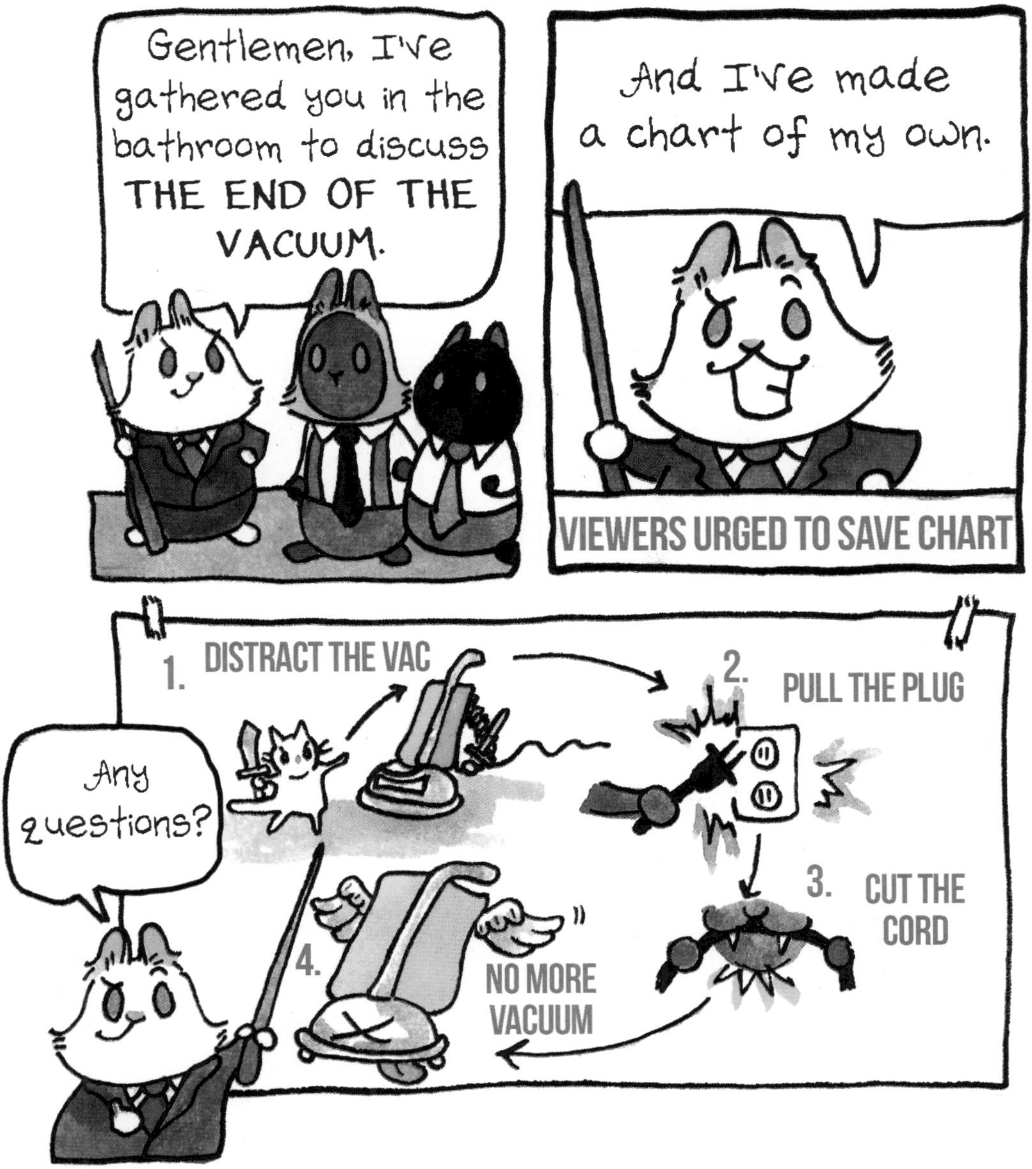
Gentlemen, I've gathered you in the bathroom to discuss THE END OF THE VACUUM.
And I've made a chart of my own.
VIEWERS URGED TO SAVE CHART
1. DISTRACT THE VAC
2. PULL THE PLUG
3. CUT THE CORD
4. NO MORE VACUUM
Any questions?

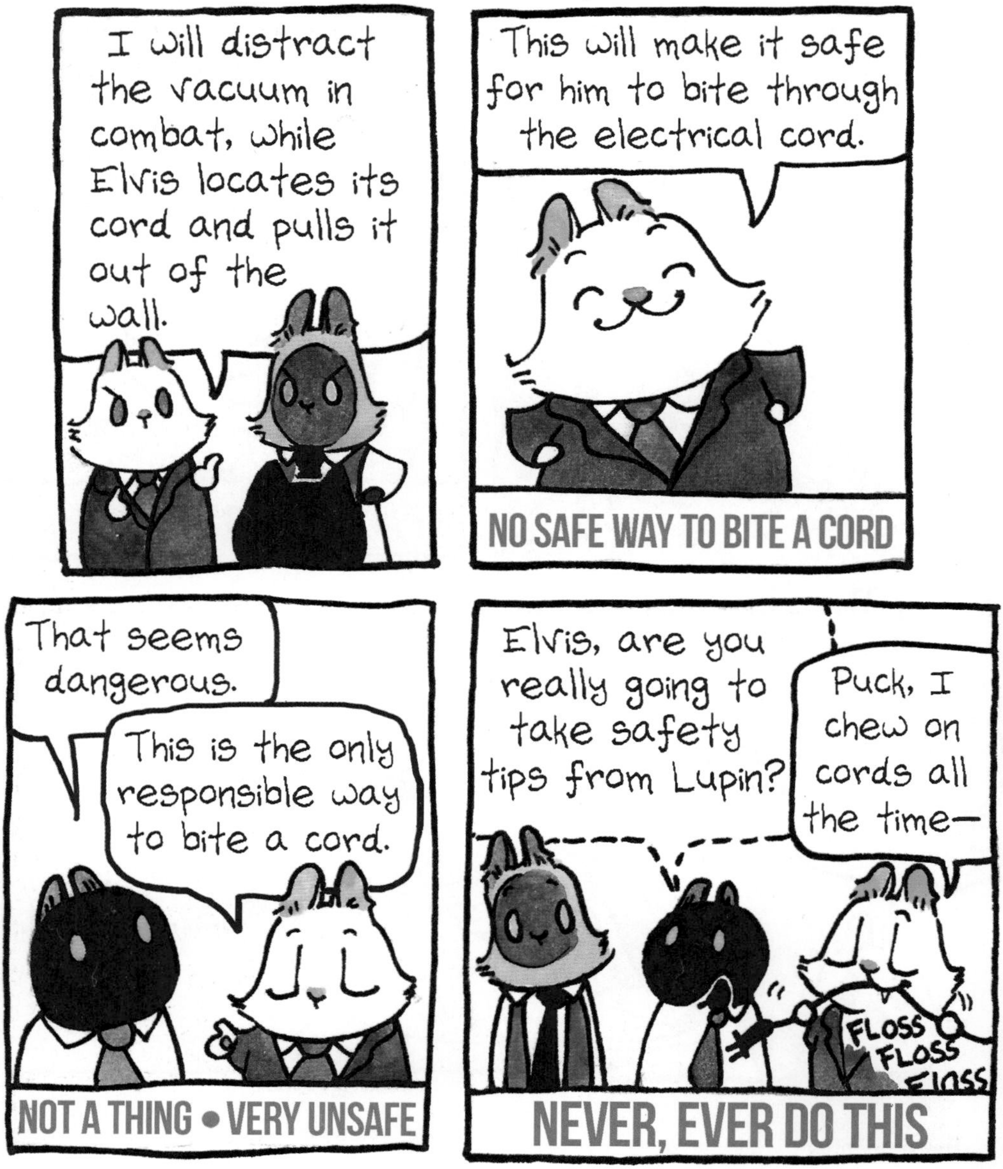
I will distract the vacuum in combat, while Elvis locates its cord and pulls it out of the wall.
This will make it safe for him to bite through the electrical cord.
NO SAFE WAY TO BITE A CORD
That seems dangerous.
This is the only responsible way to bite a cord.
NOT A THING • VERY UNSAFE
Elvis, are you really going to take safety tips from Lupin?
Puck, I chew on cords all the time—
FLOSS FLOSS FLOSS
NEVER, EVER DO THIS

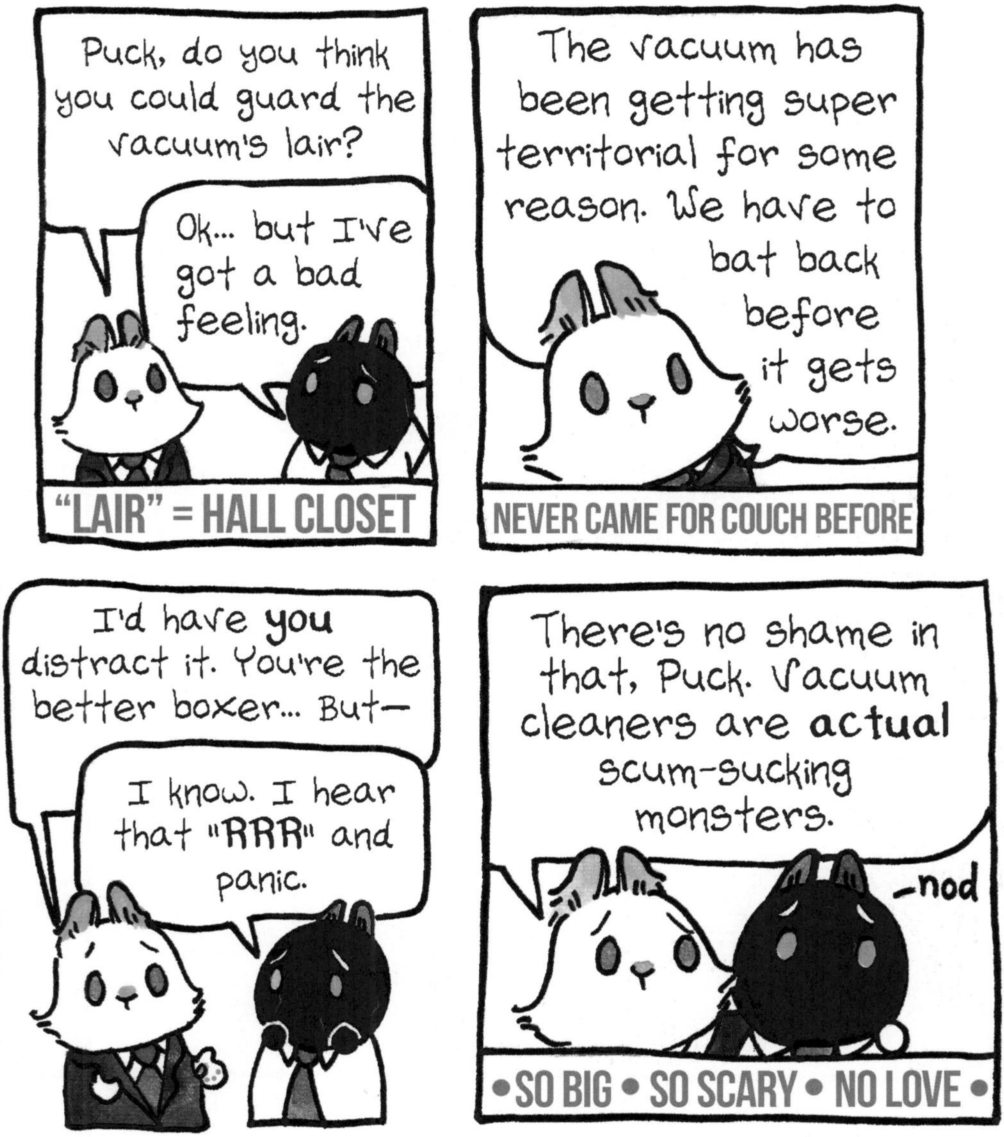
Puck, do you think you could guard the vacuum's lair?
Ok... but I've got a bad feeling.
"LAIR" = HALL CLOSET
The vacuum has been getting super territorial for some reason. We have to bat back before it gets worse.
NEVER CAME FOR COUCH BEFORE
I'd have you distract it. You're the better boxer... But—
I know. I hear that "RRR" and panic.
There's no shame in that, Puck. Vacuum cleaners are actual scum-sucking monsters.
-nod
• SO BIG • SO SCARY • NO LOVE •

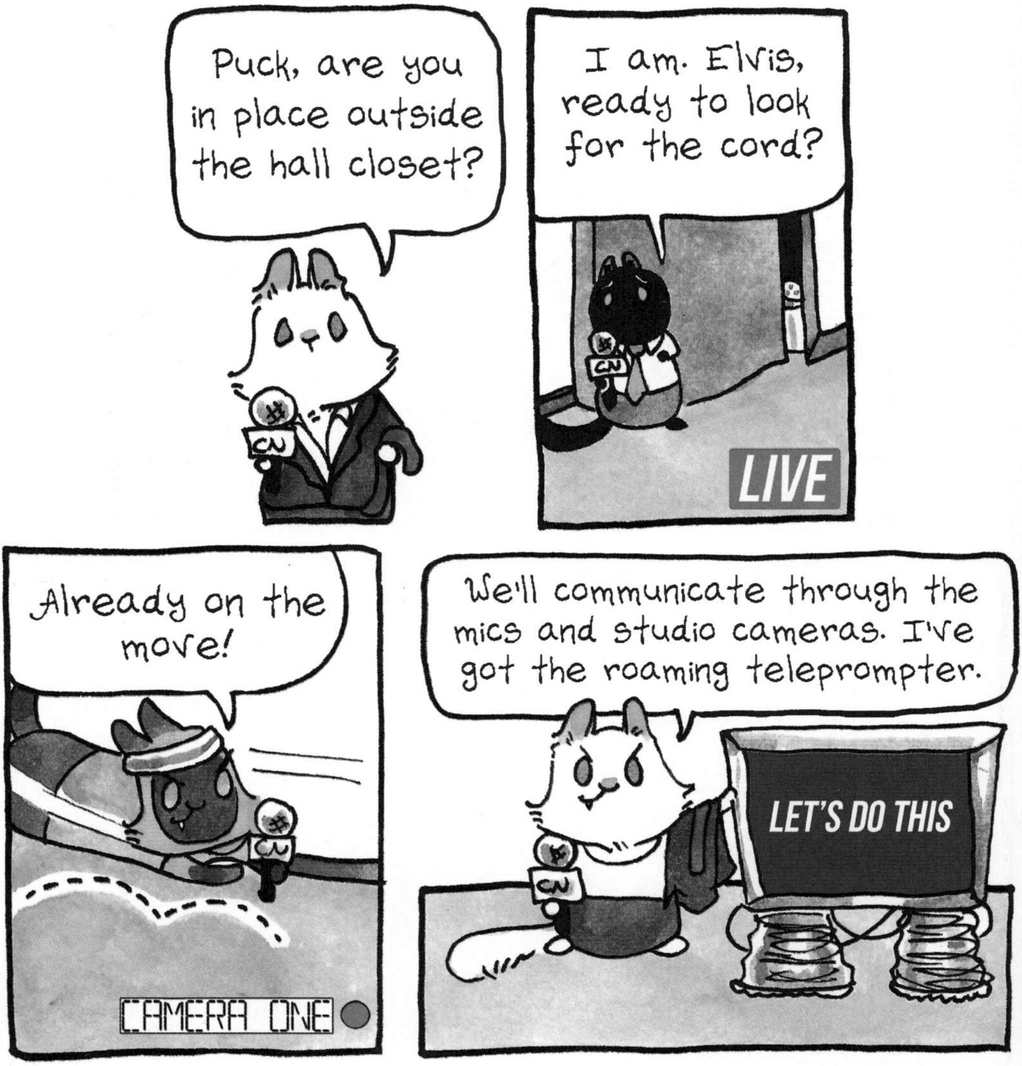
Puck, are you in place outside the hall closet?
I am. Elvis, ready to look for the cord?
LIVE
Already on the move!
CAMERA ONE
We'll communicate through the mics and studio cameras. I've got the roaming teleprompter.
LET'S DO THIS

RRRRRRR

PATROLLING HALL AGAIN

RRRRRRRRRR

CIRCLING BACK TO LIVING ROOM

RRRRR RR

RRRRRRRRRRRR

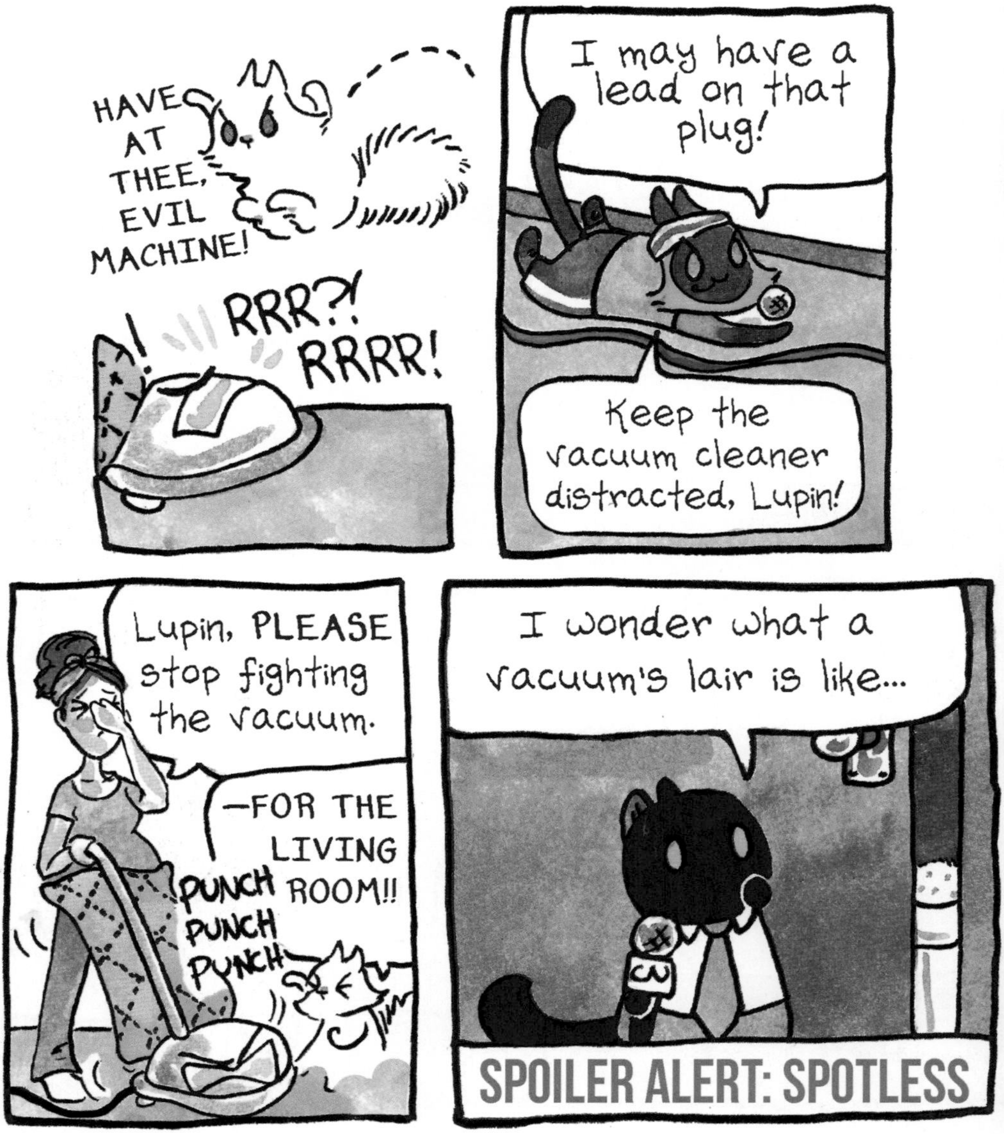
HAVE AT THEE, EVIL MACHINE!
RRR?!
RRRR!
I may have a lead on that plug!
Keep the vacuum cleaner distracted, Lupin!
Lupin, PLEASE stop fighting the vacuum.
—FOR THE LIVING ROOM!!
PUNCH
PUNCH
PUNCH
I wonder what a vacuum's lair is like...
SPOILER ALERT: SPOTLESS

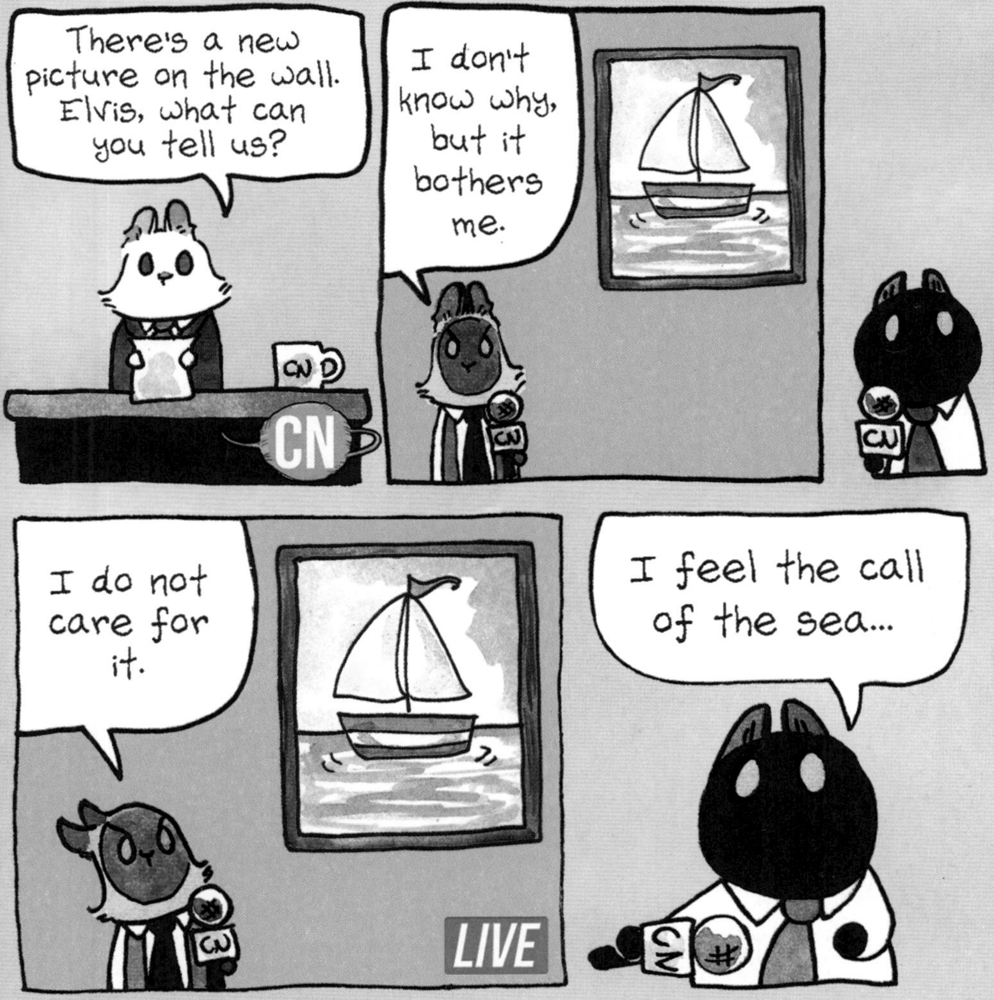
There's a new picture on the wall. Elvis, what can you tell us?
CN
CN
I don't know why, but it bothers me.
CN
CN
I do not care for it.
CN
LIVE
I feel the call of the sea...
CN

Puck, you ok?

CN

Ahoy, matey.

What

Just gonna steer the vessel this way...

Get that smug little boat away from me!

SWIPE SWIPE

THAR SHE BLOWS!

PUCKY!

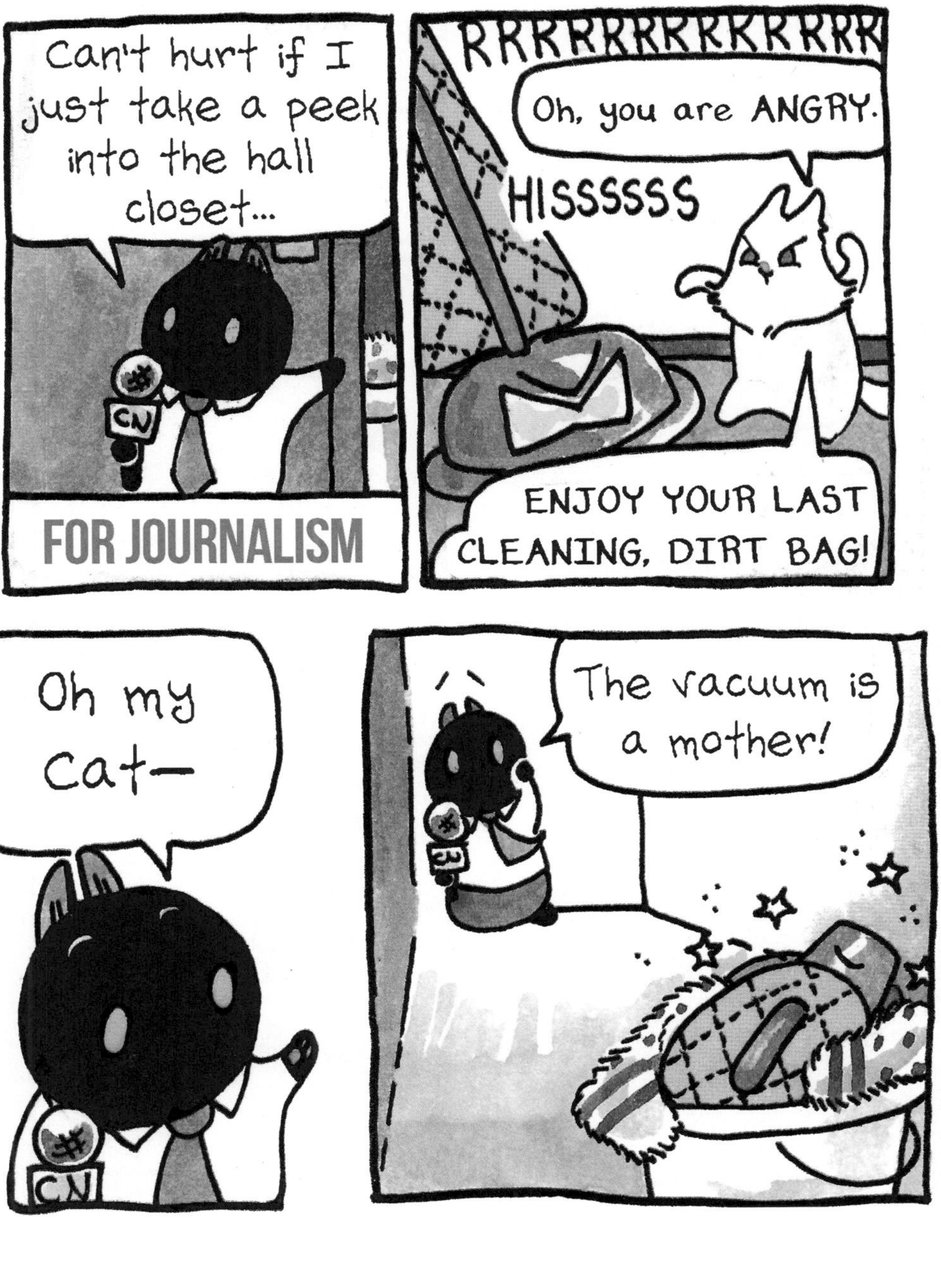

Can't hurt if I just take a peek into the hall closet...
FOR JOURNALISM
RRRRRRRRRRRRR
Oh, you are ANGRY.
HISSSSSS
ENJOY YOUR LAST CLEANING, DIRT BAG!
Oh my Cat—
The vacuum is a mother!

Elvis! Lupin!

NOT NOW, PUCK—

SHAKE
SHAKE
SHAKE

LITTLE BUSY!

I can't talk now either, Puck!

I found the plug!

Wait, no!

I know why the vacuum has been so territorial!

PULL

CUT

SO DANGEROU---

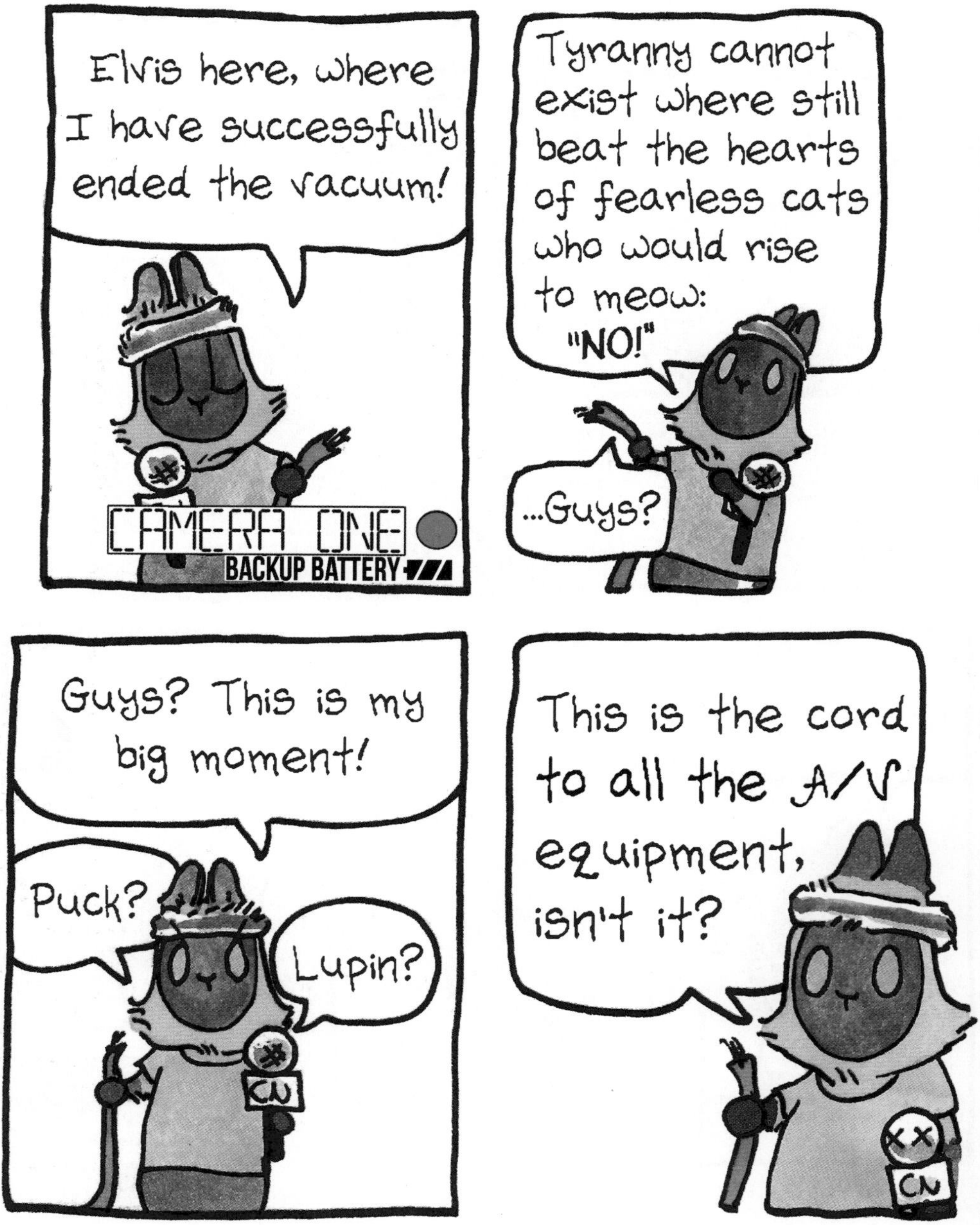
Elvis here, where I have successfully ended the vacuum!
CAMERA ONE
BACKUP BATTERY
Tyranny cannot exist where still beat the hearts of fearless cats who would rise to meow: "NO!"
...Guys?
Guys? This is my big moment!
Puck?
Lupin?
CN
This is the cord to all the A/V equipment, isn't it?
CN

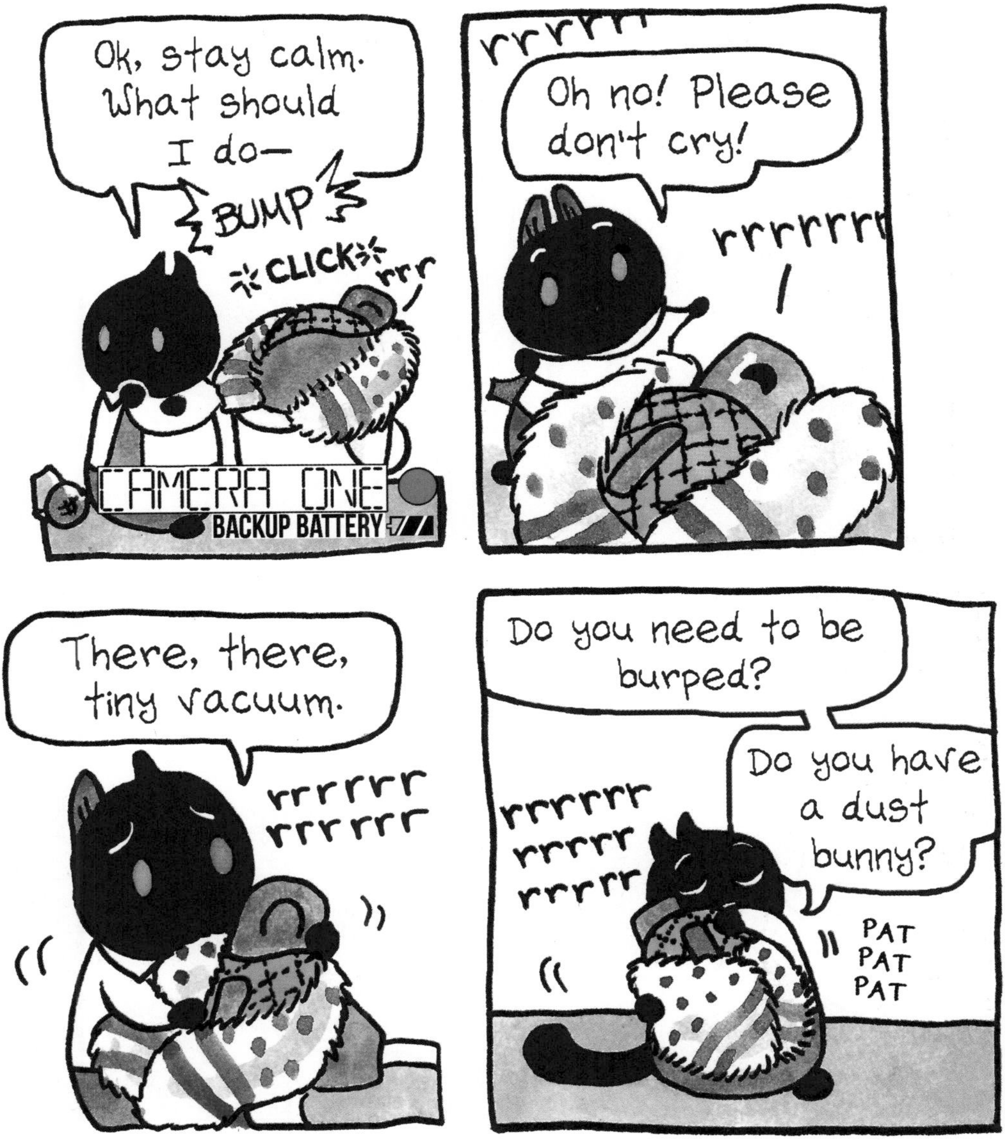
Ok, stay calm. What should I do—
BUMP
CLICK
rrr
CAMERA ONE
BACKUP BATTERY
rrrrrr
Oh no! Please don't cry!
rrrrrrr
There, there, tiny vacuum.
rrrrrr rrrrrr
Do you need to be burped?
Do you have a dust bunny?
rrrrrr rrrrr rrrrr
PAT PAT PAT

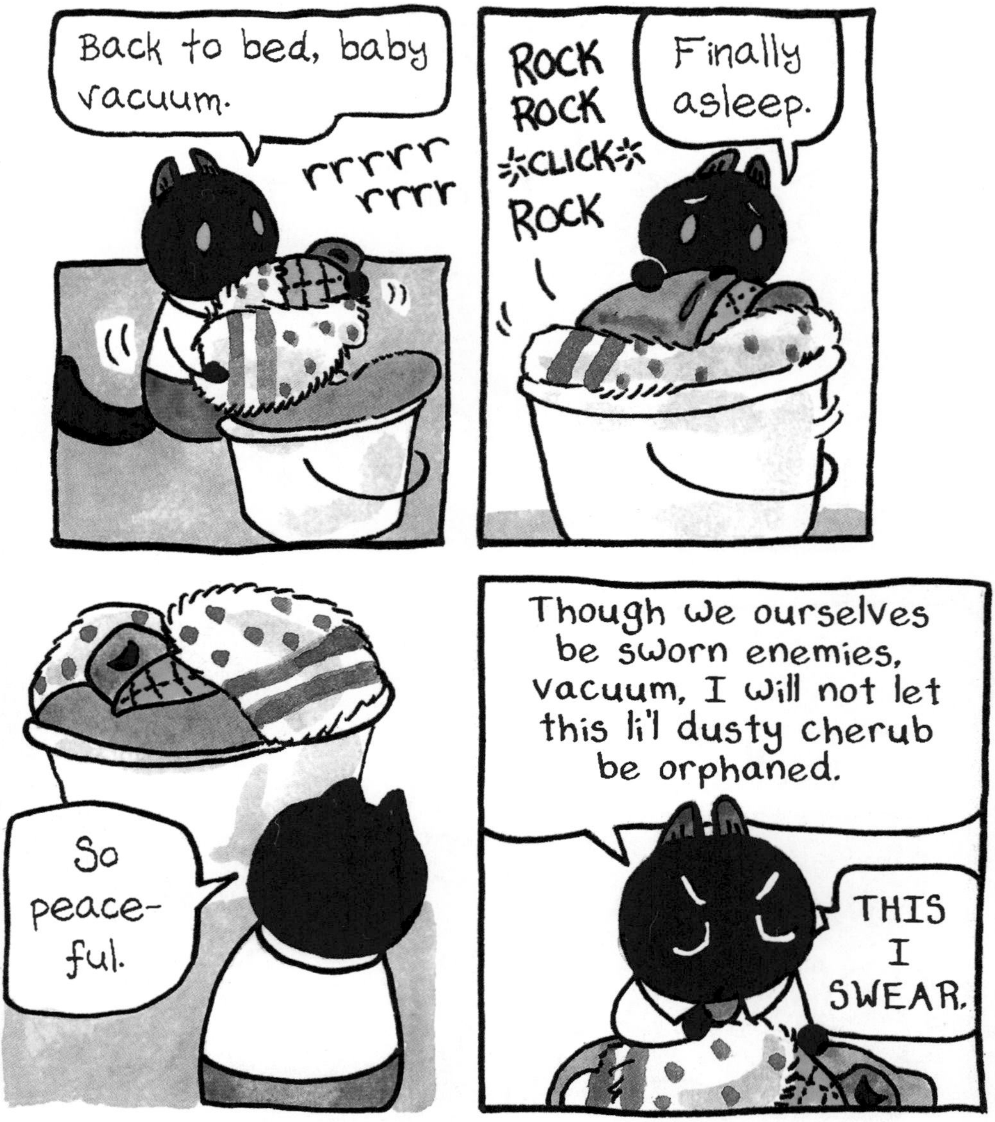
Back to bed, baby vacuum.
rrrrr rrrr
ROCK ROCK
CLICK
ROCK
Finally asleep.
So peace-ful.
Though we ourselves be sworn enemies, vacuum, I will not let this li'l dusty cherub be orphaned.
THIS I SWEAR.

The Woman keeps getting up off the couch.

Over to you, Puck!

Lupin, I'm live where the Woman's about to get up again.

And it is driving Elvis BERSERK.

Where are you going now?!

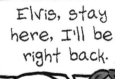

Elvis, stay here, I'll be right back.

NO.

No, no—

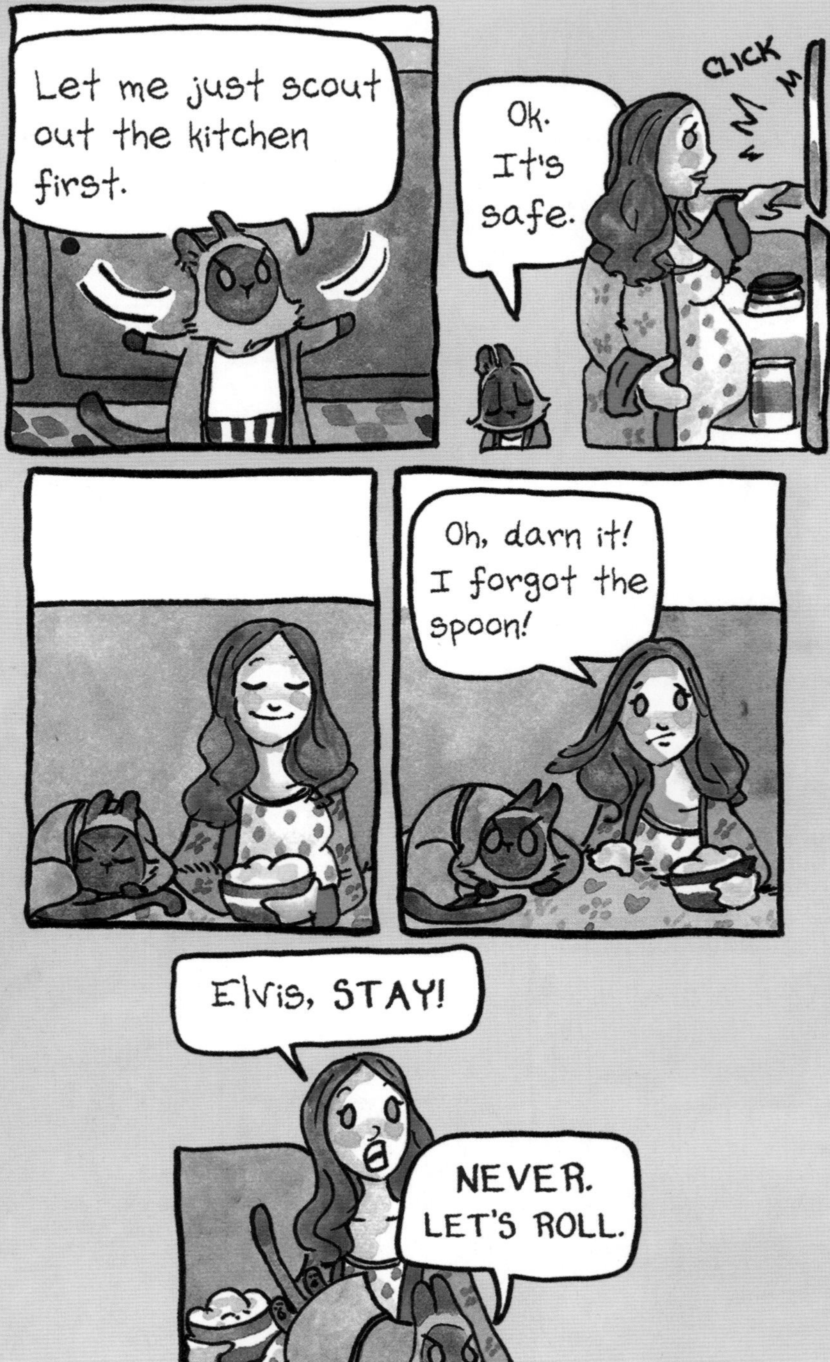
Let me just scout out the kitchen first.
Ok. It's safe.
CLICK
Oh, darn it! I forgot the spoon!
Elvis, STAY!
NEVER. LET'S ROLL.

RRRRRRRRRRR

I FEAR ONLY BOREDOM!

BOINK BOINK BOINK

KICK KICK KICK

RRRRR

LUPIN, DON'T! THE VACUUM'S A—

'BOUT TO BE SPARE PARTS! STEP ASIDE, PUCK!

RRRR

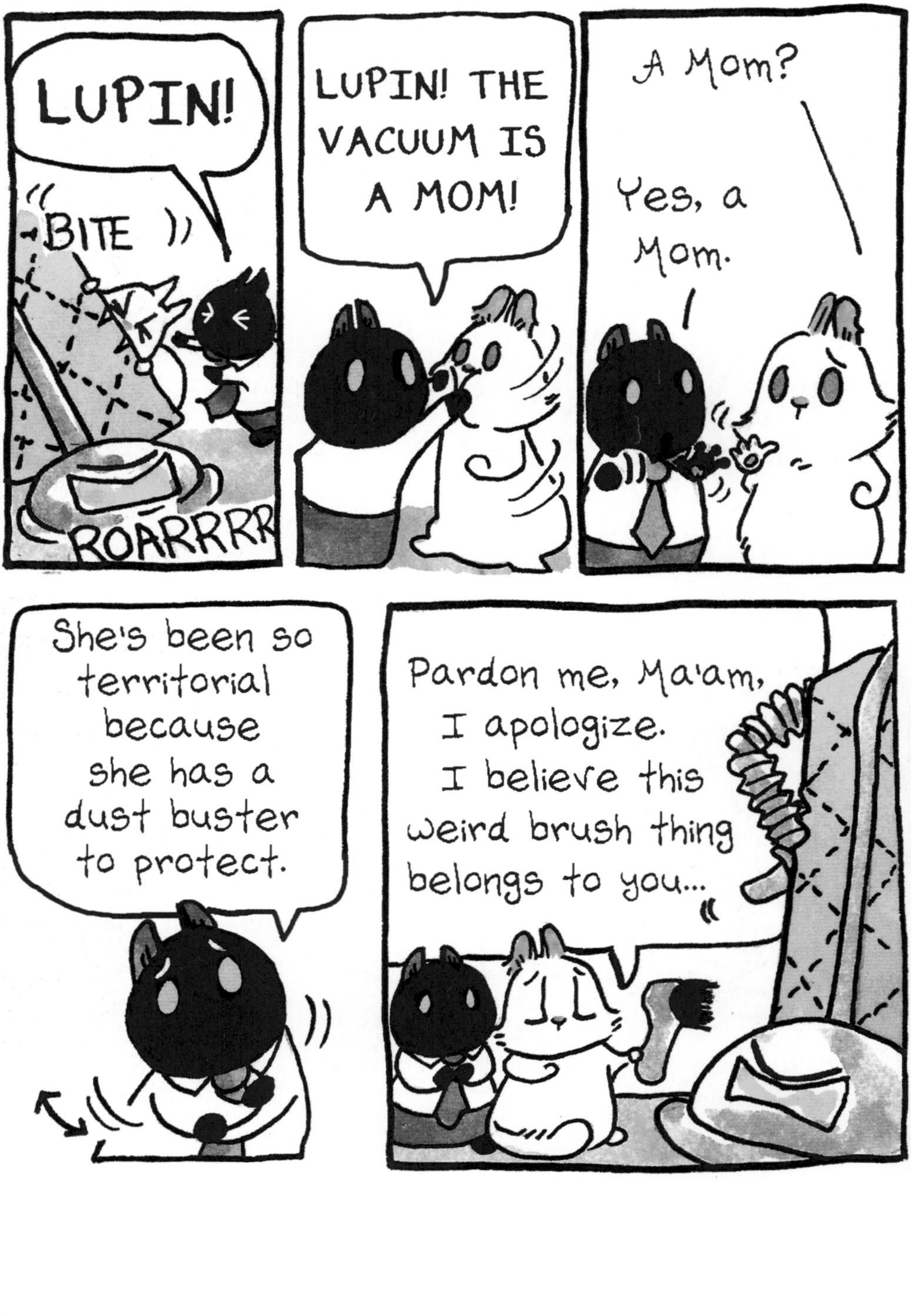
LUPIN!
BITE
ROARRRRR
LUPIN! THE VACUUM IS A MOM!
A Mom?
Yes, a Mom.
She's been so territorial because she has a dust buster to protect.
Pardon me, Ma'am, I apologize. I believe this weird brush thing belongs to you...

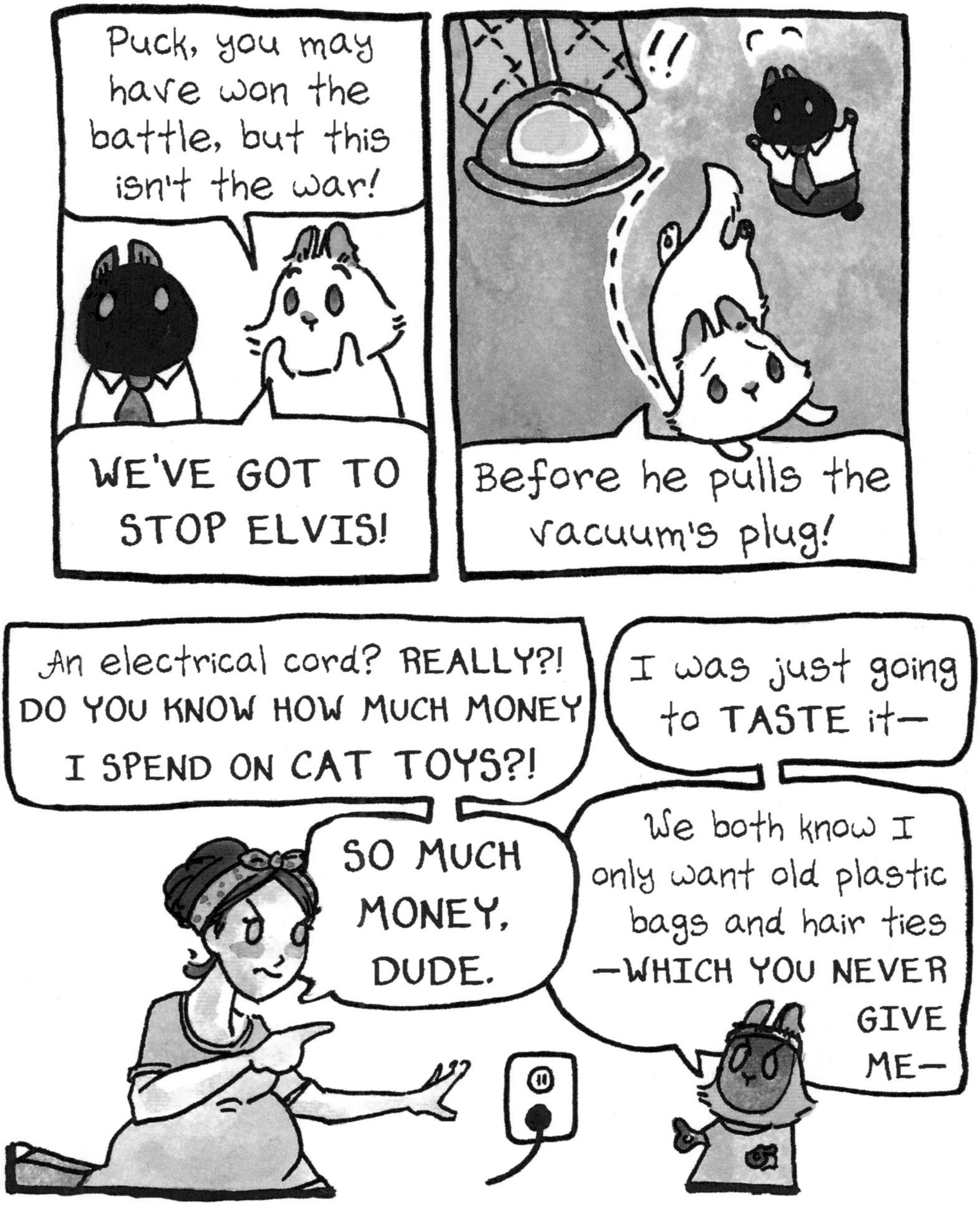

Puck, you may have won the battle, but this isn't the war!
WE'VE GOT TO STOP ELVIS!
!!
Before he pulls the vacuum's plug!
An electrical cord? REALLY?! DO YOU KNOW HOW MUCH MONEY I SPEND ON CAT TOYS?!
SO MUCH MONEY, DUDE.
I was just going to TASTE it—
We both know I only want old plastic bags and hair ties —WHICH YOU NEVER GIVE ME—

SURPRISE! I WAS WRONG!

WHAT

!

Are you protecting the vacuum?!

I can explain!

Allow me to avert my eyes first—

I'm sorry if my invisibility makes you uncomfortable.

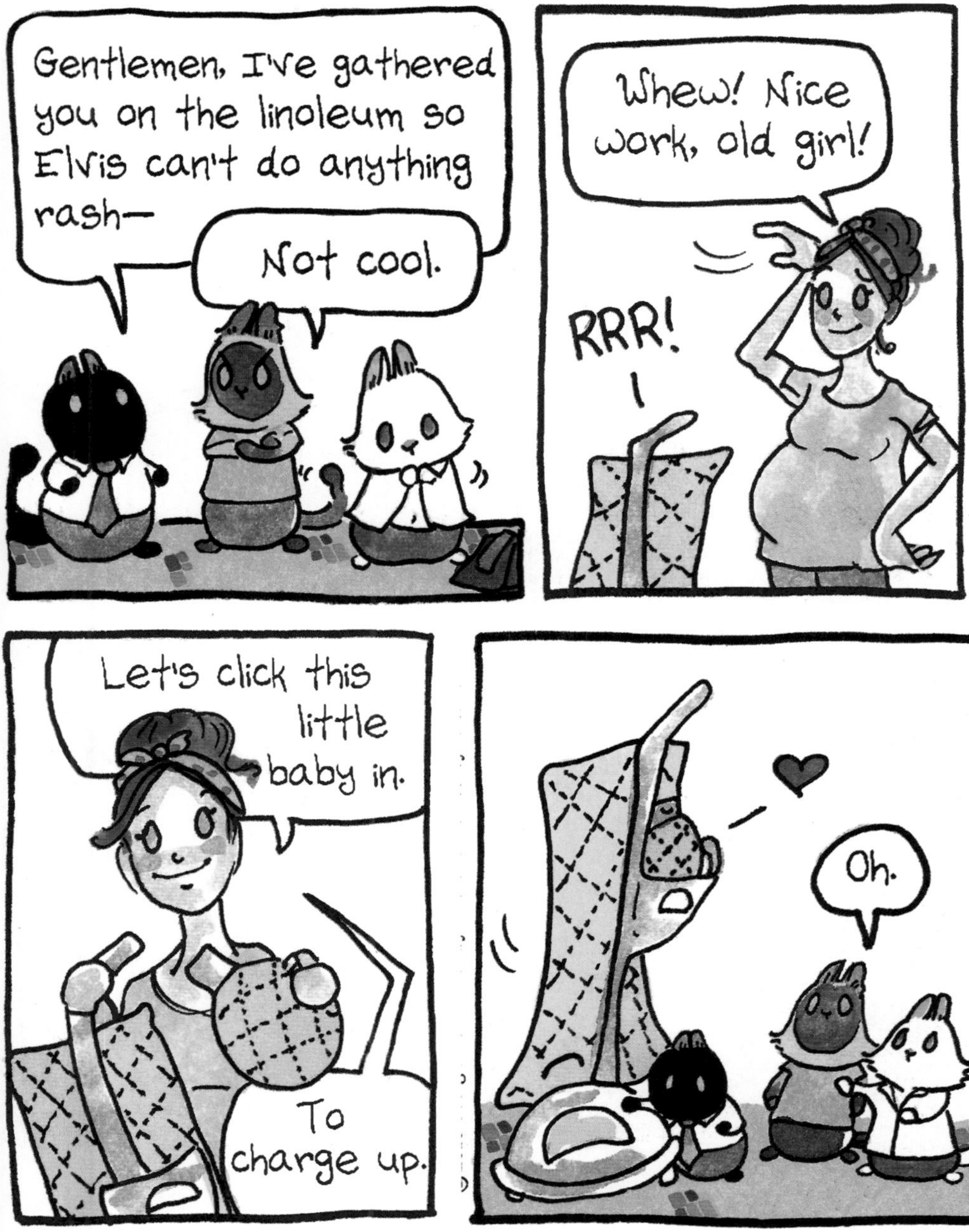
Gentlemen, I've gathered you on the linoleum so Elvis can't do anything rash—
Not cool.
Whew! Nice work, old girl!
RRR!
Let's click this little baby in.
To charge up.
Oh.

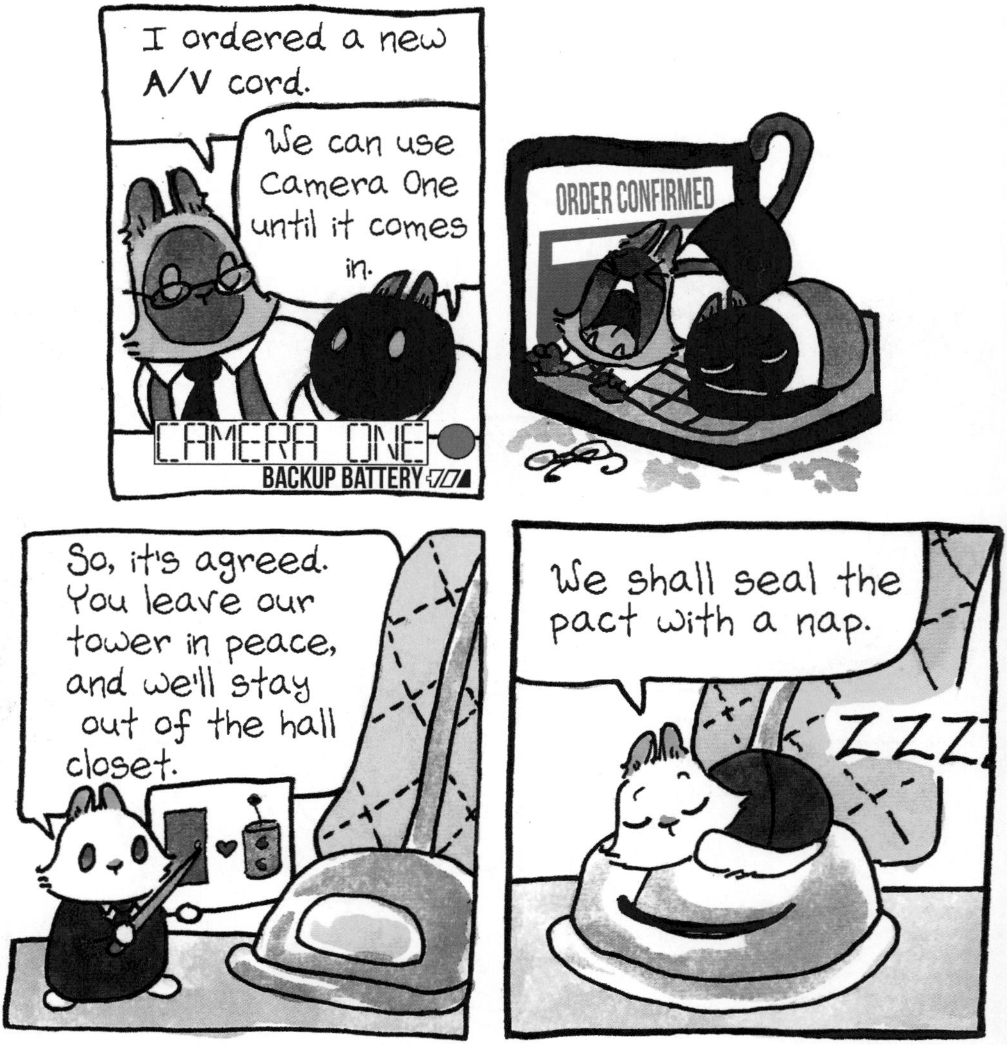

I ordered a new A/V cord.
We can use Camera One until it comes in.
CAMERA ONE
BACKUP BATTERY
ORDER CONFIRMED
So, it's agreed. You leave our tower in peace, and we'll stay out of the hall closet.
We shall seal the pact with a nap.
ZZZ

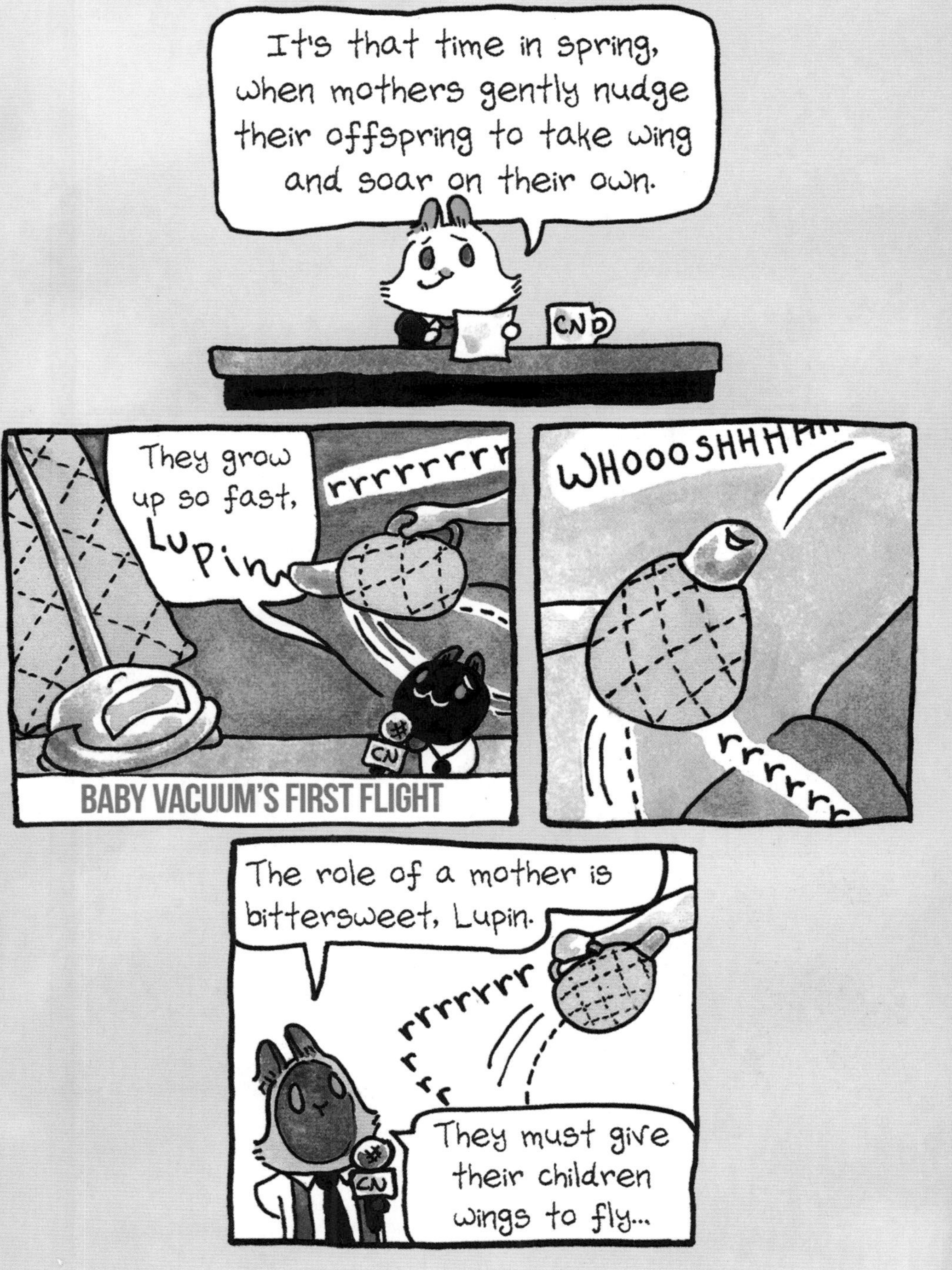
It's that time in spring, when mothers gently nudge their offspring to take wing and soar on their own.
CND
They grow up so fast, Lupin
rrrrrrrr
CN
BABY VACUUM'S FIRST FLIGHT
WHOOOSHHHH
rrrrrrr
The role of a mother is bittersweet, Lupin.
rrrrrrr
rrr
CN
They must give their children wings to fly...

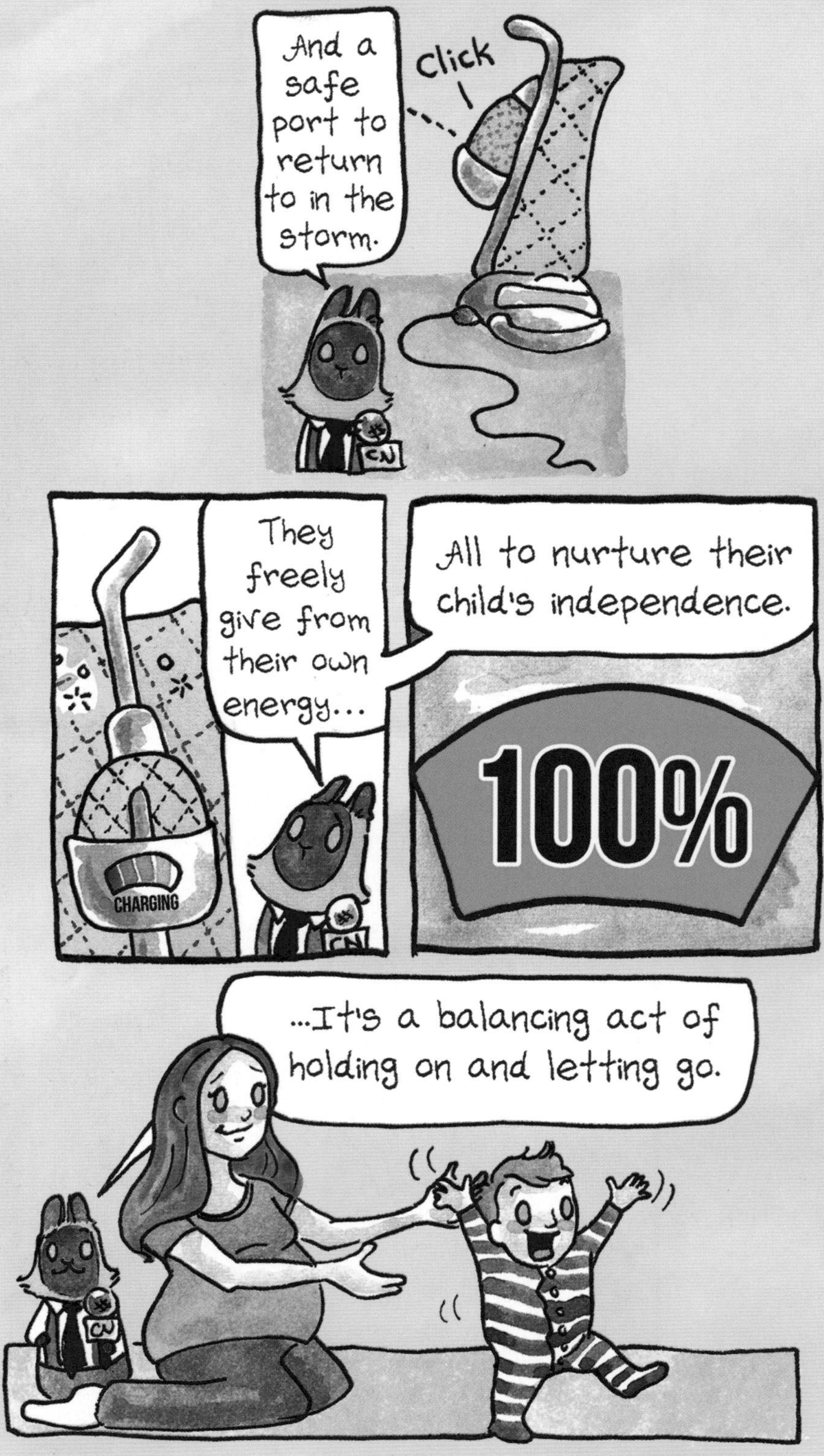
And a safe port to return to in the storm.
Click
They freely give from their own energy...
All to nurture their child's independence.
CHARGING
100%
...It's a balancing act of holding on and letting go.

The Man is repairing a mug.

We are live on the scene, being totally helpful.

Just gotta boop the super glue real quick—

OH MY GOD, LUPIN, NO! WHY—

GOTTA BOOOOP

SPLAT

LIVE

BREAKING: In a tragic turn of events, the Man now HAS A MUG FOR A HAND!!

SHAKE SHAKE

GRUESOME BUT CONVENIENT

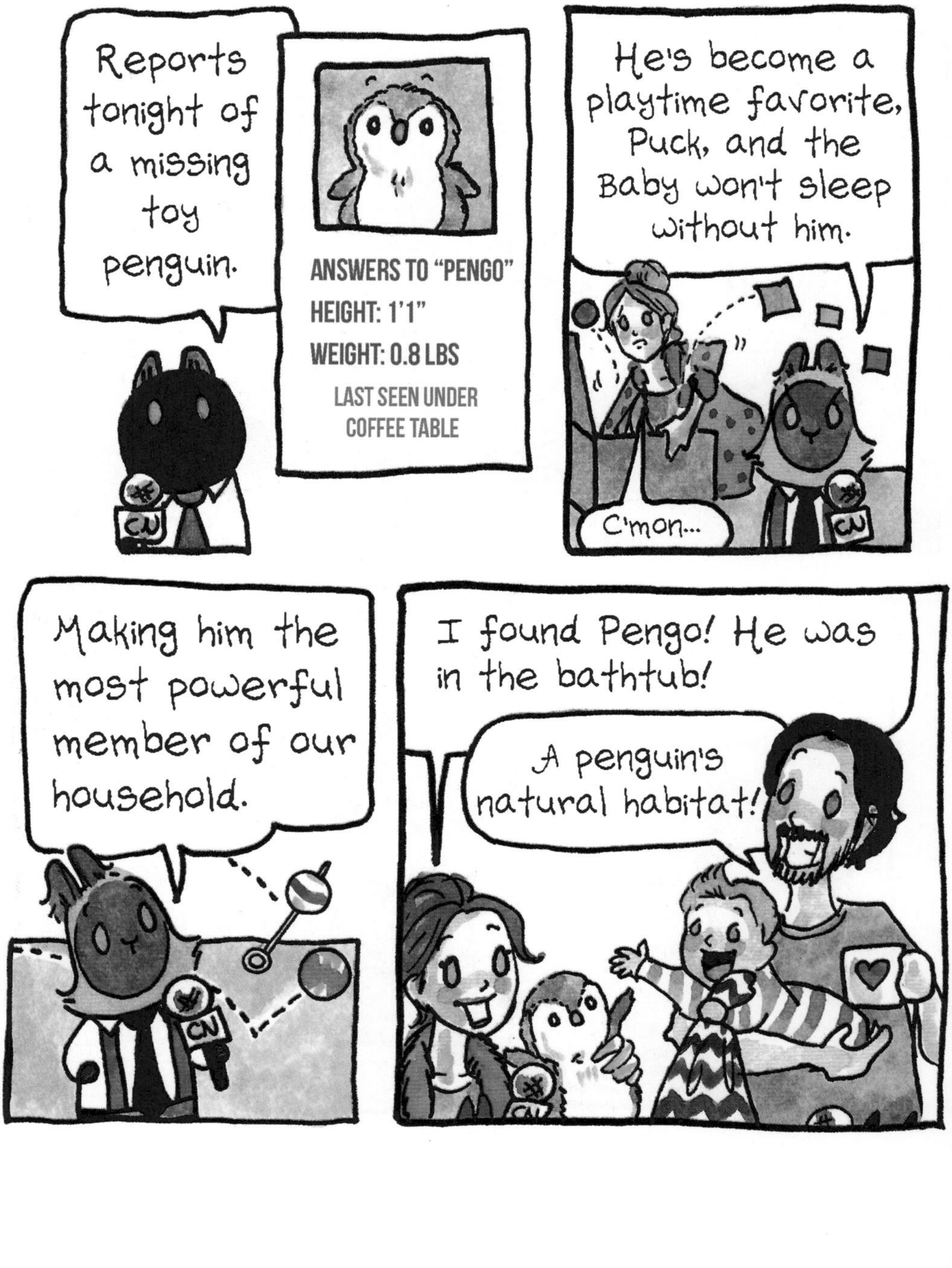
Reports tonight of a missing toy penguin.
ANSWERS TO "PENGO"
HEIGHT: 1'1"
WEIGHT: 0.8 LBS
LAST SEEN UNDER COFFEE TABLE
He's become a playtime favorite, Puck, and the Baby won't sleep without him.
C'mon...
CN
Making him the most powerful member of our household.
I found Pengo! He was in the bathtub!
A penguin's natural habitat!

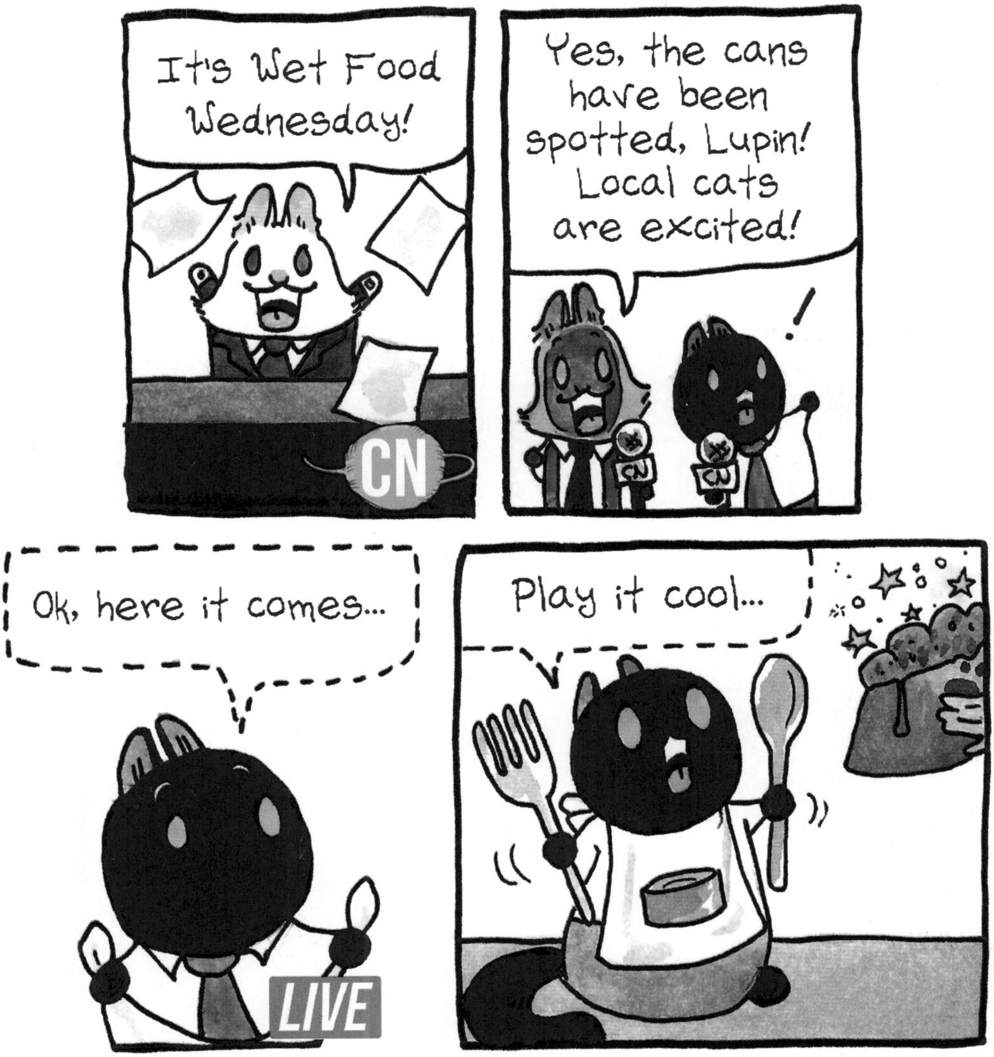
It's Wet Food Wednesday!
CN
Yes, the cans have been spotted, Lupin! Local cats are excited!
!
Ok, here it comes...
LIVE
Play it cool...

The Woman is taking a warm, relaxing bath.
And apartment residents are out-raged.
CN
Ma'am?
MA'AM?
Ma'am, CN news.
MA'AM!
Is she still in there?
MA'AM?
CN NEWS, MA'AM!
Guys, give her some space.
MA'AM?
MA'AM?!
MA'AM!
MOM!

Guess who's got two pruney thumbs and is too pregnant to get herself out of the tub?

It me

The Woman is in a delicate situation.

And wasting precious time texting her husband sweet nothings—

4:34 pm

My Man

I'm stuck.

I think my legs are falling asleep

Well, I live here now.

Tell our son his mother loved him

...

My hero!

I like a woman who lives dangerously!

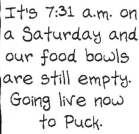

It's 7:31 a.m. on a Saturday and our food bowls are still empty. Going live now to Puck.

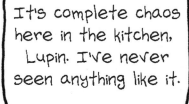

It's complete chaos here in the kitchen, Lupin. I've never seen anything like it.

My God. We've sent Elvis into the bedroom. Elvis, what can you see?

Lupin, these maniacs are out of control.

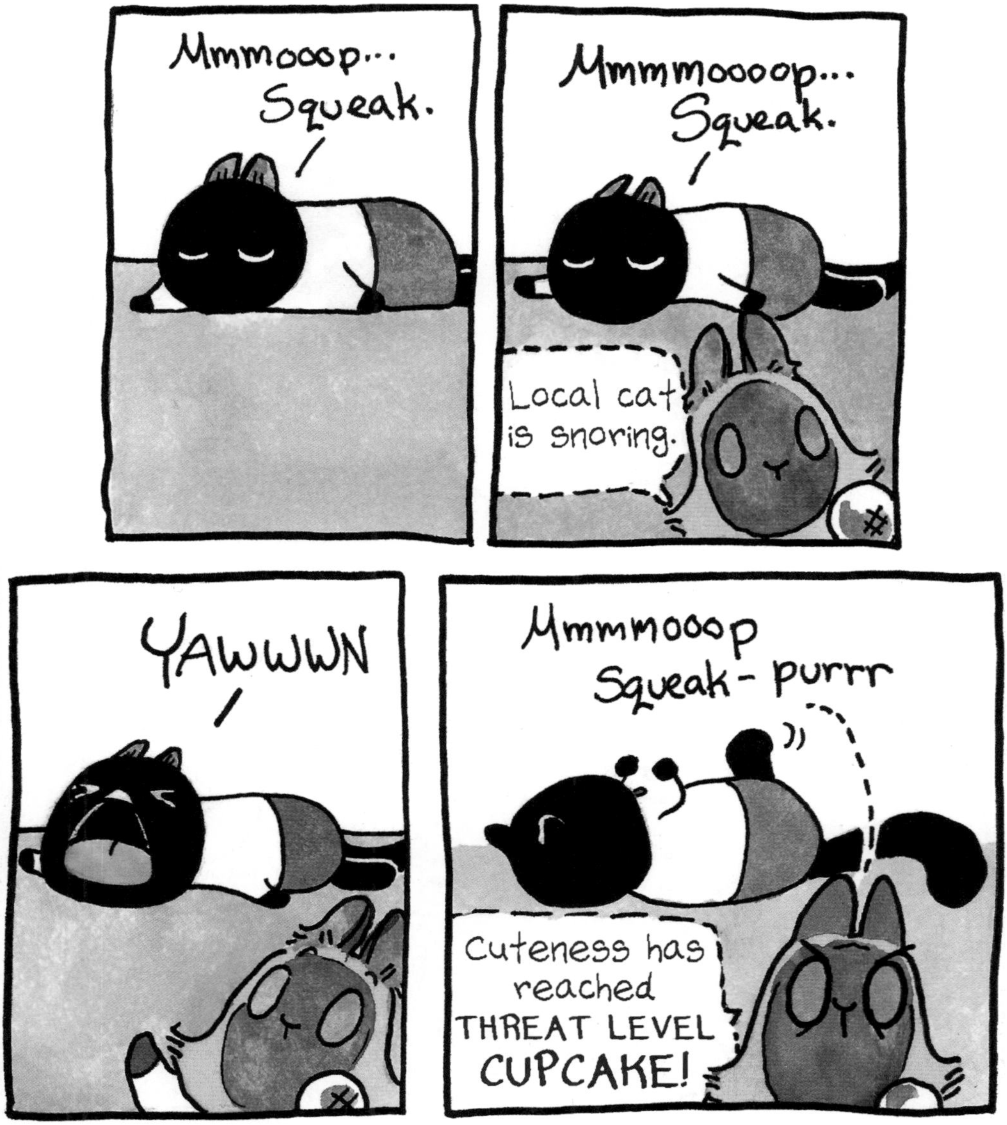
Mmmooop... Squeak.
Mmmmoooop... Squeak.
Local cat is snoring.
YAWWWN
Mmmmooop Squeak - purrr
Cuteness has reached THREAT LEVEL CUPCAKE!

Recently a cat gained control over the tiny waterfall in the bathroom!

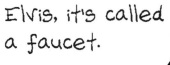

Elvis, it's called a faucet.

And there's one in the kitchen, too!

KICK

And if you leave it on, the tiny waterfall becomes A MEDIUM WATERFALL!

LUPIN!

MU-HA HA HA HA HA!

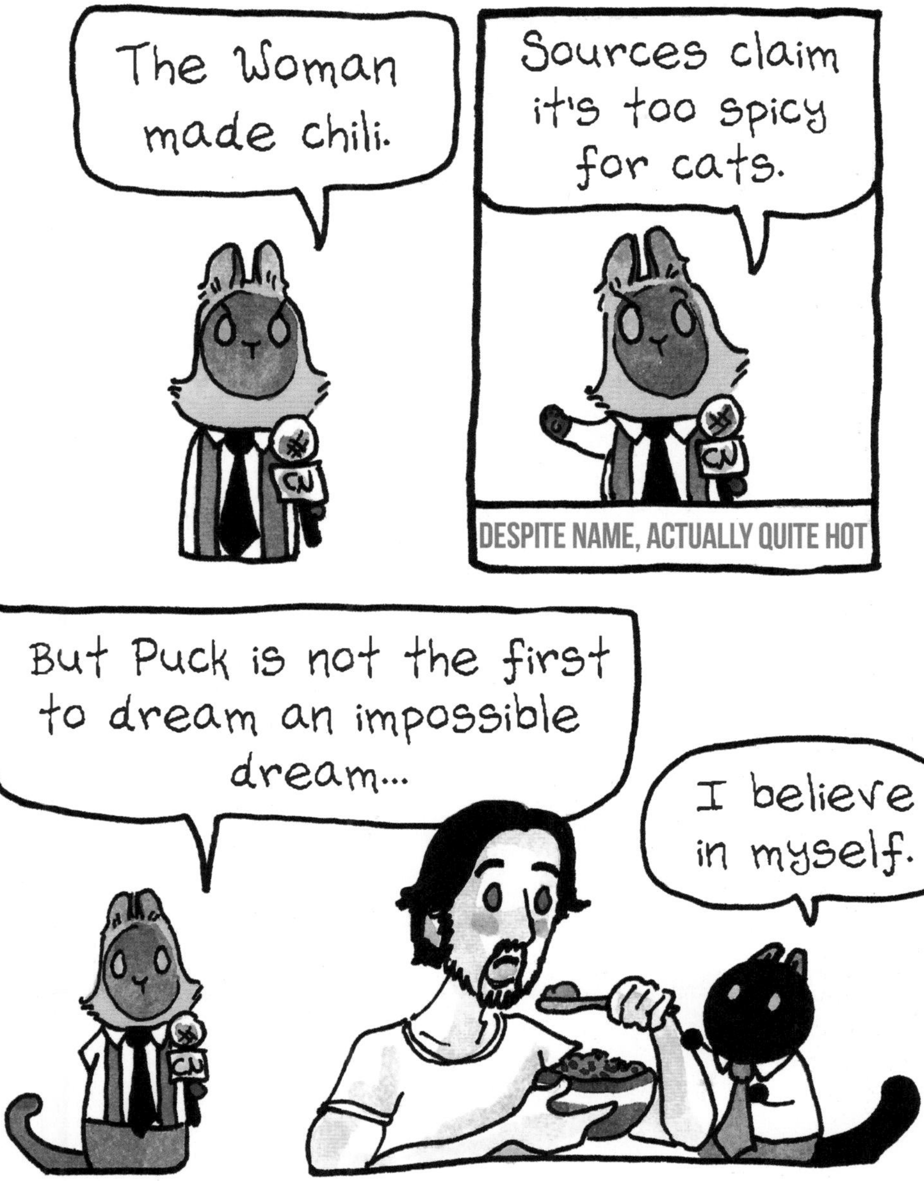

The Woman made chili.
Sources claim it's too spicy for cats.
DESPITE NAME, ACTUALLY QUITE HOT
But Puck is not the first to dream an impossible dream...
I believe in myself.

In today's forecast, it'll be perfect sun-spot weather! Get out there on the carpet and soak it up while you can!

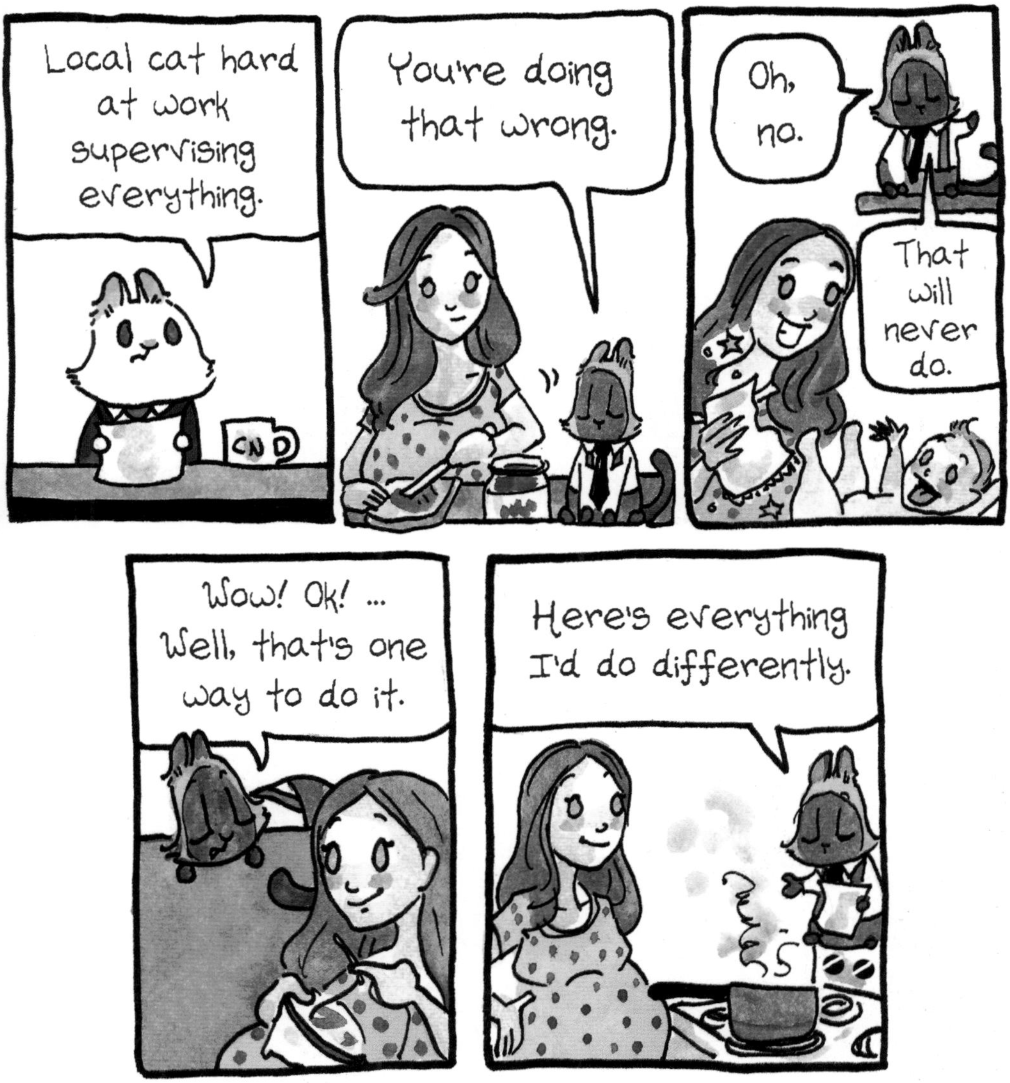
Local cat hard at work supervising everything.
You're doing that wrong.
Oh, no.
That will never do.
Wow! Ok! ... Well, that's one way to do it.
Here's everything I'd do differently.
CND

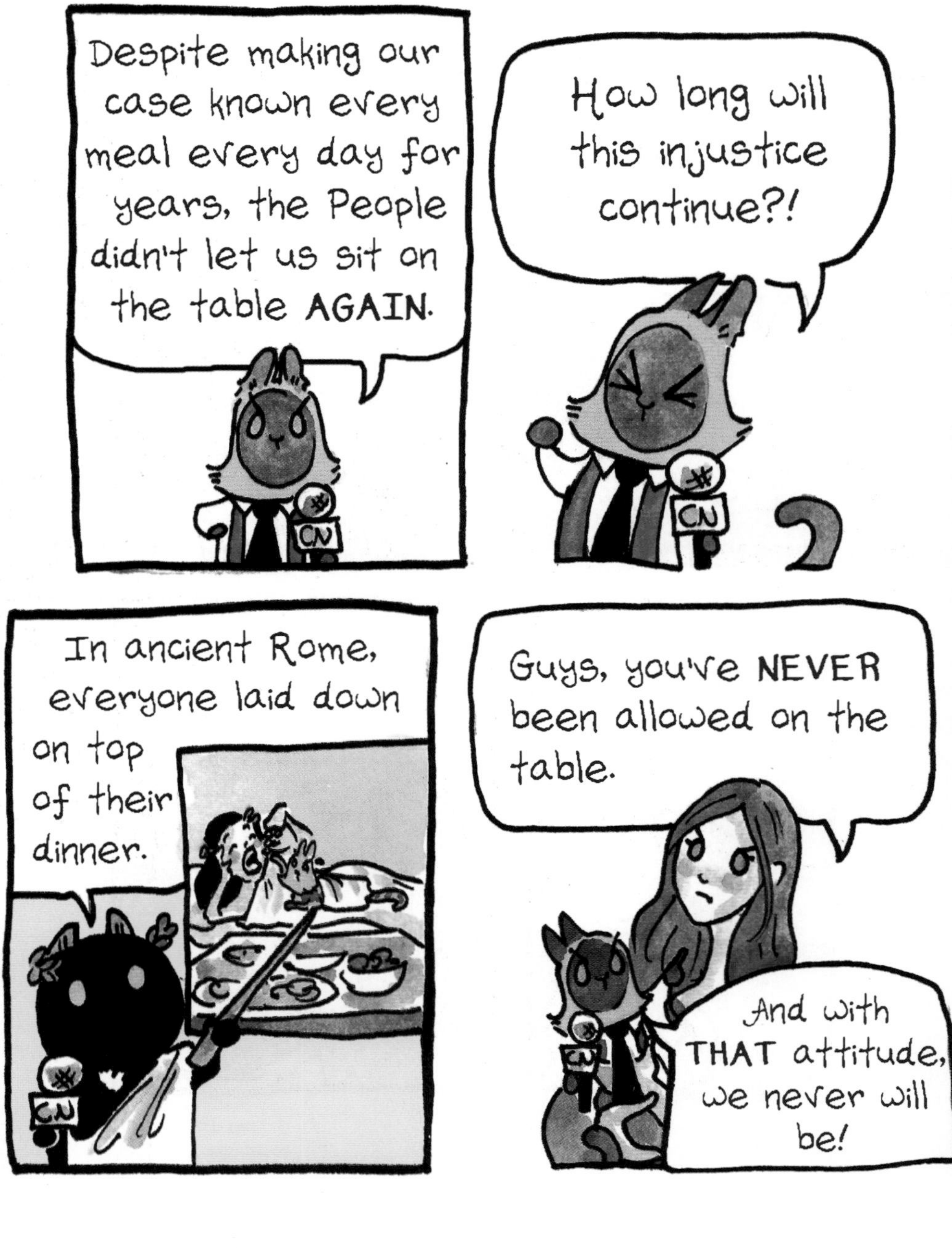
Despite making our case known every meal every day for years, the People didn't let us sit on the table AGAIN.
How long will this injustice continue?!
CN
CN
In ancient Rome, everyone laid down on top of their dinner.
CN
Guys, you've NEVER been allowed on the table.
And with THAT attitude, we never will be!
CN

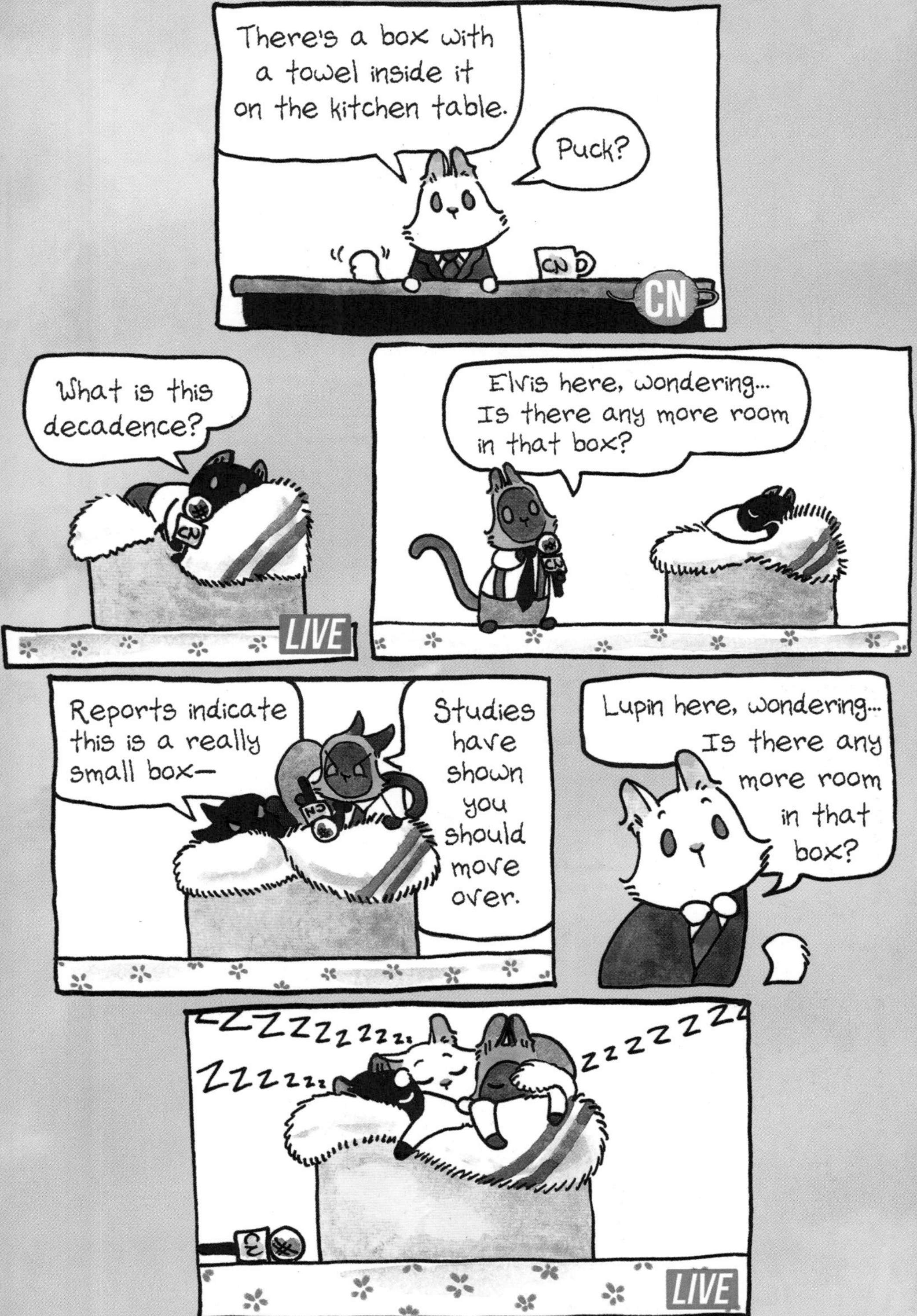
There's a box with a towel inside it on the kitchen table.
Puck?
CN
CN
What is this decadence?
CN
LIVE
Elvis here, wondering... Is there any more room in that box?
CN
Reports indicate this is a really small box—
Studies have shown you should move over.
CN
Lupin here, wondering... Is there any more room in that box?
ZZZZZZZZ
ZZZZZ
ZZZZZZZ
CN
LIVE

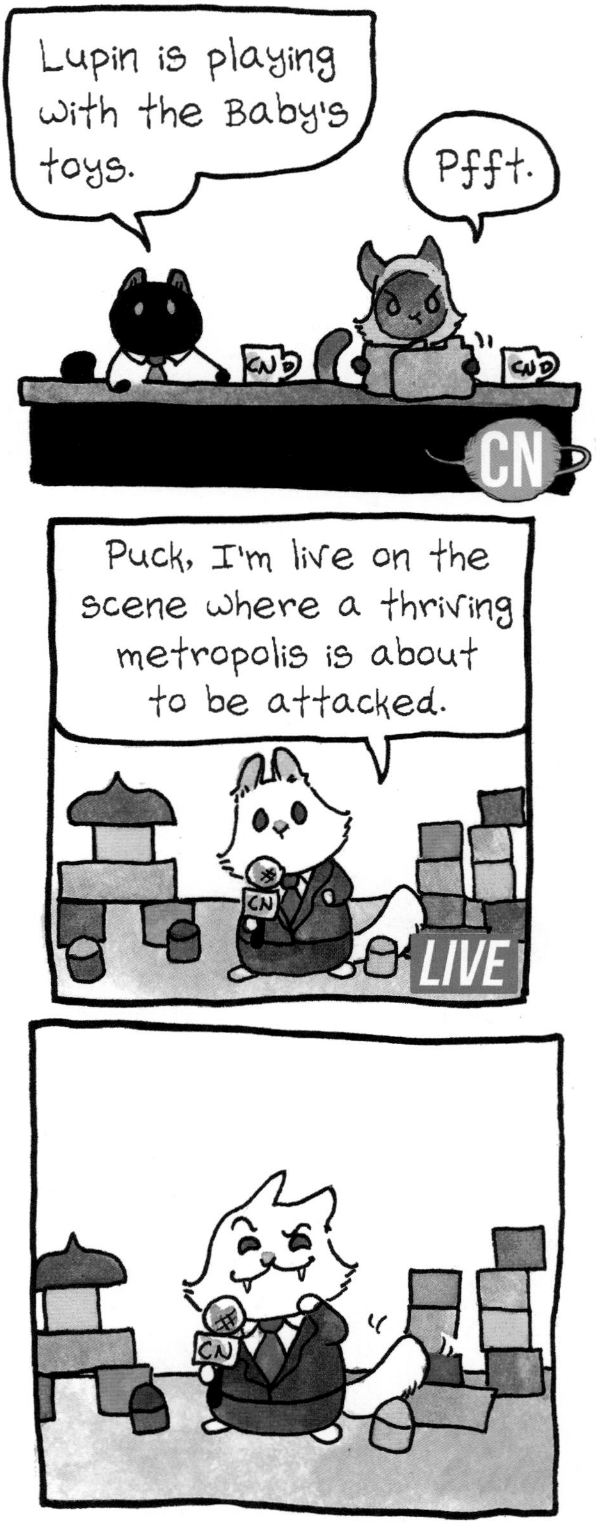
Lupin is playing with the Baby's toys.
Pfft.
CN
CN
CN
Puck, I'm live on the scene where a thriving metropolis is about to be attacked.
CN
LIVE
CN

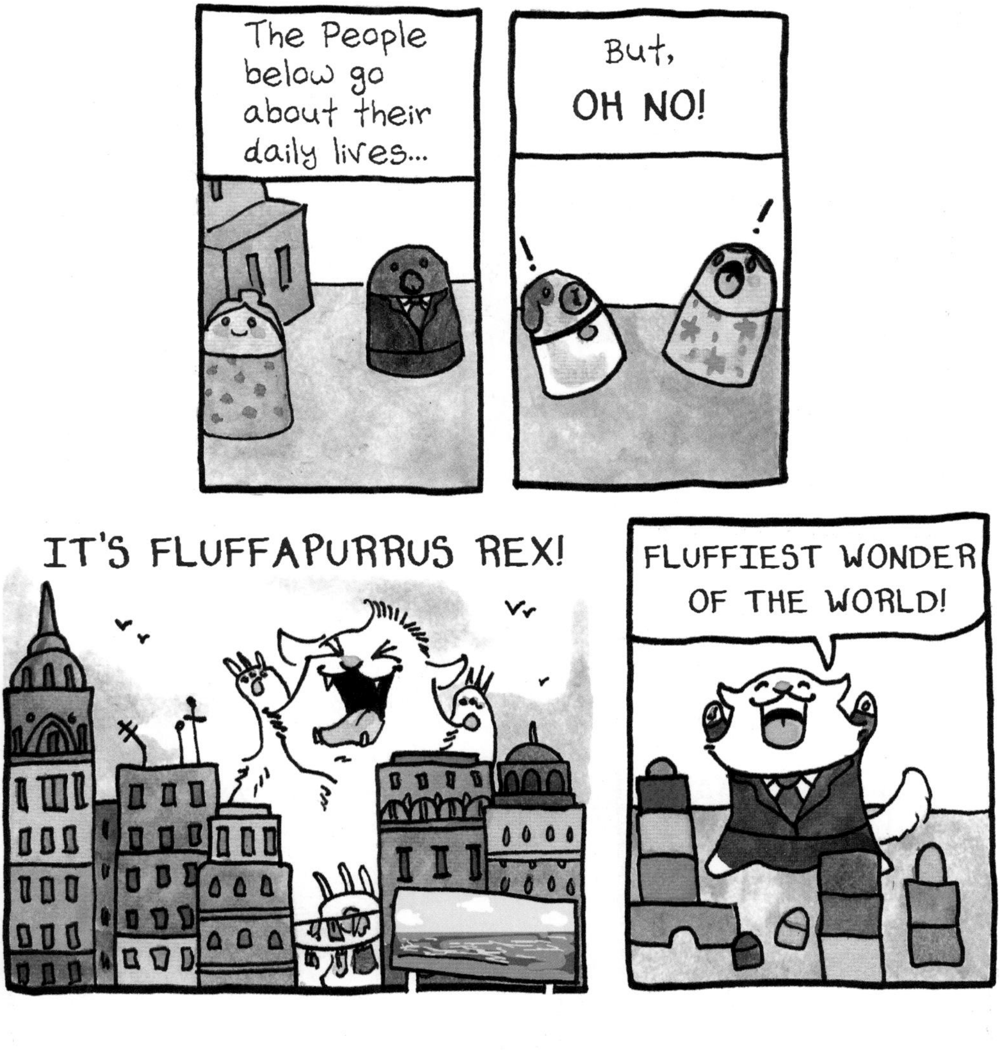
The People below go about their daily lives...
But,
OH NO!
IT'S FLUFFAPURRUS REX!
FLUFFIEST WONDER OF THE WORLD!

SWAT
SWIPE
!
TAP
TAP
I DON'T BELIEVE IT, IT'S KIDZILLA!
ROARRR!

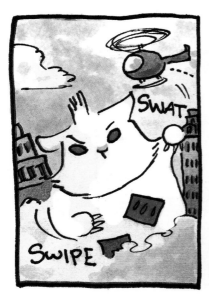

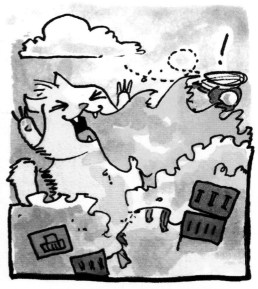

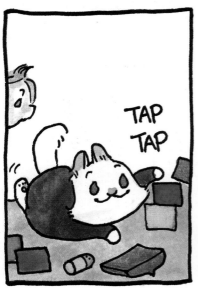

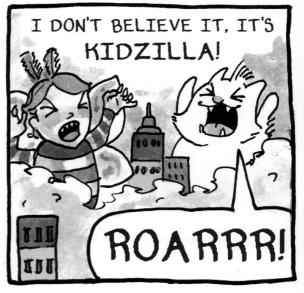

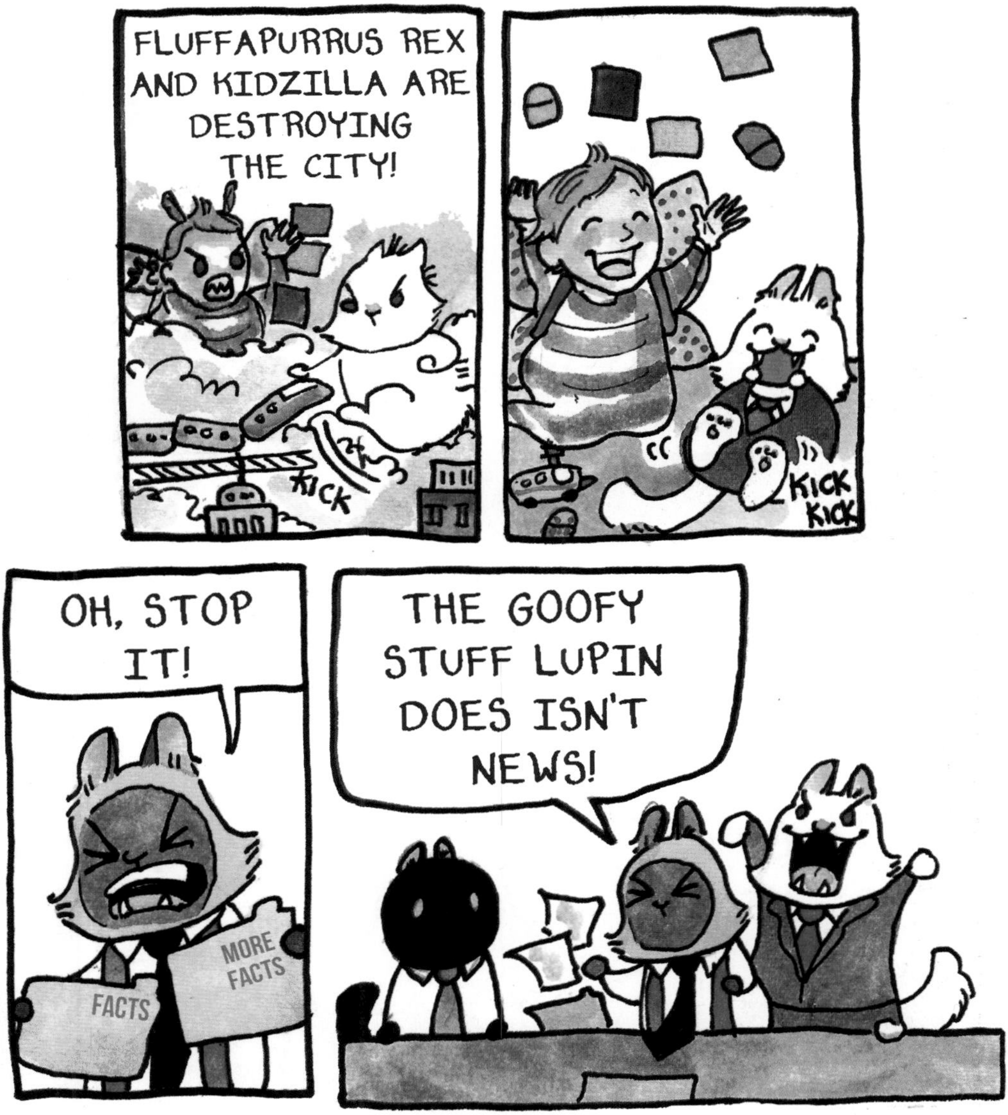
FLUFFAPURRUS REX AND KIDZILLA ARE DESTROYING THE CITY!
KICK
KICK KICK
OH, STOP IT!
FACTS
MORE FACTS
THE GOOFY STUFF LUPIN DOES ISN'T NEWS!

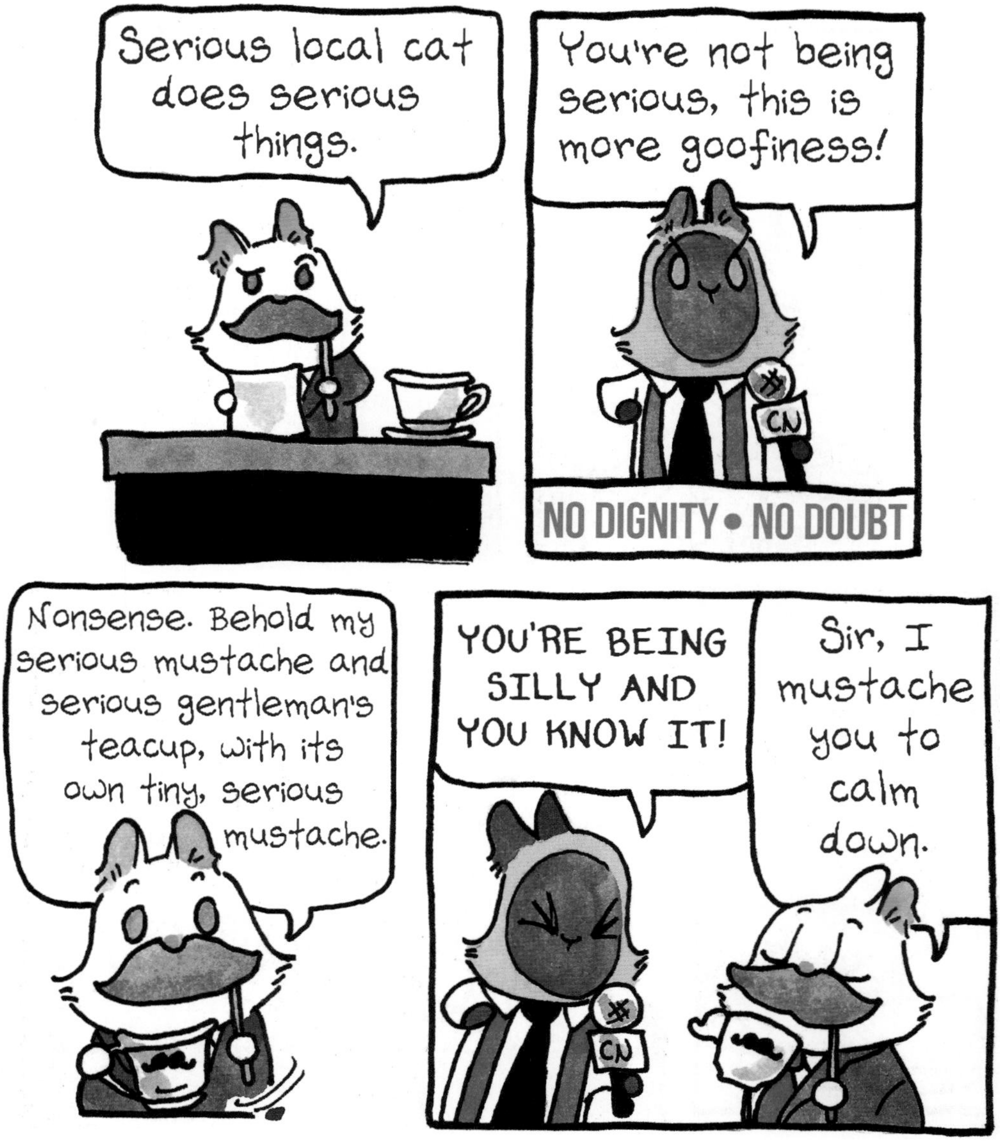
Serious local cat does serious things.
You're not being serious, this is more goofiness!
CN
NO DIGNITY • NO DOUBT
Nonsense. Behold my serious mustache and serious gentleman's teacup, with its own tiny, serious mustache.
YOU'RE BEING SILLY AND YOU KNOW IT!
Sir, I mustache you to calm down.
CN

Serious, elegant cat is not the only local with a completely serious mustache. We go live to Puck with more!

I'm so sorry, Elvis. He taped it to me.

Now if I take it off, my fur will get all stuck.

No, I get it.

SERIOUS SITUATION

I, for one, am sick of this tom-foolery!

Elvis, turn around, I think there's something on your face—

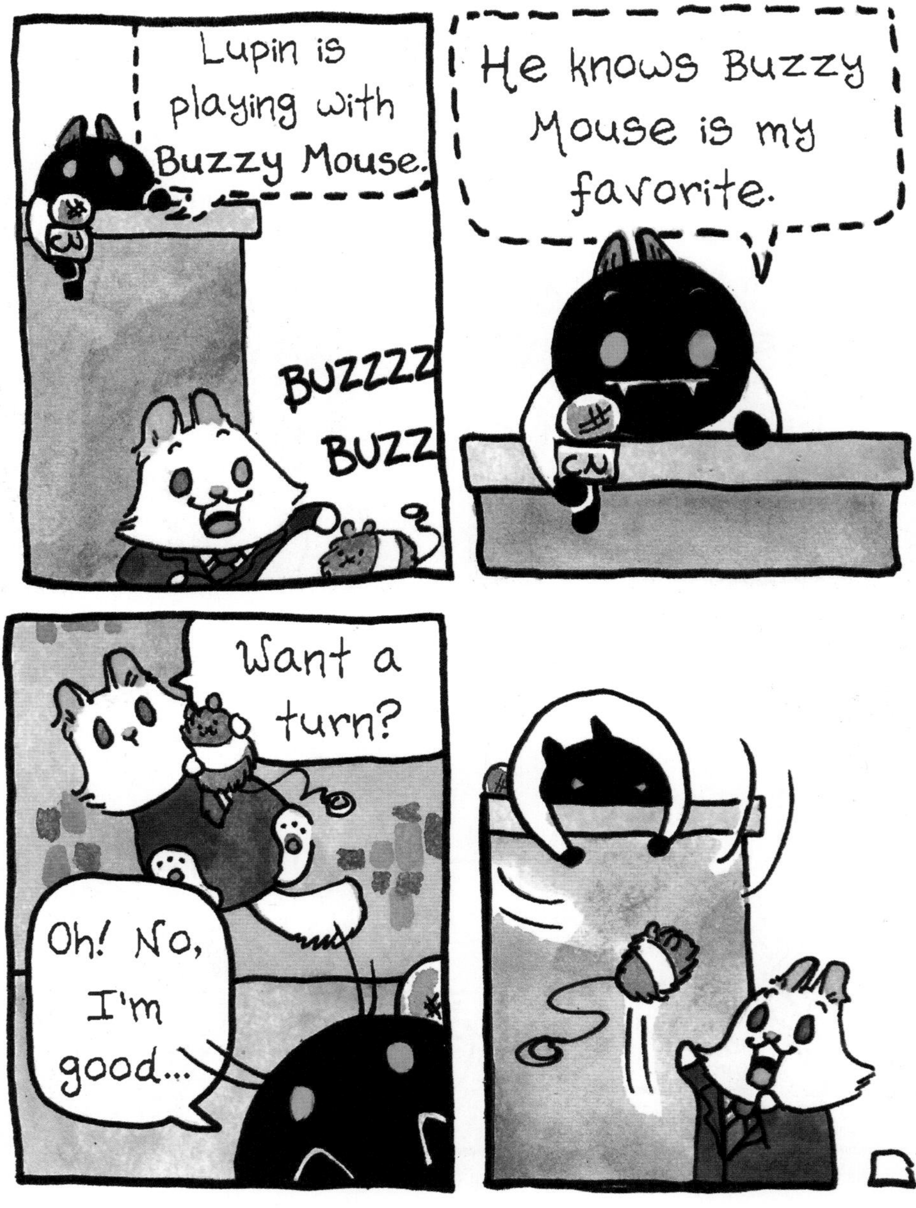
Lupin is playing with Buzzy Mouse.
BUZZZZ
BUZZ
He knows Buzzy Mouse is my favorite.
Want a turn?
Oh! No, I'm good...

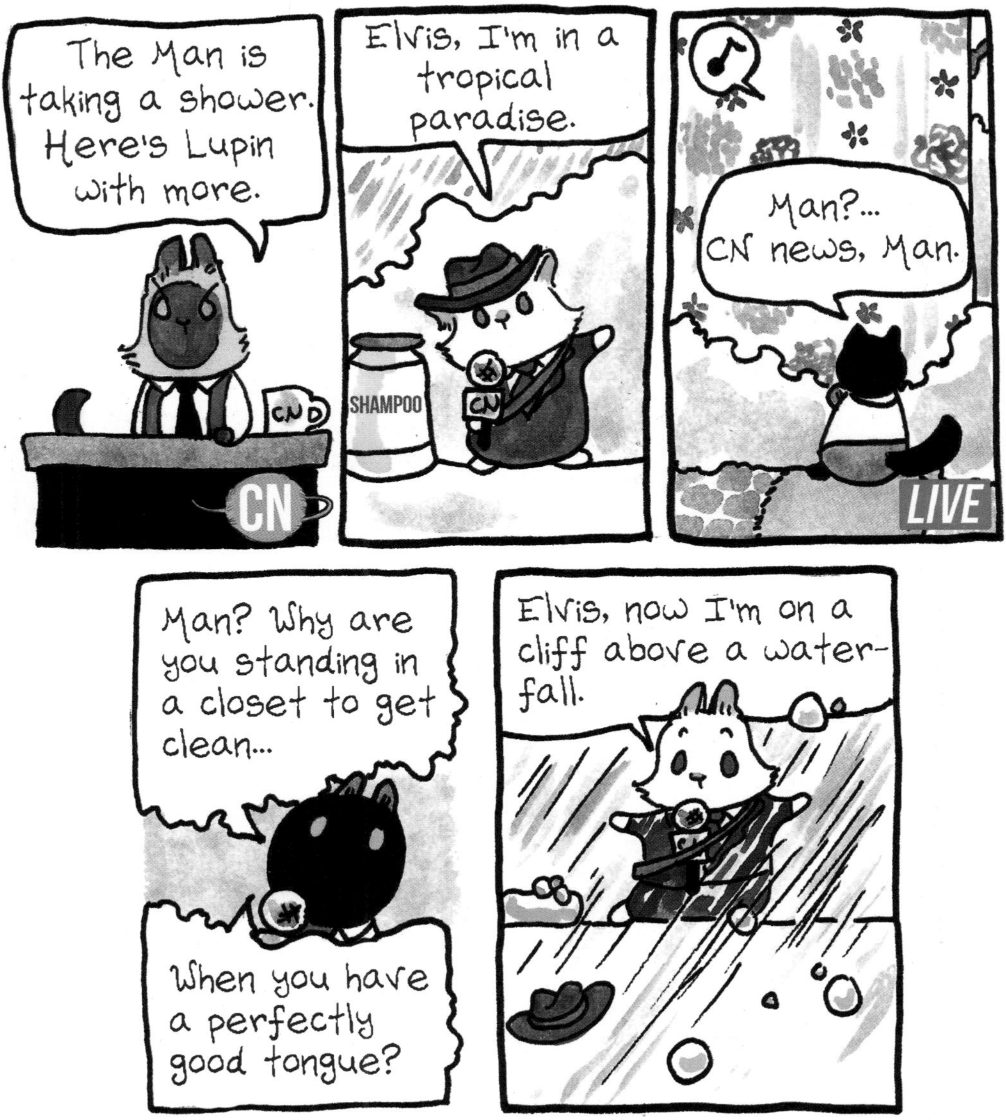
The Man is taking a shower. Here's Lupin with more.
CN
CN
Elvis, I'm in a tropical paradise.
SHAMPOO
CN
Man?... CN news, Man.
LIVE
Man? Why are you standing in a closet to get clean...
When you have a perfectly good tongue?
Elvis, now I'm on a cliff above a water-fall.

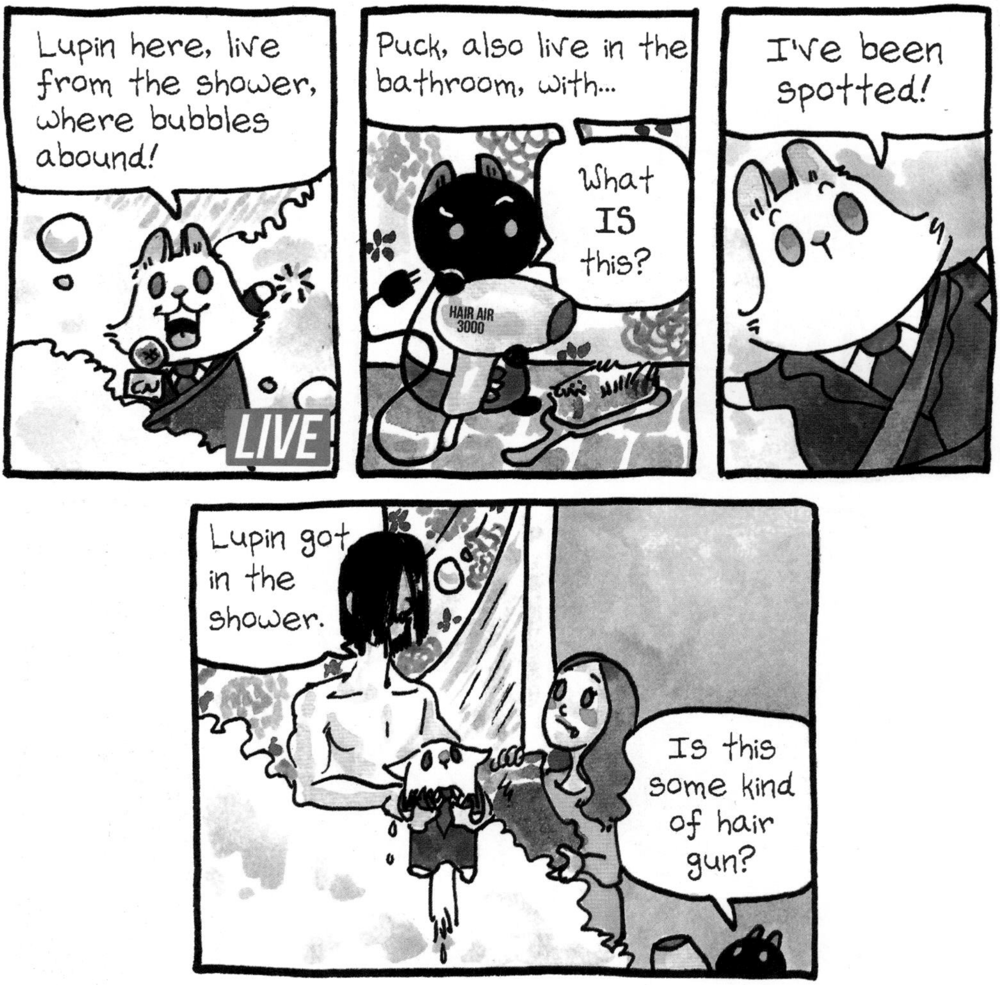
Lupin here, live from the shower, where bubbles abound!
LIVE
Puck, also live in the bathroom, with...
What IS this?
HAIR AIR 3000
I've been spotted!
Lupin got in the shower.
Is this some kind of hair gun?

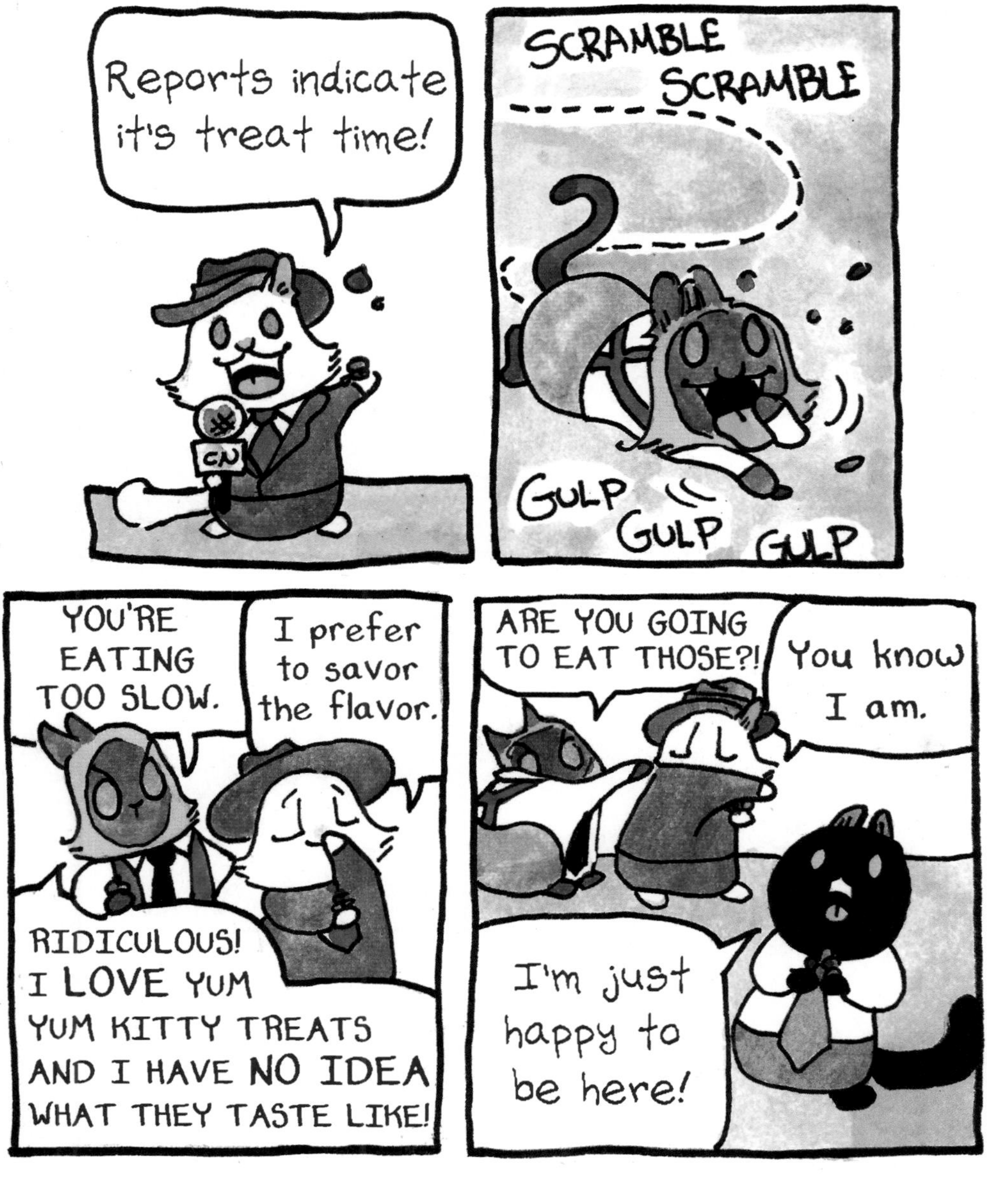
Reports indicate it's treat time!
CN
SCRAMBLE
SCRAMBLE
GULP
GULP
GULP
YOU'RE EATING TOO SLOW.
I prefer to savor the flavor.
RIDICULOUS! I LOVE YUM YUM KITTY TREATS AND I HAVE NO IDEA WHAT THEY TASTE LIKE!
ARE YOU GOING TO EAT THOSE?!
You know I am.
I'm just happy to be here!

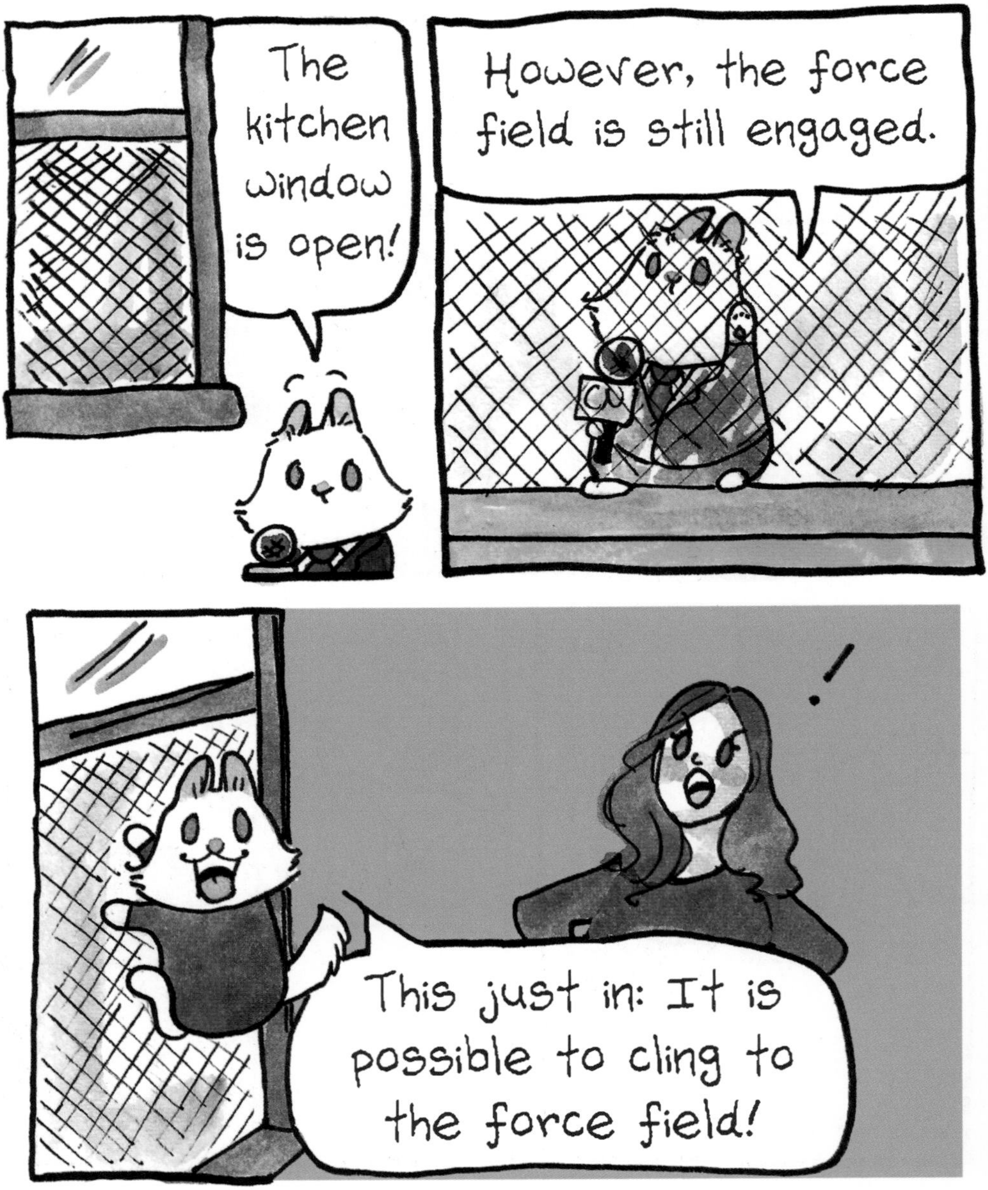
The kitchen window is open!
However, the force field is still engaged.
This just in: It is possible to cling to the force field!

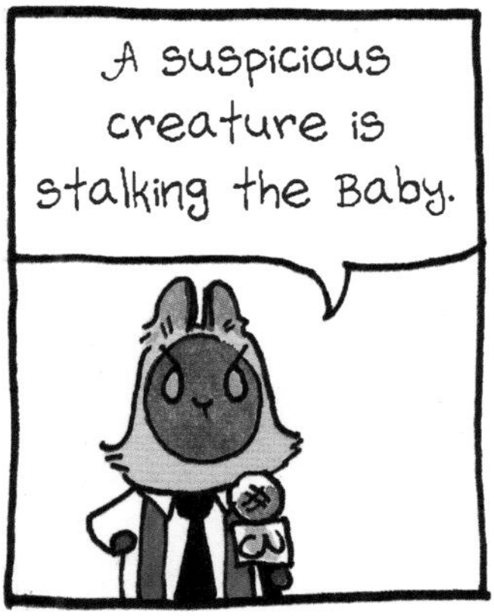
A suspicious creature is stalking the Baby.

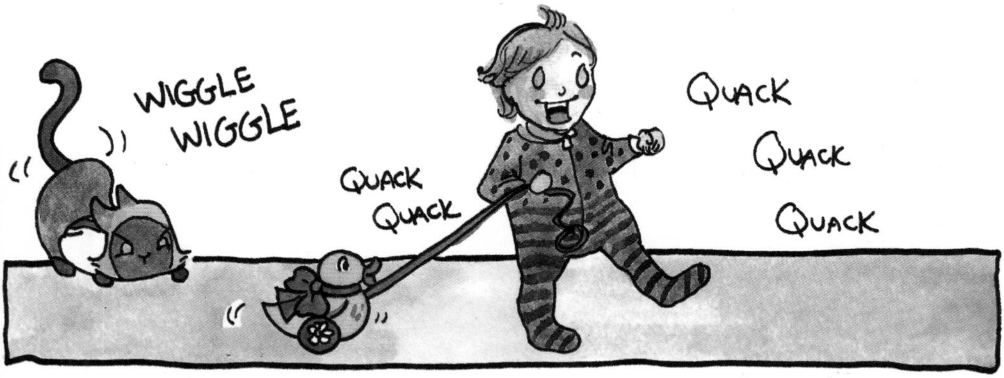
WIGGLE WIGGLE
QUACK QUACK
QUACK
QUACK
QUACK

The Man has to get up early tomorrow. Here's Elvis with continuing coverage.

Lupin, I'm here where the Man is trying to fall asleep. Let's go to Puck for more.

Elvis, c'mon.

The Man has an important job interview tomorrow. It's crucial he wake up early.

We here at CN news will not rest until the Man does. Elvis, is the Man asleep?

NOPE

SIGH.

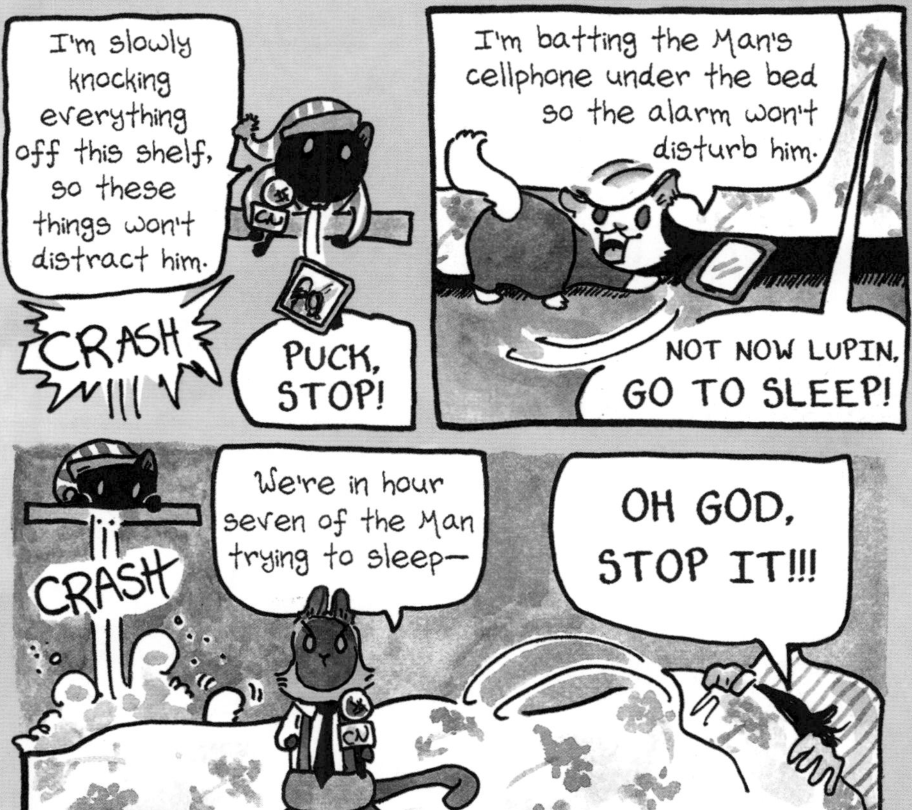
I'm slowly knocking everything off this shelf, so these things won't distract him.
CRASH
PUCK, STOP!
I'm batting the Man's cellphone under the bed so the alarm won't disturb him.
NOT NOW LUPIN, GO TO SLEEP!
CRASH
We're in hour seven of the Man trying to sleep—
OH GOD, STOP IT!!!

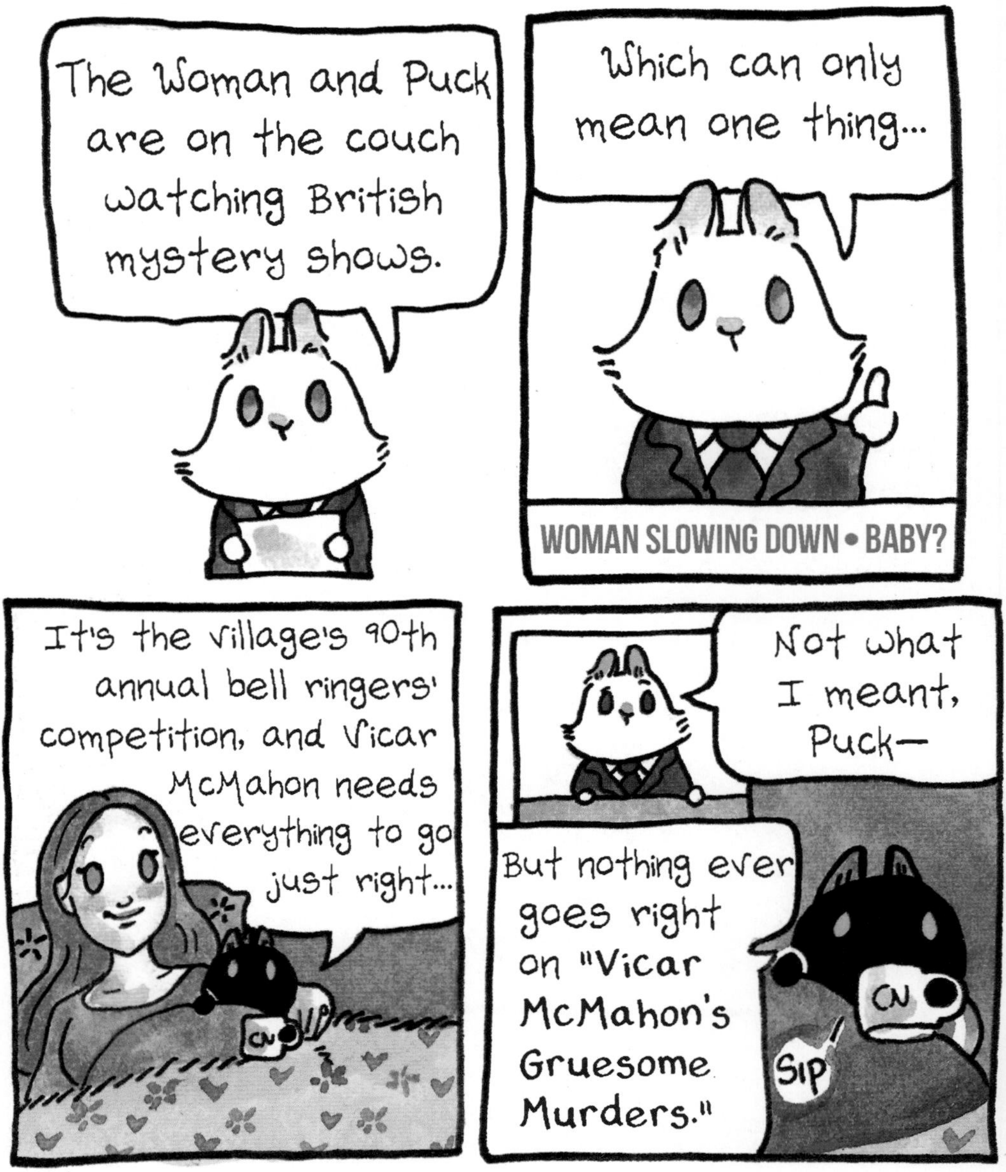
The Woman and Puck are on the couch watching British mystery shows.
Which can only mean one thing...
WOMAN SLOWING DOWN • BABY?
It's the village's 90th annual bell ringers' competition, and Vicar McMahon needs everything to go just right...
Not what I meant, Puck—
But nothing ever goes right on "Vicar McMahon's Gruesome Murders."
CN
SIP

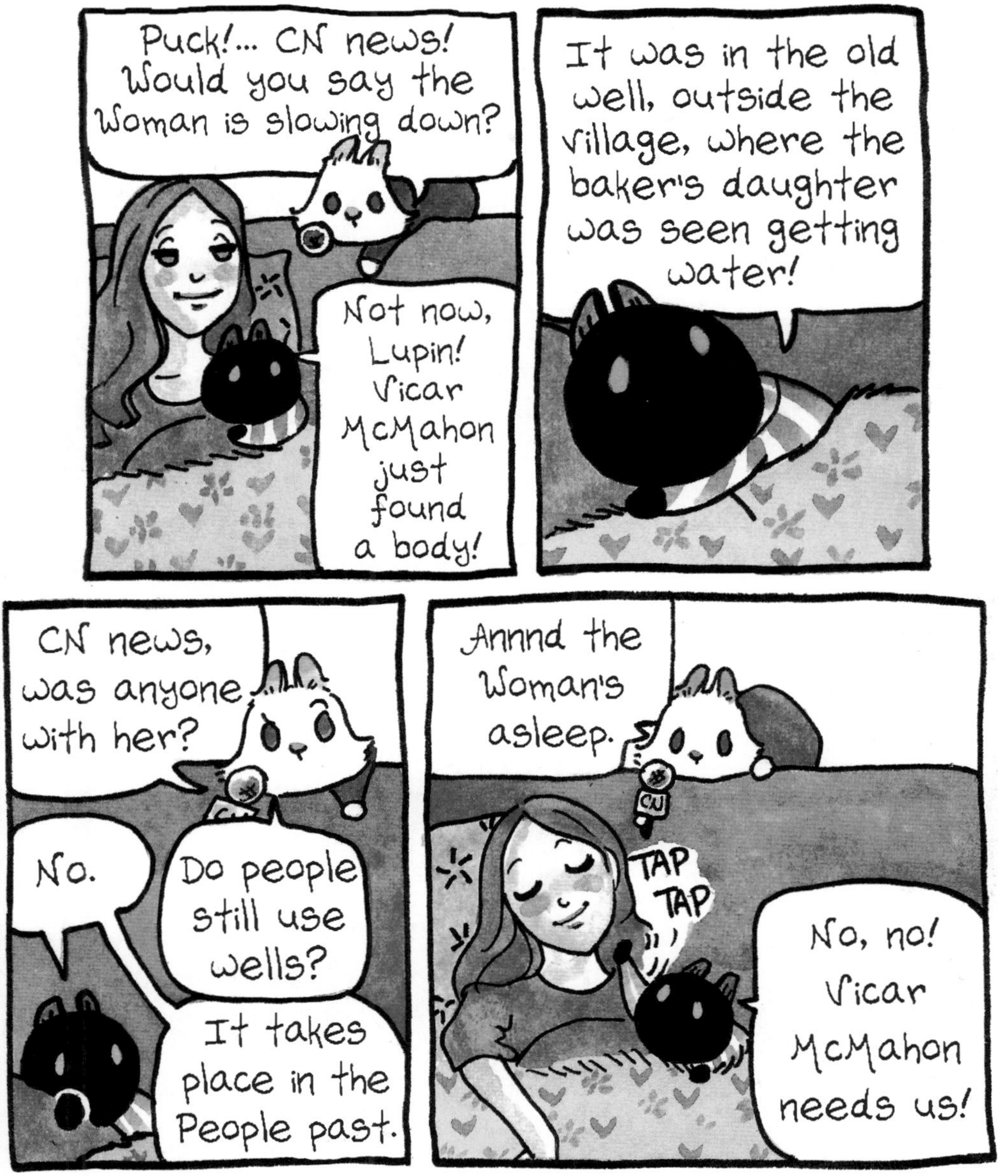
Puck!... CN news! Would you say the Woman is slowing down?
Not now, Lupin! Vicar McMahon just found a body!
It was in the old well, outside the village, where the baker's daughter was seen getting water!
CN news, was anyone with her?
No.
Do people still use wells?
It takes place in the People past.
Annnd the Woman's asleep.
CN
TAP TAP
No, no! Vicar McMahon needs us!

Tha' killer was tha' bearded man, or should I say...
Tha' baker's daughter!
ZZZZ
GASP!
GASP!
BEARD SNATCH!
Wait—tha' beard was fake?
90% of beards in mysteries are fake. It's like a red flag with side-burns.
Really?
Yup. And all fictional criminals are left-handed.

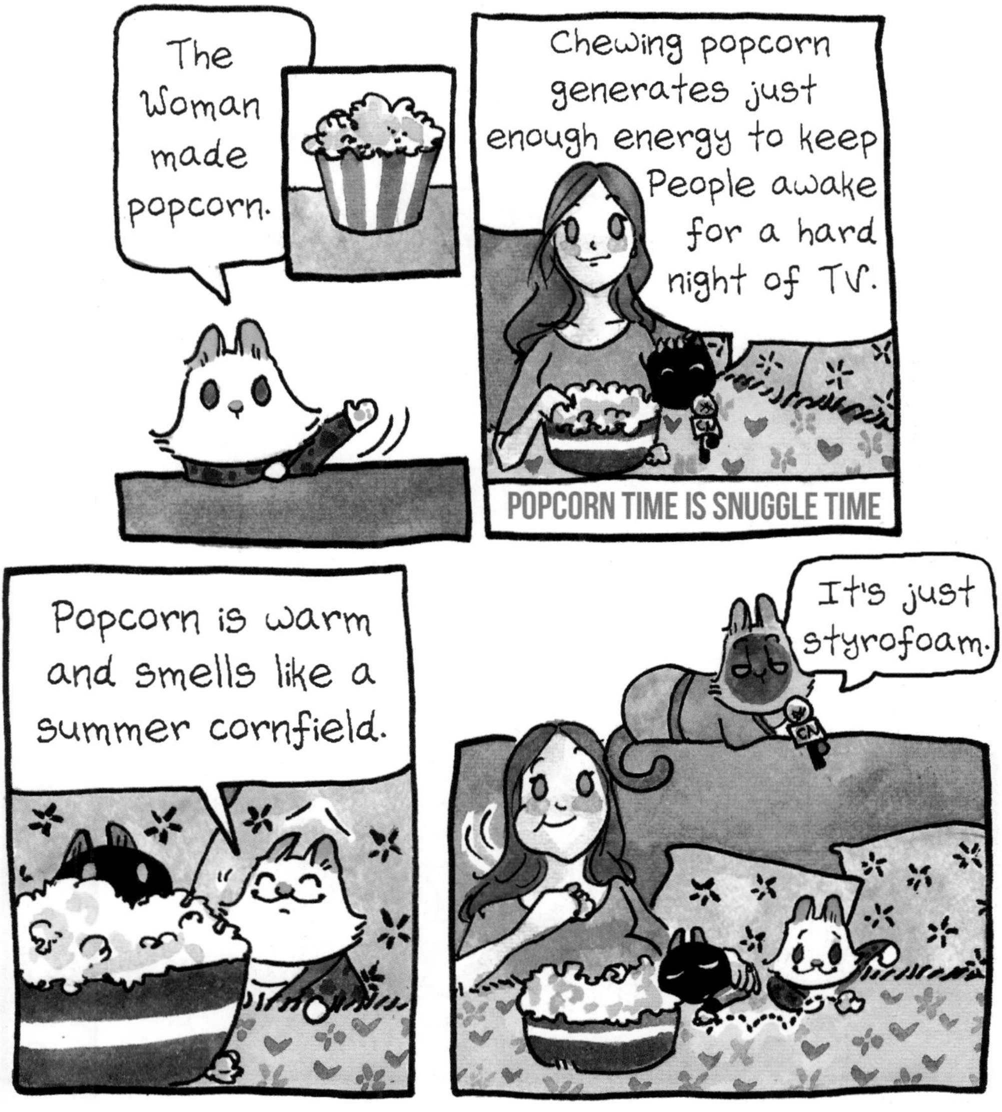
The Woman made popcorn.
Chewing popcorn generates just enough energy to keep People awake for a hard night of TV.
POPCORN TIME IS SNUGGLE TIME
Popcorn is warm and smells like a summer cornfield.
It's just styrofoam.

It's very late, and the Man and Woman are still awake.

This heart-burn is TERRIBLE.

Is sitting up helping?

A little.

AHEM.

I don't even feel like a person anymore. I'm just a weird spaceship carrying a tiny person.

You are a weird spaceship. That's why I love you. That's why I married you.

Ha.

SPIN-SPIN

STOMP STOMP

STOMP

The Woman is cranky. Here's Puck with more.

I didn't sleep well last night... It's hot. I can't get comfortable. I'm 41 months pregnant—

Uh-huh.

Oh, I hear you, honey.

I think you mean "weeks" babe—

I SAID what I SAID.

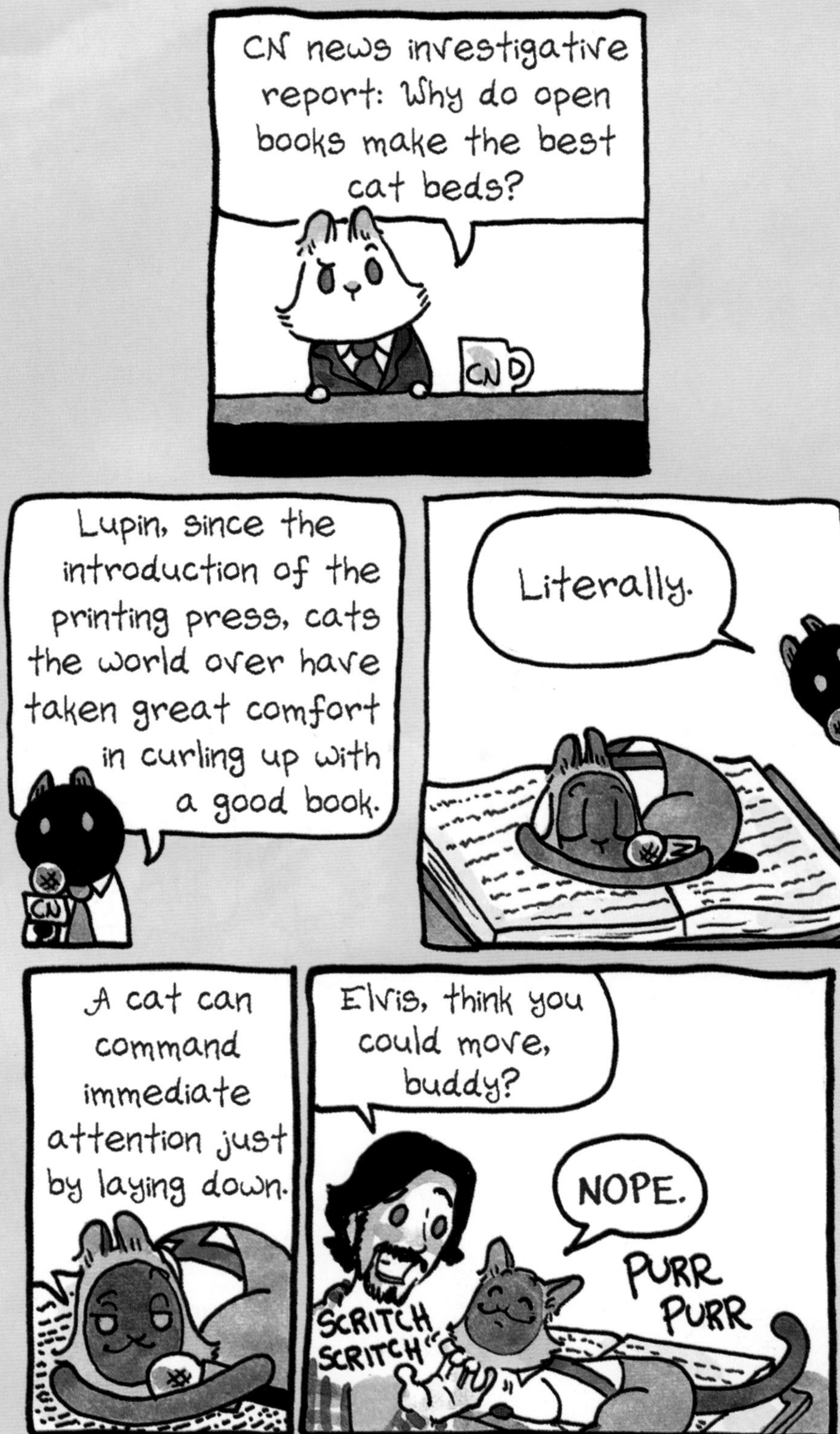

CN news investigative report: Why do open books make the best cat beds?
CN
Lupin, since the introduction of the printing press, cats the world over have taken great comfort in curling up with a good book.
CN
Literally.
A cat can command immediate attention just by laying down.
Elvis, think you could move, buddy?
NOPE.
PURR PURR
SCRITCH SCRITCH

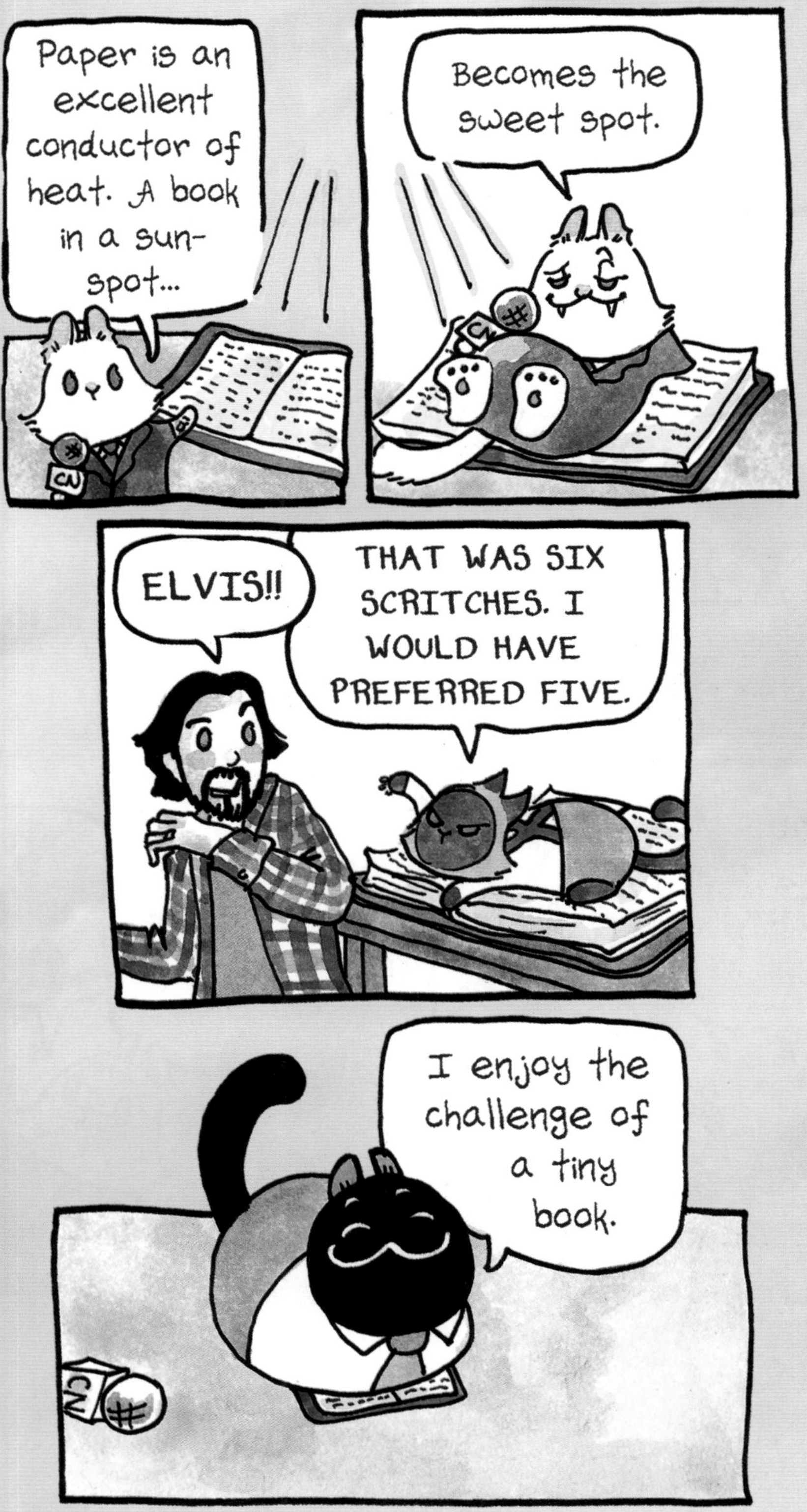
Paper is an excellent conductor of heat. A book in a sun-spot...
CN
Becomes the sweet spot.
CN
ELVIS!!
THAT WAS SIX SCRITCHES. I WOULD HAVE PREFERRED FIVE.
I enjoy the challenge of a tiny book.
CN

The People have returned—with a new baby!

HOW MANY OF THESE THINGS ARE THEY GOING TO HAVE?!

Oh my cat, Elvis, they are RIGHT THERE.

Um... My, that's a mighty small pile of human you've got!

Nice!

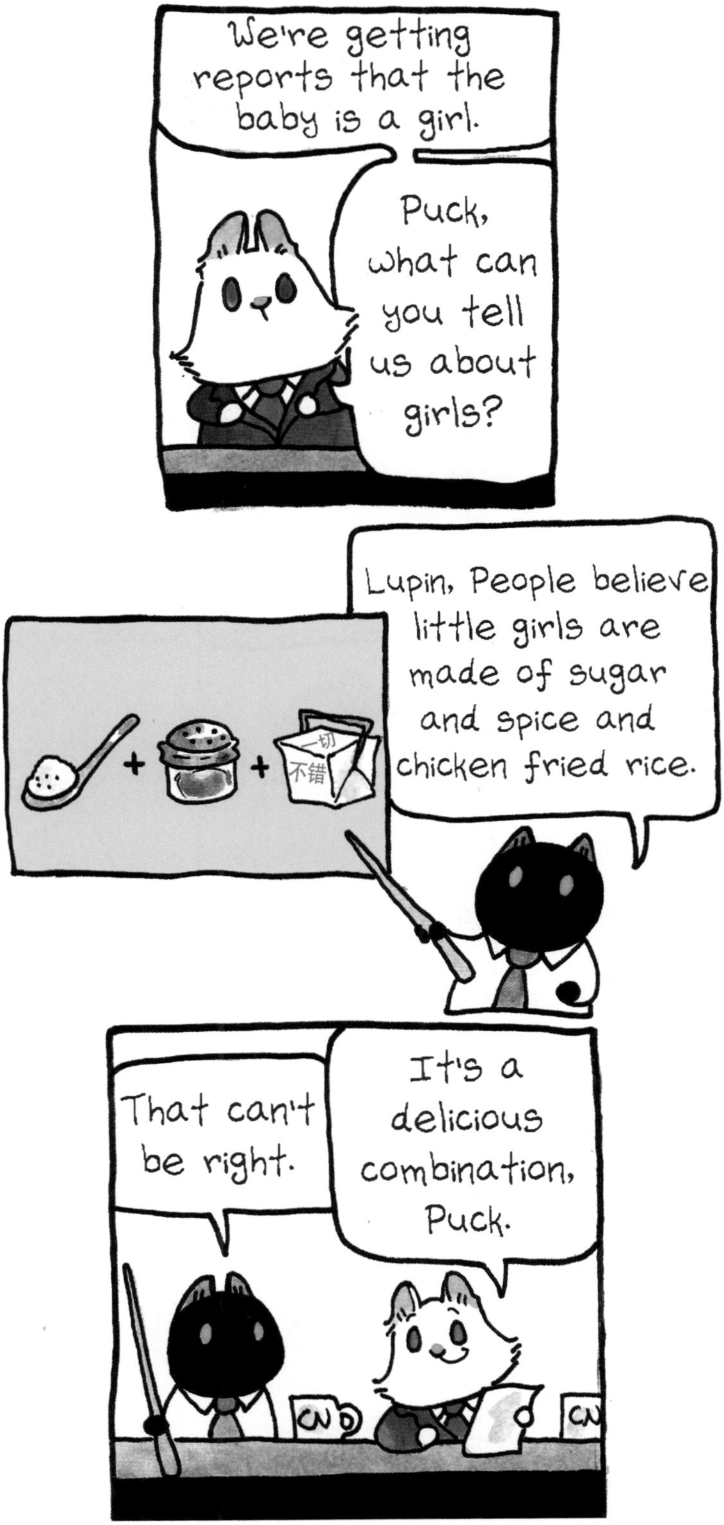
We're getting reports that the baby is a girl.
Puck, what can you tell us about girls?
Lupin, People believe little girls are made of sugar and spice and chicken fried rice.
一切
不错
That can't be right.
It's a delicious combination, Puck.

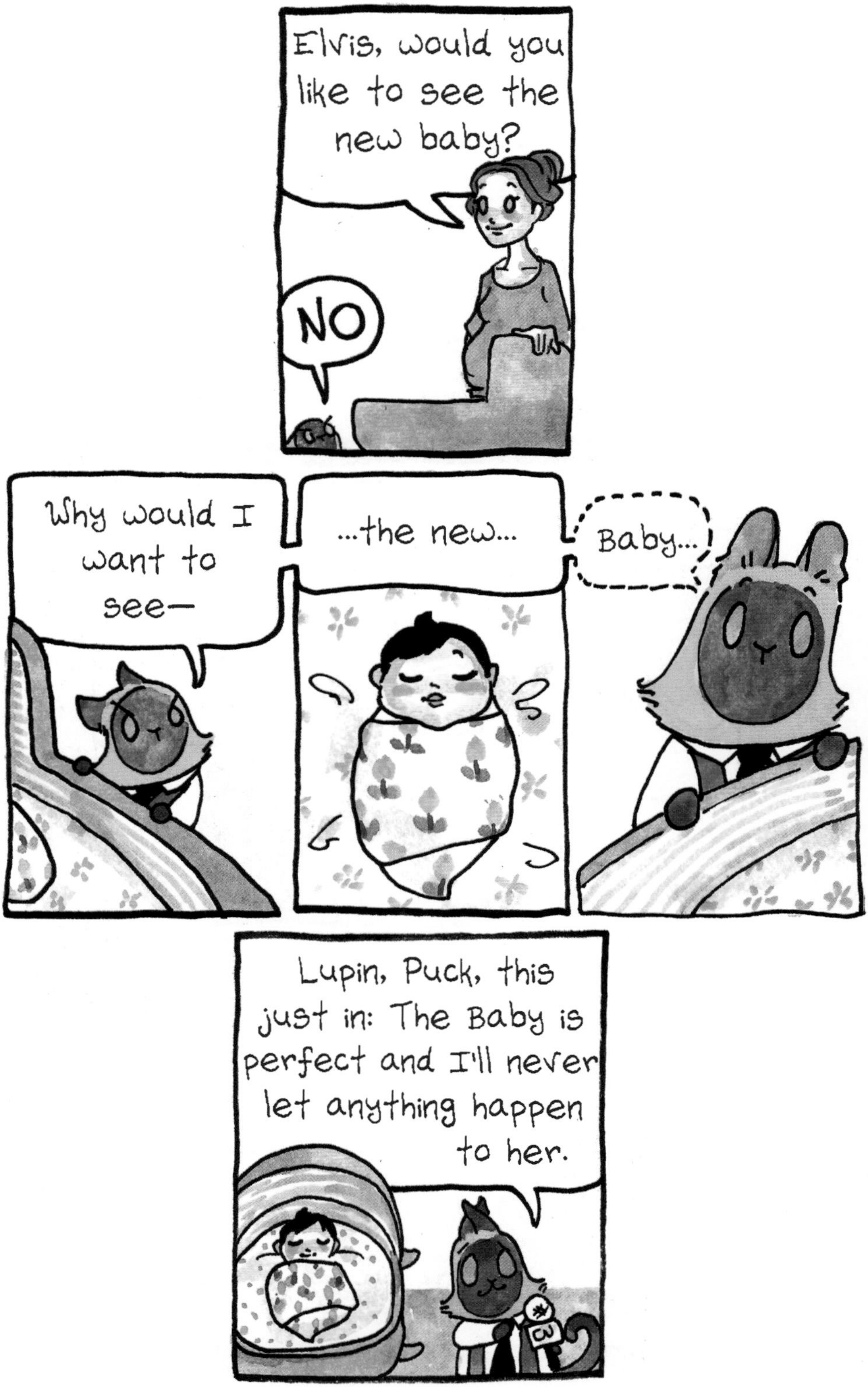
Elvis, would you like to see the new baby?
NO
Why would I want to see—
...the new...
Baby...
Lupin, Puck, this just in: The Baby is perfect and I'll never let anything happen to her.

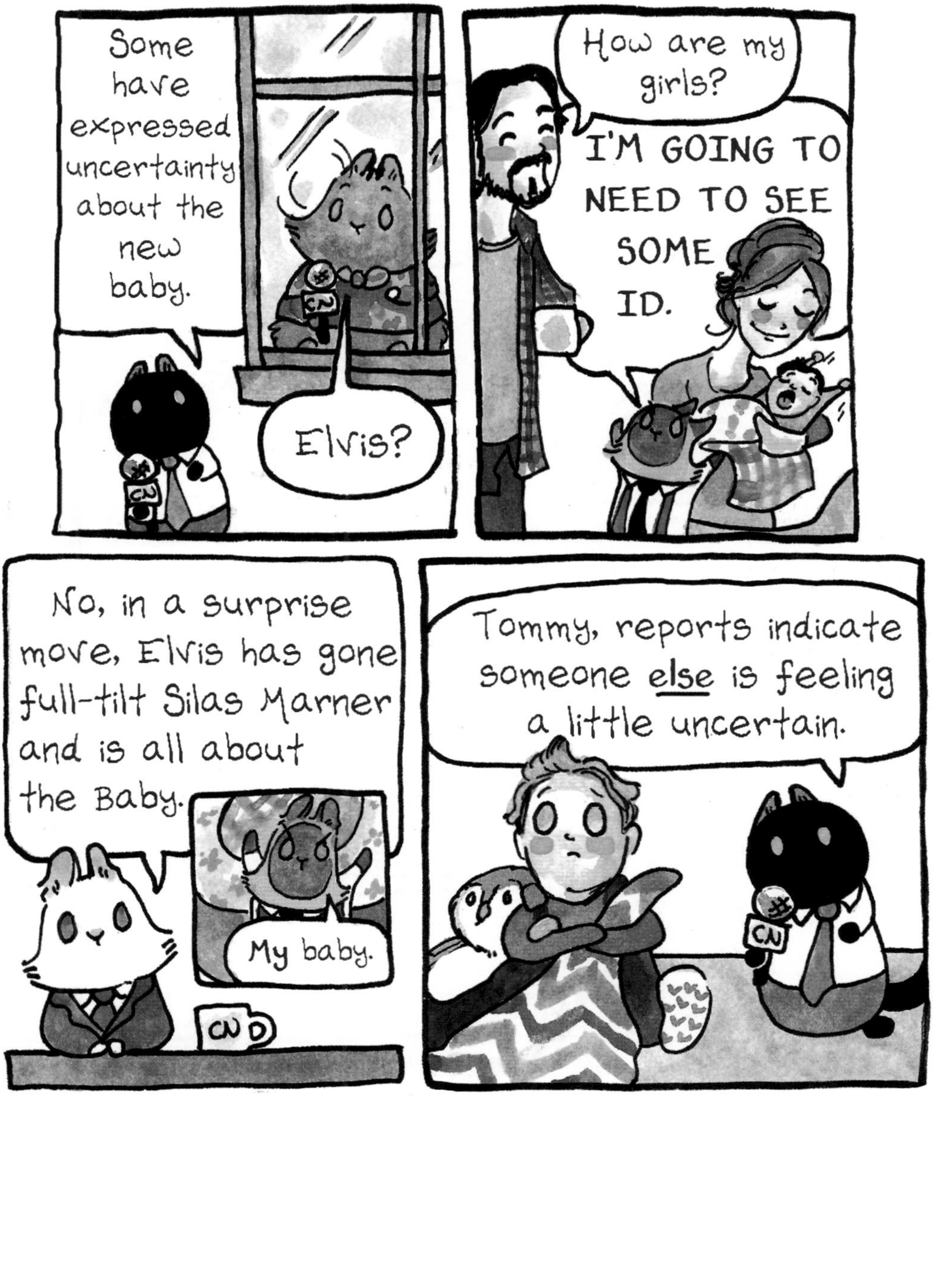
Some have expressed uncertainty about the new baby.
Elvis?
How are my girls?
I'M GOING TO NEED TO SEE SOME ID.
No, in a surprise move, Elvis has gone full-tilt Silas Marner and is all about the Baby.
My baby.
Tommy, reports indicate someone else is feeling a little uncertain.

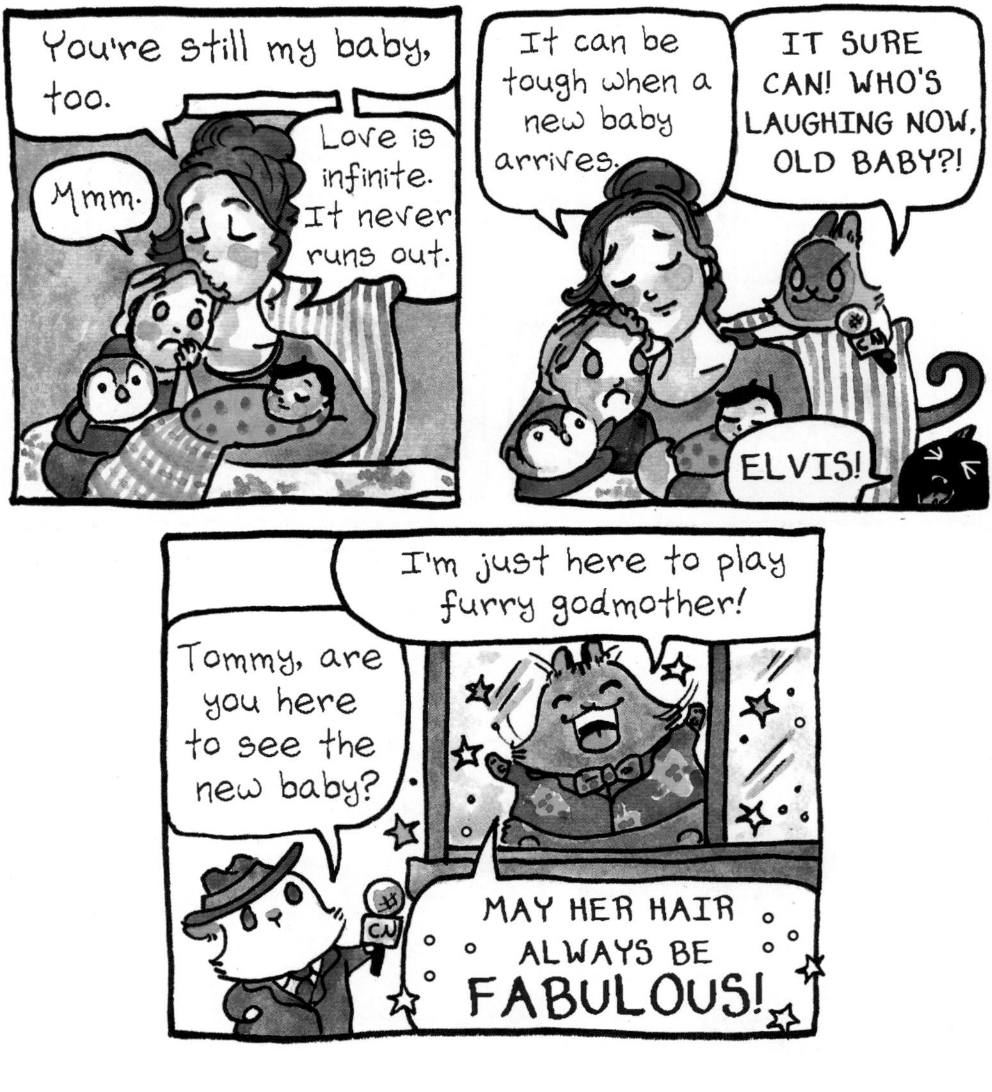
You're still my baby, too.
Mmm.
Love is infinite. It never runs out.
It can be tough when a new baby arrives.
IT SURE CAN! WHO'S LAUGHING NOW, OLD BABY?!
ELVIS!
I'm just here to play furry godmother!
Tommy, are you here to see the new baby?
MAY HER HAIR ALWAYS BE FABULOUS!

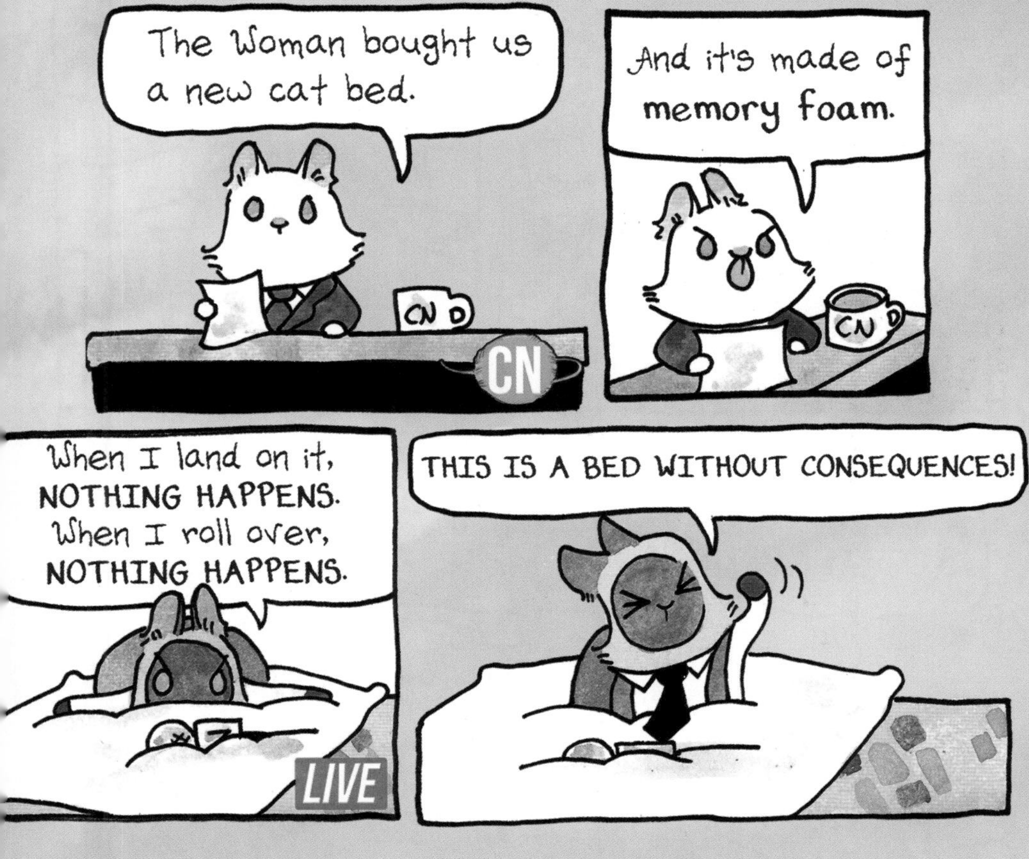
The Woman bought us a new cat bed.
CN
CN
CN
And it's made of memory foam.
CN
When I land on it, NOTHING HAPPENS. When I roll over, NOTHING HAPPENS.
LIVE
THIS IS A BED WITHOUT CONSEQUENCES!

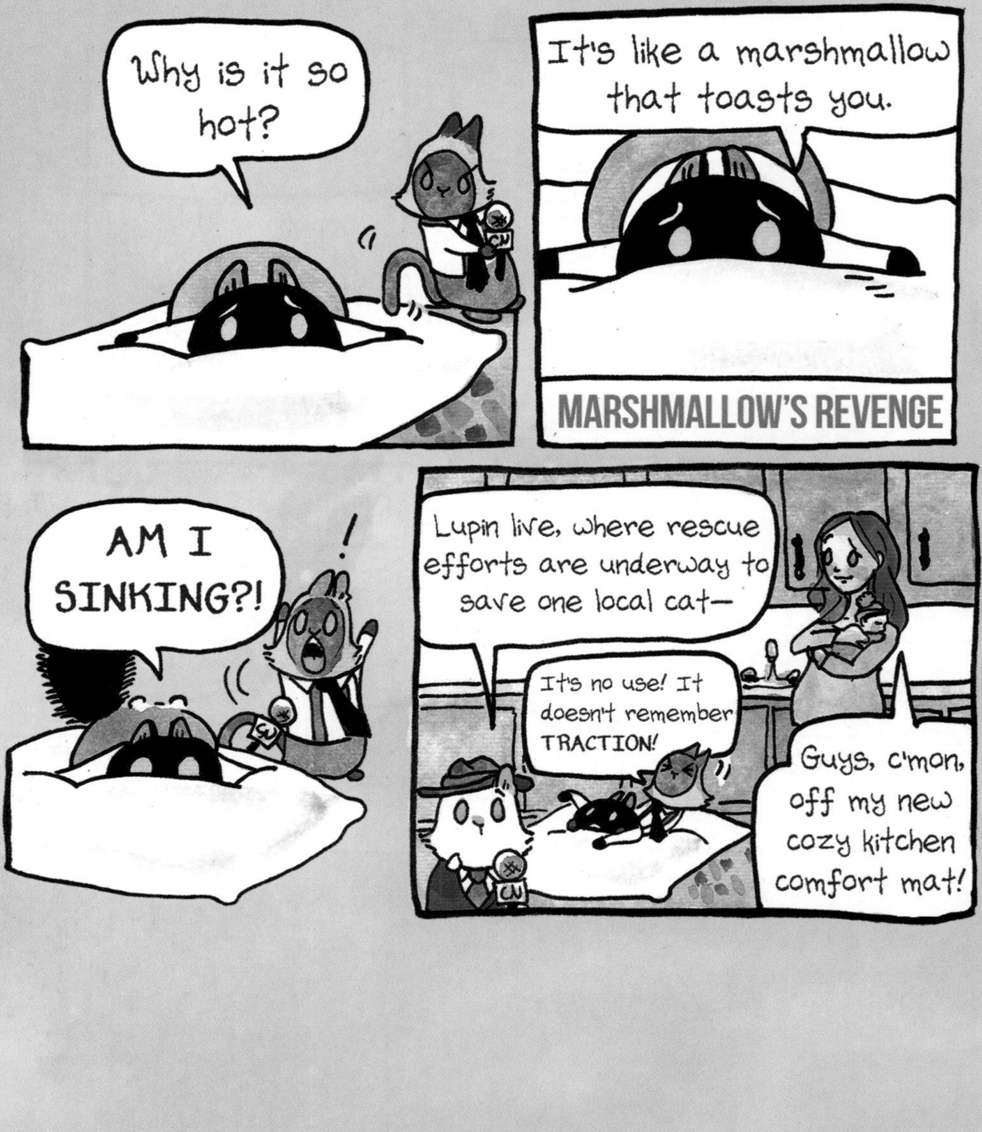
Why is it so hot?
It's like a marshmallow that toasts you.
MARSHMALLOW'S REVENGE
AM I SINKING?!
!
Lupin live, where rescue efforts are underway to save one local cat—
It's no use! It doesn't remember TRACTION!
Guys, c'mon, off my new cozy kitchen comfort mat!

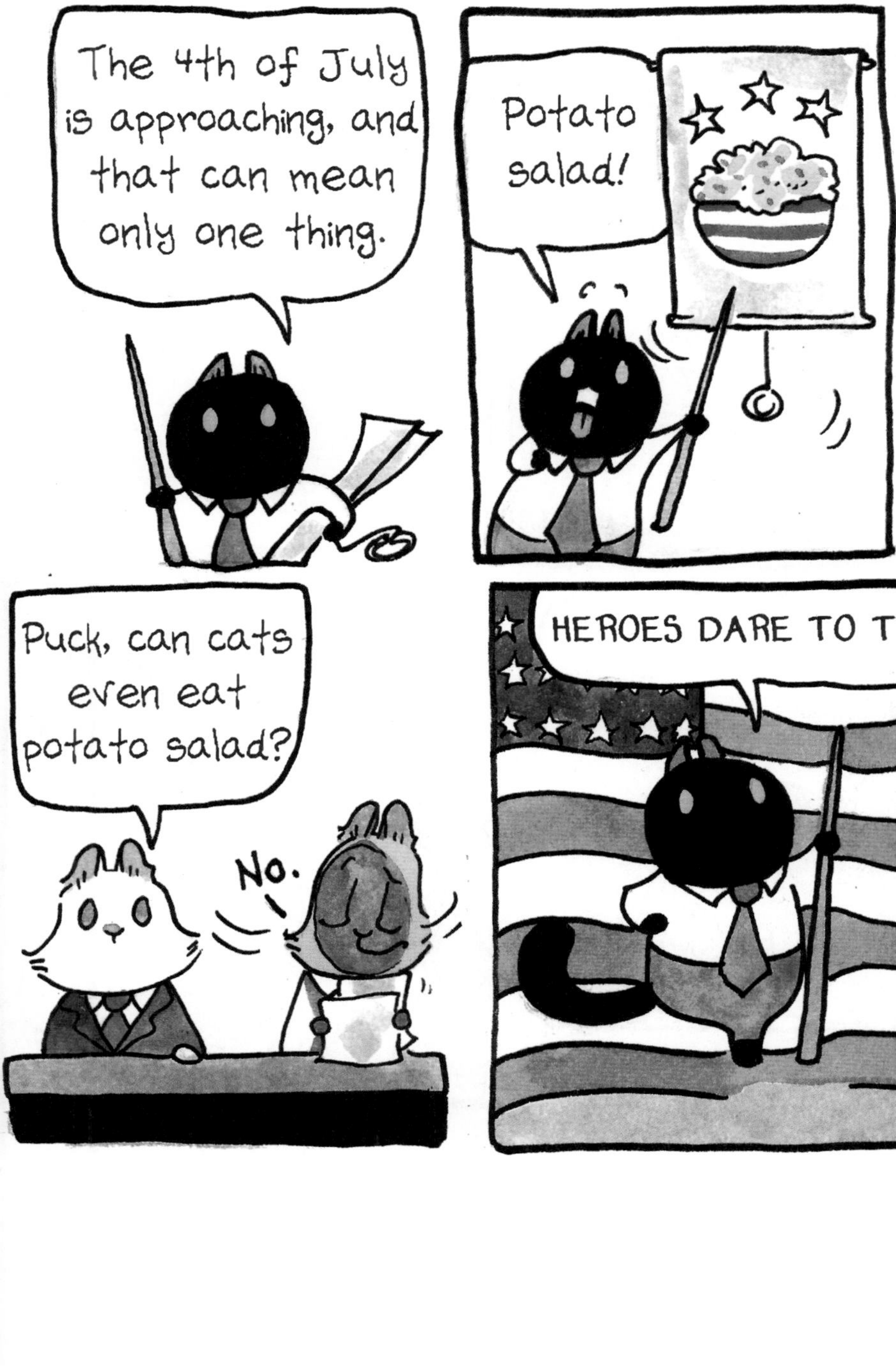
The 4th of July is approaching, and that can mean only one thing.
Potato salad!
Puck, can cats even eat potato salad?
No.
HEROES DARE TO TRY.

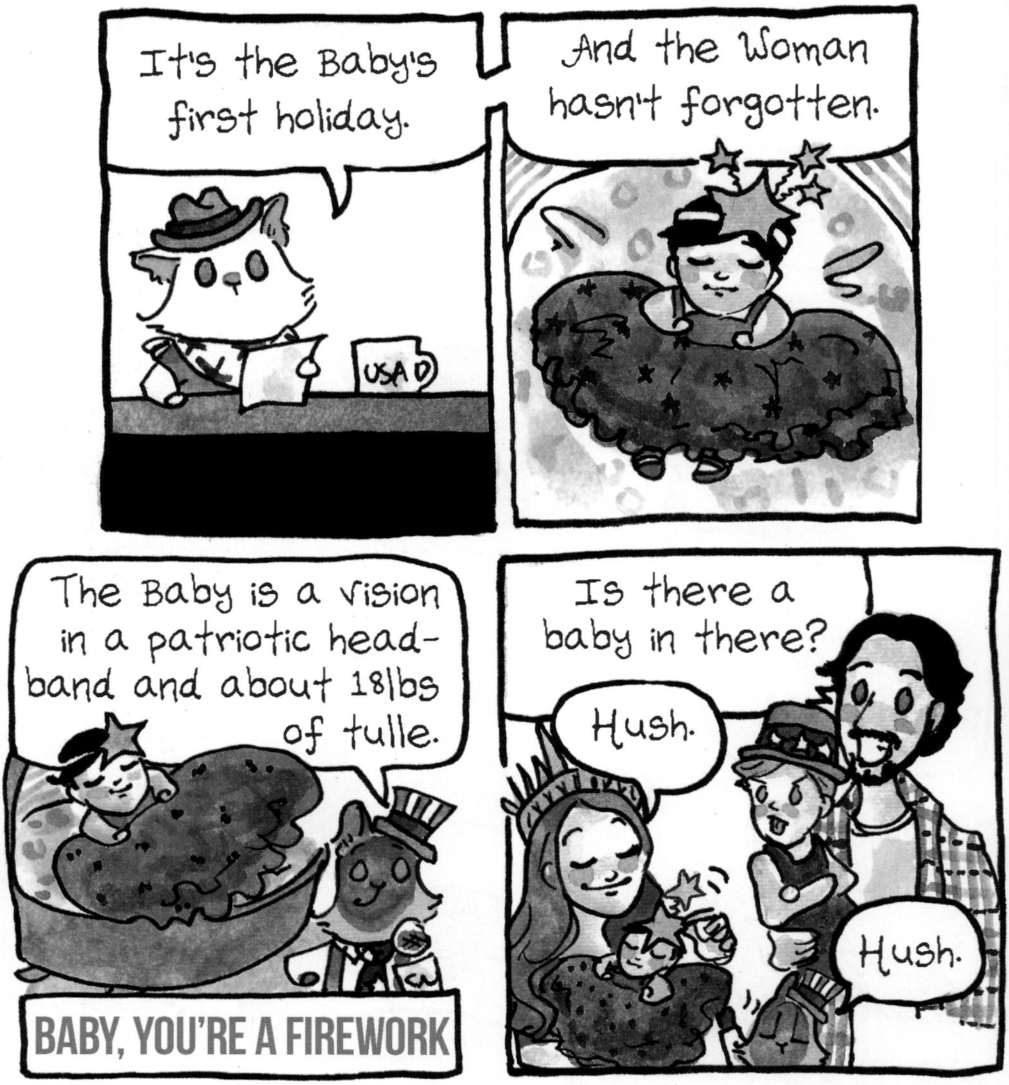
It's the Baby's first holiday.
And the Woman hasn't forgotten.
USA
The Baby is a vision in a patriotic head-band and about 18lbs of tulle.
BABY, YOU'RE A FIREWORK
Is there a baby in there?
Hush.
Hush.

Can you watch Pucky around the pork hot dogs? He's inching in.

Oh?

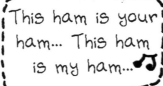

This ham is your ham... This ham is my ham...

LIVE

From the pasta salad...

To whatever this is....

THIS FOOD WAS MADE FOR YOU AND ME!

The Man's first day at his new job is tomorrow, and we've got everything covered. Puck?

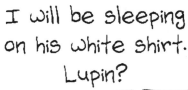

I will be sleeping on his white shirt. Lupin?

LIVE

I'm on black pants duty! Elvis, back to you!

Now all of the cats at the Man's new office will know he's TAKEN.

SNAP

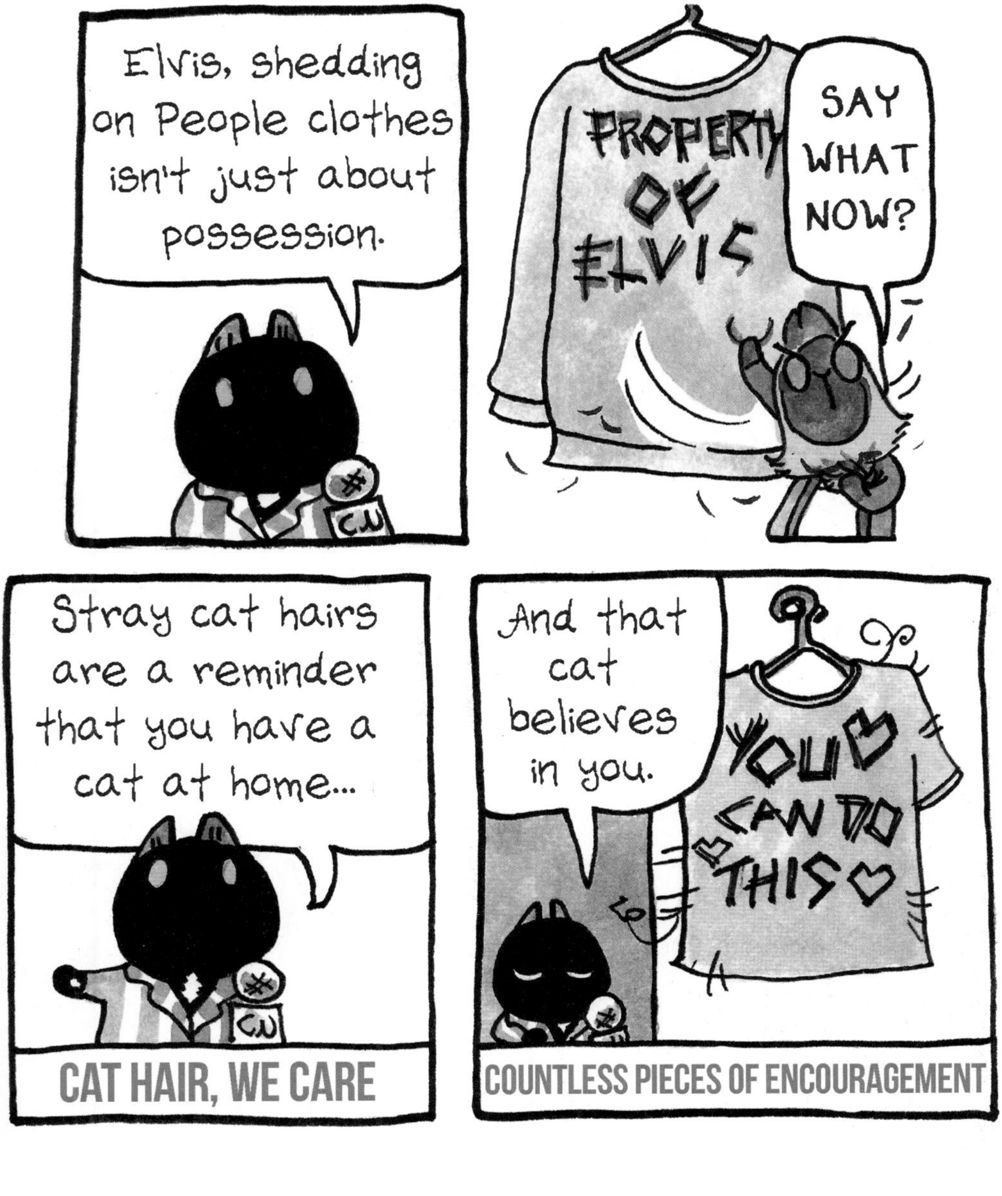

Elvis, shedding on People clothes isn't just about possession.
PROPERTY OF ELVIS
SAY WHAT NOW?
Stray cat hairs are a reminder that you have a cat at home...
CN
CAT HAIR, WE CARE
And that cat believes in you.
YOU CAN DO THIS
COUNTLESS PIECES OF ENCOURAGEMENT

We're getting late—breaking reports that the Man's new job has a relaxed dress code!

Puck, what does this mean for shedding on the Man's clothes?

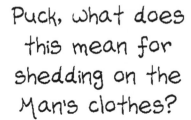

Lupin, it means the Man can wear PLAID.

WE CANNOT DEFEAT PLAID

Do you even **WANT** anyone to know you have **CATS?!**

Elvis?... ...Psst! Honey? I swear your cat is threatening me again—

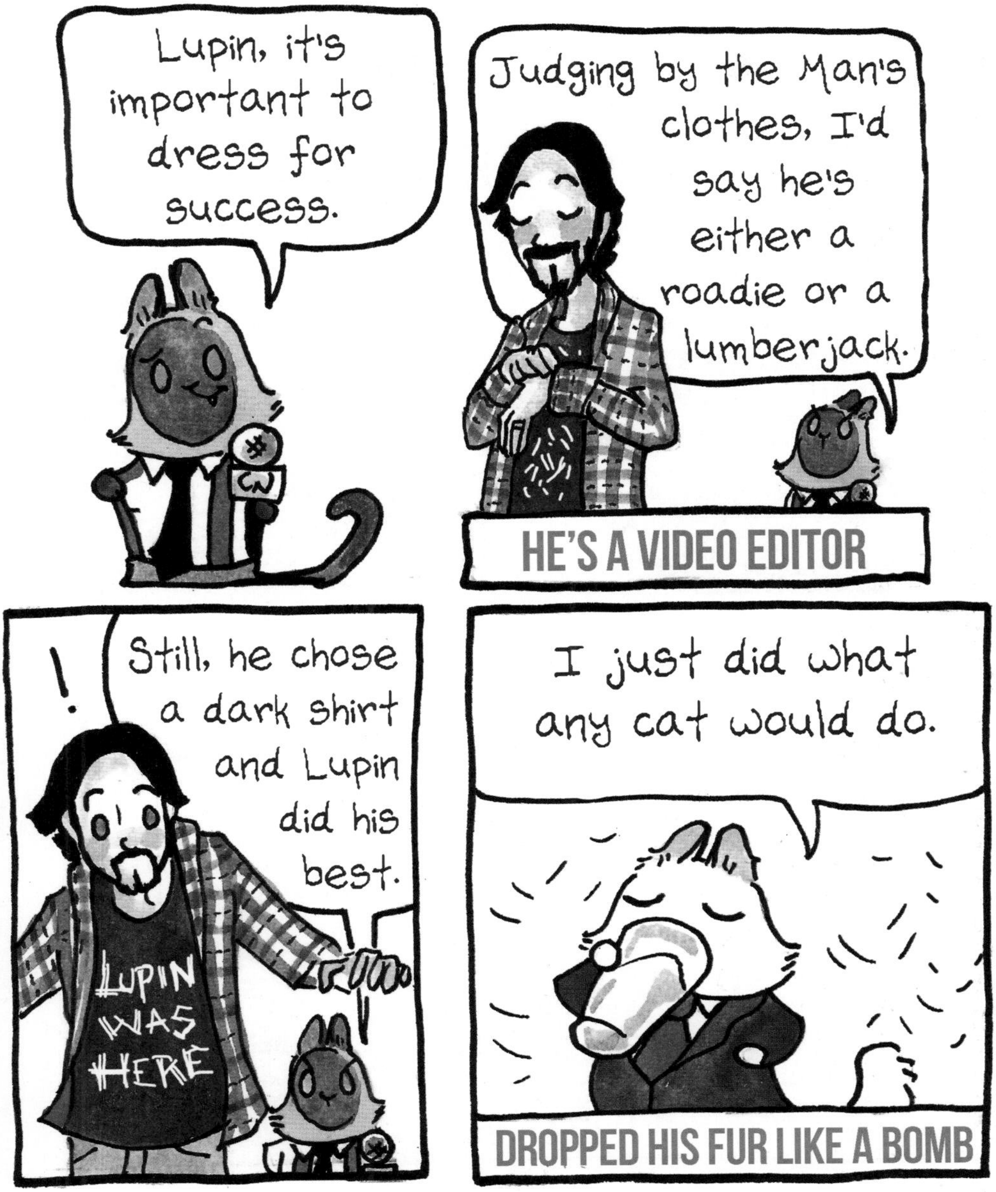
Lupin, it's important to dress for success.
CN
Judging by the Man's clothes, I'd say he's either a roadie or a lumberjack.
HE'S A VIDEO EDITOR
!
Still, he chose a dark shirt and Lupin did his best.
LUPIN WAS HERE
I just did what any cat would do.
DROPPED HIS FUR LIKE A BOMB

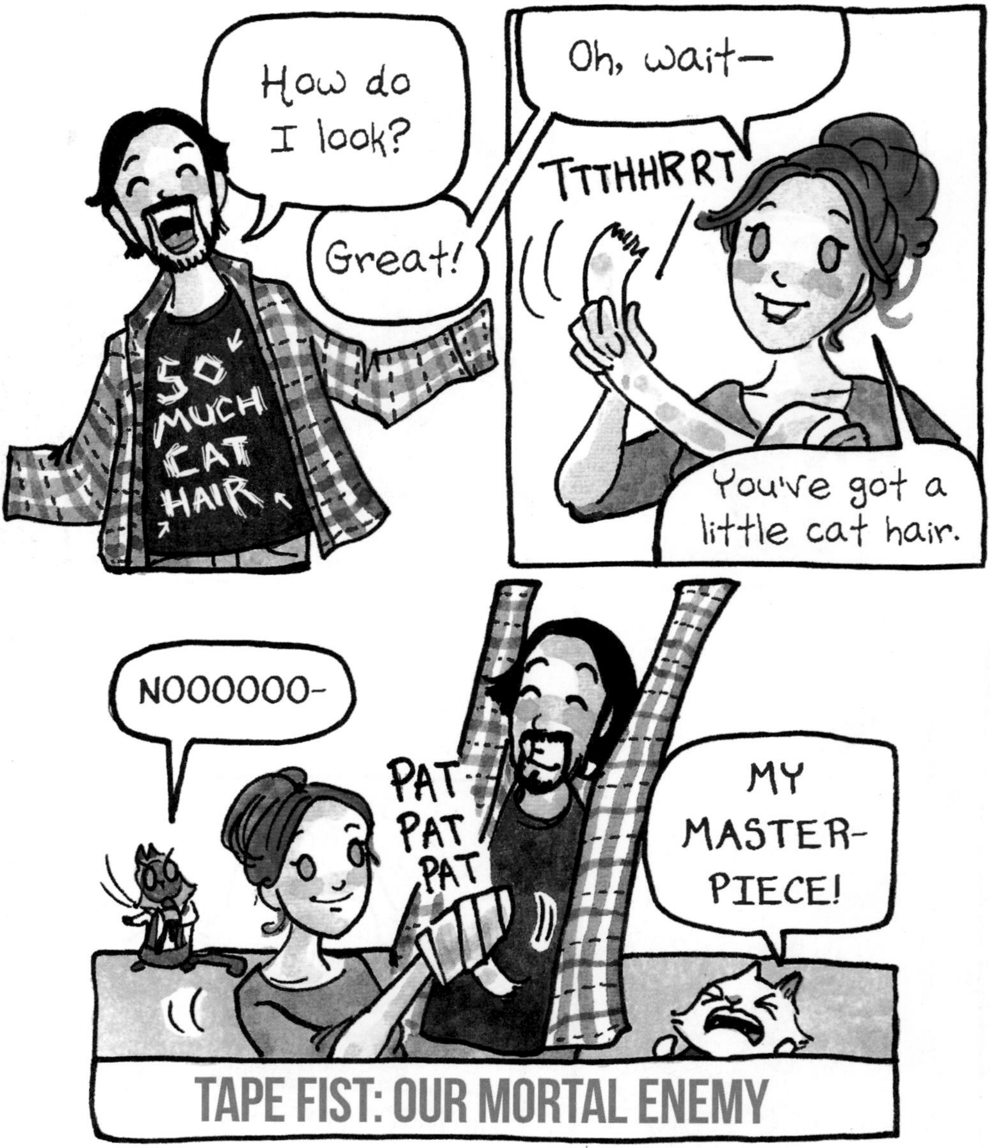
How do I look?
Great!
Oh, wait—
TTTHHRRT
You've got a little cat hair.
SO MUCH CAT HAIR
NOOOOOO-
PAT PAT PAT
MY MASTER-PIECE!
TAPE FIST: OUR MORTAL ENEMY

As the Man starts the first day of his new job...

Good luck, honey! You'll do great!

You will too! ...You'll be ok?

Sure!

We got this!

☆ CLICK ☆

...the Woman starts her first day alone with a toddler and a newborn.

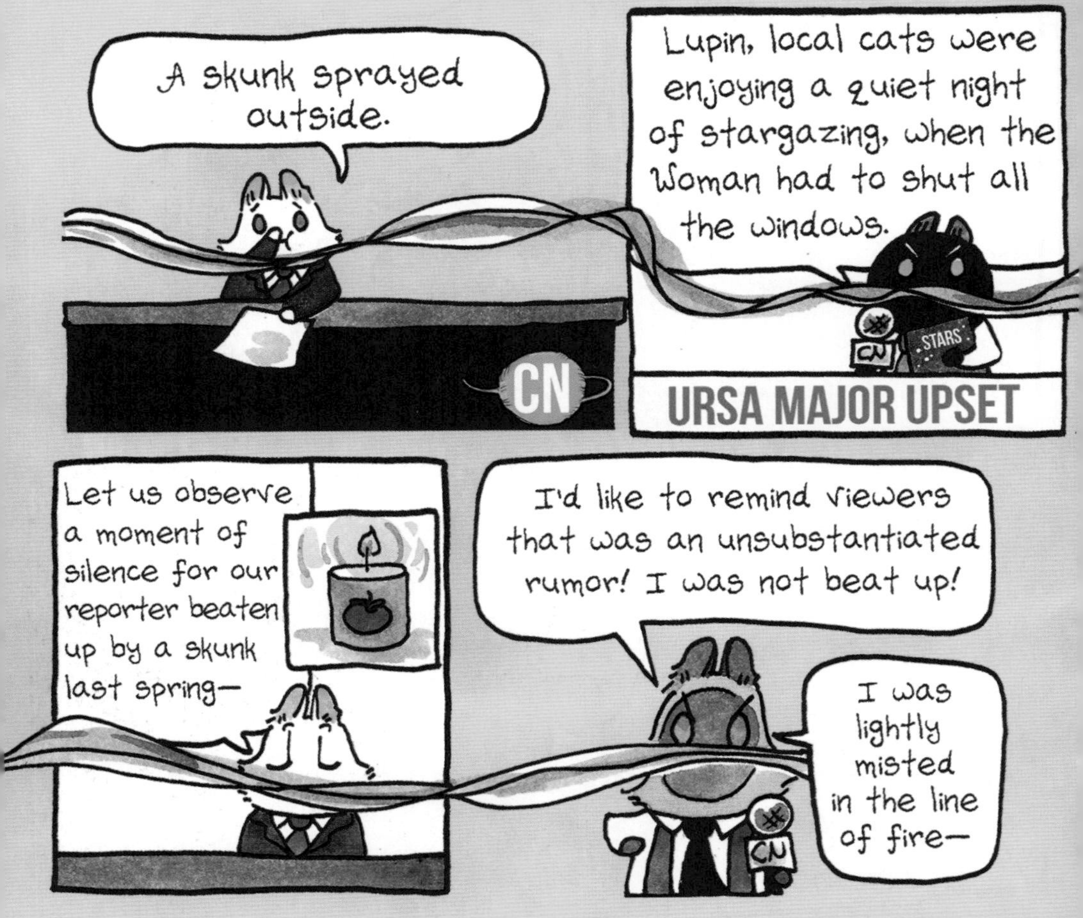
A skunk sprayed outside.
Lupin, local cats were enjoying a quiet night of stargazing, when the Woman had to shut all the windows.
CN
STARS
URSA MAJOR UPSET
CN
Let us observe a moment of silence for our reporter beaten up by a skunk last spring—
I'd like to remind viewers that was an unsubstantiated rumor! I was not beat up!
I was lightly misted in the line of fire—
CN

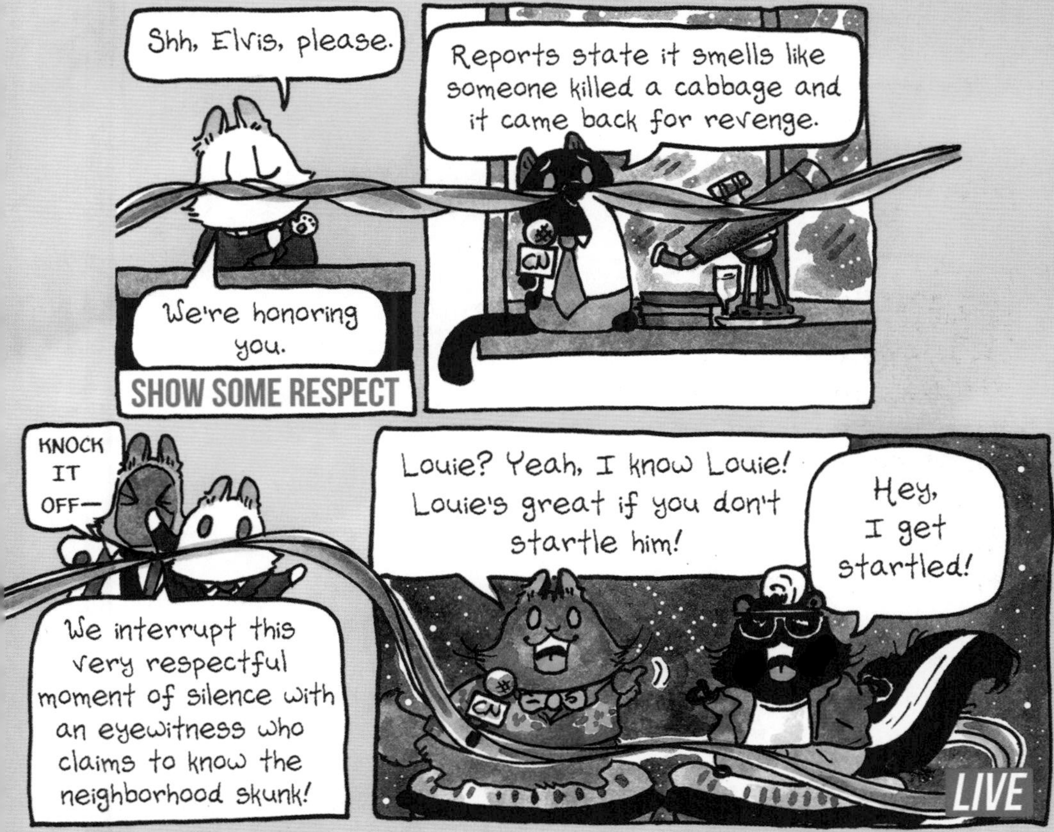
Shh, Elvis, please.
We're honoring you.
SHOW SOME RESPECT
Reports state it smells like someone killed a cabbage and it came back for revenge.
CN
KNOCK IT OFF—
We interrupt this very respectful moment of silence with an eyewitness who claims to know the neighborhood skunk!
Louie? Yeah, I know Louie! Louie's great if you don't startle him!
Hey, I get startled!
CN
LIVE

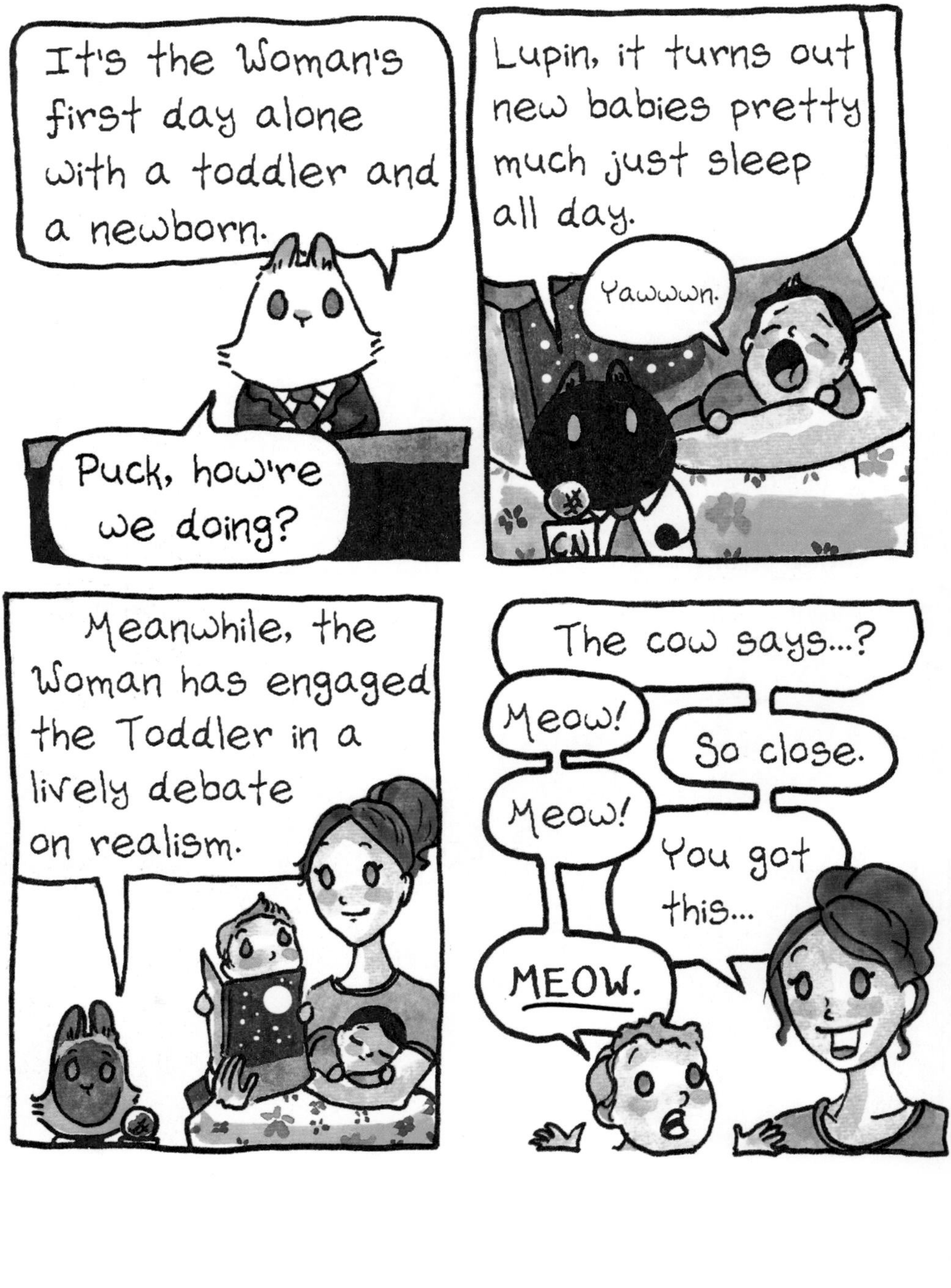
It's the Woman's first day alone with a toddler and a newborn.
Puck, how're we doing?
Lupin, it turns out new babies pretty much just sleep all day.
Yawwwn.
CN
Meanwhile, the Woman has engaged the Toddler in a lively debate on realism.
The cow says...?
Meow!
So close.
Meow!
You got this...
MEOW.

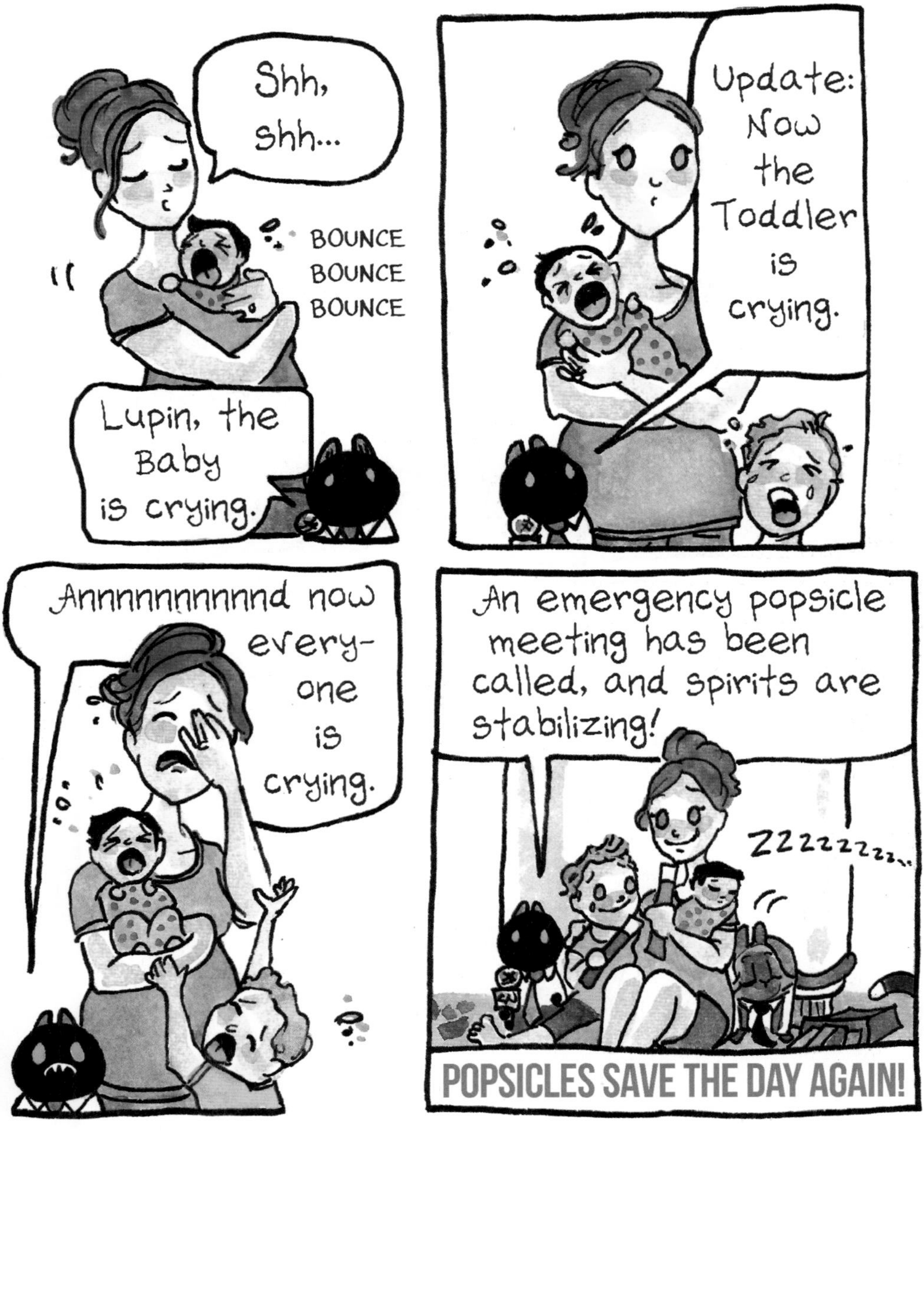
Shh, shh...
BOUNCE BOUNCE BOUNCE
Lupin, the Baby is crying.
Update: Now the Toddler is crying.
Annnnnnnnnd now every-one is crying.
An emergency popsicle meeting has been called, and spirits are stabilizing!
ZZZZZZZZZ...
POPSICLES SAVE THE DAY AGAIN!

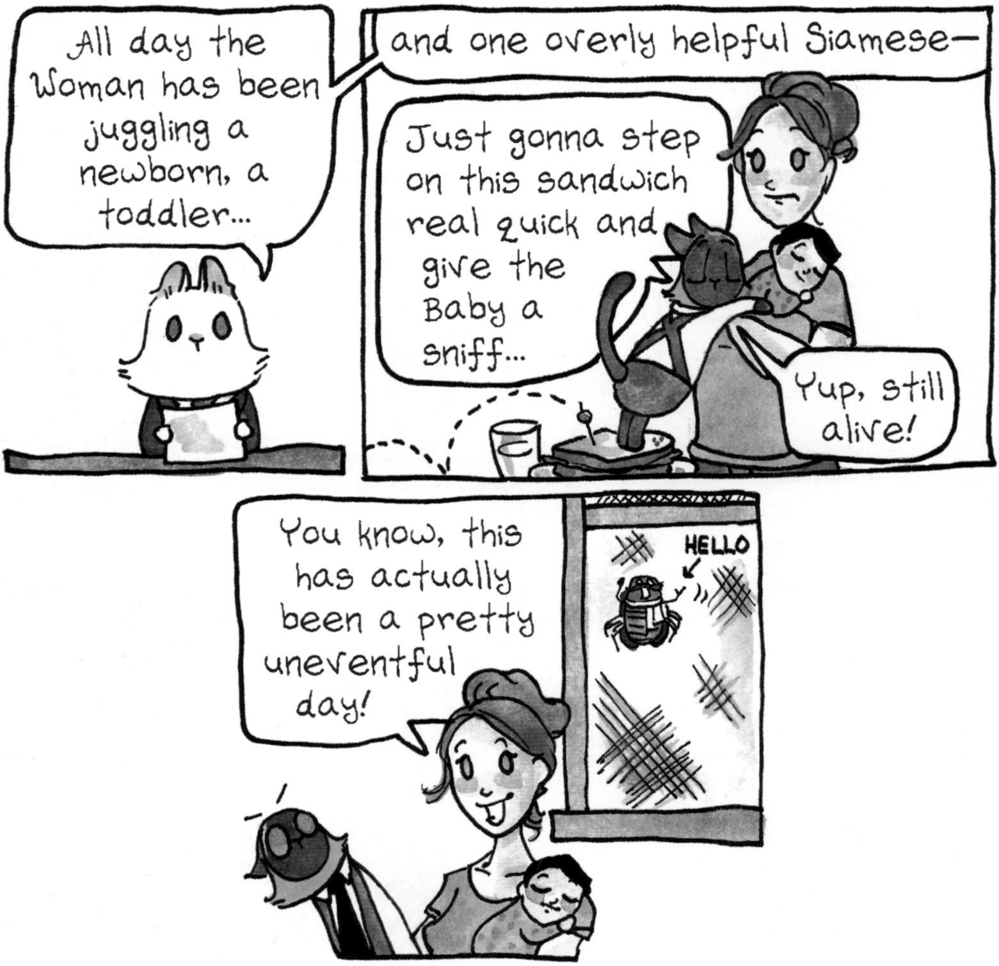
All day the Woman has been juggling a newborn, a toddler...
and one overly helpful Siamese—
Just gonna step on this sandwich real quick and give the Baby a sniff...
Yup, still alive!
You know, this has actually been a pretty uneventful day!
HELLO

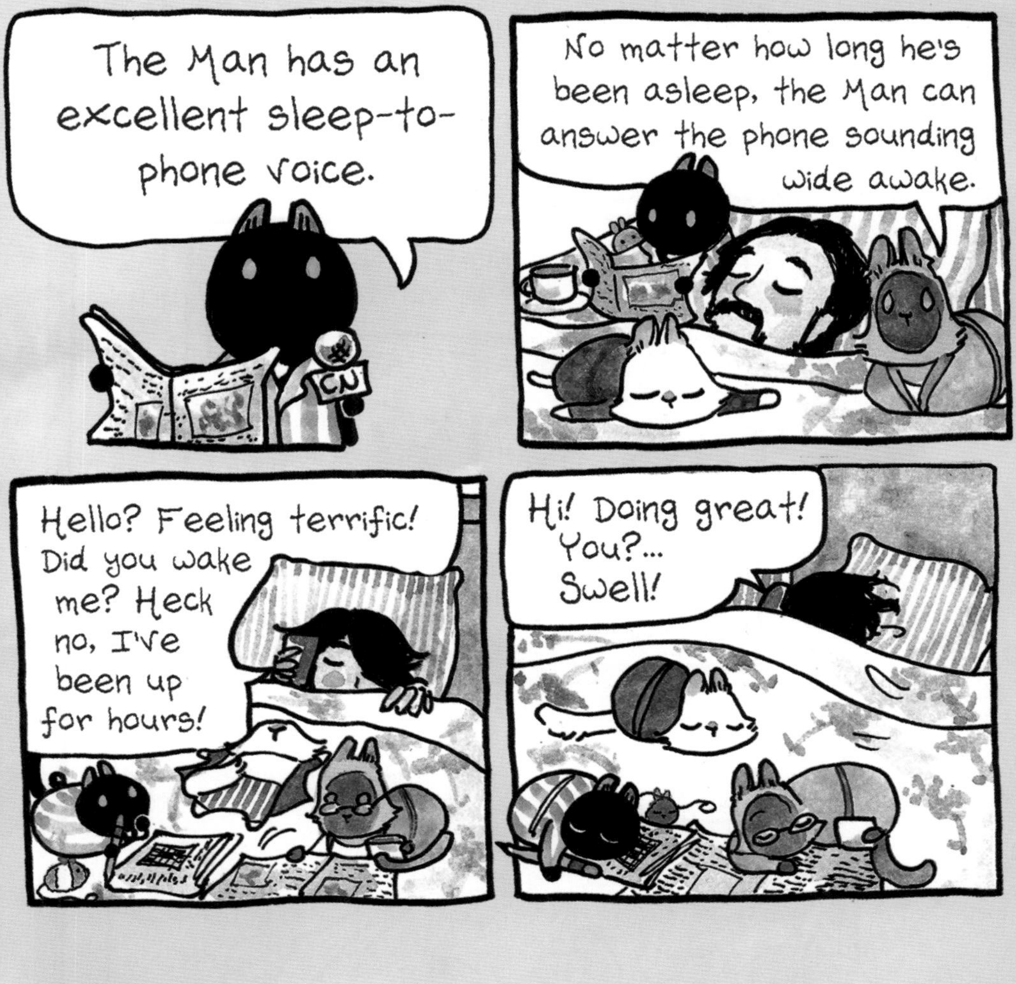
The Man has an excellent sleep-to-phone voice.
No matter how long he's been asleep, the Man can answer the phone sounding wide awake.
Hello? Feeling terrific! Did you wake me? Heck no, I've been up for hours!
Hi! Doing great! You?... Swell!

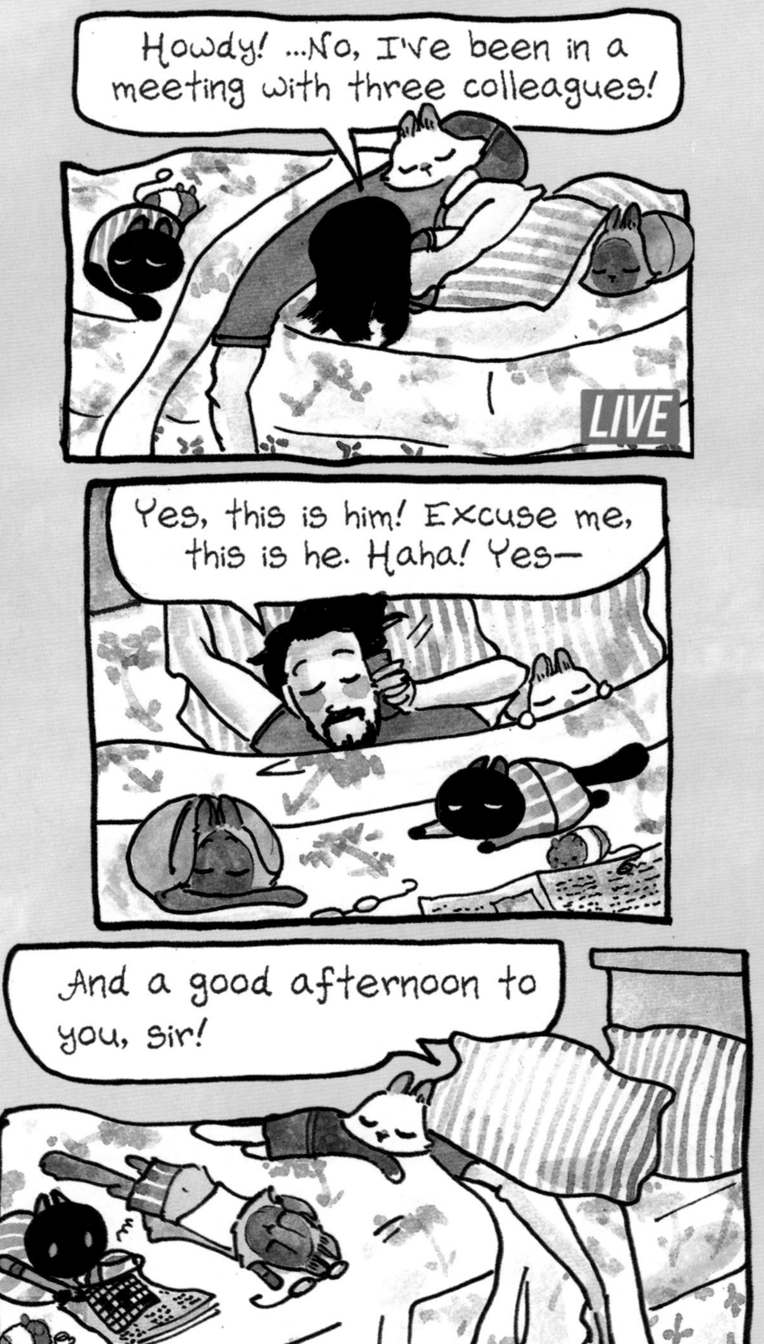
Howdy! ...No, I've been in a meeting with three colleagues!
LIVE
Yes, this is him! Excuse me, this is he. Haha! Yes—
And a good afternoon to you, sir!

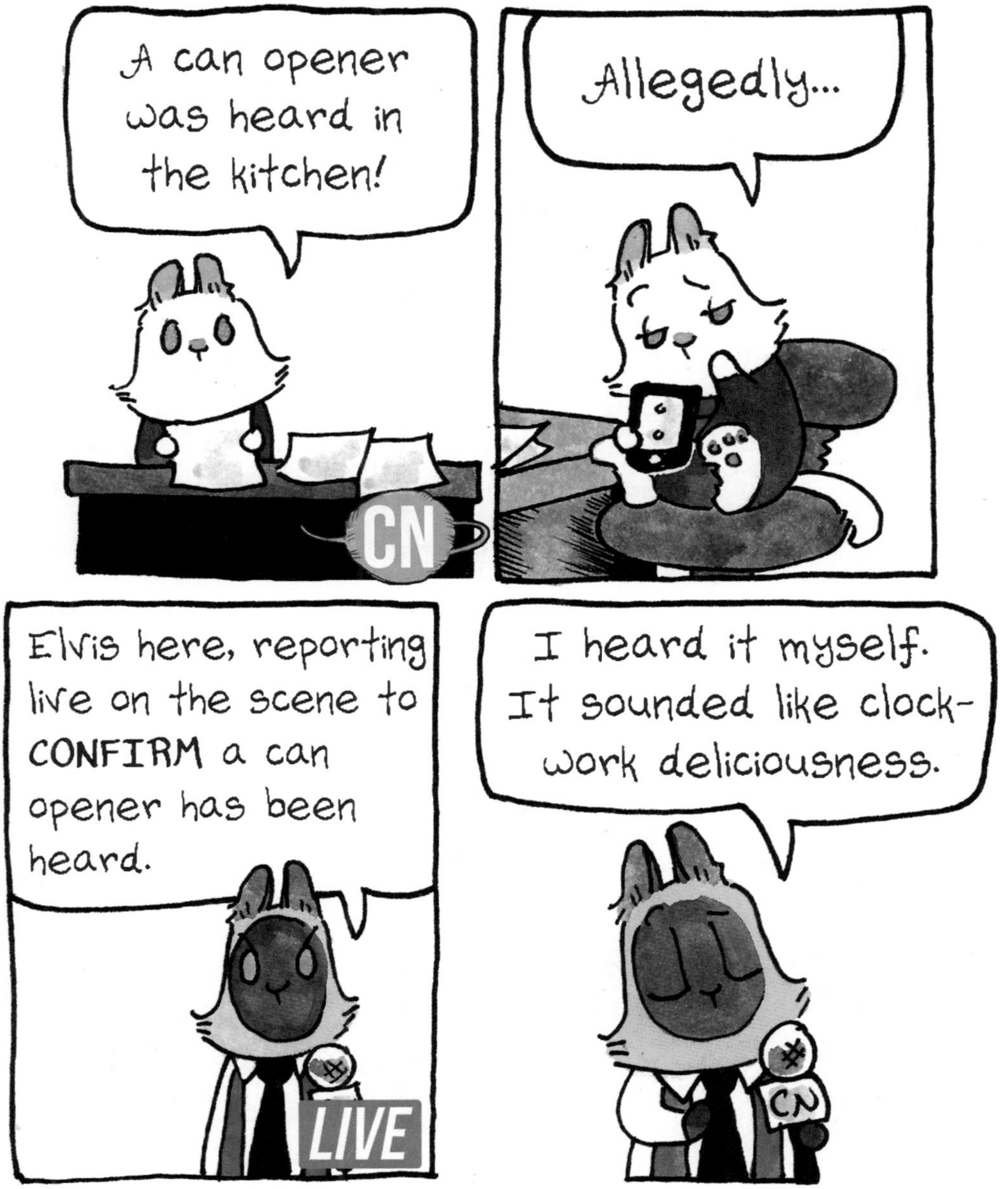
A can opener was heard in the kitchen!
CN
Allegedly...
Elvis here, reporting live on the scene to CONFIRM a can opener has been heard.
LIVE
I heard it myself. It sounded like clock-work deliciousness.
CN

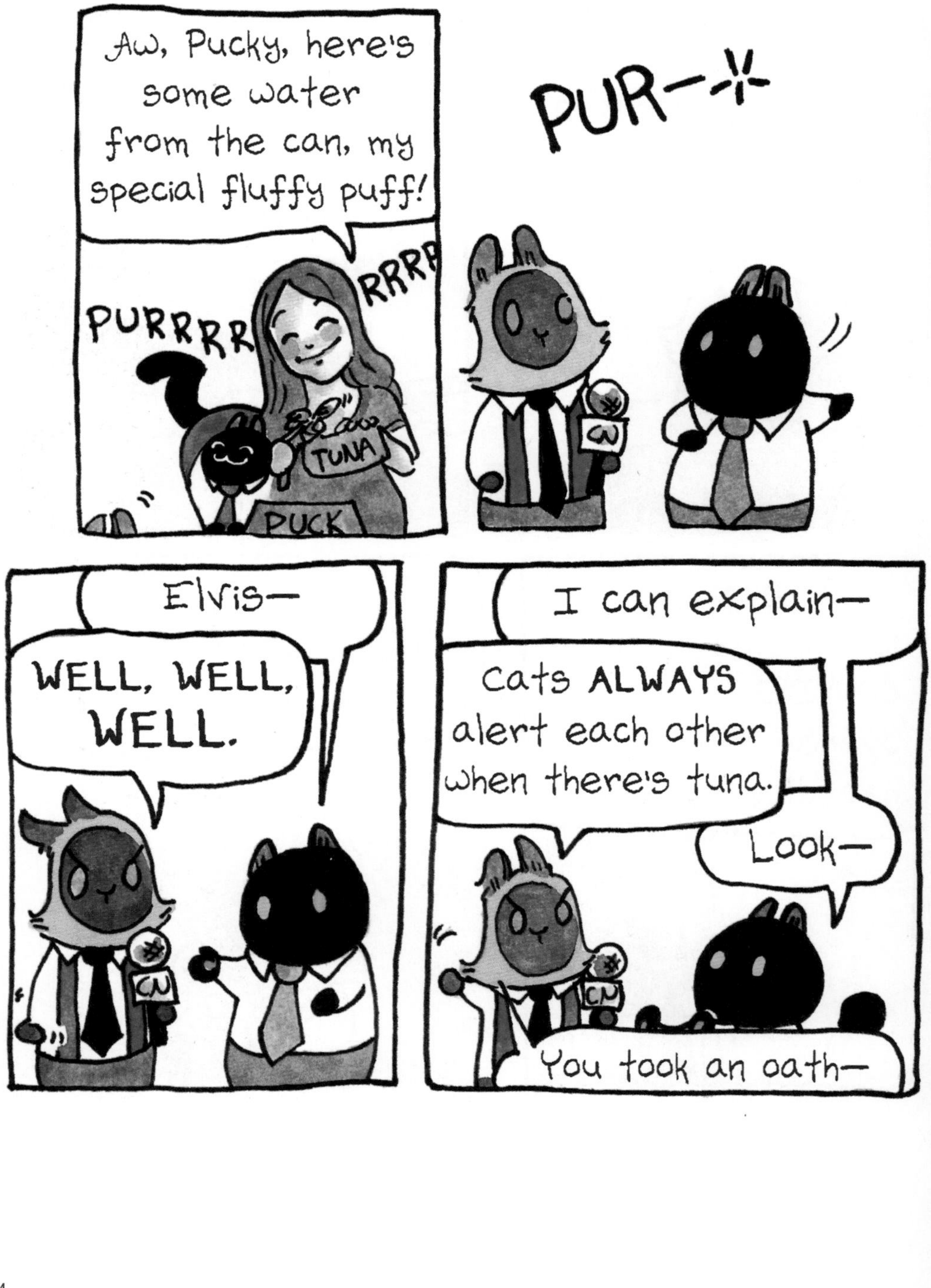
Aw, Pucky, here's some water from the can, my special fluffy puff!
PURRRRRRRRR
TUNA
PUCK
PUR—
Elvis—
WELL, WELL, WELL.
I can explain—
Cats ALWAYS alert each other when there's tuna.
Look—
You took an oath—

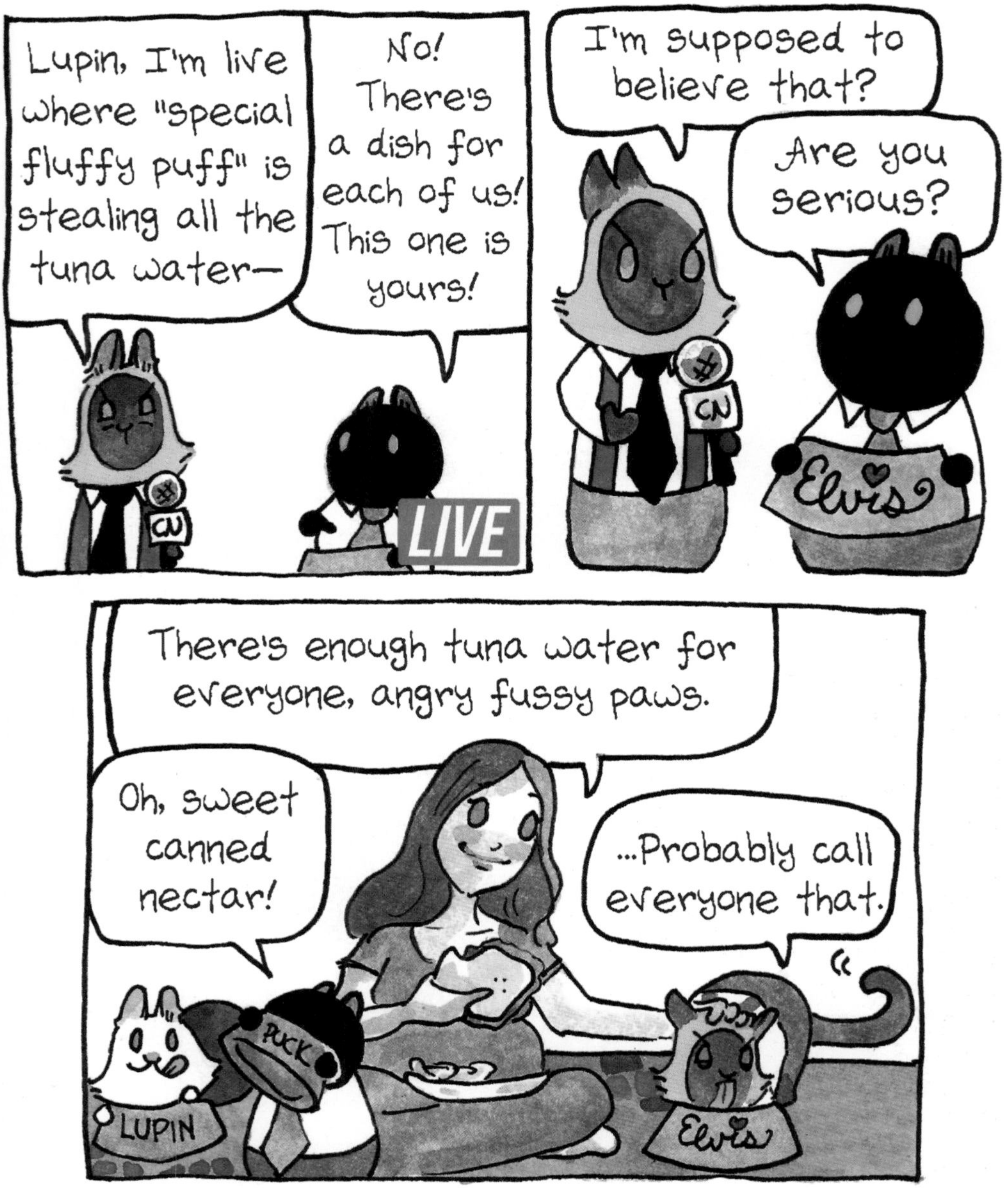
Lupin, I'm live where "special fluffy puff" is stealing all the tuna water—
No! There's a dish for each of us! This one is yours!
CN
LIVE
I'm supposed to believe that?
Are you serious?
CN
Elvis
There's enough tuna water for everyone, angry fussy paws.
Oh, sweet canned nectar!
...Probably call everyone that.
PUCK
LUPIN
Elvis

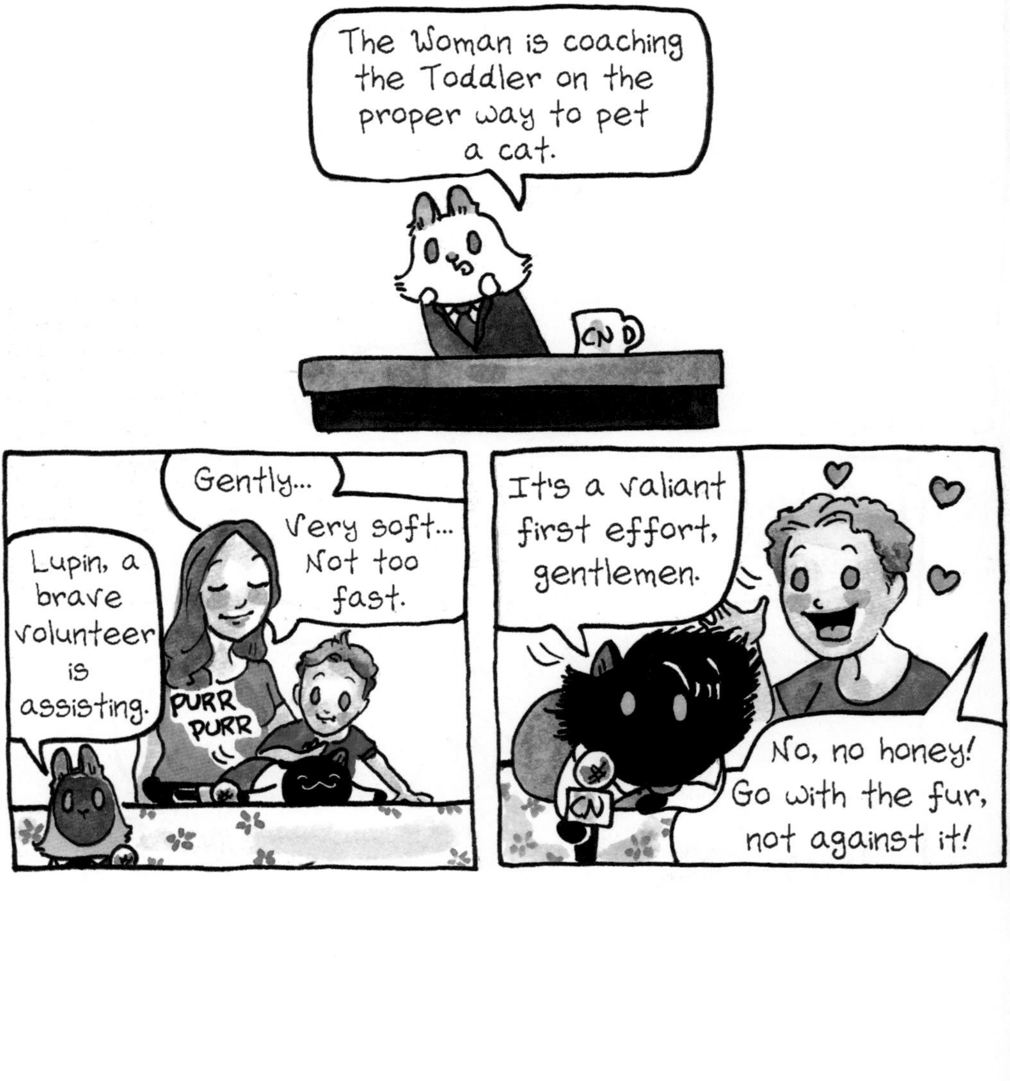
The Woman is coaching the Toddler on the proper way to pet a cat.
CND
Gently...
Very soft... Not too fast.
Lupin, a brave volunteer is assisting.
PURR PURR
It's a valiant first effort, gentlemen.
CN
No, no honey! Go with the fur, not against it!

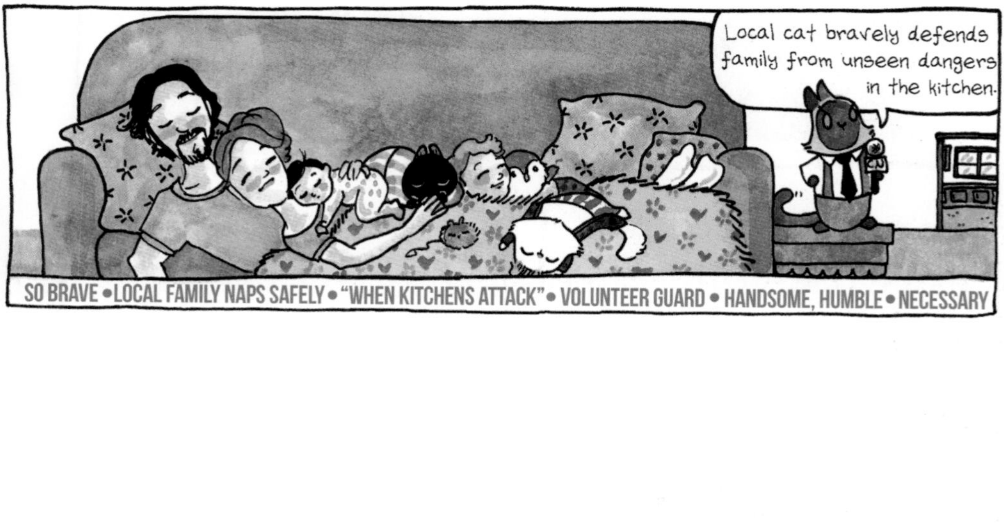
Local cat bravely defends family from unseen dangers in the kitchen.
SO BRAVE • LOCAL FAMILY NAPS SAFELY • "WHEN KITCHENS ATTACK" • VOLUNTEER GUARD • HANDSOME, HUMBLE • NECESSARY

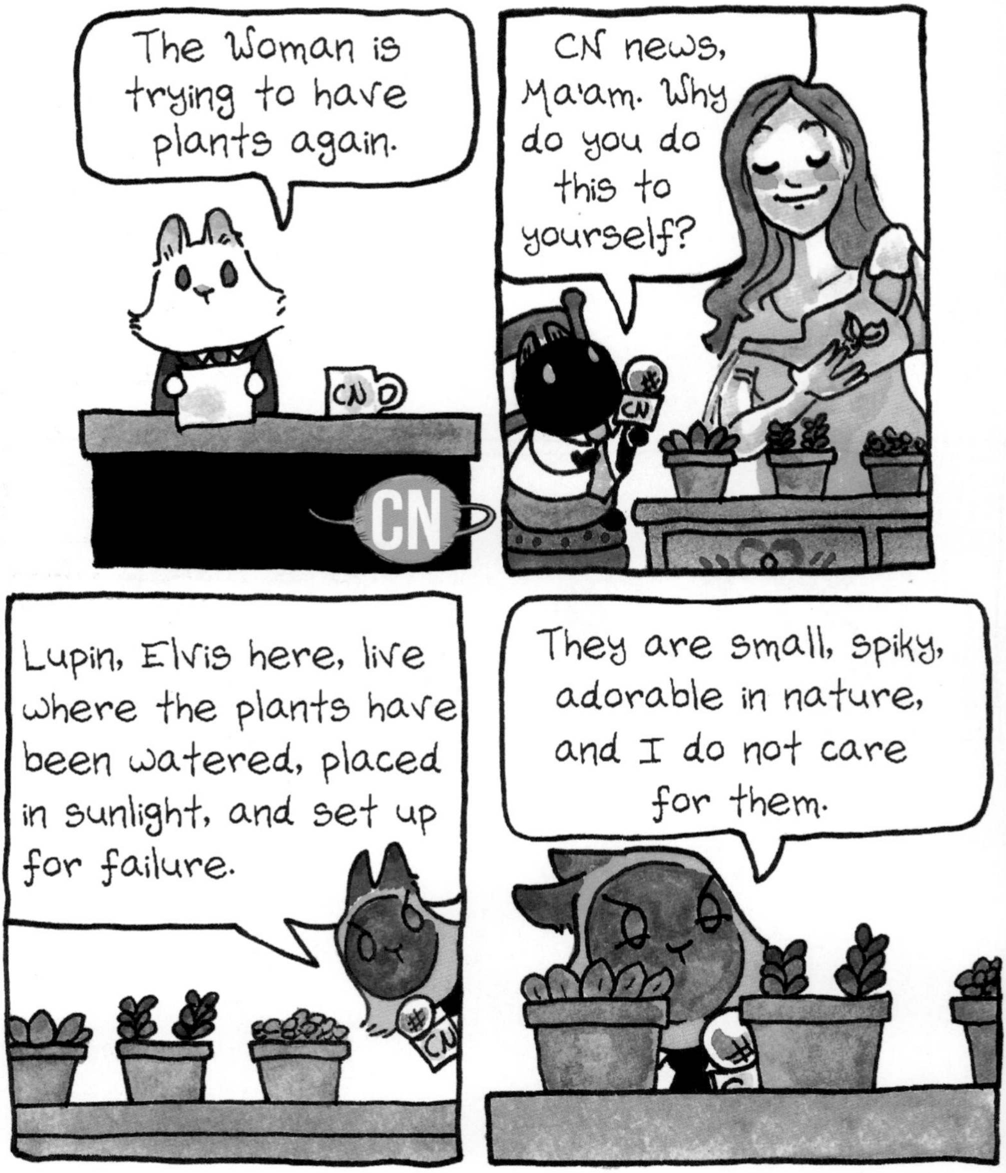
The Woman is trying to have plants again.
CN
CN
CN news, Ma'am. Why do you do this to yourself?
CN
Lupin, Elvis here, live where the plants have been watered, placed in sunlight, and set up for failure.
They are small, spiky, adorable in nature, and I do not care for them.

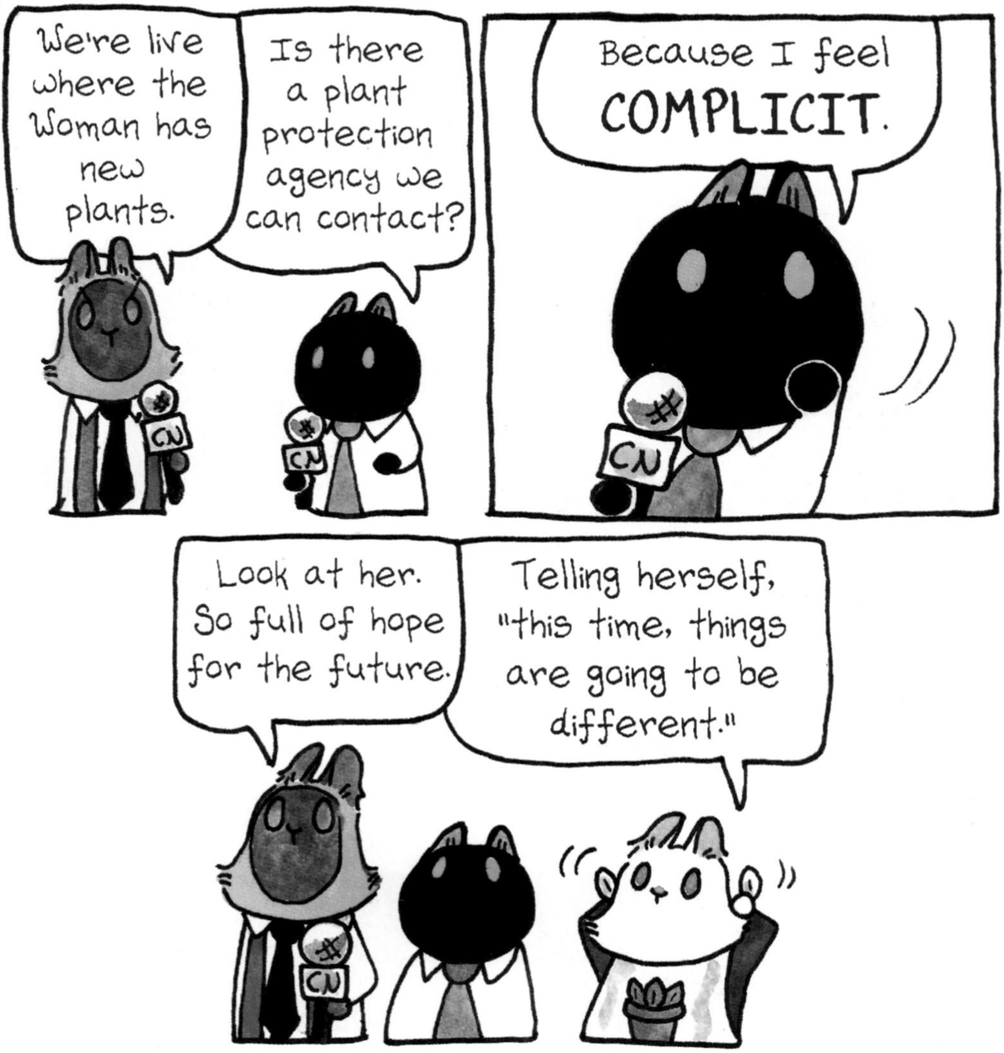
We're live where the Woman has new plants.
Is there a plant protection agency we can contact?
Because I feel COMPLICIT.
Look at her. So full of hope for the future.
Telling herself, "this time, things are going to be different."

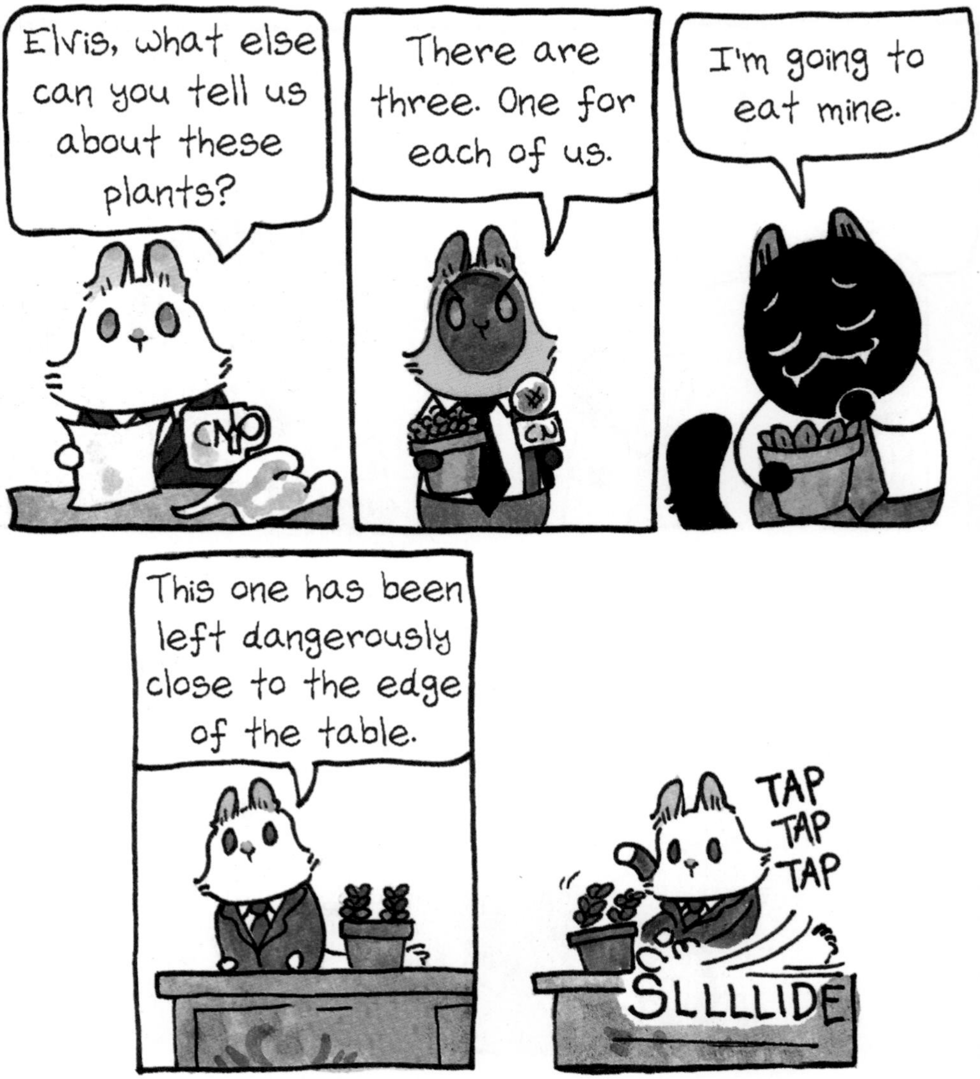
Elvis, what else can you tell us about these plants?
CN
There are three. One for each of us.
CN
I'm going to eat mine.
This one has been left dangerously close to the edge of the table.
TAP
TAP
TAP
SLLLLIDE

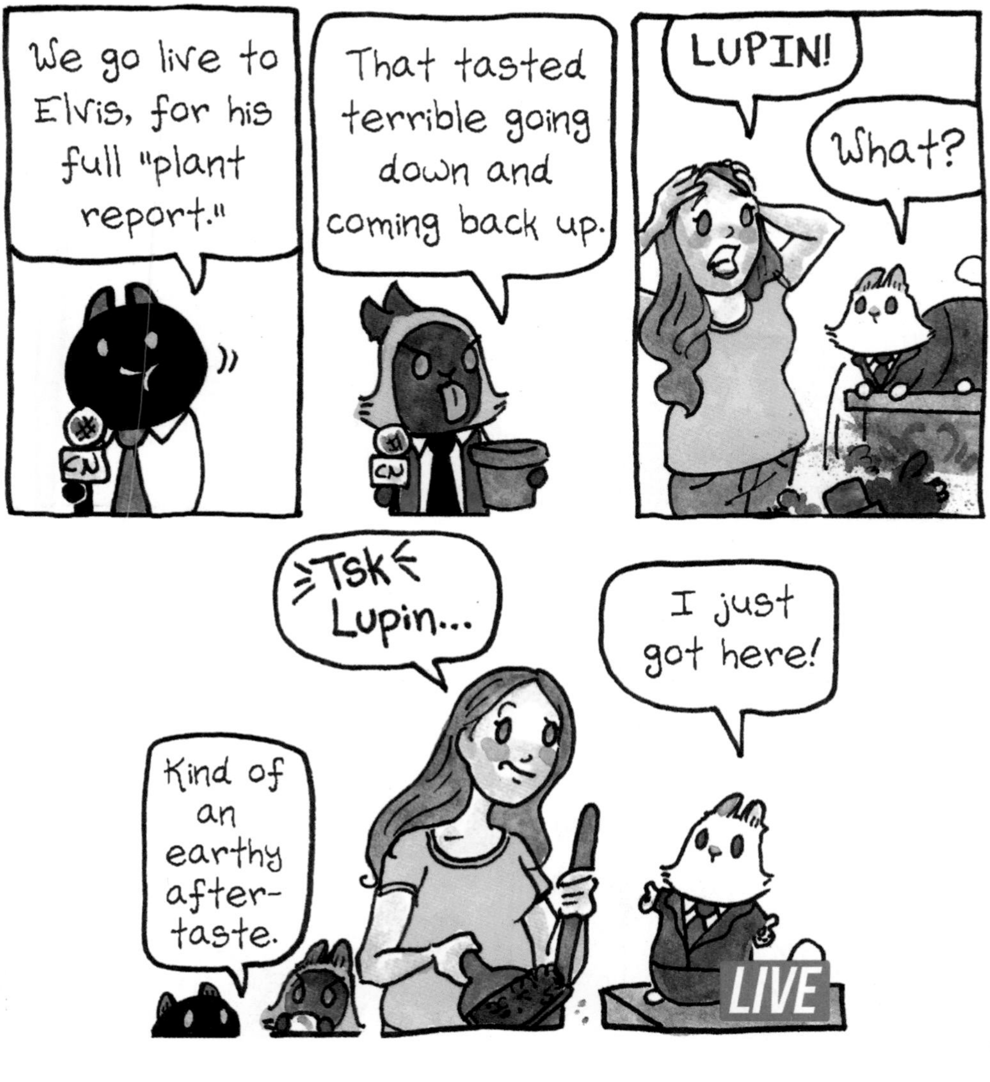
We go live to Elvis, for his full "plant report."
That tasted terrible going down and coming back up.
LUPIN!
What?
TSK Lupin...
I just got here!
Kind of an earthy after-taste.
CN
LIVE

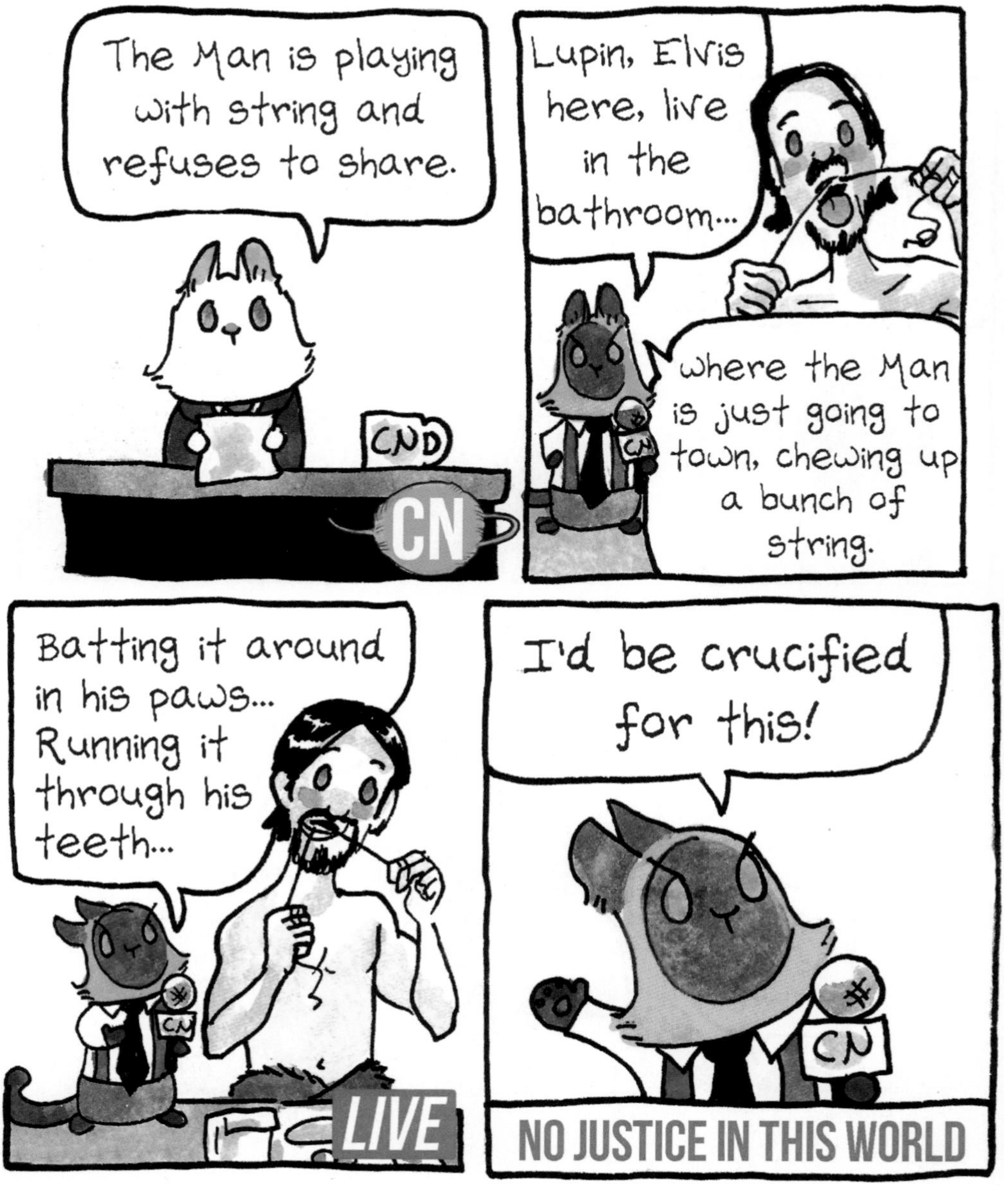
The Man is playing with string and refuses to share.
CND
CN
Lupin, Elvis here, live in the bathroom...
where the Man is just going to town, chewing up a bunch of string.
CN
Batting it around in his paws... Running it through his teeth...
CN
LIVE
I'd be crucified for this!
CN
NO JUSTICE IN THIS WORLD

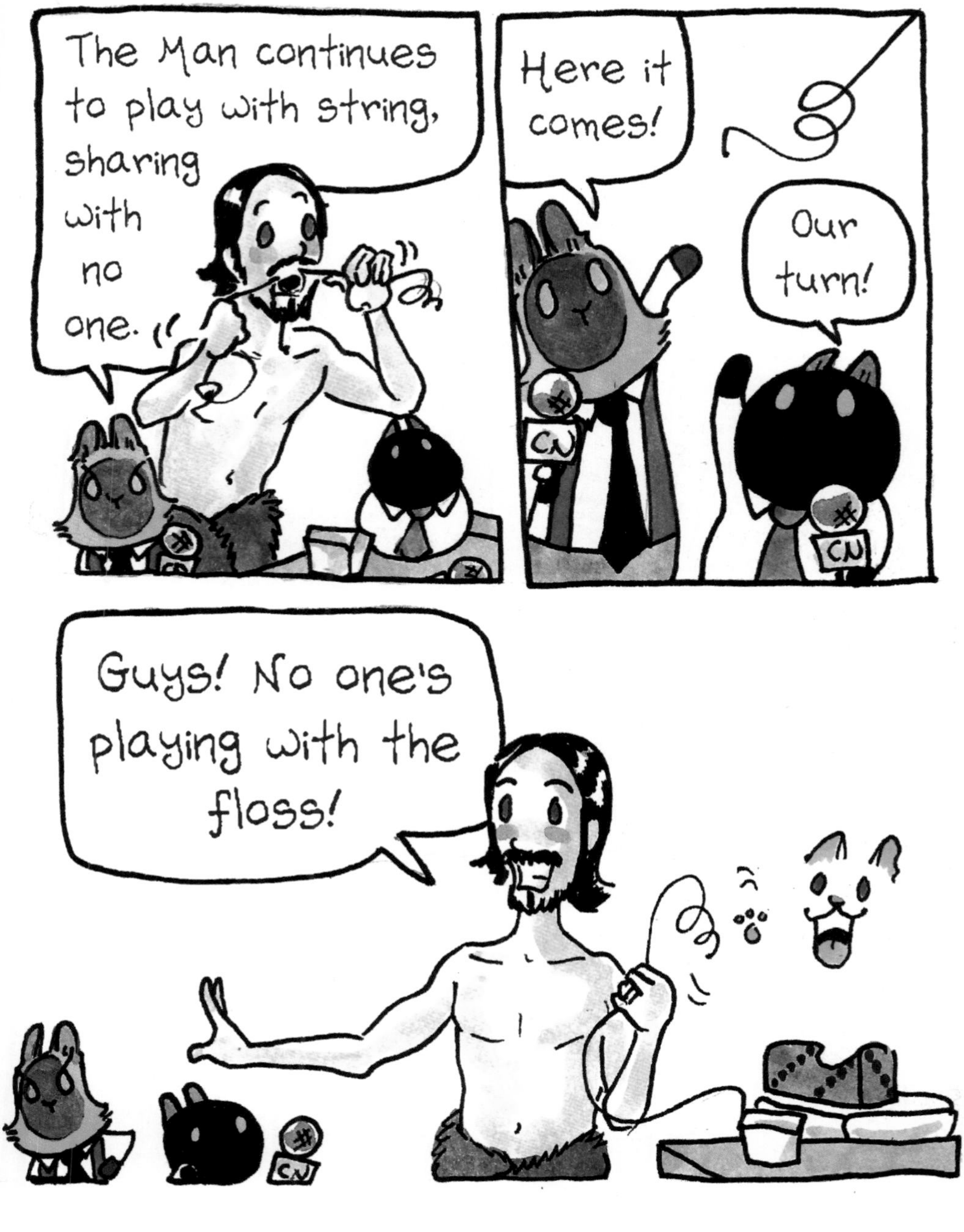
The Man continues to play with string, sharing with no one.
Here it comes!
Our turn!
CN
CN
Guys! No one's playing with the floss!
CN

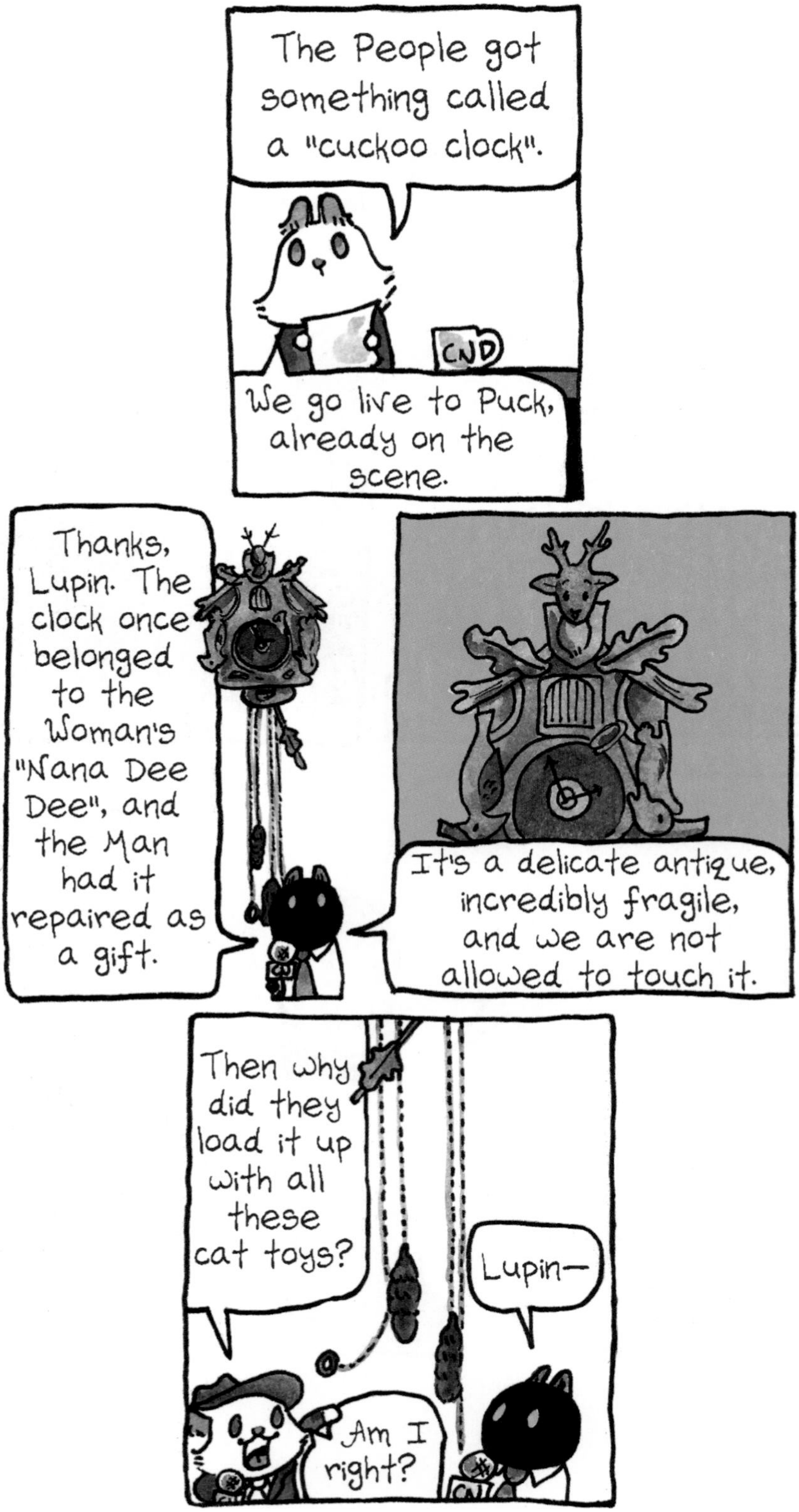
The People got something called a "cuckoo clock".
We go live to Puck, already on the scene.
CND
Thanks, Lupin. The clock once belonged to the Woman's "Nana Dee Dee", and the Man had it repaired as a gift.
It's a delicate antique, incredibly fragile, and we are not allowed to touch it.
Then why did they load it up with all these cat toys?
Lupin—
Am I right?

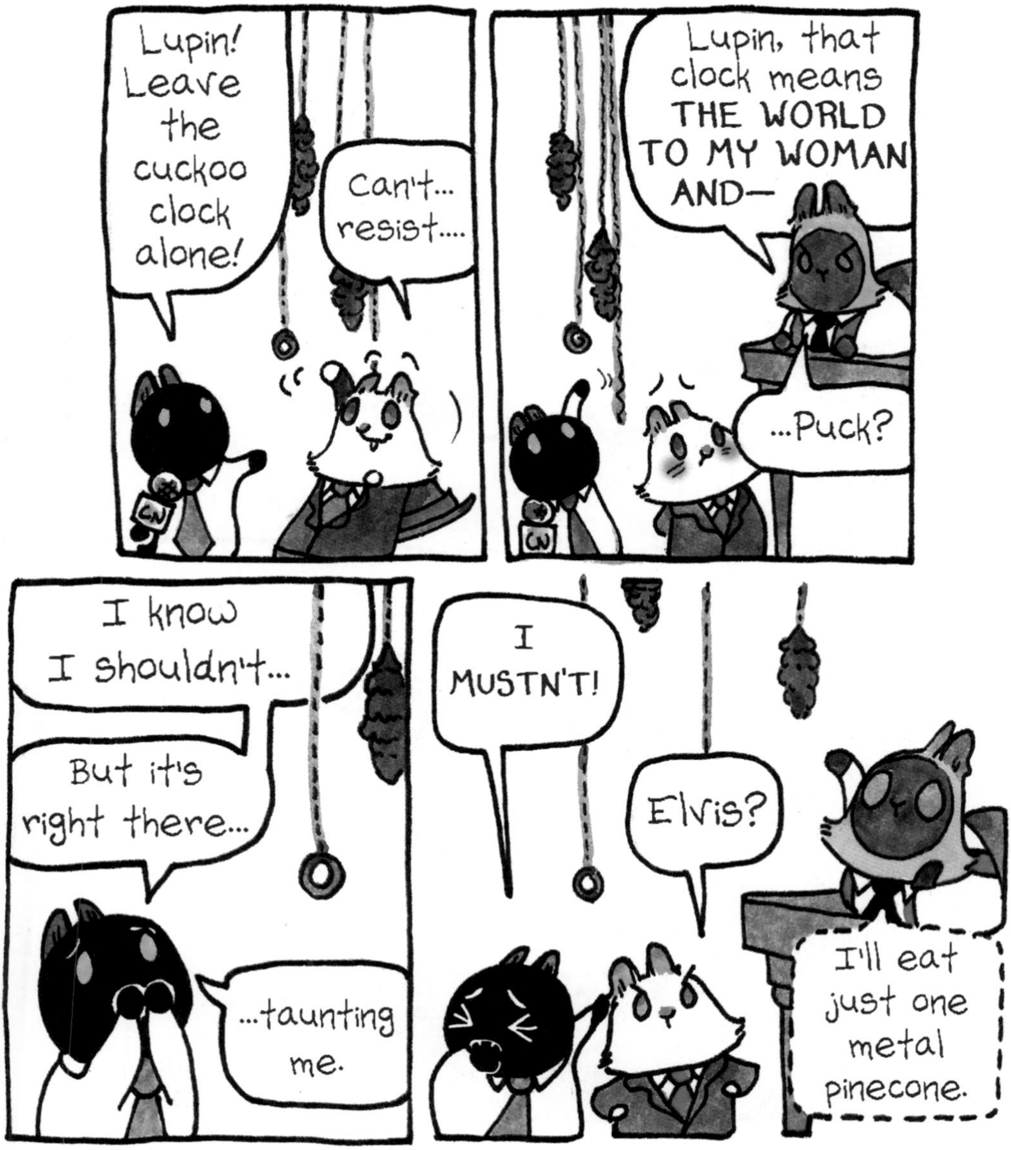
Lupin! Leave the cuckoo clock alone!
Can't... resist....
Lupin, that clock means THE WORLD TO MY WOMAN AND—
...Puck?
I know I shouldn't...
But it's right there...
...taunting me.
I MUSTN'T!
Elvis?
I'll eat just one metal pinecone.

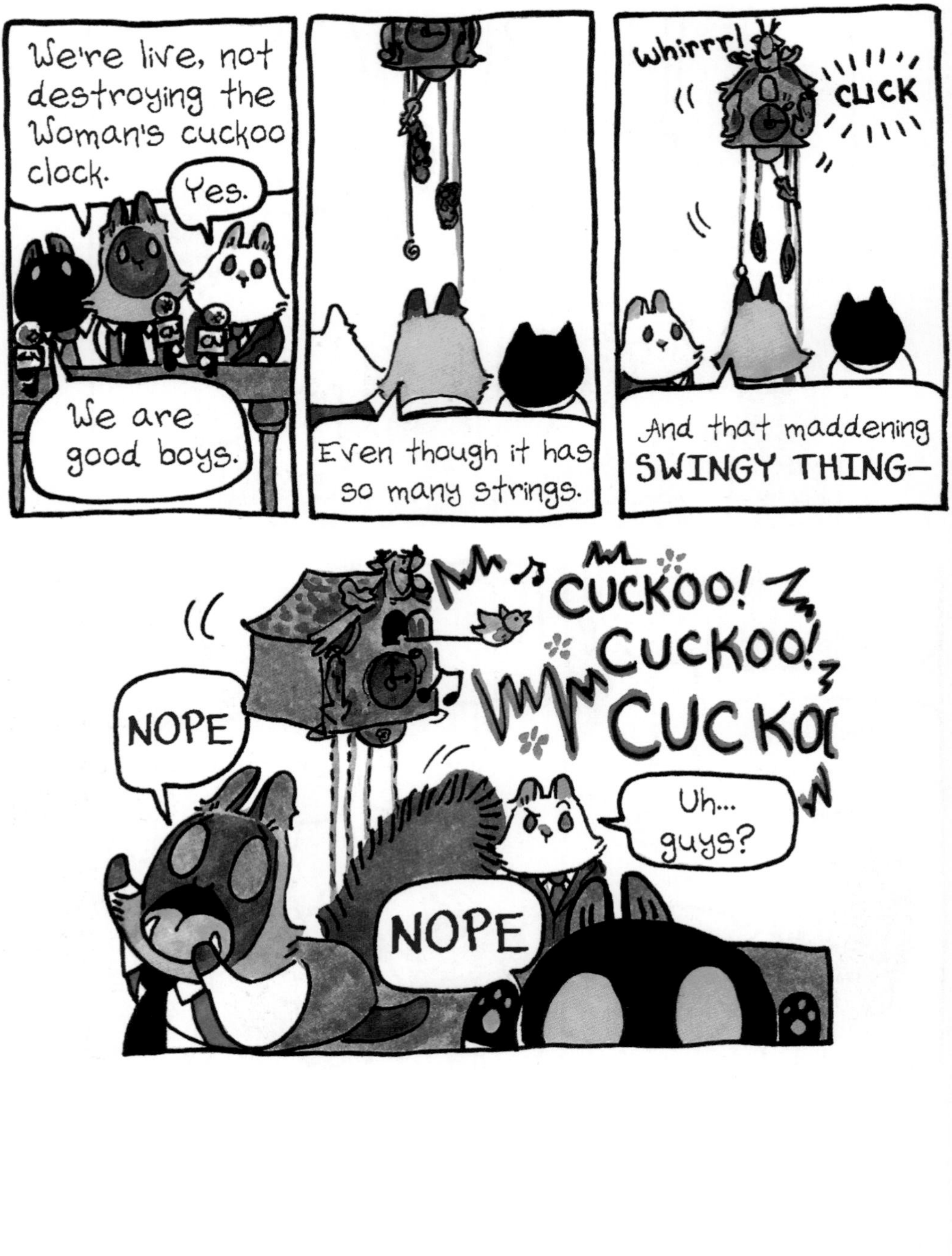
We're live, not destroying the Woman's cuckoo clock.
Yes.
We are good boys.
Even though it has so many strings.
Whirrr!
CLICK
And that maddening SWINGY THING—
CUCKOO!
CUCKOO!
NOPE
Uh... guys?
NOPE

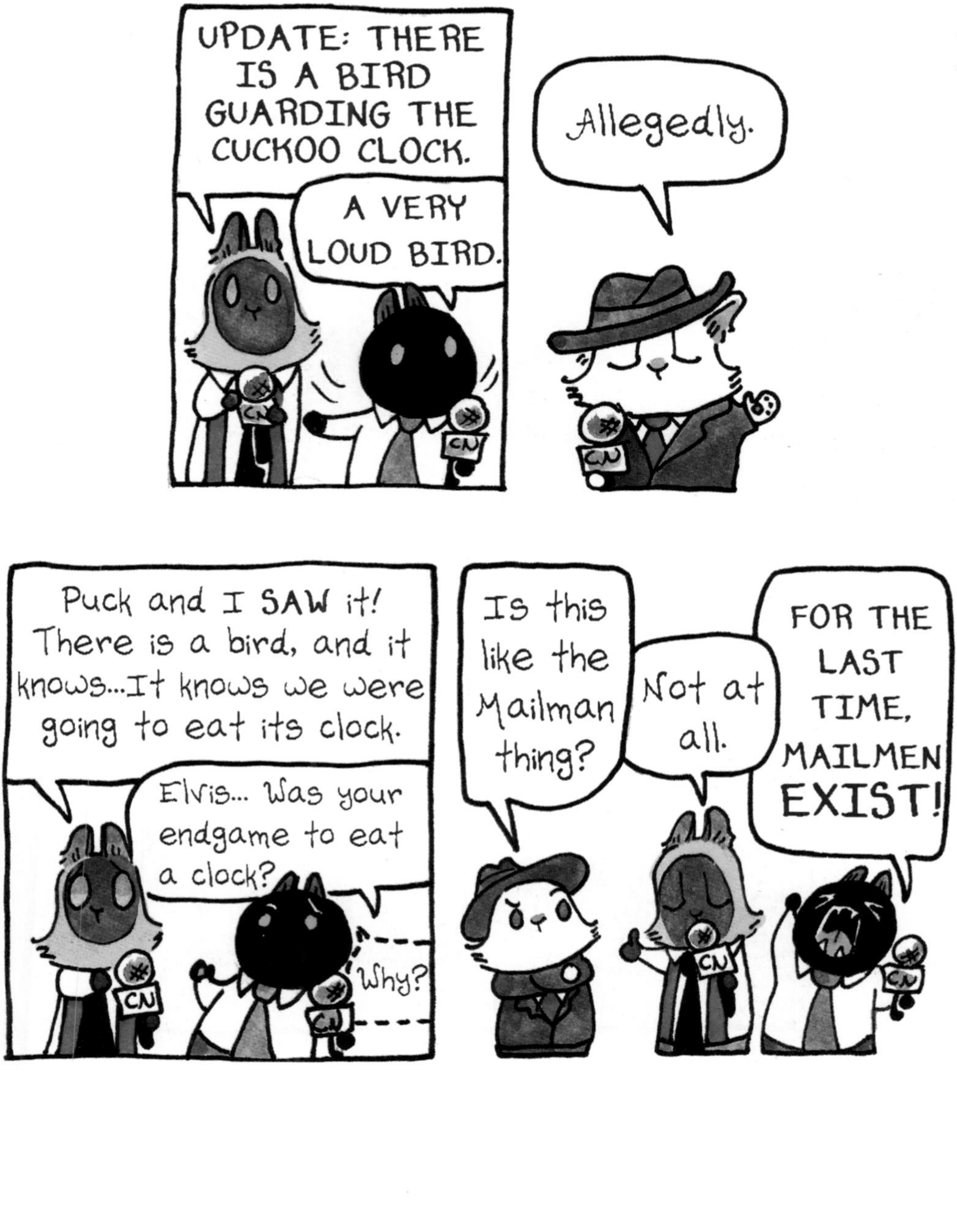
UPDATE: THERE IS A BIRD GUARDING THE CUCKOO CLOCK.
A VERY LOUD BIRD.
Allegedly.
CN
Puck and I SAW it! There is a bird, and it knows...It knows we were going to eat its clock.
Elvis... Was your endgame to eat a clock?
Why?
Is this like the Mailman thing?
Not at all.
FOR THE LAST TIME, MAILMEN EXIST!

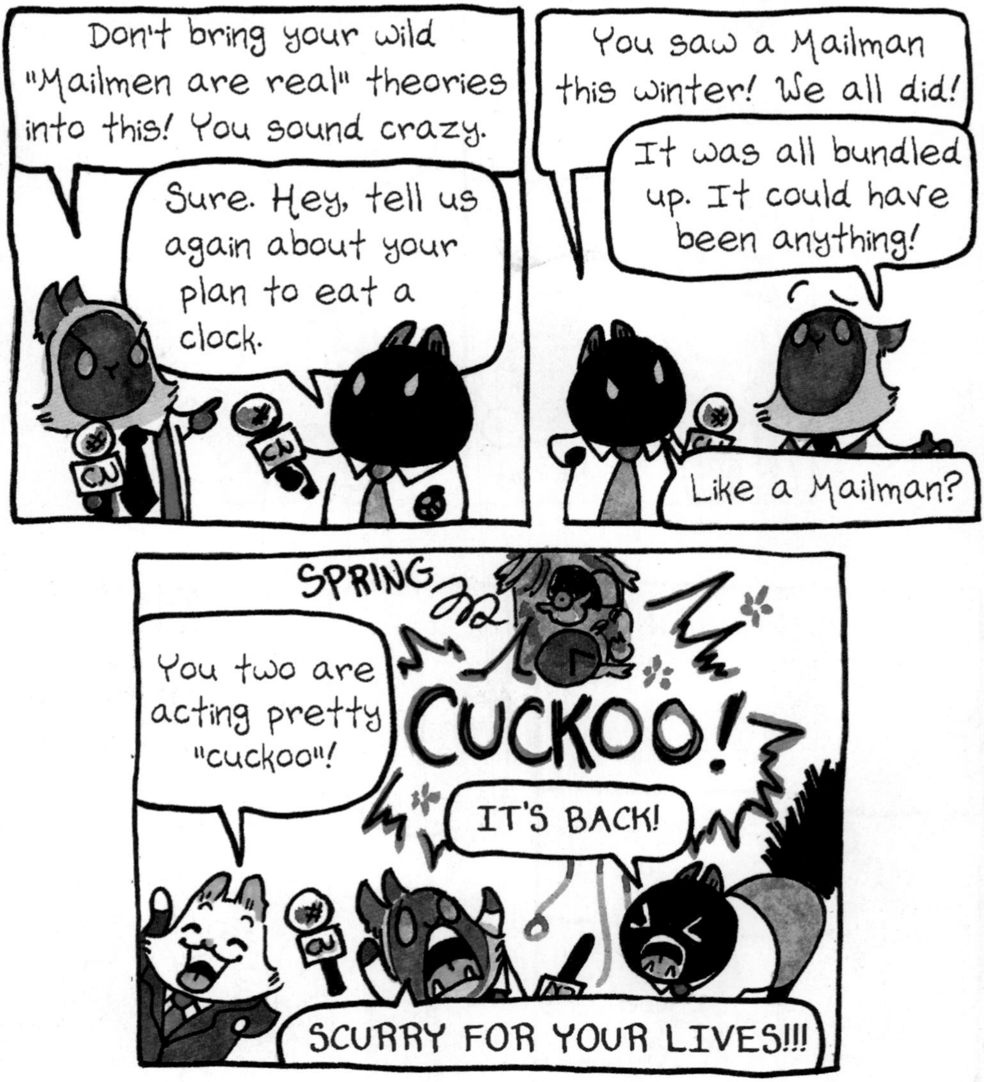
Don't bring your wild "Mailmen are real" theories into this! You sound crazy.
Sure. Hey, tell us again about your plan to eat a clock.
You saw a Mailman this winter! We all did!
It was all bundled up. It could have been anything!
Like a Mailman?
SPRING
You two are acting pretty "cuckoo"!
CUCKOO!
IT'S BACK!
SCURRY FOR YOUR LIVES!!!

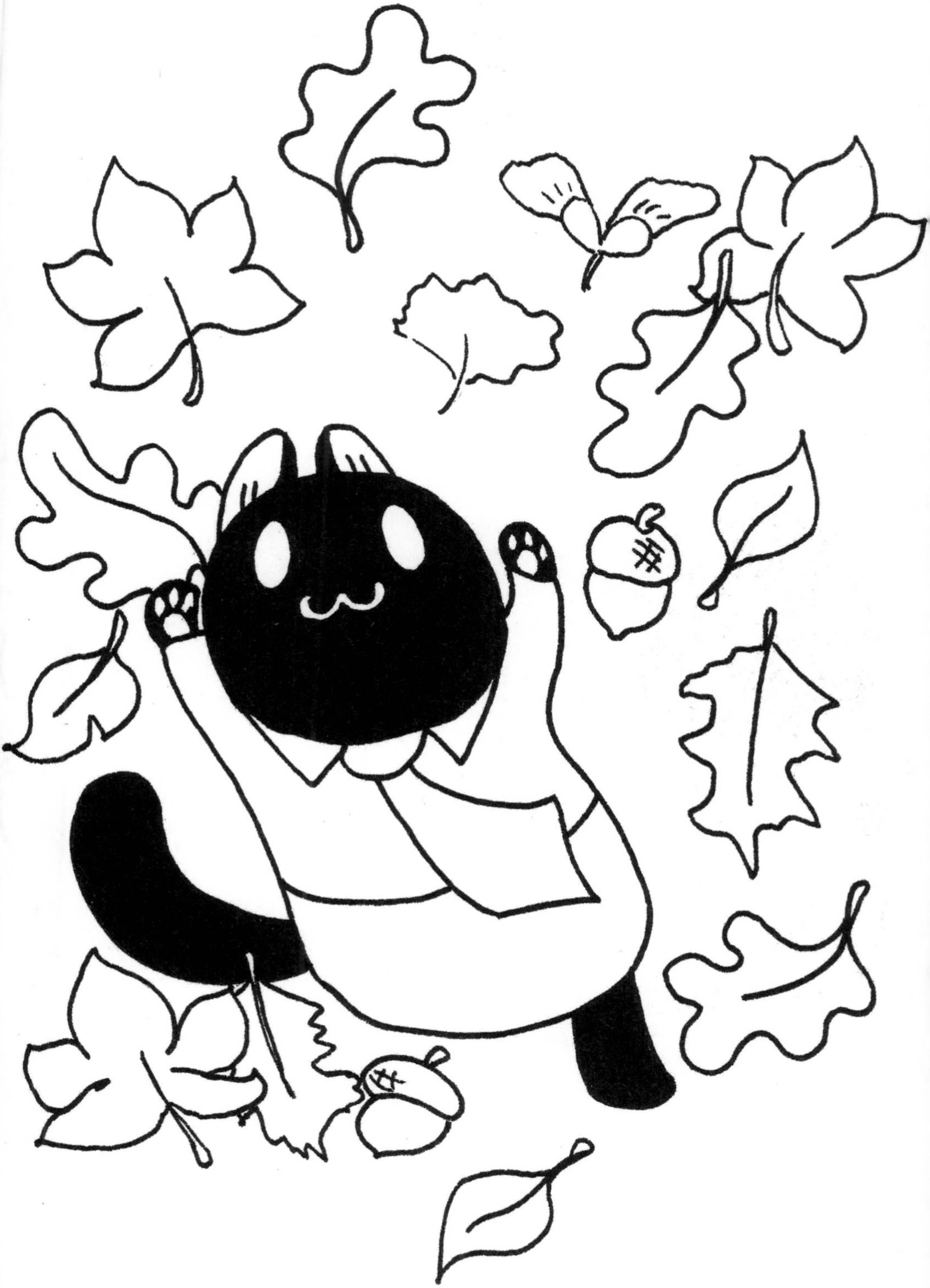

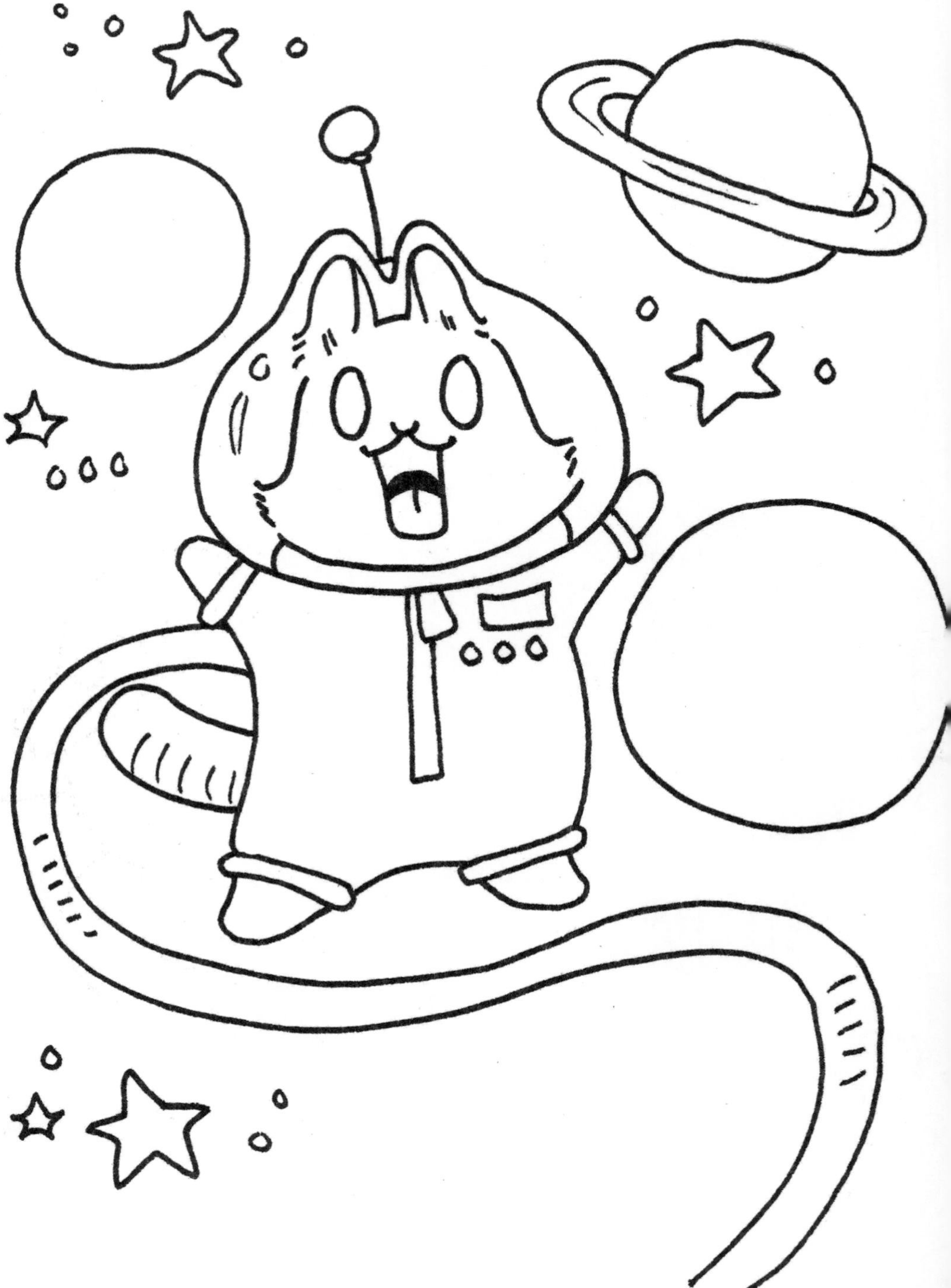

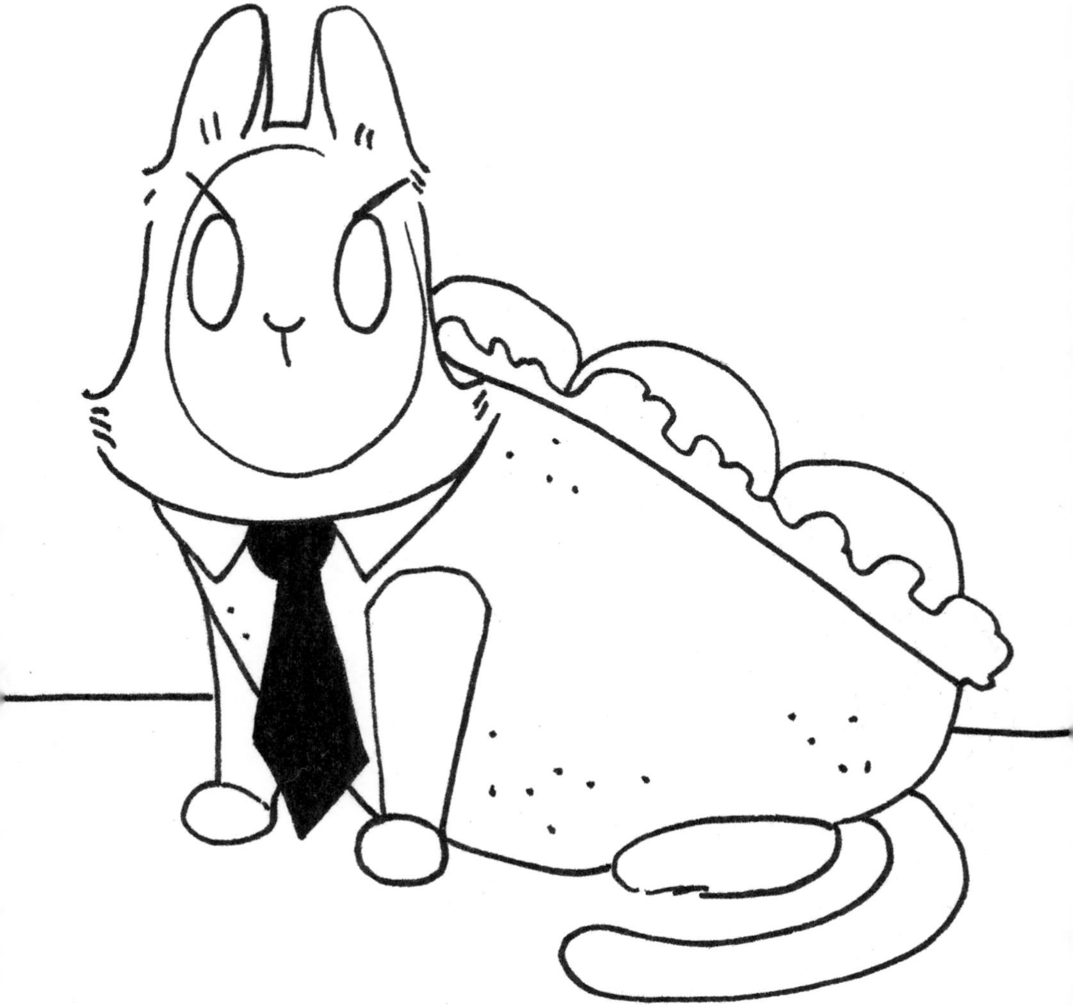

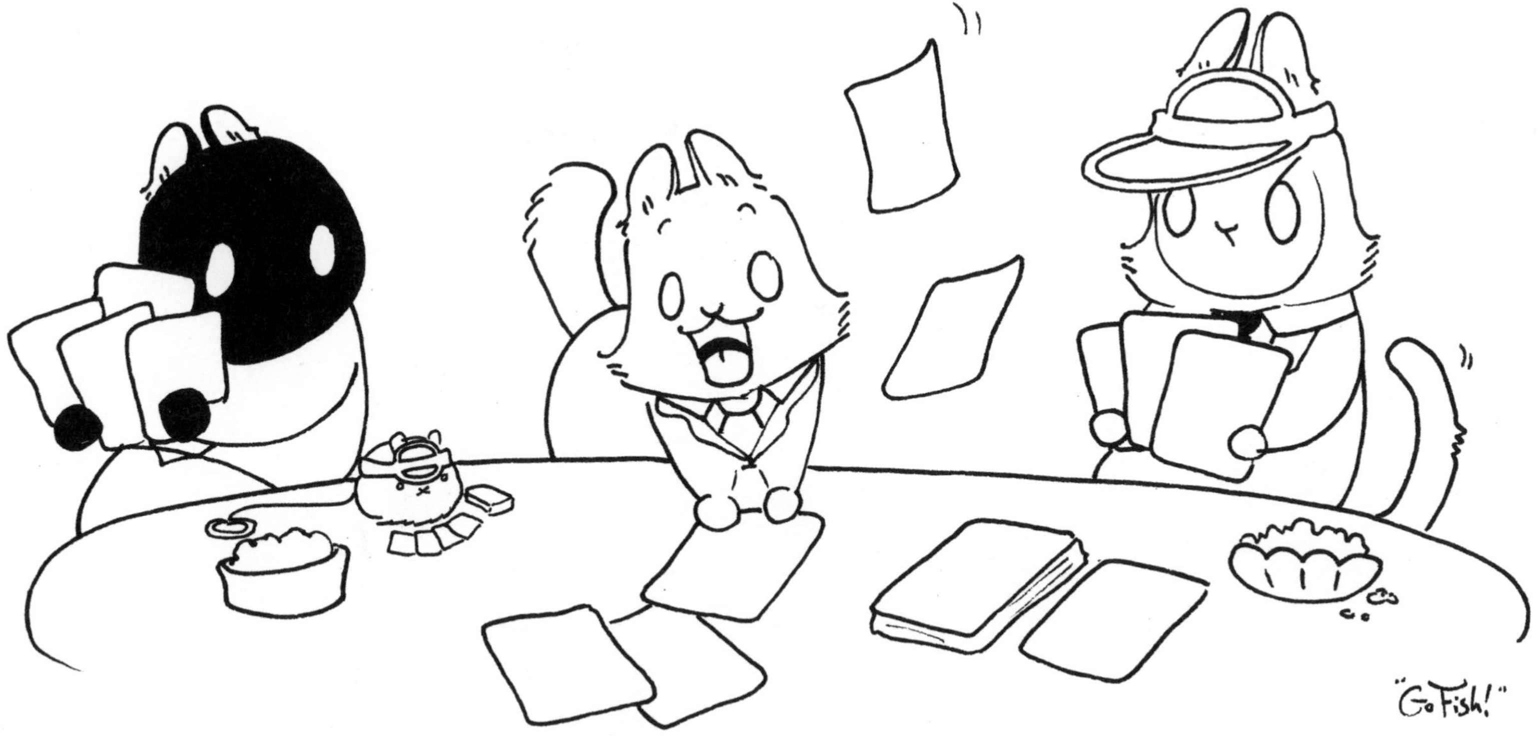
"Go Fish!"

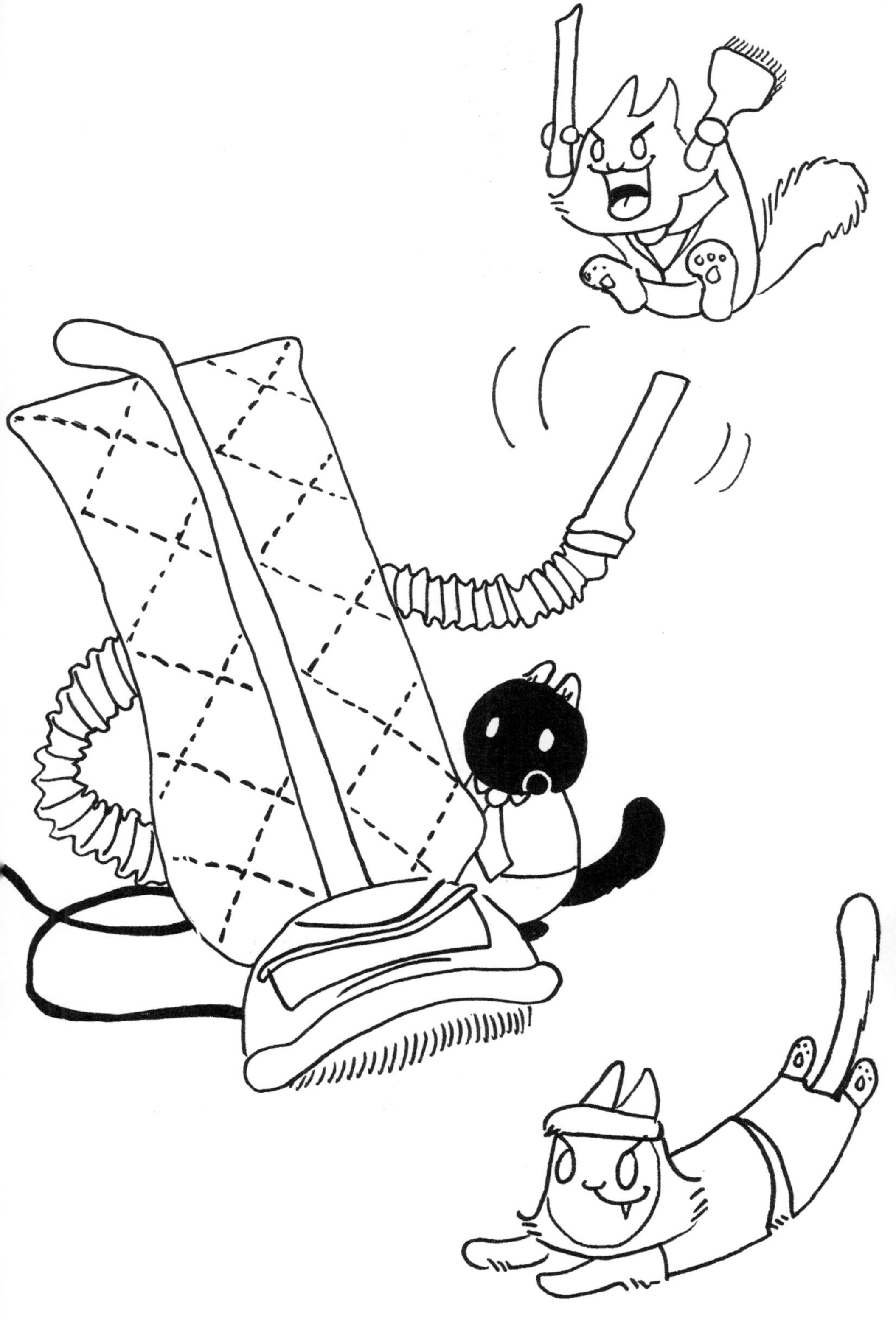

Andrews McMeel Publishing
a division of Andrews McMeel Universal
1130 Walnut Street, Kansas City, Missouri 64106

www.andrewsmcmeel.com
www.breakingcatnews.com

22 23 24 25 26 SDB 10 9 8 7 6 5 4 3 2 1

ISBN: 978-1-5248-7128-4

Library of Congress Control Number: 2022935299

Editor: Patty Rice
Art Director/Designer: Diane Marsh
Production Editor: Meg Daniels
Production Manager: Chuck Harper

Made by:
King Yip (Dongguan) Printing & Packaging Factory Ltd.
Address and location of production:
Daning Administrative District, Humen Town
Dongguan Guangdong, China 523930
1st Printing — 5/23/22

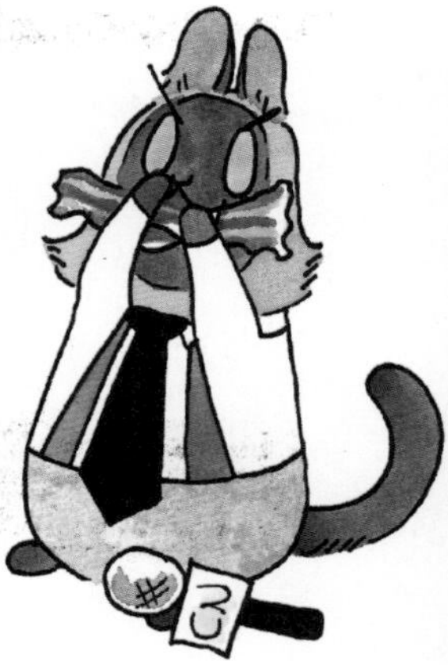
#CN